ALSO BY JESSICA HENDRA

How to Cook Your Daughter

Jennifer
Steinhauer

Jessica
Hendra

St. Martin's Press ⚬ New York

This is a work of fiction. All of the characters, organizations, and events portrayed in this novel are either products of the authors' imagination or are used fictitiously.

www.stmartins.com

Library of Congress Cataloging-in-Publication Data

Steinhauer, Jennifer.
  Beverly Hills Adjacent / Jennifer Steinhauer and Jessica
Hendra.—1st ed.
    p. cm.
  ISBN-13: 978-0-312-55182-7
  ISBN-10: 0-312-55182-7
  1. Actors' spouses—Fiction. 2. Television producers and directors—Fiction. 3. Adultery—Fiction. 4. Los Angeles (Calif.)—Fiction. I. Hendra, Jessica. II. Title.
  PS3619.T47635B48 2009
  813'.6—dc22   2008044068

First Edition: May 2009

10 9 8 7 6 5 4 3 2 1

To Wikipedia: We couldn't have done it without you.

CHAPTER 1

The trouble with starring in a network television show about a bipolar dentist who is looking for love on the Internet is that no matter how deft the flossing puns, or how diverting the high jinks with your Puerto Rican hygienist, it all comes down to the time slot. For Mitch Gold, this was the unpleasant axis upon which his world spun.

"Hello?"

"Mitch Gold, please"

"This is Mitch."

"Hello, Fiona from Creative Artists here. Can you hold for Tim Zelnick?"

"Sure."

"Hi, Mitch, it's Tim, and Angie Varone is on the line too. How's our favorite bipolar dentist?"

"Hi, guys! So how did *Molar Opposites* do last night?"

"Well," Tim answered, "it came in fourth."

Mitch stared out the window and noticed the parched garden. "Fourth? Yikes."

"Hey," Tim said, "what do you want? You're up against *American Idol*. But I talked to ABC. They're still *very* committed. They're gonna run a bunch of promos during *Brothers & Sisters* and see if they can bring in more women. They just want it to do a little better every week."

Mitch took a breath. "What were the numbers?"

"Well, it's a blue-state show, no question. The Hispanic audience eighteen to forty-nine was good, you were strong there. But you dropped in the second fifteen minutes. You pulled a 1.8. I think the network would like to see a 2.5."

"Wow." Mitch was quiet for a second. "They want a million more people. How can we do that?"

"Hey, you never know. It's a good show," Tim said. "And you're fantastic in it, Mitch, seriously."

Angie Varone piped up. "I do have to wonder why they put Rosie in that purple skirt. Wardrobe really dropped the ball there. She looked like a walking Jamba Juice."

"Really?" Mitch asked.

"*Totally*. Anyway, hang in there, Mitch."

"Thanks, Angie. And Tim. See ya."

Mitch went to hang up from the call with his agents but hit the mute button instead. In this fateful move—one that led Tim and Angie to believe that Mitch had hung up when in fact he was still listening—the truth leaped out from behind the telephonic curtain.

"Tim, you still there?" Angie asked.

"I'm here. Did you actually see that piece of shit last night?"

"No, I watched *Idol*. I saw that skirt on one of the ads."

"Well, it blows." Tim said. "That never stopped a hit, but with a 1.8, I bet it was behind the Weather Channel. I can't believe the network's gonna let it go more than another week."

Mitch heard someone—probably Angie—take a deep slurp from what he imagined was a venti vanilla latte, with Splenda.

"They won't dump that many Hispanic viewers just like that. But I agree it's a long shot." She continued, "Mitch books a lot. But man, what is this, his eighth failed series? He's had his chances. If *Molar Opposites* gets canceled and Mitch doesn't get another pilot this season, I think we should drop him."

"Yeah." Tim agreed. "Plus Mitch is a conflict with Willie Dermot, and Willie's got more cachet and a higher quote."

"Right, but if I have to take one more call from Willie's bony-ass wife sniveling about her husband getting passed over for Jack Black, I'm gonna open a vein. I'd love to know which fucking intern gave that freakazoid my cell number."

"Angie, that's why God invented caller ID. So anyway, let's give it till the end of pilot season. If Gold doesn't get anything, we cut him loose."

"Okay." Slurp. "Where do ya wanna go for lunch? Craft?"

Mitch hung up the phone, lunged for his nine iron hidden behind the door, and began smashing it on the sofa. Fucked. He was fucked. Willie Dermot was going to get a hit this season and *Molar Opposites* would be canceled. That would mean the end of Mitch Gold at CAA, and perhaps the end of his career. And that he could not afford.

Six months ago, the Golds had embarked on badly needed renovations to their 1926 Spanish-style house, but the contractor had run off with the $150,000 deposit—perhaps back to Russia, who knew?—and now they had no savings. Plus, the writers' strike had added further financial pain.

A character actor such as Mitch might easily go two years between jobs. So having no savings and no steady income was a calamity waiting to befall the Gold family.

Should Mitch be dropped from his agency, he would have damaged-goods disease, and everyone in town would fear catching it. His auditions would diminish, and the ones he got would become perilously fraught, enveloped with the stench of desperation. Desperation was repellent to already desperate producers. Mitch would be reduced to Viagra commercials and trade shows to keep the bank from foreclosing.

June must never know.

June squinted up Sunset Boulevard from out the passenger window of the town car, which had slowed in front of a low-rise strip mall. She saw a liquor store with the R in LIQUOR hanging from its sign like a fallen rock climber, a Shakey's Pizza, and a twenty-four-hour tattoo parlor. There was no evidence of a swanky nightclub. "Are you sure this is the block?" she asked her husband.

"I don't think those security guards are here to protect the pepperoni," Mitch said as the car slid through a line of beefy, beckoning men in black T-shirts gesturing determinedly like ground controllers at Andrews Air Force Base. Mitch and June had indeed arrived at their destination, that rite of winter, the ABC All Star Round Up Party, a repository of cast members from all the network shows who gather to walk the red carpet and bask in the glory of good ratings, network executive adoration, and media scrutiny.

From the backseat of their town car Mitch and June took in the mass of clipboard-bearing interns standing on the sidewalk, and beyond them, a troupe of entertainment reporters crowded around the front of the unmarked nightclub. Young women in something approximating prom wear, their faces twisted with joy at being at a Hollywood event courtesy of a college friend who worked as a production assistant on *The View*, gathered near the door.

June felt something scratching her back. She reached behind her, and pulled a caramel-coated candy wrapper from the crack in the seat. She wanted out of the dingy car. "Mitch, why are we sitting here?"

"Let's see if someone comes."

Mitch looked hopefully out the smoked window to the spot where, last year, at this very same event, one of the ubiquitous network girls had instantly materialized. At that time he had been on the massive hit *Beverly Hills Adjacent*, on which he played an alcoholic plastic surgeon. But that was last year. (After Mitch made a crack about the head writer's bald spot, his character, Dr. Hyatt, was killed off by a patient whose left breast he had rendered sans nipple.)

For three minutes June itched behind the T-strap of her sandal, mulled the difference between parody and allegory, prayed that her four-year-old daughter, Nora, would not wake up at 5 a.m. again, and wondered with vague alarm if she had remembered to buy cake flour. Mitch chewed frantically on a wooden coffee stirrer that he had pulled from his pocket, one of the many he collected at Starbucks each week. It was a habit only slightly less off-putting than his proclivity for chewing the corners of used Post-it notes.

"Enough!" said June, grabbing the masticated stirrer and shoving it in her open evening bag. "I think we are more than capable of alighting from this car unassisted."

Mitch sighed. "We got an intern last year." He craned his neck out the town car window. "I mean, look at America Ferrera over there— she's got three!"

June heard a voice in her head trilling in a loop that had become increasingly familiar after a decade of network television parties. *Who fucking cares? Who fucking cares?* But her mouth uttered the words she had also come to memorize for these occasions. "Oh, sweetie, you're reading too much into this." She leaned over and opened the car door.

On the sidewalk, eyeing the red carpet, Mitch and June were stymied. Where to go? Finally a network intern, her name badge askew (Syndee, a curious name for a pudgy white girl clearly from the Inland Empire), loped toward them.

"Uhhhhhhh . . . hi. Remind me who you are?"

"Mitch Gold."

"And friend?" Syndee said, glancing toward June.

"June Deitz. I'm his wife actually. Thanks, Syndee."

"Ah, it's SynDEE. So, do you wanna do the carpet?" SynDEE had already turned her eyes toward the limos arriving behind them.

"All right," Mitch said, and walked to the rug's crimson edge like a woman facing her bikini waxer. June trailed behind him. Suddenly the Golds were abandoned by SynDEE, who rushed toward a steel blue Prius pulling up to the curb. From the driver's seat emerged the TV megastar Michael Thomas O'Shea. His car was quickly commandeered by the valet, who ushered it away.

With the help of SynDEE, now animated, Michael Thomas and his wife, the actress Cass Martin, were escorted toward the carpet. Just finishing an eight-year run on a hospital drama, *Eye See You,* for which he had won four Emmys, Michael Thomas was instantly enveloped in a swirl of flashing bulbs and reporters screaming his name. As one of the few African American actresses who could open a movie, Cass was a singular draw herself. Her espresso-toned skin seemed untouched by a makeup artist, and she was inches taller than her shorter-than-you-would-have-thought husband.

With Cass in tow Michael Thomas ambled past Mitch and June, his phalanx of interns clearing a path around him. He wore dark jeans and a cotton T-shirt bearing the single word GREEN.

"Michael Thomas," squawked a tiny television reporter from E! "Who will Dr. Armstrong end up with in the final episode? Deb or Sandra?"

Michael Thomas countered, "You know, Brandy, tonight I really want to focus on what we in the Industry can do to heal our planet."

"Of course, Michael. So . . . um, Deb?"

June and Mitch bravely pushed on down the carpet. A shout rang out from the pack of press gathered along the side. "Mitch! *Molar Opposites* guy!" Mitch realized the voice was coming from a photographer, and he turned instinctively toward him, his face exploding into a giant smile. "Mitch, can you move? You're blocking Marta," the photographer, moons of sweat soaking his underarms, said, referring to an arriving hot newcomer from *Beverly Hills Adjacent*. Turning bright red, Mitch tried to erase from his brain what had just happened.

Once inside, the first person they saw was a stunning Thai server sporting a long ponytail and white yoga pants and a loose shirt embellished with a large sun. Ah, Ra, sun god, June noted to herself, recognizing the preferred polytheistic deity for Angelenos' yoga wear and nightclubs.

"Uh-oh, this place is full of wactors," Mitch said, his word for waiter/actor.

June looked around. "Sweetie, this is a great sign for you! Ra protected his people from the dangerous primordial waters of the underworld. Maybe that is why the network had the party here."

"Two years ago Ra was a dangerous primordial 7-Eleven on this very same corner," Mitch shouted over the din of music. He grabbed a glass of pinot noir off a passing wactor's tray.

"Touché." June laughed. Finding humor in the face of humiliation was one of Mitch's enduring charms.

"But you know what," Mitch said, draping his arm over his wife's shoulders, "your point is well taken. This is still going to be a fun night. Let's drink the network's wine, or try to find some scotch. Anyway, I'd go to a cement-mixer trade show as long as I got a night out with you." June reached up and squeezed his hand.

The room, which June noted was loosely—very loosely—modeled on the Temple of Hatshepsut in Luxor, was almost entirely white. Vinyl banquettes were arranged in circles around giant plaster lions in a crouch. The walls were adorned with relief sculptures depicting small cats and topless women dancing in what appeared to be a festival of Hathor, but who were probably modeled on a scene from that orgy movie starring Tom Cruise.

Mitch looked around to see if he could spot any of his fellow cast members from *Molar Opposites*. The show had been a midseason replacement for a failed comedy starring an extraordinarily expensive celebrity as a self-help-book publisher whose life was perfect in every way but one: relationships. Mitch feared tonight would confirm what his agents had presaged last week: *Molar Opposites* would be losing its time slot to yet another show, this one about a failing sex-crimes detective who is successful in only one way: relationships. There remained a glimmer of hope, of course, that his show would not be canceled, but the lack of an intern was the first dismal augury.

"Hey, I see Rich Friend over there," Mitch said.

"Who?"

"Rich Friend and his wife, Justine Fein. They wrote that lesbian show, *Hi Moms I'm Home*."

"You play golf with him, right? Isn't he the one who wrapped his putter around a tree at Riviera?"

Mitch chuckled. "It was a five iron, June. But yeah, I shot a seventy-eight that day. He didn't take it well."

"Isn't it hard to write with one's spouse?"

"People do it all the time," Mitch said. "Sometimes writers divide it up by genre, say action or comedy, sometimes the man writes the guy parts, sometimes the woman writes the female parts. It just depends."

Bored by the idea of chatting up yet another television visionary, but intrigued with the idea of meeting the man attached to the absurd name Rich Friend, June agreeably grabbed Mitch's hand. They sauntered over to the food station, where Rich and Justine were debating the choice of sashimi or Yorkshire pudding.

"Hey, Rich, how's it going?" Mitch said. "Nice to see you, Justine. This is my wife, June."

June studied Rich. He had the body of tennis player, thin, muscular, but without those weird bulging biceps that men in Hollywood often sported. In short: a handsome man who looked his age.

After a quick hello with Mitch, Rich Friend turned his gaze to June, looking at her with what seemed utter fascination. "Mitch told me you teach poetry at UCLA?"

"I do." June waited for him to look behind her for someone else to talk to. At network parties, few people even asked what she did for a living, and once they heard, they suddenly had to use the restroom.

Rich remained focused on her. "Is it true that you actually studied *Nibelungenlied* in its original German?"

"Did Mitch tell you that?"

"No, I Googled you."

Slightly stunned, June felt her face get hot. "I thought people in this town only Googled themselves."

Rich laughed. "Well, research first, and then conclude. So did you?"

"It was a long time ago. You forget Middle High German once you pay off your student loans."

"Well, I'm awed."

The corners of Rich Friend's azure eyes crinkled up and seemed to animate his entire face. June noticed his teeth. They did not blind her with bleach tones, and his lips seemed alert with impending cleverness. He looked like someone she knew, but she could not quite place him.

Rich's wife chimed in: "After Berkeley I devoted a summer to reading all ninety thousand verses of the *Mahabharata*. I think I did ten."

"That's not the same kind of accomplishment, Justine," Rich said.

June looked at Justine to see if she registered this as an insult, but her face revealed nothing. Her thick blond hair fell to the middle of her back, and she was swathed in silk scarves. She was in no way fat, but no one would use the word "thin" to describe her either. She had warmly rounded edges, June noted, a sort of Kate Winslet, circa *Sense and Sensibility*. Her eyes, a deeper green than June had seen before, were partly obscured by her red oval glasses.

"I love that poem. What compelled you to take it on?" June asked, though in truth she found it incredibly tedious. Justine spent several minutes explaining her fascination with India, seeded during her year as an exchange student in high school, and the two compared notes on a variety of authors. Rich chimed in: "Did Justine mention she couldn't get off the toilet the first three weeks in Bombay?"

Justine laughed a little. "It's true. Delhi belly."

June smiled at them both, wondering when the conversation would end. Mitch jumped in again, and began to talk to Rich about his new driver.

"I have an open spot at Rustic Canyon this weekend. Wanna play?" Mitch asked.

"I can't. Aspen."

"So, another time?"

"For sure," Rich said.

Justine turned to Patrick Dempsey, who had just sidled up for a bear hug and plate of sashimi. Rich joined his wife and the TV star, but not before glancing at June once more with greater admiration than both the conversation and their minimal acquaintance seemed to merit. This was a sort she had seen before, the one who professionally shines his light on you, as if you were the first person he had ever met who actually spoke English, too, until the next customer comes along. Except that June, with nothing to offer the world of Hollywood commerce, was rarely the target of such an unfettered gaze.

"It was so nice to meet you, June."

"Later, potato," June said, oddly.

Rich Friend laughed.

Mitch and June glanced around, looking for someone else to talk to. Mitch's eyes fixed on a burly ginger-haired man. It was Willie Dermot, Mitch's longtime nemesis—a possible Duke of Wellington to Mitch's Napoleon—on an undersized white seat alongside his elegant, sharp-featured wife, Larissa.

Willie and Mitch, both tall and the same age, had similar abilities to play sarcastic, law-enforcing, or unbalanced. With his dark hair and Eastern European features, Mitch was viewed generally as the "urban" (i.e., Jewish) choice, whereas Willie, redheaded and fair skinned, would be the WASP alternative. And so it had been: two decades of the weatherman in a Hollywood blockbuster (Willie); town sheriff in a horror-film spoof (Mitch); sex-crimes investigator (both, many times); wacky friend of the bride on half-hour comedy (Willie); bipolar dentist (Mitch).

"Shit," Mitch muttered. "Why does Willie have to be here? He doesn't even have a show on ABC this season."

"How do you think I feel? Now I have to listen to Larissa Dermot spend twenty-five minutes describing the color pallette choices for the preschool auction."

"Well, I hope you brought a swatch book, because they see us."

Larissa's snug sheath dress accentuated her perfectly toned biceps, acquired by daily classes between school drop-offs and pickups at a Brentwood Krav Maga studio. Her iPhone sat humming on the table, downloading e-mails about flower arrangements for teacher appreciation week and her next dermatology appointment.

June pulled on her dress. She had meant to get her hair blown out for the party, but got distracted cleaning the errant carrot tops and dried-out fennel bulbs from the bottom shelf of her refrigerator. Next to Larissa, June always felt as if her thighs were pudgy, and she tucked her legs close together as she sat down. June had an untidy elegance, with a slightly heart-shaped face, decorated with delicate features, like an antique teacup on display in a breakfront. Her auburn hair, which frizzed in the humidity, fell just to her shoulders, and she cut it when it grew beyond them. Her eyes were dark brown, and held the bulk of her emotions, daggers when angry, dancing in the light when pleased. Her face, free of anything but lipstick, and her eyebrows, which were unwaxed, pegged her for "natural," which in Los Angeles was not a compliment for a woman over twenty-five.

"Hey, man, how's the show going?" Willie asked, hugging Mitch. Over Willie's shoulder, Mitch caught sight of a large network poster festooned with a montage of all the season's shows. Among the eight-by-ten publicity shots of medical dramas, situation comedies, *Beverly Hills Adjacent,* and three glossies of Michael Thomas O'Shea solo, the promotional photo for *Molar Opposites,* smaller than a baby tooth, poked out embarrassingly at the bottom of the poster.

"Did you get picked up for the back nine?" Willie pressed Mitch. June always wondered how Hollywood came to adopt a golf expression to refer to the final nine episodes of a new show's first season. Why didn't they use a swimming term? The final nine laps? She mused about this further, tuning Willie out.

"We're on the bubble," Mitch answered, now internally conceding that the degrading spot on the poster signaled the bubble had already burst. "You guys opened huge this weekend," Mitch went on in a determinedly sunny tone, referring to Willie's role as the voice of villain Poison in the animated film *Super Roach.*

"Number one in the country and I'm a Happy Meal action figure!"

Mitch mentally added up foreign residuals, first network showing, and DVD sales of *Super Roach,* plus the toy thing. A million at least.

"That's some bucks," Mitch said. Larissa smiled and seemed to inflate like an anorexic puffer fish. June stared at Willie, who reminded her of that giant Paul Bunyan statue in Baxter, Minnesota. He had the same almost comically oversized shoulders, out of proportion to his scrawny legs. His grin was slightly lopsided, and his eyes seemed to vacillate between overzealous glee and sheer bewilderment. June stifled a giggle, thinking of Larissa as Willie's decidedly spindly blue ox.

Willie went on. "Hey, I caught your little film at the ArcLight this weekend. I wish I could afford to do quality work like that, but you gotta feed the bulldog!"

"Yeah, ten screens, and I'm an action figure at Whole Foods," Mitch cracked.

June attempted to change the conversation. "So, who do you guys like in the governor's race?"

"Whoever brings down our property taxes!" Larissa said, laughing.

"Well, property taxes are statutorily determined in California. In fact—"

"Yeah, right, I forgot about that," Larissa interjected, hoping to head off yet another one of June's newspapery blah, blah, blahs with a quick toss to the safe world of their children's preschool. "June, will you be on the coloring committee at Tot Shabbat this winter?"

June was amused by how Larissa and Willie, who were not Jewish, had thrown themselves into the world of Temple Beth Israel, joining the synagogue in order to get their daughter, Chloe, a spot at the coveted preschool. They had no intention of converting, but they had learned to pray phonetically so as to participate in the random bread blessing and Passover seder, even as they continued to attend the Church of the Good Shepherd in Beverly Hills every Sunday. "Um, I'm a little busy this semester," June said.

Mitch overheard this and began to smile broadly. "Hey, did June tell you that she won the William Parker Riley Prize? It's a huge honor in the academic community. And she's up for a big grant this year, too." Mitch was immensely proud of June's professional accomplishments, which were many, though she rarely spoke about them. Two years ago, her students had nominated her for a teaching award at UCLA—something she never mentioned, even though she had come in second.

Larissa clucked, "Oh, I could never have time to fill out papers for stuff like that. I have so much to do at home. You know, that's why I left the business when Chloe was born. It is just so hard to work and be the kind of mom I want to be. And now I'm busy looking at schools, which is a major execution, because, as you know, Chloe's very gifted."

June nodded, remembering that the last time she saw very-gifted Chloe she was chowing down on a dollop of paste. "Yes, that must be quite an execution."

June thought about trying to activate that feature which makes your own cell phone ring and reached inside her bag to grab it, and a soggy wooden stirrer fell out onto the table. Larissa looked repulsed, and June quickly stowed the stick back in her purse.

At that moment a youngish man in pleated khakis with a reporter's pad in his shirt pocket approached Mitch. "Hi, I'm Owen Thrush from the *Calgary Herald!*" he said. "*Molar Opposites!* You're big in Canada!"

And so the lovelorn bipolar dentist gave his one and only interview of the evening. *Calgary Herald.* Roughly twenty-one seconds.

> Q: Is mental illness common among medical professionals in the United States?
> A: I think we really are highlighting disabilities in an empowering way.
> Q: Are you coming back next season?
> A: Here's hoping!

Willie snickered as Owen Thrush walked away. Mitch looked sheepish. The four made plans for a family picnic at Roxbury Park, which June knew Larissa would cancel, likely under the pretense of a hideous lactose incident that had left Chloe incapacitated.

Twelve minutes later Mitch and June were back on Sunset waiting for their driver. The hem of June's dress had snagged on a plaster sphinx and her hair was beginning to frizz at the ends. June noticed a woman's head bobbing up and down in the backseat of a passing car.

"You don't see a lot of postparty blow jobs anymore. Why?"

Mitch peered over June to take in the action. "Shame, really." June giggled, but Mitch began to stare at the ground. "We're getting canceled. That's clear."

The driver pulled up and they poured themselves back into their repellent strawberry air freshener/Winston Light–smelling car.

"I seriously could puke," June said. "What kind of person creates a cardboard strawberry, dips it in toxic chemicals, and proclaims it a nice alternative to body odor?"

"You're right. No more town cars to Hollywood events. Let's move to Oregon!"

"Oregon? I don't like the shoes they wear in Oregon."

"What?"

"Those ugly rubber boots. And what would you do there anyway?"

"I don't know, do theater again. Finally read *The Faerie Queene* with you by the fireplace. Watch you make gnocchi."

"Oh, gnocchi never works at home. Anyway, I'll take that under advisement. In the meantime, here in Los Angeles, do you want to go to the Apple Pan? The food at that party was inedible."

"Why not?" Mitch raised his voice, a bit too much as usual, addressing the driver. "Take us to Pico and Westwood please." The driver tugged on his cell phone earpiece.

"Huh?"

"I said Pico and Westwood. Sorry for interrupting. *Thank you!*" Mitch pulled a new wooden stick out of his jacket pocket. "Was I just rude?"

The car had turned west on Santa Monica Boulevard and June was looking out the window, trying to see if bougainvilleas were starting to bloom. In the wash of the streetlights, she could make out their hot pink buds, licking at the night air. "Yes, you were rather rude, frankly."

"Well he wasn't listening."

The town car pulled up to the famous hamburger spot—a midcentury shack of a restaurant slumped under the neighboring low-rise, its green faux-thatched roof seemingly sunk in on itself—and Mitch and June grabbed a place at the curved counter.

Sitting under a cloud of hickory grease, among lobster-shift utility workers, hipsters on their way home, and a group of drunken teenage girls in halters who maybe recognized Mitch, the couple dug into their burgers. June poured her Coke into a white paper cup. Mitch picked the tomato off his burger, tossed it aside, and snorted: "Big in Canada."

CHAPTER 2

Mitch directed his blue Saab east on Franklin, past a store advertising "sexy" artificial plants. Every time Mitch drove along this particular stretch, as he had dozens of times on the way to his manager's office, Mitch wondered what exactly made a fake fern sexy. Tad Meier had been in a dilapidated building on the corner of Franklin and Poinsettia for over a decade, before exotic pastries were sold on Sweetzer, back when gangs and drugged-out guys selling straw cowboy hats outnumbered architects and midcentury furniture stores.

Like every actor, Mitch had both an agent and a manager. Tim, the agent, negotiated the deals, then passed the information to Tad, Mitch's manager, who relayed it back to Mitch, an inexplicable system that cost Mitch a total of 20 percent of his salary.

As in May, as in October, it had not rained for thirty-one days, and January was proving as warm as last June. But really, Mitch reflected as he felt the hot wind on his face, in Hollywood, there is only one season: pilot season.

It begins every January, when the networks choose a dozen or so each of sitcoms and dramas to make into pilots, moves through the winter as actors are cast on the shows, and ends in spring with only a handful of pilots actually making it to the prime-time schedule. As with farmers enduring seasons of drought and finally being rewarded with a wet spring and an abundant wheat yield, actors look to each pilot season to bring them a crop of Nielsen families whose enthusiasm will save the homestead—or at least upgrade the master bath. Now Mitch was beginning the cycle again.

Mitch pulled into the lot behind his manager's office, and saw Tad's black Range Rover, adorned with a bumper sticker, DOG IS MY COPILOT. Mitch walked through the parking lot to Tad's office, which was situated between a tapas restaurant and a Red Mango yogurt shop.

"Hi, Monica," Mitch hailed the woman in the long black sweater sitting in front of a computer terminal, back to the door, a telephone headset perched in her mass of blond and red-streaked hair. When she swung around in her chair, the acne-scarred office manager was not Monica, but a new addition in the seemingly endless run of Tad's assistants. Mitch knew what was coming: having to introduce himself to his manager's assistant for the nineteenth time this year, and soon she would be gone anyway, and he'd have to start again.

"It's Jamie. And who can I say you are?"

"I'm Mitch Gold. I'm on Tad's list."

"Oops! Totally. I haven't gotten through that yet."

"Okay, can you . . ."

Jamie glanced back at her *Us Weekly*.

"Can I go in?"

"Fine with me!" she chirped.

Mitch walked past Jamie's desk as an ailing German shepherd, eyes watery, whiskers foamed with drool, holding a mangled teddy bear in his mouth, limped toward Mitch, who not so gently pushed the dog out of his way and walked into the office, where he found Tad on the phone.

The office was surprisingly decrepit, considering Tad's high-profile client list. The paint was peeling and the rugs were stained with animal life. On the walls were nearly a dozen photographs of Tad and his most famous clients, hung in cheap frames, and almost as many of women whom Tad had met at his favorite haunts, decked out in gold lamé costumes.

Forced to choose between a black chair and a couch where two mangy cocker spaniels were snoozing, Mitch opted for the couch.

"Well, if it doesn't have financing now, you can't wait on it," Tad said to whoever was on the other end of the line. "I know, sweetie. I get it. But you've got this other abuse movie and it has money. Your abuse clock is ticking. This is Oscar bait. Scarlett has hers lined up. And the thing is psychological abuse—really more fresh than sexual abuse anyway. Two words: Dakota Fanning. Exactly. Uh-huh." He listened to the other end a second more, then glanced toward Mitch. "No, honey, I've got time."

Mitch tore a small corner off a script lying on the couch, balled it up, and began to chew it. Tad looked at him and silently mouthed: "That's disgusting!"

Tad was the essence of medium: average height, brown eyes—a forgettable face. His black hair was slicked back, emphasizing a high forehead, and his mouth twisted in a perpetual smirk.

Mitch pretended to pat one of the dogs but actually just caressed the script. He picked it up and started scanning it, looking for lines that might be attached to a forty-year-old comic Jewish man. It seemed to be some menopause movie. Maybe there was a doctor he could play? He was unnerved by Tad's endless phone patter.

"You deserved that best body on the beach award. That's you. Anyway, Urth Café, Wednesday right? Okay, babe. See you then. Uh-huh. Okay. I'll let them know—we pass on the sex abuse, we're in for the psychological deal. Okay. Bye-bye!"

A white parrot with a giant shock of green feathers on his head was perched on a bird swing in the corner of Tad's office. Mitch glanced at the parrot, which was now squawking: "Gotta go! Gotta go!"

"New friend?" Mitch asked Tad.

"Yeah. I'm training him to shut up when a client calls. He was flying around the canyon. An escapee I guess. I found him on a hike."

"So, thanks for telling me you have another assistant. What happened to Monica?"

"She never showed up after the Zeus thing."

"That ferocious rottweiler?"

"Zeus is a sweet dog, Mitch. He had a tough childhood—it's not his fault he took a chunk out of her leg."

"Do dogs have childhoods?"

"SQUAWK! GOTTA GO! GOTTA GO!" the parrot screeched.

"Oh, are you hungry, little buddy?" Tad said in the general direction of the bird, fumbling around for a Cheese Nip.

Tad looked back at Mitch, his voice transforming from parrot daddy to disgruntled former employer. "Monica claims she's gonna sue me. Hate her. Listen, anyway, it's a drag about *Molar Opposites* getting canceled. You were really good in that. So, what else is going on?"

"You tell me. I like to eat. So do Nora and June. What have you got? Any movies?"

"Well, features are down. That sucks. But there is one thing, a low-budget deal, but it's shooting in Morocco all August. Scale plus ten and a hepatitis shot. Don't count on air-conditioning."

"Uh-huh. Well I'd work for scale if it's a really good script."

"Oh, it's a shitty script."

"So why did you mention it?"

"Options. Options."

"Okay. Pilot season starts in two weeks. What's on the breakdowns?" Mitch started to riffle through the pile of printed papers sitting on Tad's desk, each one a synopsis of the proposed show and the available roles.

"Give me that," Tad said, snatching the pile from Mitch. "Please don't go through my stuff, Mitch. Okay? What do we have. . . . Lemme see, here's one, *Cane Mutiny*, about a blind renegade cop."

"Umm . . ."

"Here's a half-hour sitcom about a polygamist and his wives. Working title is *Too Many Cooks*. I think the husband is out to Danny DeVito. Maybe they'll see you for the minister."

"I can do Christian."

"Are Mormons Christians?"

"I think so."

"Okay," Tad continued. "And there's *Cro-Magnon*, a half hour about cave people living in modern times who run a fast-food restaurant."

"That's incredibly stupid. Get me in on it."

"Right." Tad resumed rifling. "Oh, and what about the Fein/Friend thing?" He began reading from the breakdown: 'High-powered single political reporter adopts a child from Ethiopia and tries to balance home and family.' There are some good co-worker parts."

More parrot sounds from the corner of the room. "Squawk! Gotta go!"

"So submit me for this stuff, Tad."

"I have."

"Then why are we talking about it?" Mitch asked.

"Because I'm your manager. I take care of you. Whenever, wherever, even when you come here without an appointment."

"Squawk! Make an appointment!"

"Thanks for the reminder, um, bird," said Mitch. "So, how's Lori?" Tad had been seeing the stripper for the past month.

"Oh that. That's over. Cat person, didn't like the dogs in the bed. Whatever."

"Too bad. She was, you know—"

"Stacked!" Tad snickered.

"I was going to say bright."

More snickers.

"I almost forgot," Tad said. "Joy Wainscott called about you."

"Joy?" Mitch felt a weird tingling sensation in his legs. Joy Wainscott was a playwright and director with whom he had worked in New York many years ago, who had developed what could only be characterized as an unhealthy obsession with him, best marked by the pair of lavender panties she once placed folded up in his stage makeup case. Then there was the anonymous poetry left on his fire escape, which Mitch realized was written by Joy only when he discovered her at 3 a.m. hanging from the last rung of the suspended ladder eight feet above Second Avenue. He was once at dinner with his parents at Acme Bar and Grill and saw her sitting at a table alone, wearing a wig and giant tortoiseshell glasses, reading *No Exit*, glancing at their table occasionally.

Through the years Mitch had heard news of Joy moving from off-Broadway to Broadway, then on to independent features. These days, she was making a name for herself in Hollywood. But, as much as it would help his career to be in one of her projects, the mere thought of Joy Wainscott gave him the serious creeps.

"Yeah," Tad said. "You know her last film was huge at Sundance, right? She won best screenplay and was up for best director. I guess she's written something for Sony. Ridley Scott's directing this one. There's a part you're right for. Apparently she wants to talk to you about it directly, which is a good thing."

Mitch reached across the desk and grabbed the crumpled PETCO receipt where Tad has scribbled Joy's name and cell phone number.

"Okay. I'll call her." Mitch took a deep breath. "So anyway, Tad, what do you hear about people getting dropped from CAA?"

"People get dropped all the time from the Death Star. Why? Need another thing to be neurotic about?"

"Well, you know it's a huge agency. I just want to make sure I'm secure there."

"Hey, Brad Pitt isn't secure at CAA. Getting dumped from CAA would be really bad, man. Nowhere to go but down from there. But you're a great actor. You'll get another show this season. Are you still stressing about the runaway-contractor thing?"

"Always. We're waiting to hear from the district attorney."

"Well, you'll get work. You always do," Tad said.

Mitch felt a sharp pain in his left temple. The parrot began its squawking again, and the intercom lit up with Jamie. "Tad, Jessica on line one."

Tad barked at the parrot: "CLIENT! BIG CLIENT!" and stunningly, the bird hushed.

"Jessssssssssss. Hi again. Uh-huh. Uh-huh. No problem." Tad swiveled away in his chair, and a cocker spaniel tried to sidle up to Mitch as he pulled a final edge of a script for some chewing material to go.

Mitch waved vaguely in the direction of Jamie on his way out. She looked up at him with a smile. "Bye, Mark!" she said.

CHAPTER 3

June prayed she would not be late for the meeting at Nora's preschool. She had lost track of time dishing with her colleague Carol about the temerity of a professor who had gotten tenure three years ago and not published a word since. She glanced at the clock on her dashboard. Damn! She had thirteen minutes to get to Kindergarten Kibitz. Not enough time to fight her way through rush-hour traffic from Westwood to Rancho Park. June foresaw her familiar fate—being marked "the tardy mom" by sideways glances from those parents who had arrived two hours before the meeting to "set up" three baskets of cookies and arrange forty bottles of Fiji water into tidy rows.

She sat at a light on Wilshire gazing at a black Lexus with tinted windows and the license plate D D FAKE. Was the driver Breasts, the artificially endowed woman she saw each morning running around the golf course in full makeup, her streaked hair flying behind her, skin tanned the color of butternut squash?

June glanced down at her cell phone resting in the dirty cup holder of her car and resisted the urge to dial Mitch at home to check up on Nora. June was making an effort not to talk on her phone while driving anymore, given that all things car-related—staying in her lane, parallel parking, discerning north from south, finding the entrance of an underground lot on the first try—remained challenging for her, even after years in LA. She heard the blare of music to her right, and looked over to see a young guy in a camouflage green Hummer, with a skinny pale face badly in need of a shave, motion to her to roll down her window. June pushed the button and watched her window descend.

*"I wanna let allllll y'all niggaz know in here tonight
that this is that Wu-Tang shit!"*

"Yo, which way to Robertson?"

June made an apologetic shrug and responded, *"Absit invidia ego
hospes sum."*

Mr. Hummer yelled, "FUCKING ILLEGALS!" and sped off.

Again at a lengthy light, June was no longer able to resist the
phone. She pushed her earpiece awkwardly into her ear and quickly dialed her friend Adrian in New York. Adrian worked as a restaurant
critic for *New York* magazine and so was often available to chat at odd
hours, which worked well with the difference in time zones.

"Hey, friend," June said. "What are you up to?"

"I'm eating a huge pig," Adrian answered. June imagined him sitting at a restaurant in the West Village, bottles of excellent red wine
and a large roasted sow on the table, surrounded by six friends who were
licking their fingers.

"Fun," June said. "What are you up to this weekend?"

"Fellating, I think. But I need to run because I don't want to be
rude to my guests. Everything okay?"

June talked quickly so she could hang up before the light changed.
"Here is my day so far: a jerk in a Hummer asking for directions, three
students who neglected to turn in their papers on Spenser, and now I
am off to a meeting at school with a room full of mothers who don't
know the name of the mayor. One highlight, though, I finally mastered
my pie pastry. Seeyabye."

Adrian, June, and their friends Amanda and Ian had been a gang
of four in New York before June left for Los Angeles. During the college
years, they were an inseparable force at the dimly lit Hungarian Pastry
Shop on the Upper West Side, where they would study for exams, drink
coffee, and, in Ian's case, flirt with the young Hungarian waitresses.

After locating a parking spot that might or might not be big
enough for the Honda, June backed in unsuccessfully then lunged forward, planting the front tire up on the sidewalk. Reversing, she bumped
the SUV behind her and watched it sway. Then she pulled forward
again, hearing a horrible crunch as the front hubcap ground against the

curb. She began sweating and twisting the steering wheel, hoping this was going to straighten out the car. It didn't. She locked the door and walked away.

June made her way to the preschool, a low orange and yellow building adjacent to a synagogue with banners inviting early enrollment and the name "Temple Beth Israel Preschool" in childlike lettering. June rushed toward one of the classrooms, already three-quarters filled with women dressed in tight exercise clothes commenting about the excellence of their child's artwork, which was Scotch-taped along the classroom wall. June squeezed herself onto a toddler chair and turned her gaze toward the teachers sitting before the group.

"Oh, hi, June." Of course: Larissa, balancing her sculptured ass on a tiny seat. Willie, sitting next to her, was dozing. "Mitch couldn't make it tonight, huh?" Larissa asked, turning the corners of her mouth up in the way one might while getting a passport photo taken.

"Actually, he's home with Nora."

"Surrrrrre. You know, on nights like this I just feel sooooo lucky to have a live-in. Then Willie and I can both be a part of the school community."

"Uh-huh," June said.

Larissa raised her eyebrows a little. "I'm guessing with your construction situation things are a little tight though, huh?"

"That's an understatement. But we're fine, Larissa."

"You know, I don't want to be a bummer, but there are only so many failed shows an actor can sustain. I've been in this business. I *know*."

Larissa's time "in the business" consisted of one season on a Disney show about kids who lived in an upscale hotel (three lines each month), a bit part as a nurse, and a Vagisil commercial (two lines: "Feeling discomfort?" "Ask your pharmacist.").

"I mean, thank God for *Super Roach*. Ya know," Larissa continued, looking at Willie, who was snoring gently, a small dab of drool on his chin. Larissa dabbed at the wet spot absently, as if Willie were her toddler.

At that moment a woman came rushing into the room—it was Lexi, head room mother, a position she had fought long and hard for last year, besting the other three contenders by organizing several

23

teacher-appreciation lunches. Lexi, mother of Walker, wore tall high-heeled boots and an open-necked sari over an expensive pair of jeans.

"Hi, Lexi," June started, eager to escape Larissa, and remembering something she had wanted to do for Nora. "I notice you started a playgroup after school."

Lexi crinkled her nose almost imperceptibly. "Oh darn, June. No nannies in playgroup."

"Well, maybe I could come every other week, when my class gets out early?"

"You know, June, our group is pretty small, and we like to keep it consistent for the kiddies. It must be so hard to work."

June tried to think of something vaguely neutral to say. "Before I forget, Lexi, you didn't RSVP for Nora's birthday party. Can Walker come?"

"Oh, that's on Saturday the twelfth, right? I am so sorry, but we have a conflict that day."

"Actually it's Sunday the thirteenth."

Lexi looked over June's shoulder. "Oh. Sunday. You know what? I have a girl's brunch. But thanks for the invite."

June, her face burning, moved her seat over.

To open the meeting, Barbara, one of Nora's teachers, the one who wore a large beret each day, spoke first. "Welcome to Kindergarten Kibitz! I want to start tonight's discussion with one CRITICAL issue, and that concerns *snack*."

A mom in Lycra sweatpants and a T-shirt imprinted with a monkey face piped up. "I'm totally confused. Are we a peanut-free school or a totally nut-free school? And by the way, I think you serve too many Ritz crackers. Could you work on skills that keep the kids from eating too many?"

The snack talk continued. Is goat's milk okay? How about grapes? Soon the lanky dad who had spent the first fifteen minutes of the meeting whispering into his cell phone said, "I'm really wondering what the goal of the year will be. Is anyone else as uncomfortable as I am with the fact that the teachers have really not articulated any clear academic goalposts for the year?"

June quipped, "I'd like Nora to master decoding DNA."

June was new to the preschool, while most of the parents had been taking their children there since they were babies, beginning with Mommy and Me music classes, graduating to a program for two-year-olds, and on through something called developmental pre-K, which was filled in large part with boys whose parents did not want them to go to kindergarten until they were six.

Because she had not bothered to send Nora to preschool until she was four—June thought she got more at home with her nanny, Olga, reading and going to the library—June was always two steps behind the other parents, a place she seemed doomed to for perpetuity. By now, social groups had long been established, playdates formulated, classroom volunteer assignments made, rhythms learned.

June had tried her best in the first half of the year. She had hosted a back-to-school coffee, but lost track of the details while preparing a lecture on Grendel's oedipal complex in *Beowulf*, and made the unfortunate mistake of inviting half the class for 1 p.m. and the other for 3 p.m. This made for a confusing and endless afternoon that she had failed to recover from. Then there was the whole problem with never leaving enough spare underwear and socks in Nora's cubby; for the first three months of school, her daughter, who often dirtied herself with paint or mud from a puddle on the slide, would come home wearing the jeans and underpants of some other child whose mother had made sure to keep her child's cubby well stocked. Often it was boy's underwear, which Nora occasionally stuffed with socks.

June had run out of time to do things like help set up for the Thanksgiving parties and buy corn on the cob for Shavuot, and had no patience for spending drop-off time comparing the relative merits of the city's gymnastics programs, children's boots, and napping schedules. Her ability to feign interest and give time dissipated quickly. But Nora loved the school, so for her sake June was trying to just get through the rest of the year.

Lanky Dad ignored June's joke. "I think it would be incredibly helpful if you sent out weekly e-mail reports on what they do each day in preschool. In fact, what would be really great is if you could send one out on Monday with the week's goals, and then follow up on Friday with an update on how it all went."

"Well, we don't really have computers in the classroom—," Barbara began.

Agent Dad (Nora said his son threw blocks) chimed in. "Seriously, that is a great idea. Like last semester, I remember you did a bunch of stuff with the color blue. Now see, if you had informed the parents ahead of time, we could have reinforced knowledge of all things blue at home, because we really like to feel a part of things." Agent Dad's cell phone rang, and he excused himself.

Before the academic goals of preschool could be further discussed, it was time for Lexi to speak: "Let me tell you how passionate I am about this school. And we need parents like you to have passion, too, when it comes to traffic duty, bake sales, and all that good stuff. Gentle reminder! If you invite any child from the class to your child's birthday party, you need to invite every child. We don't like hurt feelings."

June began to panic. Traffic duty. Baking pies. Tenure papers, grant proposals, helping Mitch with auditions, class hours. She looked around to see if anyone else was visibly riled. Instead, parents—mostly mothers, June noted—began to sign on the sheets passing through the classroom, jotting their names in ink along the dotted lines for volunteers.

Then conversation turned back to the relative nut-oil qualities of sandwich breads. Quietly grabbing her bag, June got up and stole from the room. Larissa shot her a dirty look, but June didn't care. If she hurried she might just have time to read Nora a bedtime story.

June ran to her car, and found it with a fifty-dollar ticket attached to the windshield for parking too far from the curb. Damn it.

The lavender light of dusk had long faded to black when June stepped up onto her porch and leaned down to gather the latest bits of flotsam left to greet her: one Thai food menu, a card for a landscaping business, and another goddamn notepad featuring the grinning face of a real estate agent. She walked in to find Mitch reading *Go Dog Go* to Nora, who was cuddled in his lap, sucking on the end of her blanket. June sat on the foot of the bed listening to Mitch reading. "'Do you like my hat?'" he said in a midcentury Minnie Pearl voice. "'No, I do not like your hat,'" he answered himself, suddenly low and menacing.

Nora was spellbound. As soon as he finished she begged, "One more, Daddy, pleeese!"

"Not tonight, baby. I'll read more tomorrow."

Nora turned to June: "Hi, Mama." Too sleepy to get up, she held her arms out to June, who buried her face in Nora's neck. It smelled of baby shampoo and mowed grass. Nora's tiny face was festooned with giant Harry Potter glasses, which brushed June's cheek as she kissed her. June lifted Nora from Mitch's lap and tucked her into bed. "Mama, I think I want to be a paleontologist when I grow up. Or, maybe an artist."

"That sounds terrific, Noony. Take off your glasses now, okay?"

Nora insisted on wearing the glasses, beginning each day squinting as she rose from the bed, professing that she couldn't see without them. She wasn't allowed to wear them on the playground, so June had developed a long ritual of pretending to put contacts into Nora's widely opened eyes before the school day began.

"Today was silly with Daddy."

"How so?"

"We were driving by the grocery store, and these guys tried to bang us with their big car, and then Daddy started saying bad words at them, and they took our pictures."

"Oh. I'll have to ask Daddy about that."

"Oh wait, I forgot, he told me not to say it to you. Mama, can people really shrink?"

"No, sweetie, they can't."

June sang a few bars of Amy Winehouse—children's songs made her ill at ease. "'They tried to make me go to rehab, I said no, no, no. . . .'"

"Can I have water?" Nora asked.

"Sure." June walked into the kitchen, and the phone rang.

"Hello?" she said into the phone, which she wedged between her ear and shoulder as she rummaged through the cabinets for a sippy cup for Nora.

"It's potato."

"What?"

"Potato. As in later."

With surprise June recognized the voice of Rich Friend, a sort of caramel oozing over the line.

"We were wondering if you and your other half wanted to join us for dinner Friday night. Just Orso. Hope that's okay?"

27

"Well, I think that's fine. I mean, I'm sure it is." Mitch would be consulted, but face time with the creator of a new pilot was not an invitation he would likely decline.

"June, I look forward to it."

"Me, too," she said, a bit too eagerly June suddenly felt, and her face got hot. "I love the idea of eating there."

Stupid! Who loved eating at Orso?

"Excellent. Oh, Willie and Larissa will be coming. Is that cool?"

It wasn't. But the die was cast. She put the water next to Nora's bed, but the child was already asleep.

"Who was that?" Mitch asked.

"Rich Friend. They invited us for dinner Friday. Willie and Larissa are coming."

"Jesus, can't we get away from those two once in a while?"

"I know. They were both at the meeting," June said, plopping down into a kitchen chair.

"Willie was at a school meeting during pilot season? Did he have a script with him?"

"No, he appeared to be asleep."

"Good. He's not busy yet."

"Mitch, could you be more obsessed with Willie's career?" June remembered what Larissa had said about Mitch's show being canceled. "Is this year special?"

Mitch poured himself a glass of water. "'Special,' what means 'special'? I need to get a job if that's what you're asking. By the way, I played golf with Martin today. He has a new horror movie in the works. Werewolves this time, shoots in Bulgaria, says there might be a part for me."

"Playing a human?"

"Nah, the humans are all eighteen. But I could make a lot of overtime with a heavy prosthetic role. A couple of extra hours in the makeup trailer every day add up. Remember how much I raked in playing that Cardassian general on *Deep Space Nine?*"

"Do you want to play a werewolf?" June asked.

"Sure, why not? And listen, I need your help with a pilot audition for tomorrow. In fact, as it turns out I have five auditions tomorrow. FIVE."

June quickly inventoried the things she would rather do than practice a pilot audition with Mitch: watch *The Colbert Report*, flip through
Gourmet magazine, cut her toenails, clean under the kitchen sink, and
fantasize about actually getting a door to the kitchen, which now, thanks
to Uri the contractor, was only an unfinished frame.

Some people dreaded winter and the ill effects of diminished light.
Others lamented the start of summer, with the midday sun beating down
on their necks and their homes filled with children with nothing particular to do. June hated pilot season, with its script reading at all hours,
crises of self-confidence in her otherwise relatively even-keeled husband,
and abject misery forever seeping into the dinner hour during a time of
endless uncertainty. Her role, never to be acknowledged at the Emmys,
was the spouse, ever bucking up her husband.

Mitch walked out to his garage office to gather up his "sides"—the
pages of the scripts that contained the scenes he would be auditioning
for. There were five pages for Detective Joey Murphy, seven for the boss
on a half-hour, six for the part of a book publisher on an hour-long
drama, ten for a recently divorced wacky dad, and another eight for the
principal on a one-hour show about a troubled school in the Bronx.

June followed Mitch into their bedroom, sat down on the bed, and
took a copy of the pages Mitch handed her.

"Which one are we doing?"

"I think I have the best shot at the one-hour procedural. So let's
do that one."

"Okay, what's the premise?" June asked.

"Bunch of detectives. Serial killer is after prostitutes."

"Shockingly original."

"Why don't you e-mail Steve McPherson about that, honey? I'm
just the actor."

June laughed. "Right. So what's your role?"

"Joseph Murphy." Mitch handed June the breakdown, sent by the
casting director to the actor along with the sides. June read it silently.

*Joseph "Joey" Murphy—Series regular. 40–50. Police captain. Any
ethnicity. Joey is a good honest cop who has seen it all in this
tough Hollywood precinct. Gang members murdered his wife*

after Joey collared their leader, and he is now bringing up his teenage daughter alone. When she begins to run with the wrong crowd, Joey worries he may lose her, too. MUST BE GOOD WITH COMEDY.

"I am failing to see the need for comedic skills," June said.

"I know. Stupid. Can we work?"

"Okay. Who am I?"

"Lieutenant Johnson."

"Johnson! What a boring name. Anyway, action!"

Mitch stood in the middle of the room. *"Well, what have we got, Lieutenant?"*

June read her line: *"Another dead hooker. White, maybe sixteen. This one was stabbed with a steak knife twenty times. It's not pretty."*

"Sixteen, that's my daughter's age. Any witnesses?"

"Not yet."

"Stabbed twenty times on Hollywood Boulevard and no one noticed? Where's the body?"

"Over by the patrol car," read June, distracted by what appeared to be a large brown spider making its way up her dresser.

Mitch took a few steps, then squatted down and pretended to unzip a body bag. *"Jesus, what a mess."*

"Mitch, it looks like you're considering a can of diced pineapple, not staring at a corpse."

"I know, it's just hard with nothing there. If I was shooting they'd have a body bag."

"Do you want me to be the body?" June offered. "I could lie down there and be a corpse if it would help."

"That would really help actually, thanks. I wish I could get the casting director to do that, too."

June got off the bed, smacked the spider with a magazine, and lay down on the rug, attempting to look lifeless.

Mitch kneeled down close to June, "unzipped" "the bag," and tried the line again. *"Jesus, what a mess."*

"That was better," June said, looking up at him. "Now it looks like you are seeing something."

"Yes, but I'm not seeing a chopped-up sixteen-year-old hooker. I'm seeing my incredibly sexy wife lying on the floor. I am not sure I can run these lines right now, sweetheart."

Mitch helped June up and led her over to the bed. He began to kiss her behind the ear. Aroused, June pulled him on top of her. She noticed the duvet cover was ripped. Her skirt was pulling uncomfortably, with the zipper twisted around to the front. "Let me get out of this," June said, standing up, and she pulled the skirt off while Mitch tinkered with the belt on his golf pants. June quickly took off the rest of her clothes and walked over to the closet, where she stood, naked, carefully returning her skirt to its hanger.

"You can probably do that later," said Mitch, who was standing in his underwear and socks, pulled up midcalf. Some men are tall but Mitch was more elongated, as if he had been pulled from the womb and stretched across the delivery room, then left to fill in as the years went by. His face was not so much handsome as notable, with protruding brown eyes and an elastic mouth through which his voice exploded.

"Sorry, sweetie," June said as Mitch pulled her carefully to the bed. Just as he put his mouth over his wife's Mitch's cell began to buzz. "Let me just check that."

"Now?" June asked.

"Oh man, it was Tad," Mitch said, looking at the caller ID on his cell phone.

"So? He'll call back if it's important."

"Let me just call him back quick-like! When he calls at night that always means I got a bite." Mitch began to dial.

June reclined onto her pillow, feeling that this rare spontaneous romantic interlude could not be revived. She reached down over the side of the bed and picked up her panties, pulling them back on inside out.

Tad answered after several rings. "Hey, Mitch, what's up? I'm at the Lakers game."

"You called me. I thought you might have a new audition to tell me about."

"My Sidekick must have called you by accident. Sorry, no news!"

Mitch hung up and turned to June. "It was nothing. You know, I

31

really should work on the other four auditions, and polish the detective thing."

"Go ahead, Mitch, I'm spent."

"Sorry about that, June-June. I really know what a pain in the ass I am. Do me a favor, just give me a pass on this one. Pilot season."

June didn't answer.

"Hey, sweetie, could you hand me my bleach trays?"

Without looking up, June reached onto their nightstand and seized the plastic molds Mitch used to whiten his teeth. He squeezed a bit of clear gel into the molds, then stuck them in his mouth. This made his lips stick slightly to the plastic, causing him to talk like a gopher with seeds in his cheek pouch. "Goodnough, Junnn."

"Uh-huh." Out of her dresser drawer June pulled the oversized stagecoach-themed pajamas that Mitch had gotten her on a whim at Costco. Dressed for sleep, she picked up the guidebook to the Greek Isles. June and Mitch had visited the area long before Nora was born, but she enjoyed reading guidebooks only after she had already been somewhere. Somehow all the places she had been came more to life in retrospect. Her mind occasionally turned back to the spider, wondering if it was actually dead.

June fell asleep while reading about a baklava festival near the Aegean and hearing Mitch muttering beside her, an endless loop: "*Well, WHAT have we got, Lieutenant? Well, what have we GOT, Lieutenant? WELL, what have we got, Lieutenant?*"

CHAPTER 4

"Well, what have WE got, Lieutenant? . . . Sixteen, that's my daughter's age. . . . Jesus, what a mess. . . ."

Mitch was hunched over his second venti latte on a stained chair in a Burbank Starbucks, practicing his lines. Detectives, police chiefs, and coroners—those were roles Mitch scored. The series' starring role would always go to some handsome kid in his twenties—but this part was a series regular and a potential forty-five thousand a week.

The constant running of his hands through his hair had caused it to mat strangely on one side of his head. He had a bit of foam clinging to the corner of his mouth, and was muttering lines to himself. Other customers kept their distance. Barely looking up from his script, Mitch went to order another coffee.

"Another venti?"

"Huh? Yeah, same thing, thanks. *Well, WHAT have we got, Lieutenant?*"

Mitch paid for his drink, crinkled his change in his hands, and walked over, still reading, to the counter that held milk and his beloved wooden stir sticks. He hoisted the sugar container, but some crystals were stuck to the dispenser flap. Mitch banged on the container's bottom, and a giant pile exploded onto the counter, in the process splashing a bit of his coffee on the cashmere scarf of a nearby woman who was stirring her Chai. She immediately shrieked, "Jesus, what the hell is wrong with you?"

Mitch fixed his eyes on a short, not unattractive woman with thick, blown-straight blond hair. "Sorry—I'm so sorry," he said.

"I mean what are you on that you can't work a sugar shaker?"

Mitch started to feel himself unravel slightly.

"I really am sorry about that."

"Seriously, are you going to pay to dry-clean this?"

"Excuse me?"

"My scarf! Are you, or are you not, going to pay to dry-clean it?!"

Mitch peered at the minute speck of coffee on her pale pink scarf. He balled up his five dollars in change, now damp from his sweaty hand, and chucked it toward her. The woman's eyes widened dramatically, eyebrows shooting to midforehead.

"Here you go! Knock yourself out at the dry cleaner's." Mitch's voice rose to something just short of a shout. "I know what it's like to have a bad day. I had to share a sugar shaker with you before your Zoloft kicked in!"

He turned and stomped out of the coffee shop, feeling her stare on his back.

Ten minutes later Mitch pulled up at the gate of the Burbank studio where his audition was to be.

"Hey, Mitch," the guard said.

"Hey, Leo."

"How's it going?"

"Show got cancelled."

"Right. Me and my lady friend caught it once. Back pounding the pavement, huh? What are you in for today?"

"*Hollywood Beat.*"

Leo scanned the drive-on list inside his booth, looking for Mitch's name among those entitled to bring their cars directly onto the lot.

"Here you are, Mitch Gold. Got your ID?"

"ID? I've been coming here for a decade."

"Homeland security, man. No pass on the car, you gotta show ID."

"Okay, whatever."

Mitch reached into his pocket, pulled out his wallet, and flashed his driver's license. Leo handed him the pass. Mitch waved and headed to the enormous parking structure to the left of the gate.

Sides in hand, he walked across the lot to the casting session. All around him were squat buildings named after classic stars: Hepburn, Stewart, Pickford, Harlow, and Fairbanks, where Mitch was going. Just being on the lot again made Mitch's stomach tighten as he thought about all the things that could go wrong in the casting office: What if this was the last audition he ever got? He might sweat through his shirt. What if he was flat? What if he forgot his lines? He had managed to survive the year of the stolen money, but he wasn't sure about the mortgage money for next year. How many Starbucks were there in Ashland? He started to think hard on Oregon, and felt his face relax.

Production assistants, their dreams perhaps still intact, careened along the narrow paths on bicycles or in golf carts. Trailers filled with costumes, makeup, or actors were parked at every intersection. Mitch passed sound stage 15—one of the many warehouses where the shows were filmed. This was where he had shot *Molar Opposites*. The sound stage had since been completely transformed into the set for a new reality show, *Twelve Stepping*, in which alcoholics raced to stay sober. Crowds of tourists, waiting to watch the taping of the results, lined up behind metal detectors. One woman pulled out her cell phone, nudged her husband, and began snapping pictures of Mitch. Pretending to ignore her, but actually pleased to be recognized, Mitch walked on. He made out his old dental chair tossed to the side of the stage, waiting to be carted away, and tried not to feel despondent.

At Fairbanks he found guys in various shades of dark suits (de rigueur attire for detective auditions) wandering around outside the building. One was dragging on a Benson & Hedges. Another was doing stretching exercises. Two were simply muttering.

"Well, what have we got, Lieutenant?"

Mitch knew each man and his position in the hierarchy of TV character actors. There was Dan, with whom he frequently competed for jobs as various law-enforcement officials, and whom he usually bested. Dan was never happy to see Mitch. There was Scott, who kept claiming he would quit the business and become a wind farmer. Scott mostly did commercials. Translation: bottom feeder. And then there was the vast middle of fellow character actors he saw at nearly every audition: tall, forty-something, not-exactly-hot, not-exactly-weird-looking, the good guy, the bad guy, and the best friend. Never the star. Most of these guys

Mitch beat out in the great hunt for roles. The only real threat was Willie Dermot. And Mitch's nemesis was nowhere in sight.

"Hey, Mitch," said Dan, looking irritated. "Here for Joe Murphy?"

"Yeah."

"Christ, do you need to get every job in town?"

"My show got cancelled, Dan."

"Oh." Dan lit another cigarette. "Well, good luck. Not really. Just kidding. More or less."

"You too, Dan," Mitch said, actually a bit sorry for Dan. His wife, who was a receptionist at Jenny Craig, insisted on sending all three of their kids to private school. Plus Dan lived in Rancho Cucamonga.

Mitch's own detective outfit, a dark gray wool suit, felt stifling. He wondered if he should take off his jacket. And what about rolling up his sleeves and loosening his tie? Why hadn't he asked June what was best? Mitch decided to go down the middle: jacket off, but sleeves unrolled and tie tight but not too tight. Too tight made his neck look fat. Did the elliptical machine address neck fat? Maybe he should add ten minutes to his workout?

Mitch took the stairs up to the casting office. The small beige-carpeted room was packed with more "detectives." Mitch sat in the waiting area—a long hallway really—with a bunch of highly uncomfortable chairs lined up. Mitch tried to breathe in through his nose, out through his mouth, to calm his pounding heart. He rooted around in his jacket pocket for a beta-blocker, knowing it was fruitless.

Each audition was just as unbearable as his first. In fact, they were perhaps worse now, after fifteen years. A young actor was invigorated by even a hint of interest expressed by the casting director of a gum commercial, believing it would get easier. It didn't.

The rejection of an actor's performance was the repudiation of his essence, a flat statement: I do not like you. You. But that was the business Mitch had chosen, and so there he sat, waiting for his turn.

Behind the closed door of the casting director's office, Mitch could hear another actor giving *"Jesus what a mess"* his best shot, and resisted the urge to press his ear to the door to better hear his rival's rendition. Mitch said hello to a few more of the actors he knew, told his tale of *Molar Opposites* woe several more times, making up a few lies along the way to make it more interesting: He had thrown up once during makeup. He polished his co-star's nails with the dental equipment during breaks. The wardrobe girl gave everyone on the set crabs.

Mitch had to pee. He made his way down the hall to the men's room, passing the half-opened door of the casting assistant's tiny office.

"Hey, Darren, its Alicia," the assistant said. "Donna wanted me to follow up with you about Luke Perry. Did he get a chance to read the script? Oh great! And he liked it? We think he would be PERFECT as Joey Murphy. No, he's not too young. Terrific. I'll let Donna know his quote is sixty thousand per episode. Okay. Cheers!"

Abruptly the assistant noticed Mitch huddled in the hallway. She stood up, glaring, and slammed the door. Mitch ducked into the men's room. On his way out he heard "Mitch Gold!" and saw that another casting assistant with a clipboard was calling him from the waiting room.

Mitch followed the girl into the office, where the casting director, Donna Lawrence, sat at her desk just finishing up a phone call, and four producers and the director were crammed onto a small brown sofa.

Mitch said his hellos and then stood in the tiny space left in the middle of the room facing another casting assistant who looked about twelve. This was the stand-in whom Mitch would be reading the scene with. Mitch had no choice but to carry on even though the part had just been offered to Luke Perry. Walking out of a session would ensure that he would never be welcomed into this casting director's office again. He had to give it his best shot. Plus, he reasoned, Luke Perry could get a DUI before shooting and end up in rehab.

"Whenever you're ready, Mitch," Donna said cheerfully.

"Sure." Mitch took up his Detective Joey Murphy stance. "*Well, what have we got—?*" Mitch began as her cell phone rang.

"Oh, so sorry, gotta take this. Go ahead, Mitch. I'll be right back," Donna said, squeezing past the others in the room.

"Oh, hi, Darren. No, no, I can talk. Uh-huh. Yes, the network okayed sixty thousand," Mitch overheard as she walked down the hall.

She came back and gave the room a discreet thumbs-up.

"Please continue, Mitch," she said, bobbing her chin quickly, like a hamster attacking a carrot.

Mitch sped through the rest of the audition.

"Great, Mitch! Thanks so much for coming in!" Donna squeaked, and shut the door on Mitch's departing back.

Mitch hit Tad's number on his speed dial.

"Yo!"

"They hired Luke Perry when I was in the fucking room."

"Luke Perry? Huh. I wonder what his quote is these days."

"I heard sixty thousand. That's sixty thousand a week that I am not going to get!"

"Well you never would have gotten sixty anyway, man," Tad said. "But you've got four more auditions today, right? Mitch, you'd be much calmer with a bird in your life."

"Who is calmed by a bird? Who?"

"I am."

"Noted."

"Hey, Joy Wainscott called here again. Haven't you called her back yet? This project is green-lit, my friend. What's the issue?"

"No issue. Just forgot," Mitch said.

"You forgot? Call her. Okay?"

"Okay, I promise I'll do it today."

Mitch opened the door of his car and threw his scripts, somewhat stained with latte, on the passenger seat next to his cell phone. He turned his car toward traffic and began to mull his options. He could take the 5 to the 110 to the 10 to National, but who knew what the 5 would be like at this time of day, given the trucks and all. There was the Olive-to-Barham-to-Cahuenga-to-Highland option. But then he'd be headed right into Hollywood traffic. He began to sweat, in spite of his air conditioner. Shit. Did he remember to bring a hand towel? Okay, surface streets. Mitch made his way past giant billboards of Ellen DeGeneres and Jay Leno, and the tiny houses that lined Olive Avenue, filled with rarely employed actors obsessively watering their minuscule lawns.

He thought about calling Joy. The payment for all the great stage roles of the past had been enduring her love letters, which stank of clove cigarettes; her midnight poetry drops; and her constant sexual entreaties in the wings, none of which he had been able to overtly reject. Freak that she had been in those days, she was the talented freak at Joe Allen's eating lunch with Wendy Wasserstein.

But even before he met June, he'd never been remotely interested. Joy's hair was like a Brillo pad, her eyes were too close together, and her legs reminded him of vermicelli noodles. Her collection of historic-monument-themed pincushions gave him the creeps. He wasn't sure that a job, even though it was a feature with Ridley Scott, would be worth having to deal with Joy Wainscott again.

Sixty-three minutes later, as Mitch finally arrived at a studio gate in Culver City, exhausted and still rattled, his cell phone rang, and he peered down at the seat and saw that it was Tad.

"Turn around."

"What are you talking about, Tad? I'm at the studio for the publishing thing."

"They called to cancel."

"What! I just came all the way from freaking Burbank."

"Sorry, Mitch, they rewrote it last night. Made it a woman, an Asian Judith Regan type."

"Damn it!"

Mitch made a U-turn at the gate and headed toward Sawtelle, and the on-ramp for the 405 Freeway on his route straight back to Burbank, where the Bronx school pilot was being cast. He hoped to shave at least ten minutes off his return trip.

He flicked on the only country-western station in Los Angeles—a secret obsession of his—and listened for a Sig alert, which would indicate a massive delay on the freeway.

"Rush-hour traffic report brought to you by Los Angeles Plastic Surgery, where anesthesia is always included! Big trouble on the 405 North with an overturned big rig in the right lane. Look for alternate routes. That trouble has you backed on the westbound 10 from Overland to Boyle Heights. A mess through downtown. And trouble on the Antelope Valley Freeway, where a fatal motorcycle accident has yet to be cleared. Have a great day, Southland!"

Mitch cursed his traffic fate and tried to relax to Kenny Chesney. One upside of the new Asian Judith Regan was he now had an extra hour built into his travel time. He would need it. The cars inched along at five miles an hour. He considered getting off at Sepulveda, but realized that surface streets would be no better at this time of day. In the midst of mopping his brow with his already moist towel, he narrowly avoided rear-ending a canary yellow Lamborghini with a license plate he couldn't wait to tell June about: U NV ME.

As Mitch finally merged onto the 101, the morning haze was beginning to burn off and the palm trees looked almost iridescent against the midafternoon sky. This part of the freeway had numerous signs for gentlemen's clubs. Mitch gazed impassively at one for the Spearmint Rhino and thought he recognized the pouty-lipped pole dancer on the billboard as one of Tad's exes.

Nearly an hour later, Mitch found Dan sitting on a seat in the hallway of the Pickford Building wearing a pair of strange, slightly bent horn-rimmed glasses.

"Nice touch, Dan."

Dan grunted in Mitch's direction. Mitch also waved to Sam, the perpetual fat guy, who longed to go on a diet but feared he would never get a job again.

A gay Minnesota-escapee type, common in casting offices, his shirt worth possibly a week's salary, poked his head out of the auditioning room. "Mitch Gold?"

Mitch took a deep breath, grasped his rolled-up sides, and stepped over the threshold of the casting office door.

Gay midwestern assistant smiled brightly: "Do you all know Mitch?"

"We certainly do," said a woman in the back of the room. Mitch followed her voice. She looked vaguely familiar. Had they done that awful zoo-based pilot a few years back? Or maybe the alcoholic clown thing? Who was she?

Annie, the casting director, quickly went through the room, stopping at the familiar woman, who Mitch could swear was glaring at him. "This is Bonnie Green, creator of the show."

Bonnie Green. Bonnie Green. Was she glaring?

"Whenever you're ready," Annie said.

Mitch began the scene. *"Jose, I'm telling you the way it is. You don't get a diploma, you'll be on the fast track to Rikers."*

"Listen marycone," said Mr. Trendy Shirt, who had the most unlikely street Spanish Mitch had perhaps ever heard. *"You some smart grrrringggggooooo. You don't know nothing 'bout what it like on the street. . . ."*

Mitch was put off by the accent of the assistant and a feeling of discomfort. He was hitting all his lines. It seemed to be going well. Or was it? Did he get a word wrong? June would have noticed that, but they didn't run lines together for this one. Shit. He could feel someone was staring at him, and not with pleasure. He looked up. Bonnie Green's eyes were locked on him, cold and hard. That hair, blond, the cashmere scarf around her neck. Cashmere. Oh shit. Starbucks.

Back in his car Mitch called Tad. "I am not going to get the troubled-school-in-the-Bronx show."

"Why! You're perfect for that part."

"I know, and I was good. But I'm not gonna get it."

"Why?"

"I had a thing with the show creator."

"What 'thing' Mitch?"

"Um, we had a little run-in at Starbucks, a latte thing. Wasn't my fault. Honestly, Tad, I said a little something, but it was only because she was going nuts over a tiny spill!"

"You insulted Bonnie Green? Mitch, do you know how many shows that woman has going?"

"I don't know who these people are! I am telling you, Tad, she was deranged."

"Listen, do me a favor. Try not to leave the house without June."

Mitch's next audition, for corporate boss D. J. Powers, was in Hollywood.

Feeling slightly grimy at this point, Mitch was greeted at the casting session by a handwritten note taped to the front desk: ATTENTION: NEW SIDES. Mitch discovered that every line he had memorized for D. J. Powers had been changed.

The casting director, Marilyn King, a short, middle-aged woman, slightly shlumpy in elastic-waist pants and flowing sari, smiled at Mitch.

"Hey there! Did you get a chance to look at the new material?"

"For about thirty seconds."

"Great! Let's go!"

"I'm not sure the word I would use is 'great,' Marilyn. I mean, I spent two hours learning the old material."

Marilyn looked at Mitch the way June gazed at Nora when she tried to march up the down escalator at the Beverly Center. "I'm sorry you're feeling that way, Mitch. You can pass on this audition if that would comfort you."

Hearing the word "pass," Mitch realized he had gone too far in his outburst. You can mouth off to your manager, to your agent, maybe, your wife certainly. Not a casting director.

"I'm sorry, Marilyn. God, I mean I am so, so sorry. Pilot season jitters. Pass? No. I'm here. Let's go."

Mitch took a deep breath yet again, sat down on the tiny stool in the center of the office, holding his knees akimbo to stay centered on it. He tried to imagine himself sitting in the expansive leather chair of a corporate bigwig.

"HEATHER!"

"Yes, D.J." The assistant reading this time was a pretty girl of twenty or so.

"Where is that report I asked for?" Mitch looked down at the paper in his hand. "Oops . . . I mean good job on that report . . . oh shit. Can I start over?"

"Sure!" said one of the show's creators, a thirty-something woman, Oprah-esque. "But while you're stopped, I need to say I think you are barking at her too much."

"Oh. I thought I was supposed to be a tough corporate boss," Mitch said.

"Um. The character has changed a little. Now you're in love with Heather. We need you guys to have a TON of chemistry."

"Really?" Mitch asked. "What about my wife, aren't I married to the CEO of the company?"

"Not anymore."

Marilyn added: "Didn't you get the revised material? That role was cut."

Mitch nodded slowly and tried again. *"Heather,"* he said, attempting to look at the young assistant with lust in his eyes, but unable to peel away from the script, *"you look . . . uh . . . you look nice in that shirt."* His face was almost completely buried behind the new sides.

"It looks just as good off," Heather read.

Mitch could not remember the line, and had lost his place on the page. "Well then take it off!" he ad-libbed.

Everyone stared at him.

The last stop of the day was in Studio City, for wacky dad. After passing through two miles of traffic on Ventura Boulevard, Mitch made a quick change into a polo shirt, then walked into the waiting room and saw Willie Dermot lounging on a chair, cracking jokes with the other "dads" and casually showing off pictures of his new Mercedes-Benz E500. "You can't believe this machine, dudes, three hundred and two horsepower, single overhead cam. I got it up to one twenty on Mulholland last night. Hey, Mitch my buddy!"

"Hey, Willie. How's it been?"

"Busy, busy. A bunch of features and this stuff. Busy man! You?"

"Same, same."

It was Willie's turn.

"Good luck," Mitch lied.

Two minutes later Mitch winced as laughter exploded from the casting office. Willie was nailing it. He was soon escorted out by a slobbering casting director. "Oh, you're always so good, Willie." She beamed, then glanced at her clipboard. "Scott Pinicke?"

"Warmed 'em up for ya, big guy!" Willie laughed.

"Thanks, Willie." Scott tripped on the rug. "That's the first time I've ever been in the room with speed bumps," he joked as the casting director shut the door. Silence.

Mitch began to panic slightly. He made it outside, turning on his cell, and reached into his pocket for the crinkled PETCO receipt with Joy's number. It was still lunchtime. Hopefully she wouldn't answer.

"Hello?"

Mitch was instantly transported back to his dressing room at the

Manhattan Theater Club, where Joy, smacking a wad of gum, would often catch him in his underwear because she never bothered to knock.

"Joy, its Mitch Gold."

"Oh hey." Mitch was struck by her indifferent tone, as if they had just spoken yesterday about the call time for the matinee.

"Nice to hear your voice again, Joy." Silence.

He continued. "I know you've been doing really well the last few years." Still nothing. "So, um, you've got a feature with Ridley Scott at Sony. That's great! Have you been working on it for a while?"

"Yeah, thanks, Mitch," she said, tersely. "I'm swamped at the moment. But I have something for you in the film. It's a family drama with some adventure—think *Hancock* meets *Mamma Mia!* If you're interested, I'll have my assistant set up coffee."

"Sure," Mitch said. "I look forward to reading the script." Then he added politely, "It would be nice to see you again."

"Tawny?" Joy called out. "Can you pick up Mitch Gold on my cell phone to set up coffee?" She added: "Mitch, do me a favor, call on the landline next time," and hung up without even a good-bye.

Mitch returned to the casting session just as Scott Pinicke slunk out of the room. It was his turn.

In the room, he happily spotted a writer he had worked with before—a Harvard guy who was one of the original writers of *The Simpsons*, perpetually unshaved, a Red Sox cap pulled low over his head.

"Hey, Rex."

"Hey, Mitch. Whenever you're ready."

"*Chelsea, come down here!*" Mitch bellowed, and laughs exploded throughout the tiny office. Mitch felt hopeful for the first time all day. He rolled with it. "*What is with this cell phone bill?*" More laughs.

"*I told you I had to call Kevin in Denver,*" said a sprightly woman in her fifties, probably the director's mother, who wanted to watch him at work, now playing the role of sixteen-year-old Chelsea.

"*For three hundred and six minutes?*" Mitch said, louder still. Guffaws.

"*Daddy, we just like to listen to each other breathe.*"

"*Well, don't breathe on my dime!*" Again, outsized laughter.

By the end of the scene Mitch could barely hear himself read. Fantastic!

That evening June walked into the house and found Mitch giving Nora a bath, imitating the slightly unhinged voices with her tub toys. "Heather!" Mitch wiggled the tiny plastic frog. "What a mess! You're on the fast track to Rikers!"

"Hey, how did it all go today?" June asked, sitting on the closed lid of the toilet and pulling her laptop out of her briefcase. She flicked it open and quickly checked her e-mail. There was one from Amanda, e-mailing from New York, where she was an investment banker. Amanda and her lawyer husband, Sebastian, had recently had twins.

To: Junejune@gmail.com
From: Amandamalone@smithbarney.com

Hey friend! What's new there? Max is finally finished throwing up, but now Rose has the stomach thing. Fun times around here. Wondered: how do you render animal fat? Lots of love . . .

June began to type her reply as she listened to Mitch.

"My day was ninety percent disastrous—I nailed wacky dad. But Willie was there," Mitch said.

"Um, well I'm sure you were just as good as he was," June said, still typing.

To: Amandamalone@smithbarney.com
From: junejune@gmail.com

First, make sure it's totally free of impurities: little leftover bits of herbs, etc.—strain through a coffee filter or cheesecloth-lined strainer. Then if going to use as a butterlike emollient, freeze in ice cube trays, pop out, and save in freezer. Or for more immediate use, just refrigerate till firm. (Fat debacle warning: I used some chicken fat instead of butter to make cookies the other day, and it turned out to be spoiled and so they stank to high heaven.)

"Stop typing, June, please? How was your day?" Mitch asked.

"Oh, a pill," June said, closing her laptop. "You remember that professor I told you about who is always making inappropriate sexual references, like, 'Had Ted Hughes possessed better appreciation for both Sylvia Plath's sense of play and verbiage, to say nothing of her luscious behind . . .' "

"What?" Mitch asked.

"Are you listening, Mitch?" June continued: "Anyway, he decided that he would abandon the somewhat arbitrary though perhaps pedagogically correct method of picking students at random in class to answer questions—"

"Another brilliant UCLA hire," Mitch interrupted.

"Actually, he's done some rather important work in poststructural theory," June went on. "Anyway, you're not letting me finish. So he decides he will assign each student a tarot card at the beginning of the semester, and then, whenever he pulls a student's card—"

"Wait," Mitch interrupted again. "Before you finish that story I have to tell you what happened with this show creator at Starbucks."

June raised her voice. "ANYWAY, THE POINT IS THAT SOME EVANGELICAL CHRISTIAN STUDENTS WERE REALLY MAD ABOUT THIS METHODOLOGY AND COMPLAINED TO THE DEAN, AND I WAS ASKED TO SERVE ON A COMMITTEE TO ADJUDICATE IT ALL, AND COULD I JUST TELL MY STORY?"

June walked out of the bathroom to answer the phone, which had been ringing incessantly, and returned a few seconds later.

"It's Tad."

Mitch wiped the bubbles off his hands and took the phone.

"Hey there, buddy," Tad said, warm and soft. This meant something good.

"Hey, Tad!"

"Good news, my friend. They loved you for *My Dad Is Totally Weird*. So it is on to the next stage. You're going to the network!"

"Thanks, Tad," Mitch said, wondering which three other actors had made it to the final audition for the network executives.

"I'll start working out your deal tomorrow. Then the network will give us a date for the audition."

"Did you find out who else is going?" Mitch asked.

"David Hasselhoff."

"I can smoke him. Anyone else?"

"Willie Dermot."

CHAPTER 5

Friday nights were always pleasurable to June. A week of classes behind her, but Sunday, when she had to grade essays, far off, so she drank in some rare free time. Often, if she wasn't preparing a lecture or an article, she might try a new cookie recipe after work and was generally loath to go out. But she had been oddly looking forward to this dinner, even making a point to get her hair cut. But now she was five minutes late. She had missed the entrance to Orso twice, which really most people could only do on purpose. Before she was even out of the car, a valet sidled up and took her keys. She was slightly embarrassed. Not by the make of her car—only idiots cared about what car they drove; but she felt a little sad about the crushed goldfish crackers and creased MapQuest directions on the passenger seat. The valet handed June a pink ticket, and she barely nodded at him before he zoomed off, screeching her tires as he rounded the corner.

Running a hand over her hair, June rushed into the restaurant and looked for Mitch or the others. She made her way to the outdoor patio, where heat lamps were flickering over a series of round tables. She saw her husband and other dinner companions seated next to several other tables of agents, producers, and Bette Midler. Orso's food was good enough—but the restaurant was preferred by industry denizens for its high walls, which kept the paparazzi away.

Mitch had his back to June and his chin in his hand, ostensibly listening to Larissa, who was gesticulating madly. Justine and Willie were leaning toward each other talking in more hushed tones, and June immediately caught the eye of Rich Friend, who flashed a row of teeth at her.

"Hi, everyone. So sorry. Wilshire was a nightmare," June said to the table at large.

"No worries. Good to see you," said Rich, who went to kiss her cheek but pecked her slightly at the tip of her nose. June turned to Mitch to see if he had taken in this mis-aim, but he was still listening to Larissa.

"If I want body sprays in the master bath, and those are really good for resale, then we have to change some plumbing thing underground, which is another three thousand dollars. Which I am fine with, but isn't that, like, something the plumber should have told me six months ago?"

Mitch pretended to listen but was furtively glancing at Willie and Justine. Were they talking about a show? Her show? A job? Maybe Willie would get something else and pass on the wacky dad.

"Hey, June!" said Willie in his usual slightly-too-boisterous voice. "'Take a sad song,'" he sang, off-key. It was a deeply boring shtick of his. Justine waved silently and excused herself, walking through the restaurant with a cell phone pressed to her ear. The table was already well into several bottles of San Pellegrino, and June reached into the untouched breadbasket.

"Phew, I'm starving!" she said, pushing an oily piece into her mouth.

"We'll get a waiter right here for you then," said Rich.

"Hi, sweetie. How did your *El Cid* lecture go?" asked Mitch.

"Well, they stayed awake. Hi, Larissa, nice to see you."

"Hiiiiiiii."

June noticed a small silver vial hanging between Larissa's prominent clavicle bones. "That's pretty, Larissa. What is it?"

Larissa tugged on her vial, which was hanging from a chain that appeared a bit too delicate for it. "Oh, that's my Rescue Remedy. I carry it everywhere these days. I really find when I am superstressed, a dab on my tongue totally changes the way things go for me. After I had that whole colon-cleanse debacle last year, it really made a difference."

"Uh-huh." June walked over and peered politely at the vial.

"I know it sounds crazy to a book person. But this stuff is superpowerful. That's all I am saying," Larissa said.

June noticed the bottle had Larissa's initials engraved in tiny script on the bottom. The waiter ambled over, asking if everyone was ready to order. "Can I have a glass of Sancerre?" June asked.

"Right on," the waiter said, appearing puzzled.

June raised her eyebrows. Rich noticed, winked at her, and then asked, "So what's new?"

She smiled. Too broadly, maybe. She tried to furrow her brow as if confused. "Not much. You?"

"Just more Hollywood crap. What are you teaching this semester?"

And so it was that June found herself telling Rich about all the things she had meant to detail for Mitch earlier this week—the departmental committees that had been set up this month to review her tenure file; the epic-poetry teacher at USC who was angling to get on the tenure committee to undermine her; and the intellectual disputes that can fell an associate professor in this quest. And of course her book, the cornerstone of her tenure package, which concerned the themes of male anger in the epic poetry of the Greeks, the Romans, and the medieval Crusaders.

Rich seemed fascinated, and his blue eyes stayed riveted on June's as she wove him into her world. "I'm interested in what you said about 'disputes,'" Rich said. "What kind of disputes?"

"Well, for example," June began, "let's consider chansons de gese which are Old French epic poems that celebrate historical figures. So they take place in the Middle Ages, correct? But whether or not they were actually written then or were translated from what were really oral traditions from an earlier time is the subject of great debate. Now I have my own thoughts on this—"

The waiter reappeared. "Are we all ready here?" He had forgotten June's wine.

Larissa spoke first. "I'll have the Cobb salad. No bacon, no corn, no cheese, no avocado, and can you do dressing on the side?"

"We can do that, but that is like, not really a Cobb."

"Gino knows me, and he makes it that way for me all the time," Larissa said.

"Yeah, Gino's not here tonight."

"You know what? Just tell them in the kitchen, okay?"

"Um, well, it's pretty hectic back there. But I'll ask for ya." The waiter, definitely a wactor, looked at June. "How about you?"

June looked over at a plate of fish on the table next to theirs. She tapped the shoulder of a tall guy who was poking his fork into the dish. "Sorry to reach. That looks interesting. What is it?"

Appearing amused, he answered. "Halibut. It's fantastic."

Larissa looked mortified. She hissed at June: "You do realize that was Tim Robbins?"

"Seriously?" June asked. "He looks way too young! *Even Cowgirls Get the Blues* was written in the midseventies."

Rich grinned. "That's Tom Robbins, hon. *Tim* toils in the same salt mines as the rest of the men at this table."

"Should I come back?" The wactor seemed impatient.

"No. I would like the halibut. And can I please have my wine?" June asked again.

"Did you order wine?"

"I did. A Sancerre. Maybe you forgot?"

"You never ordered it."

June gave up.

"Oh, wait," said the wactor, "there are specials. Did you want to hear them?"

"Do go on," Rich said.

"Um, grilled trout with cockles, some kind of risotto, I can ask the chef if you're interested, oh yeah, and one appetizer, free-range escargot."

Rich looked at June and pulled his lips in to stifle a snicker. "Free-range?" June asked. "Where do they range?"

Rich chimed in: "How far can a snail get?" June could not contain her laugh.

The wactor glanced at his notes. "Uh, I'm not totally sure."

Mitch looked up, annoyed, from the other end of the table. "Can we order? Don't find out about the risotto. I've had a hectic day and I'm starving."

Mitch looked at Willie to make sure he'd heard him, and hoped he would infer that "hectic" meant busy with auditions. Then Mitch glanced toward Rich to see if he had heard him too, but he seemed to be lost in his menu. Willie did not even look at Mitch, but instead piped up: "I'll take the penne puttanesca. And a salad."

"Which salad."

"Surprise me!" Willie said.

After a while the conversation turned to *My Dad Is Totally Weird.* June looked at her watch—twenty minutes seemed a long time to wait for salads—but the waiter finally reappeared.

"So, did you do your deal?" Mitch asked Willie.

"It's not closed," Willie answered, digging into an heirloom tomato.

Larissa snapped her head in their direction. "Willie's quote is sixty thousand, but Mark and Tim are asking for eighty." Mitch suddenly felt a little chill in his back. He knew CAA would never ask for eighty thousand dollars for him. He would be lucky to get forty-five.

"We're holding out," Larissa said. "There's a ton of pilots for Willie this season."

Mitch looked frantically toward June, but his wife was laughing with Rich. A busboy arrived back at the table, a large tray teetering on his palm, and the wactor followed behind him, dispensing the dinner plates, placing the wrong ones in front of every person.

June picked up the plates and distributed them around the table correctly, surreptitiously dipping her pinky finger into Willie's puttanesca sauce so she could give it a taste. Not bad. A little salty. Larissa waved frantically at the busboy. "Excuse me! There's avocado in this. Can you take it back please?"

June tucked into her halibut, and was pleased to find it silken and perfectly seasoned. She had chosen well.

"Do you have children?" she asked Rich conversationally.

"Not exactly. Justine's dogs function more or less as our children."

June had long realized that the toniest neighborhoods in Los Angeles were roughly divided between dog people and kid people, and each group preferred the other to stay out of its way. "What kind of dogs do you have?" she asked politely, bracing herself for a doggist conversation about runs in the park and the merits of organic dog food over commercial.

"English setters, Wendy and Peter."

"Fun names."

"Yes they are. But I would rather have real children, not animal stand-ins."

Justine, who had missed most of the dinner standing on the sidewalk and talking intently into her cell phone, sat down and apologized to everyone. She looked at Rich. "That was Steve. He said he doesn't like Samantha's baby coming from Ethiopia. He says the place is a downer. He's thinking France. It's got a better look."

"France! That's absurd!" Rich said. "No American woman would adopt a baby from France! The whole point of the show is that she adopts from Africa."

"I warned you about this, Rich. The network wants what the network wants. Anyway, I'd better go home and start working. He expects the rewrites by tomorrow morning. I for one want to get the show on the air."

"Justine, let's discuss this later."

Justine looked at June and placed her hand, which was peering out from a velvet oversized jacket, on her arm in apology. "I am so sorry, June. I was looking forward to tonight. I never seem to get a full meal during pilot season."

June looked carefully at Rich, but his attention had turned from her at last. He was staring at a spot on the wall, frowning. Andy Flynn. That was it. June had been trying to figure out why Rich Friend seemed familiar, why the things she expected him to laugh at, he did, and why his smile was comforting, like a friend she had missed. He looked remarkably like Andy Flynn, a college boy she'd had a crush on in high school, but whom she hadn't thought of in years.

She met Andy Flynn at the wedding of a friend's sister her senior year in high school. The reception was in the backyard of the house, and June had been sitting alone, fanning herself with a dinner napkin, when he walked by. Andy Flynn had been taken by her simple cotton dress, which stood in contrast to the low-cut rayon numbers worn by the older girls. He asked for her number, and he called her. He was twenty-three! On their first date, he took her to his apartment—her parents thought she was going to a party—and served her Chianti, the first time she tried red wine. On their next date he took her to the art house to see *Do The Right Thing*. He made her a tape of rare reggae songs by Steel

Pulse and Burning Spear, which she played for friends in her Honda Civic and felt extremely sophisticated. He knew the bouncer at Club Soda, the college bar in town, who let June slide by.

Then one day, when she called him from the hall pay phone between classes and Andy Flynn heard the fourth-period bell go off, he realized the error of his ways. June was dumped. She drove by Andy Flynn's apartment many times after that, and coerced her friends into crank-calling him late at night. (Liz Lopez: "Hi, Andy. I heard you're a hot number.") Andy Flynn remained a pleasant, if vaguely embarrassing, memory of June's, and she always wondered what had happened to him. Apparently, he had become Rich Friend.

"I hate pilot season," June said quietly. For the first time all evening, Rich remained silent. Their plates barely cleared, the wactor inquired about dessert.

"Red Jell-O," Larissa said. "And a decaf coffee, with a straw."

"Yeah, Jell-O is not on the menu."

"I always get it here. I like it in a champagne glass. And can I have some water without ice?"

The wactor looked at June, who was still eating her halibut. "Are you still working on that?"

"Working? I'm enjoying it, if that is what you mean. But I'd like the *panna cotta*, please."

When June's *panna cotta* arrived, she took a small bit and considered it as it melted on her tongue. "A bit too much almond extract."

"Really?" inquired Rich.

June absently spooned up a bite and offered it to Rich, who licked the dessert off it and smiled at her once again.

Larissa sipped her coffee carefully through the straw. "June, I love how you always eat dessert even when no one else orders it."

Rich and June ignored the comment. "You're right," Rich said to June. "Too much almond."

The wactor walked over with the check that no one had asked for, and squinted down to where Mitch was talking in an increasingly agitated tone to Willie, who was ignoring him and pouring packet after packet of sugar into his cappuccino. Plunking the check down, the wactor made his way toward Mitch. "Man, I finally figured out where I've seen you. You were in that *Dumb Ass* movie, right?"

"Uh-huh. *Dumb Ass.* Yep."

"Yeah. *Pursuit of Happyness* too, right? I didn't get what you were doing in that movie."

Amateur film critics were a nuisance that vexed Mitch at many unexpected places in his life—on line for Mr. Toad's Wild Ride at Disneyland with Nora; at the mall in Tulare, where he went to visit his sister, who was married to a date farmer; at the podiatrist. Then there was Morris, the next-door neighbor: "Aren't you glad you're not on that stupid show anymore?" Mitch: "Well, no, actually." Morris: "You mean you're not glad to be off a show that made people vomit just to watch it?"

The wactor also recognized Willie. "Oh, man, you were just too funny in that airplane thing when you got locked in the toilet!" Willie grinned.

Having paid their thirds of the check and gathered purses and jackets, the couples poured out of Orso and walked to the valet stand. June shivered, as the temperature had dropped at least ten degrees since the sun went down, and she had left her sweater in the car. Mitch was standing slightly apart from everyone else on the sidewalk, staring at Willie with barely concealed panic.

Willie, oblivious, was now playing some kind of tickling game with Larissa, who was swatting at his hands and giggling. June could not help but feel a little envious, not of being tickled but of being noticed by a husband, as she hugged herself to stay warm.

"June, I parked on the street," Mitch said. June knew saving eight dollars on valet parking was a habit of his when he was not working, less a matter of fiscal restraint than of twisted self-deprivation.

"I'll see you at home, okay?" He gave June a dry kiss on the forehead, said his good nights to the rest of the party, and made his way down the street, lost in his own thoughts. His neck looked stiff and his upper back hunched.

"Cold?" Rich asked, offering his suit jacket to June. She did not protest when he placed it around her shoulders. It smelled slightly of shaving cream.

"Thank you," June said, and went over to the man standing in front of rows of car keys and handed him her valet stub.

"This the wrong ticket."

"What are you talking about?" June asked.

"Our ticket white, this pink."

"But that's the one the guy gave me when he took my car!"

"Our ticket white. This pink," The valet insisted.

Larissa walked over to investigate. "Are you sure you understand what she's saying?" she asked the valet in a loud voice. She looked back at June. "Let me take care of this. Senior, her billete! Es pink-o!"

"I think you mean 'rosado,'" June interjected.

The valet stared at Larissa and June. "What is 'rosado'?"

Larissa piped up again. "Don't you speak your own language?"

"I from Bosnia," the valet said.

"Oh, for Christ's sake," said Larissa.

After searching the box at the valet station for her keys and coming up empty-handed, it started to dawn on June that she had been a victim of a scam that she had read about in the *Los Angeles Times*. Men wearing fake valet vests preyed on confused-seeming women, pretending to park their cars while actually stealing them.

"Who the hell wants a dirty Honda?" she said, to no one in particular. "I guess I'll call a cab."

Rich seemed genuinely disturbed. "Well, of course I'm going to take you home."

Just then Willie's new Mercedes pulled up to the curb. The valet opened the door for Larissa as Willie took the driver's seat.

Larissa looked at Rich and smiled sweetly. "This might be June's first time in a car worth over twenty thousand dollars."

She looked back at June, who was searching for a reply. "Good luck!" Larissa yelled, getting into the Mercedes. She and Willie drove away. June called Mitch on her cell to tell him about the car, and he was, unsurprisingly, furious. "June, only tourists and one-hundred-year-old ladies would fall for that."

"Hmm, well, which am I? Anyway, I was running late. Rich will give me a ride home, and I'll file a police report in the morning."

"Do me a favor!" Mitch asked. "Don't talk about any poetry stuff with Rich."

"Excuse me?"

"He's a Hollywood guy—he doesn't care about poetry. I may need to get in for their show. Willie is going to get wacky dad. I just know it."

"You know, Mitch, Rich seemed interested in my poetry stuff actually."

"Trust me, he's not."

The valet pulled up Rich's silver Porsche Cayman. June felt slightly embarrassed at how beautiful she found the sports car, not dissimilar to her attraction to the sparkling and intricate webs woven by her house spiders. Rich opened the door for June, and she slunk into the spotless leather seat, feeling somehow fraudulent at being in such a fancy car. As Rich turned them toward Robertson, shifting the gears in a way that June found both anachronistic and sensual, he explained how he had waited so long for this car that when he finally decided that it was stupid and unnecessary and that he'd rather have a hybrid, it was too late.

"Sunk cost fallacy," June observed.

"What's that?"

"It's the notion that once you've already invested time waiting for an item, starting from scratch with another one would be a deprivation. Some academic theorists believe the time you waste continuing to wait for your object of desire mitigates the time you wasted up front."

"I thought your expertise was medieval poetry," Rich teased. "You know, since I first met you at the All Star dinner, I've been thinking about a new show. What about a woman? Like you. Beautiful, of course, brilliant academic, fighting it out for tenure. Making captivating statements in sports cars. What do you think?"

"I can't think who would watch such a show," June said, already imagining Mitch gunning for the part of her department head, and reading the sides with him at eleven at night. Was Rich Friend calling her beautiful? She wasn't sure if "like you" had been actually connected to the word.

"I think it is a novel idea. A *Judging Amy*—type thing. But in a university. Do you think I could visit your office sometime at UCLA? Get a feel for it? Maybe run a few ideas by you?"

"Well, sure." June felt a prickle of heat rise to her cheeks. "I mean if you think that would be helpful. And I'm not suggesting it would be."

"It would. And let's just keep this between us for now. Justine has a way of hijacking my projects."

"Don't you work together?"

"Well, yes. But even spouses have to watch their backs in this town," he said, and then winked, but, she felt ironically.

"Don't worry. I don't take a lot of meetings."

Rich laughed.

After thanking Rich for the ride, June moved to get out of the car but could not get the door unlocked. Rich clicked the locks open and shut from his control panel, open and shut, making it impossible for her to escape. She looked at him, confused. Rich started to laugh, and she joined him.

"I'll call you next week, June," Rich said, punching her cell number into his phone.

"Okay. Well, thanks again. My car problem was embarrassing and you were kind."

June quickly made her way up her front steps, shivering in the wind. She looked back and saw that Rich was still sitting in his silver Porsche, chivalrously waiting for her to safely make it through her front door, and smiling.

CHAPTER 6

Two days later, it was broiling again, and the Santa Anas were blowing. June was volunteering at the Temple Beth Israel Purim Festival, roughly in the manner terrorism suspects volunteered information at Guantánamo Bay. She had chosen the bake sale, the least hellish assignment, in her view, but had spent the better part of the day preparing. She had gone to the farmers' market to get fresh ginger, and driven her rented Chevy all the way to Culver City to get Valrhona chocolate, because she wanted to make the sort of cookies she would like to eat. She had blanched her own almonds for a torte, and used the almond paste Adrian had brought her from Italy.

June yawned. She was still exhausted from Nora's birthday party. Having gone to six parties already this year—three at Dan the Man's play space in West LA, two at Under the Sea, and one at the Culver City ice rink—June had offered Nora an old-fashioned home party. But having never been to a party in a house, the other kids were befuddled by pin the tail on the donkey and pass the parcel, and one child, in spite of excessive private training by his father, had wept bitterly when his egg fell off the spoon during the egg and spoon race.

As she trudged toward the festival, June's phone rang. Amanda, from New York, sitting in her office monitoring the Asian markets.

"Hi there. I've been missing you. How's tricks?" Amanda asked.

"Oh, I'm on my way to a friend-raiser."

"What the hell is that?"

"It's school-director-speak for 'We are really not shaking you down for money, we're making friends!' Which I hate, and you would too."

"Oh dear. Well, you're not missing much here. It was seventeen degrees last night and I had to take the twins down the subway stairs by myself because Sebastian is in London."

"At that smart people's conference?" June asked. Sebastian, Amanda's husband, went to London every year to meet with other professionals to discuss ideas. Or something like that.

"That's the one. Hey listen, before I forget, how's your grant application going?"

"It's been hard to find the time. I can't seem to ever get out from under here."

"June, you're the only person I know who wins publication awards in her free time and gets asked to be the keynote speaker at five conferences a year. So cut the shit."

"Okay. Say, how's your nutty sister?"

"Oh, not great. Her husband is back to surfing the Internet for porn when she's at work, and now she has fibromyalgia."

"Is that the hurt-all-the-time thing?"

"Yep, but *The New York Times* says it's a made-up disease."

"Huh. Well, I wish you were here today," June said. "Although it's a bit hot, eighty-four and clear."

"Isn't it that way every day?"

"Pretty much. Gotta run. Talk to you soon."

Cookies and torte in hand, June arrived at the fair. She looked up and down the blocks where the festival was being held, noting that this seemed more like a Hollywood set than a preschool festival, with stunningly few details left unattended. On the street corner, a DJ dad, who hailed from some band called August, was holding a freeze dance contest. Each carnival game booth was embellished with brightly stenciled signs—cup stacking, fishing for treats, and the lollipop toss—and the prizes were wrapped in dark blue vellum with velvet ribbons. Enormous inflatable slides were at each end of the block, and a bungee-jumping station, too. In the center were miniature ponies, who had been in the business of carting children around so long they had acquired the disposition of old men sitting on broken beach chairs outside the corner store.

Up and down the blocks, moms wearing *American Idol*–style headsets marched around officiously, barking orders. "We need more raffle tickets! Irene is late for her dunking-booth shift! More juice boxes on table two! Pony droppings near Pico! Get a dad, STAT!" All in all, the Temple Beth Israel Purim Festival appeared to have the budget and planning process of a Doug Liman film.

June approached the bake sale table, which was covered with wicker baskets of all sizes and shapes, several Magic Markers, and roll upon roll of tape. She felt the sun begin to burn on her back. Before she could put down her purse and cookies, she was advanced on by Tasia, a mom from Nora's class, whose strong smell of patchouli oil was completely out of synch with her cop costume. There was a giant handlebar mustache attached to her upper lip, and a pair of handcuffs swayed from a belt loop of her shorts.

"Hi, Tasia. I'll just put my cookies in one of these—"

"April, I've been chairing the bake sale for FIVE YEARS, and I can tell you that if you put cookies that small in a tiny basket NO ONE WILL SEE THEM! USE A LARGER ONE!"

"Um, it's June. Okay. I see your point."

Tasia glanced around. "You didn't bring Nora did you? I think I was very clear that kids and bake sales don't mix."

"No, I didn't. She's coming to the festival later with Mitch."

"Uh-huh. So start stacking all the goods into baskets and price them. You'll figure out the system."

June found it interesting that the mothers who were the first to cluck their tongues at June for working were the first to drive up with store-bought cookies for the bake sale. June grabbed a handful of little signs fashioned out of toothpicks and scrap paper, and began to write out prices for the various treats. Her background in baked goods was limited to preparation, and she was thus forced to make assumptions about supply and demand. She stuck a tag in a basket of chocolate chip confections (two for one dollar), oatmeal cookies (fifty cents each), and store-bought cupcakes (three dollars). She fingered the little red signs with the sad face stuck to them that read NUTS, but was not quite sure what to do with them.

"OKAY, YOU UNDERPRICED THOSE OATMEAL COOKIES!" barked Tasia, her eyes a laser beam on each basket. "You need to make them at least one dollar apiece at this time of day. Also, I *told* you, small cookie, large basket." Looking over a forlorn but well-meaning batch of misshapen, fingerprint-smushed butter cookies made by Nora's Panda Bear class, Tasia's verdict was swift and uncharitable: "NO! Don't put those out. NO ONE WILL BUY THEM UNLESS THEY FEEL SORRY FOR THEM!! WE PUT THOSE OUT AT THE END!"

For the next hour, June attempted to hawk her wares to small children with dirty hands who felt compelled to paw ten or eleven cookies before making their choices. Their squinting parents repeatedly passed over her ginger snaps for packages of Oreos, which caused June to feel despondent. When she didn't have a customer, she alternately fretted about her tenure package and eavesdropped.

"I'm not letting Jacob go to that birthday party. The invite said they'd be having a squirt-gun fight."

"My husband says I have back fat. I've got to fire my trainer."

"Well my twins are still co-sleeping, but it's a real issue now that they're three, because they fight each other all night to nurse. I tell them: The milkies are tired and need to sleep. That works for my son. He just crawls into bed to pat the milkies and then goes back to sleep."

"Hi, you!"

June looked up. There stood Larissa in a pink tank top with the phrase "Open your heart" etched at the bottom next to an image of Vishnu, and a matching pair of tight sweatpants. And that engraved vial again. Larissa gingerly placed a big white box of cupcakes from Sprinkles, the famous bakery on Santa Monica Boulevard, on the table.

"I stood in line for an hour for these! They're the best."

June disliked the cloying paste that made up the frosting on Sprinkles' overpriced confections, but said nothing. Right behind Larissa was her best friend, demi (originally Dolores, shortened to Demi in the mid-1980s, and brought into lowercase with the new millennium), who had arrived at the bake sale in enormous sunglasses and an entire lululemon yoga outfit.

"Awesome, girlfriend! Sprinkles? I love those! June hon, do you have a knife?"

"Here," June said, handing demi a plastic knife. "I think they use too much frosting."

"No way, these ROCK!" demi countered. She picked up a red velvet cupcake and cut it into twenty small pieces, offering one to Larissa.

"Oh no," Larissa said, backing away slightly, like a vampire from garlic. demi took a large handful of the pieces, chewing them with her eyes closed, moaning a bit. Seconds later, she spit the entire contents into the garbage bag hooked to the end of the table and said, "Yummy. *Delicious.*"

June, three hours' worth of crumbs encrusted under her nails, face beginning to smart from sunburn, glanced across the playground and noticed Trash Lady, a sunken-faced, black-toothed middle-aged woman wearing three tatty sweaters and a dirty Oakland A's baseball hat. Trash Lady, who lived a few blocks from school in a house in which she entombed her ailing mother in garbage she pilfered from her neighbors, approached the can where demi had spit the contents of her cupcake wrapper, and began to root around. June made a point of avoiding Trash Lady on her way to school each morning because Nora was afraid of her. But June became oddly thrilled watching the pile of garbage grow around Trash Lady's house all year on the otherwise stately block. Trash Lady was the uninvited guest at the festival, and no one would comment on her disheveled state or garbage picking. June carefully placed a large flat of untouched peanut butter cookies next to a large garbage container, and did a silent prayer that Trash Lady did not have anaphylactic nut allergy. Of course, anyone who ate from the trash took that risk, she supposed.

June looked around to see if she could see Nora or Mitch. Where were they anyway? She fumbled through her expansive purse for her cell phone, and grabbed it to see if she had missed a call. Nothing. She dialed Mitch at home.

"Hello?"

"Mitch, where are you?"

"Sorry, we're watching the Honda Classic. There are only a few holes left."

"Oh come *on*, Mitch, please bring Nora here. I want to take her on some rides."

"Okay. Give us ten," Mitch said.

June had had enough of being trapped behind a small table, haggling with her peers over the price of oatmeal cookies, hearing about people's traffic troubles that prevented them from arriving on time to do their bake sale shift, and the never ending conversations around her about which children were now writing their own names.

"Uh, Tasia, my shift was up thirty minutes ago. I'm heading out."

"You can't leave!" Tasia hissed, her mustache now askew. "These other women don't know what they're doing!"

June was irritated, but Tasia's complete dedication to overseeing such a daunting if totally banal event made her feel guilty. June had skipped the parents' association meetings, she had spent only a hundred dollars at the silent auction—many paychecks fewer than those who had bid on Lake Arrowhead weekend homes and buffalo loin dinners for two at the Saddle Peak Lodge in Calabasas—and she had begged off serving on committees. She could do another ten minutes at the bake sale.

June's phone rang. Not looking at the caller ID but assuming it was Mitch, she answered with irritation. "Yes."

"Hello, I'd like to place an order for a dozen free-range escargot."

Rich Friend! June plopped down on a large flat of water bottles.

"Sorry, our snails are grazing in the pasture right now."

Rich chuckled. "How are you, June? Any news on your car?"

June felt her mouth start to tingle a little bit. She imagined Rich on the other end, his hair maybe messy from the morning, sitting on an expensive couch.

"I have a rental car for now while they look for mine. Chevy Malibu. Pretty much like yours. Thanks again for the ride, by the way. Anyway, how are you?"

"Great. I was hoping to set up our meeting for me to visit you at UCLA," Rich said.

Children screamed in the background, and Trash Lady was loudly discarding aluminum cans that apparently did not meet her specifications for house garbage.

"Where the hell are you?" Rich asked.

"Purim festival. Don't care to discuss. When would you like to come?"

"This week is bad. Next?"

64

"Sure," June said. "I'm free every day after about three o'clock."

"Actually, I was thinking night. It is easier for me to get there, and less traffic."

Night. June was never in her office after five thirty. "Sure. Any night. Just let me know."

Her heart was pounding. She reached down to put her cell phone back in her purse and knocked into a table of giant cakes. A pink frosted one, covered in a thousand tiny purple sparkles, descended from the table as June reached her arm out in a fruitless attempt to block the cake's plummet, knowing full well that the space between her and it was vast. She watched in horror as the cake plopped gooily onto the blond head of a small child in a stroller. June recognized her victim as Thor, the spindly boy in Nora's class whose mother did not allow him to run on the way to school, the boy who came to every pool party in a thick black rash guard and enormous inflatable chest pads, the kid who constantly pulled Nora down from the slide, breathlessly warning her, "That's too scary for you, Nora!"

"Thor! Baby!" screamed his mother, Nancy, running red-faced toward the stroller. "He has a terrible gluten allergy! And he is not allowed to have sugar at all!" She glared at June. "How could you?!"

June fumbled for a pile of napkins. "Nancy, I'm so sorry, I don't know what happened."

"Water, towels . . . oh, honey!" Thor, animated in a way June had never seen him, began laughing uproariously, wiping copious slabs of pastel frosting off his eyelashes and chin and then licking his fingers eagerly. "Thor! Thor! No licky!" Nancy wailed.

June made an effort to wipe Thor's face and swatting arms, and mumbled an apology to Nancy, who was too busy dialing her pediatrician to notice. June, embarrassed, quietly snuck away.

At the exit, June glanced at a sign-up sheet advertising career day. Remembering she had to enroll for this latest obligation, June grabbed a ballpoint pen and looked over the list, already thinking about how she would talk to Nora and her classmates about what it was like to be an associate professor and read poems. Of the forty-four parents in the class, only two moms had signed up—one a nurse, another a set designer—and three dads: the so-involved-in-things agent, a computer programmer, and a dentist, who last year used career day to hand out coupons for free cleanings. June did not see Larissa's or demi's name—but she did see the name of demi's nanny, who was apparently coming in demi's stead to discuss her career in child care.

June walked to her car, passing a blue minivan with a license plate she knew from their neighborhood: OY4BOYS. On her rental car was a ticket—sixty dollars. It seemed she had parked in the one residents-only spot on the block.

Exhausted and dirty, June walked into her house. On the kitchen table was a bag of rocks, often left in the driveway as "business cards" from landscapers. Nora must have brought them in. Why? June never understood.

"Mitch? Nora?" No one answered. June went to the back door and into the yard, and saw Mitch's head in his garage office window. Furious, she made her way across the lawn, stepping on a golf ball, which hurt. "Shit!" she said, steadying herself. She heard Nora say, "Daddy, I don't want to watch Phil Mickelson anymore." Mitch countered, "It's the last hole, honey. I promise."

June walked into the office to see Nora on the floor petting the family's tuxedo cat, James, who was lying in her arms purring loudly.

"Where were you?" June said. "Why is Nora forced to sit here and watch golf with you? It was really unfair to make her miss the festival, Mitch."

"June, it's pilot season. Golf helps me relax."

"Mitch, what does pilot season have to do with a Purim festival on a Sunday afternoon at your child's preschool? Do you hear yourself talking? Because you make no sense."

"Festivals make me feel claustrophobic," Mitch said. "Too many kids."

"Too many kids? It's a festival. For KIDS!"

"I know. I'm just so stressed about going to the network this week."

June looked at Mitch with irritation, then turned to Nora, who was still in her pajamas, her hair matted with pancake syrup. "Nora, sweetie, do you want to go with Mommy?" June glanced at her watch. They would be taking down most of the activities by now, but she might be able to get a pony ride in.

"June, you promised to make dinner and then run lines with me."

"Mitch, you're not going to the network *tomorrow*, are you?"

"I need to be ready. You don't know when they are going to call. It's like the army. I've invested a lot in this audition, you know that."

"Yes, I know, sunk cost fallacy."

"No, it's not a fallacy!" Mitch raised his voice. "It's our mortgage. And Uri's dacha, of course."

"Why do you always rub my face in my bad choice of contractor?" June asked as James the cat leaped out of Nora's arms and scampered away into the yard.

"Well, I did want the Irish guy with the lower bid."

June, who had long ago accepted that Mitch blamed her for all matters awry in their home, did not respond, but walked back into the house and into her kitchen. There would be no festival today. She stood staring at her pantry. She had tomato paste, garbanzo beans. She pulled open her fridge. A whole chicken. A pound of ground beef, still half frozen. Some leftover rosemary. Carrots.

She trudged back out to the office. "Mitch, we don't have any milk, and I don't have enough stuff here for dinner. I'm going to have to run to the store." She didn't even consider asking him to go; he would buy the wrong size of everything and call her three times from the cereal aisle.

"Okay, June. Come here, Nora honey, I'll play with you while Mommy is out."

Nora grabbed her Bitty Baby and waved it in Mitch's face. "Be Kylie's voice, Daddy!"

Mitch hung his head a little. "Okay. Hi, I'm Kylie."

Nora frowned. "Not like that, Daddy! Make her funny!"

"I don't feel funny right now, Nora."

Nora began to whine. "I feel funny! Why . . . can't . . . you be funnyyyyyyyy, Daddyyyyy?!"

June stared hard at Mitch, who cracked his knuckles and then began to tap the table nervously. June said, "Nora honey, you can come with me. Kylie can ride in the cart. Won't that be fun?"

Nora wiped her nose on the arm of her dirty pajamas. "Can we go in the rental car?"

"Sure. Let's get some clothes on first, Noony." June turned on her heel and walked out of the room, leaving Mitch to examine the script for My Dad Is Totally Weird yet again.

Three hours later, June was cleaning the counter of the last bits of chicken grease and red wine. Mitch had put Nora to bed and wandered out into the kitchen. He stuffed a stale cupcake that June had made earlier in the week in his mouth.

"June, please can we do My Dad Is Totally Weird?"

"Aren't you just supposed to do it the way you did it the other day? They loved you."

"You have to be better every time, June. It's me or Willie. Hasselhoff is out. My dad is totally drunk and eating Wendy's? I don't think so. With a video like that on YouTube, you're not on anyone's list. Anyway, I need more polish. I need you."

June sighed. "All right." She wiped her hands on her pant legs and followed Mitch to the bedroom. She sat down on the bed with her copy of the sides and stared at a small crayon mark on the wall. She hoped it was washable.

"June, are you listening?"

"Go."

"Chelsea, come down here!" Mitch bellowed, and looked up anxiously at June. "What is with this cell phone bill?"

June responded: "I told you I had to call Kevin in Denver."

"For three hundred and six minutes?!"

June looked down, trying to find her next line. "Daddy, we just like to listen to each other breathe."

"Well, don't breathe on my dime!—I can't do this," Mitch said. "You haven't laughed once."

"I was studying what you were doing,"

"Clearly I'm not funny!"

"Mitch, I am trying to help you. As you asked me to."

"It doesn't help me if you're not laughing."

"Well, it's just not funny!"

Mitch looked defeated. "Okay, June. Thanks a lot. You've helped my confidence a ton."

June's whole body began to hurt with a pain that began at her neck and seemed to snake all the way to her large left toe. Fibromyalgia? "I'm sorry, Mitch. I shouldn't have said that. I know pilot season is tough. Do you want to try again?"

"Too late, June." Mitch stomped out to the garage office. June lay back on the bed and stared at the ceiling, trying to remember the first time Mitch got annoyed at her for not responding correctly during a practice audition. It was an exercise she knew too well by now—Mitch, stymied by pressure, became manic and oversensitive for a good three months each pilot season, returning to something resembling reasonable once he started work again. It hadn't always been this way. When they lived in New York in their one-bedroom apartment in Chinatown, they used to run lines for whatever play Mitch was working on, pausing for the subway to rattle beneath them every ten minutes. June would sometimes dress up for the role she was reading just for the fun of it. Mitch rarely pouted. He used to enjoy his job.

June and Mitch had met at a production of *Death of a Salesman* on Broadway. June had gotten a last-minute ticket, and Mitch was there with a friend. At the end of the play, when Willie Loman's wife gives a cathartic speech at her husband's grave, June began to weep inconsolably. She was stunned to notice that the tall guy sitting next to her, who had made witty comments about the line for cappuccino during intermission, was crying too. "That play was cathartic. Truly cathartic," June said, still shuddering from her sobs.

Mitch snuffled back, "Every Arthur Miller play is brilliant."

"Classic tragedy." June blew her nose. "I have to think about it. It was overwhelming."

"Do you want to have coffee?"

A few weeks later, they were rarely apart. Mitch would read aloud to her from *Cosmopolitan* magazine while she got her hair cut, giving her the Cosmo: What Kind of a Friend Are You? quiz in a variety of accents. June would take Mitch to obscure corners of the Columbia University library, showing him where first editions of Wordsworth and Yeats were held. They would go to performance-art shows, and usually walk out, and Mitch would then do dramatic reenactments of the dreck they had just seen as they sat on the G train on their way to Greenpoint for Polish food. Those early years in New York were characterized by modest means, mutual interests, and free time. Eclairs at La Fortuna, browsing books at a Shakespeare & Co. bookstore, noodles at Kelley & Ping, standby tickets to Broadway. While June studied in her tiny studio with a skylight in Morningside Heights, Mitch would run over between auditions and bring her good chocolate that he had splurged for at Fairway Market.

Mitch ran a small theater company on Thirteenth Street with a group of friends from New York University, and June sometimes sold lemon bars and coffee at the concession stand, catching Mitch in eighteen performances of *Rhinocéros*.

They were married the standard two years later, and moved to Los Angeles. In time the farmers' markets, warm nights at the beach, and the Hollywood Bowl somewhat filled the void that leaving New York had formed.

Then came Nora. June's life became consuming, such that she did not notice the little fissures that Mitch's increasing neurosis and obsession with his career had formed in their marriage. It seemed the more successful he got, the less confidence he felt, and the more acting was a chore, not unlike waiting on tables or raking the yard. June, while empathic, could never fully understand this trajectory. And, in truth, it was boring. She had signed up for watching great theater and sitting on their futon reading *As You Like It*, not making small talk at Hollywood parties with anorexics discussing *My Dad Is Totally Weird*.

Well, another Mitch tantrum, what could she do? June noticed the *Los Angeles Times* sitting on her nightstand. She flipped through it absently—bra ads, war photos, problems in city hall. She stopped on her horoscope, and realized it had been several days since she had looked at it. She tried not to let Mitch see her do it. Experts on classic poetry were not supposed to be astrologically obsessed, and her fixation with her horoscope irritated him. *VIRGO: Your interpersonal relationships are taking a toll. Step back and reassess.*

June went to check her e-mail.

To: junejune@gmail.com
From: amandamalone@smithbarney.com

Hey. How was the "friend-raiser"? Give me news.

To: amandamalone@smithbarney.com
From: junejune@gmail.com

News? Let's see. I dumped a whole cake on this kid with a
gluten allergy and now I have to deal with the fact that no one
is going to speak to me ever again at school, not that they did
to begin with. Plus things with Mitch not great. I was running
lines with him for some show called my dad is really weird or
something like that and he lost it with me. Plus I never know
what season it is. Plus can't find Girl Scout cookies. Please send
thin mints. Your depressed friend. . . . . . . J.D.

June was delighted to see within a few minutes that Amanda
replied, even though it was after midnight in New York.

To: junejune@gmail.com
From: amandamalone@smithbarney.com

Forgive me, sweetie, because I know this is your life, but this
is one of the most hilarious e-mails I have read in weeks.
Childhood gluten allergies? These moms should stop speaking
to Gluten Boy's mom for bringing him to a BAKE SALE,
not the other way around. And Mitch getting mad about
a television show? Maybe you should remind him that he
could be in Iraq picking camel spiders off his tush. In the
meantime, who are these awful women anyway and how can
you get away from them? Surely there are at least one or two
award-winning associate professors balancing work, home, and
puff pastry? Perspective, June. Have some. Thin mints arriving
anon.

71

June smiled. She was about to reply when her phone rang. She glanced at the clock. Maybe it was Adrian, who often phoned after a dinner out, even when it was 1 a.m. in New York. The caller ID read "unavailable."

"Hello?"

"He-llo. It iz Hilda, I hope I aim not disturving you."

June instantly recognized the thick German accent of Cat Empress, the neighbor across the street who was Nora's rival for the heart of James. Hilda was obsessed with the cat and constantly fed James treats to lure him, the way the witch in "Hansel and Gretel" lured the children with her candy house.

"Hi, Hilda."

"James is sitting in my kitchen talking to meee. I am vondering what you are feeding him? I am vondering, does James have a happy home?"

"Happy home?"

"James, I am talking to Mommy! She says come home. You know, June, he does not vant to come to you. So sorry."

"I've told you to stop feeding James, Hilda. He'll come home if you don't feed him."

"I cannot do that, June. He is so beauuuuuuuuuutiful."

"I'm coming to get James, Hilda."

June walked out of her house and found Hilda in the street holding the tuxedo cat. "You don't know what it is like to lose your love June. I have no vone."

June reached for James, and Hilda clutched him tightly to her breast.

"Hilda, please give me the cat." June took the hot, lumpy mass of silky fur out of Hilda's arms and carried James back into her own silent house.

CHAPTER 7

To: MitchGold@aol.com
From: Tad@Tadmeier.com
Re: My Dad Is Totally Weird/deal

> Got them up to 45! Two and half percent bump per year, seven
> years. Up from honey wagon to double banger, favored nations.
> Cheers, T.M.

Mitch examined the e-mail from his manager. He had made $42,220 a week on *Molar Opposites*, so $45,000 was pretty sweet, though assuredly less than Willie's would-be deal. All pilot deals were made in advance of being hired for seven-year periods, even though 90 percent of shows never even made it on the air. This gave the networks the upper hand, so that once they had made their choice, an actor could not begin to negotiate hard. That said, 2.5 percent raises per year seemed pretty paltry. Of course, if he got fired, always a possibility, he would get paid only for the pilot, or two weeks' pay. If a big star got fired, he got paid for the whole first season. Never mind. He was not a big star. A double-banger dressing room trailer—show business speak for a duplex trailer—was good, better than a honey wagon, otherwise known as a horse trailer. Mitch knew that getting a pop-out, a trailer that expanded or even had a second story, was a pipe dream. Favored nations—the promise that everybody in the cast was getting the same trailers—was clearly a crock.

But what about billing? Mitch *needed* his name up high on the credits. Plus, he usually got a health club membership to compensate for the craft table full of junk food. Of course, all of this was for a job he didn't even have. Still, if this show got picked up, he wanted what he wanted.

To: Tad@Tadmeier.com
From: MitchGold@aol.com
Re: My Dad Is Totally Weird/deal

> Good work on the $45,000. But what about billing? I shouldn't get worse than third position, right after the kids. And parking? Try for a reserve spot, no farther from the sound stage than the second lead. How about the health club? And I need a couch no smaller than seven feet long in my trailer. Reasonable, right?

To: MitchGold@aol.com
From: Tad@Tadmeier.com
Re: My Dad Is Totally Weird/deal

> I'll negotiate about the billing, and try again on the health club. A couch?????

To: Tad@Tadmeier.com
From: MitchGold@aol.com

> I am a tall man, Tad. Let's say I get to the set at 5 a.m., rush into wardrobe and makeup, and then sit in my trailer until 3 p.m. until they're finally ready for me. One likes a couch at that time. Not unreasonable. And while we're on that, can I have cable? (Golf Channel.) Health club a must. Don't they want me to look good?

To: MitchGold@aol.com
From: Tad@Tadmeier.com

> Health club? This is a show about teenage girls! No one is looking at you.

Disgruntled, Mitch picked up his golf club and walked outside to wait for the mail. It was time for his afternoon ritual to begin.

He stood on the front lawn, a few feet from the mailbox, club in hand. He leaned forward slightly, then pulled his four iron behind him and took a huge swing, holding the finish, imagining his ball soaring through his neighbor Morris's window across the street. Mitch pictured the midcentury light fixture hanging from Morris and his wife Rose's living room shattering into a million pieces with the impact of his Titleist.

Mitch stared down the street looking for the mailwoman, Gloria. There she was, far down the block, sporting her blue government-issue sun hat and matching shorts. Why did mail people/men/women in Los Angeles always wear shorts, even in the winter? And couldn't she walk a little faster? He returned to swinging, and failed to notice Morris emerge from his home, one of the few two-story houses on the block. No escape.

"You've gotta keep your head down. And you're taking the club way past parallel."

"Thanks, Morris."

"You working?" Morris asked.

"Not at the moment."

"You know, you should get on that 24 show. Now, that's good. Not like some of this garbage you're on."

"Well, you know you have to audition for shows, Morris. You don't just 'get on.' "

"Yeah, I know. I know how you big Hollywood types work. Listen, I need you to sign my petition to limit parking on this street to residents only."

"What for, Morris? We have plenty of parking on this block."

"Well, Mitch, in case you haven't noticed, the Mexican guys who work at the car wash on the corner are always parking their jalopies around here, and that brings down property values. No one wants to live on a street with beat-up Pontiacs all around."

"I think most of those guys are from Guatemala."

Morris looked incredulous. "Guatemala, Guadalajara? What's the difference? I'm just asking you to sign this. How about protecting your home value? Did you ever think of that?"

Blessedly, Gloria was walking toward him, a bundle of mail in her hands.

"Hi, Mitch," said Gloria, sort of stretching out the *ch* in the way she always did. "Looks like a couple of envelopes today." Gloria knew what Mitch was waiting for—residual checks, which came at least twice a week, but with wildly varying contents. Recently, he'd hit the mother lode—a check for twenty thousand dollars for DVD sales of a horror spoof he'd made five years ago.

Residual checks served as a scrapbook of Mitch's career—the odd five hundred dollars for a network showing of a movie he made a decade ago; a check for less than the postage of the envelope for a cable episode of a sitcom he made in his early twenties; a four-thousand-dollar voice-over residual for the voice of Noah. "Thanks, Gloria," Mitch said, taking a slightly oversized pile from her hands.

"You have a good one, Mitch."

Morris ambled back toward his house to castigate the gardener, who never seemed to prune the tea roses to his satisfaction.

Mitch gave his club a final swing, then took his *Golf Digest*, the Verizon bill (too high as usual, he had to switch carriers), a notice for another in June's endless series of parking tickets (Jesus, June, read the signs), preschool invoice (again!), some junk mail, and three envelopes from the Screen Actors Guild into the house.

He arranged the mail spinach to cake—bills first, then the magazine, then the checks—and placed them on the kitchen counter. A large glass of orange juice was poured. The golf club was set in the corner of the kitchen where June would later trip over it when she walked in, then begrudgingly put away.

June put up with a lot, he knew that. He meant to apologize. And for getting angry at her while he was trying to practice his audition. He would do it at some point. He adored June—her weird expressions, her indifference to Hollywood, her appreciation of his sarcasm, the fact that she put curry paste in the sweet potatoes—but sometimes he wondered if she really understood how much was at stake with these auditions. One day they would actually have to finish the work Uri had started, and before they knew it, it would be time to pay for Nora's college tuition.

The OJ in one hand, mail in the other, Mitch repaired to his favorite leather club chair, in a sun-drenched spot in the living room. First he opened the Verizon bill. High, but a write-off. Temple bill—shocking as usual. *Golf Digest* with the cover line "Finally, a fix to your swing." Yeah! The cream-colored envelope, addressed to him, was from something called the Neptune Society: *"Free Prepaid Cremation! Details inside!"* He opened June's ticket—huh, this one was for parking too close to the curb. He made a note to self: Give June refresher course on parallel parking.

Lastly, the checks. Mitch carefully took each check one by one as he always did, ripping it slowly along the right side of the envelope, so that the old movie or television show he was being paid for was revealed first, allowing him to guess, with amazing accuracy, what the payment would be. Today: basic cable, *Dr. Quinn, Medicine Woman.* Ugh. Next up, basic cable again, *Buffy the Vampire Slayer.* Last hope: goddamn basic cable, *Walker, Texas Ranger.*

Three checks: $4.23.

Irritated with his take for the day, Mitch decided to call Tad to see if there was news on his network deal.

"Tad Meier's office."

"Hi, Jamie, it's Mitch Gold."

"Right on."

"Yeah, is Tad around?"

"Please hold."

Mitch waited. Three minutes passed. He flicked on the television and began to surf the channels. Midday news. *Oprah.* Home and garden show. Click. Whoa—there was his own face, ten years ago, final episode of *Murphy Brown.* He'd look for that two-dollar check. Three more minutes passed.

Finally—" Yo, Mitch, what's up?"

"You tell me."

"Yeah, I talked to Tim. . . ."

Hearing the name of his agent at CAA made Mitch's stomach drop. "And?"

"You're good on billing, you'll be third," Tad said.

"Exxxxxxxxcellent."

"Let's forget about the couch. The network was being dickish about that. I get why you want it, but no go."

Mitch felt his throat tighten. "And how about the gym?" Mitch was sure that CAA must have gotten Willie a better parking spot for his phantom deal, plus, no doubt, the gym membership.

"I tried to talk to Tim about that."

"Yeah, so what did he say?"

"He wasn't being supportive. Let's just let it go."

"Come on, I want to know what he said, verbatim."

"Verbatim?"

"Uh-huh."

"He said, 'I'm doing four other deals on this show. Why is Mitch busting my balls about couches, and gyms, and where he fucking parks?' Um, he also said if you're worried about the size of your ass, you should speed-walk from the parking structure to the sound stage."

"Hmm. That doesn't sound good," Mitch said, his heart sinking. "Did Tim say how much Willie Dermot is getting?"

"Don't worry about Willie Dermot. Focus on Mitch Gold. Kick ass at the network like you always do."

"When is that audition, by the way?"

"A week from tomorrow. They have too many sessions for other shows to do it earlier."

"A week!" Mitch said. "That means I can't audition for any other pilots for a week!"

The networks had an unwritten rule: As long as an actor was in position to get a series regular role, he was not considered for anything else until the decision was made.

"I know it sucks, Mitch. But you're now under contract—"

"For a part I don't even have!"

"Yep, Mitch, but that's the way it is."

"Okay, but let's say I don't get the part on *Weird Dad*. Is there anything new on the breakdowns?" It was imperative to Mitch to keep his fingers on everything. This was the season for work, and he needed to audition for all the pilots he could.

"Well, there's tons of stuff," Tad said. "You could go in on *Lone Star Gals*."

"What's that?"

"Bunch of divorced chicks living in a house in east Texas going after their ex-husbands' girlfriends. You'd be a recurring ex-husband."

"Tad, recurring ex-husbands are dead by episode five. I need to be a series regular, not recurring, at thirty-five hundred a week."

"Right." Tad continued, "there's another show, untitled, two roommates meet in a mental hospital and live together. Kind of a psycho-odd-couple kind of thing. You'd be good for that."

"That's in my wheelhouse. Hey, what ever happened to *Cro-Magnon?*"

"Rescheduled."

"To when?"

"To a date not on the books."

"Uh, doesn't that mean the audition's been cancelled?"

"No, Mitch, it's rescheduled."

"To when?"

"To a date not on the books. When it's on the books, you'll know."

"Tad, in modern standard English, that means cancelled. Anyway, what about *Cane Mutiny*, the blind-cop deal? Is that on?"

"Hmm . . . let me check on that. But right now let's try and focus on *My Dad Is Totally Weird*—I get the feeling from casting that you're first choice. And then there will be midseason replacements, so don't stress."

"Talk to you later, Tad. I gotta run anyway."

"Oh right, you're doing *Police Line* tonight, right?"

"Yep. Coffee with Joy Wainscott and then I'm doing a night shoot."

June stood in front of her afternoon class, longing for a coffee. In the back of the room, the hand of her favorite student shot up.

"Professor Dietz, I chanced upon Robert Fagles's translation of *The Aeneid* at Book Soup over the weekend and I found myself wondering about your thoughts."

"Well, I have some questions as to how literal the translation is from the original Latin. But what was your reaction?"

June could not help but appreciate Taylor Steiner, who had taken each of her classes over the last two years. An enthusiastic poetry reader, Taylor stood out among both the premeds, who snoozed through "The Rime of the Ancient Mariner," and June's most accomplished English majors. Oddly pretty for the sort who seemed to spend every Saturday night at poetry slams at downtown artists' lofts, Taylor was perpetually prepared, and enthusiastic about all types of poetry.

"Well," Taylor began, "no doubt he wants to avoid vulgar overlit-eralness—he knows that the Romans didn't feel the full specific and literal impact of every verbal stem. But instead of deepening the accuracy through attention to idiom, I feel that his choices insert just a bit too much stuffiness between me and Virgil."

June looked around the classroom to see if someone wanted to chime in, but her students were pushing back their chairs and flipping on their phones, some already deep in text messages. Class over. Time to go get Nora.

"Well, Taylor, by way of comparison I suggest you also look at Mandelbaum's translation."

"I have it at home," said Taylor, beaming.

"Great. See you next week."

June went out to her rental car. She arrived at the gate that led to Nora's classroom. Ugh. She had tried to time her drive to get there exactly at three so she could be in time to pick Nora up but too late to have to stand around with the other mothers. The stay-at-home exercisers had already lined up, their faces still red from their afternoon race-walk, debating the most effective swim diapers. June found a spot at a nearby picnic table and began looking over the first few pages of her book. Her first chapter dealt with *The Iliad*. For what must have been the thousandth time she considered the opening of Homer's poem:

Rage—Goddess, sing the rage of Peleus' son Achilles,
murderous, doomed, that cost the Achaeans countless losses . . .

Once again June mulled how long it would have been before Agamemnon dumped Chryseis if Achilles hadn't insisted on sending her home to her father.

She glanced up at the moms and saw Nancy, who glared at her and looked away. Suddenly, the gate was opened by Autumn, June's favorite teacher, a willowy twenty-two-year-old from New Orleans who spoke with a gentle lilt and taught the children yoga.

"Hi, June. Nora is right here. By the way, I had to take away her Tamagotchi. It went off during morning circle."

"Oh, I'm sorry, my husband always forgets the rule about electronic toys in school," June said, tucking the toy into her purse.

Thor, dressed in thick tube socks and covered in zinc oxide, his tiny face obscured by a giant brimmed hat, stumbled out toward Nancy. "Hi, Mama."

Nora came rushing past Thor and jumped into June's open arms. "Mommy! Can we go get a cupcake from Sparkles?" Nora pulled on the waist of her painter pants.

"Do you mean 'Sprinkles'?" June said, heart sinking slightly.

"Uh-huh. Carly's mommy says they are the best. And plus she said they deliver."

"Yeah okay, Nora. Sure."

June turned away from the other mothers, whom she knew were off to some outing of the afternoon playgroup from which she had been barred by Lexi, who, along with being room mom, organized all the playdates. She saw Libby, an older, single mother who had quit her high-powered Hollywood lawyer gig when she finally got pregnant four years ago. She had tried hard to court the younger, fitter mothers, but had been rejected. June watched her make yet another attempt.

"You guys off to Roxbury Park?" asked Libby hopefully, as her daughter Jo-Jo stood by, shyly.

Brown-Sweat-Suit Mom flicked her eyes toward the gaggle of other women in tank tops, then back to Libby. "We have a gymnastics class right now, Libby. Sorry about that."

Jo-Jo piped in. "I wanna do gymnastics, Mommy!"

Brown-Sweat-Suit Mom leaned down toward her. "Oh, sweetie,

you had to sign up for it months ago. I am sure your mommy will get you in next year."

Libby, looking defeated, pulled her too-tight purple leggings out of her butt and smoothed her shirt over her slight belly roll. "Come on, honey, let's go to the park."

Feeling embarrassed for Libby, June tried not to make eye contact with anyone as she scooped up Nora to better race off the school grounds. June's impulse was to invite Libby along with her. But she had promised Nora all week they would have special time alone. With guilt, she walked away. She had almost made it out, but was trapped at the front door by Town Crier. Town Crier was married to Cheerleader Mom, who was always volunteering to hold class parties at her house and ran the temple Thanksgiving soup kitchen, where she regularly forgot to stock the soup.

Cheerleader Mom and Town Crier took turns putting their poetry in the class newsletter, which they made sure to copyright. Town Crier (whose real name was Brant) had exhaustive information on every family in the class—name, birthday (child and parent), place of employment, college affiliation, car make, and who had slighted whom at Tot Shabbat and what was being done about it. June had had several interactions with him because Nora was very fond of their daughter, Charlotte, who was a charming child. His wife was intolerable, but in a cheerful way, and June vacillated between appreciating Town Crier's omnipotence—*when was spring break again? where does one get one's kid's hair cut? ask Town Crier!*—and feeling unnerved by it.

"Hi, June. I saw you pull up in a Chevy. What happened to the Honda?"

"It's a long story. What's up?" Nora was pulling June toward the large tree in front of the school, which Nora was too small to climb, and June wanted to avoid a battle.

"Oh, nothing," Town Crier said portentously, leaning his head a little to the side, as if weighed down by what he was about to report. "I just wanted to mention a little something I thought you might like to know."

"Oh?" June felt sense of dread.

"Yeah, well, some of the moms have been telling me that you're kind of, well, I don't know, rude at meetings and stuff. I guess you graded some papers or something at a birthday party last weekend? I dunno. Anyway, the gals are thinking maybe you, sort of, you know, judge them, because they have more money than you, or because you have to work."

"Uh-huh." June started to form a defense, rife with examples of the many slights she had suffered at the hands of "the gals" that year. She quickly looked down at Nora, who was beloved by most of the children in the class but rarely invited to play with them. She sucked it up. "Um, I can try harder to make conversation, I guess."

"I'm just telling you so you can make some friends. There are a lot of really wonderful moms in this class. And I know that you're not able to be as involved as you'd like, given your work, but I'm sure you could find a way to hook up with them."

"Town Cri— Um, Brant, I am just as involved as the other mothers. I am here every day for drop-off, and at least twice a week for pickup. What I do while my child is at school has nothing to do with parenting."

June wanted to go on, and point out that no one criticized any fathers for working. But with Nora watching she bit her tongue and smiled tightly. "But your advice is really appreciated and I'll try harder, at parties and other events."

"Great, June. It's all good! Oh, one other thing. Some of the moms have noticed that you, or I guess it's your nanny, packs peanut butter in Nora's lunch."

"I pack Nora's lunch, Brant. And it's soy butter. But thanks again for being so thoughtful."

"Just trying to help!" Town Crier said cheerfully.

June pulled Nora away, hoping to shake off the encounter. Soon they were in the car and heading to Beverly Hills.

"How was school, Noony?"

"Good, Mama. Except you know what? You know what? You know what happened, Mama? Jack G. spilled all the paint on purpose, and Autumn told him no that's not good and he did it more and he got a time-out and I didn't."

"Wow." June was now inching her way through traffic on Little Santa Monica Boulevard, and noted the long line snaking out of Sprinkles.

"Mama, will I still be in the Panda Bear class next year?"

"No, you will be in kindergarten next year. Won't that be exciting?"

"But I don't know how to be in kindergarten."

"Oh, you'll be great at it, Nora. All you have to do is play and have fun." June began the hideous trial of finding parking in Beverly Hills. She made her way into a tiny parking structure with six meters. Full. Nothing on the street. Finally, she approached a giant structure on Rodeo Drive, near an elaborate fountain, decorated with plump cherubs.

"Mommy, I want to have a playdate with Jenny P."

"Okay, I can call her mom."

"Can you call her at nighttime? Jenny P. said her mom doesn't get up during the day."

June and Nora joined the queue a few feet from the frosted-glass door of Sprinkles, which was closed tightly. Customers came out one at a time, biting into oversized red velvet cakes.

A sign on the door warned: PLEASE KEEP THE DOOR CLOSED. THIS HELPS TO MAINTAIN THE FRESHNESS OF OUR CUPCAKES.

In front of them was a woman with a small dog, which Nora moved to pet. "They have a special selection just for you, Be-boo!" the woman crooned, patting the animal's miniature head. June could not understand the phenomenon of baked treats for dogs—especially at $3.50 a pop. Nora was singing quietly to herself to the tune of "God Bless America." "God bless my underwear. My only pair. Through the washer, and the dryer . . ."

Suddenly a yellow Hummer with tinted windows double-parked in front of the store, and out poured a mass of young women in Ugg boots. They coalesced around Moxie, who even June recognized as the recently incarcerated hip-hop star–cum–talk-show host, her hair a massive weave of braids and Swarovski crystals. Moxie and her crew whisked past the line, which receded slightly to let her by.

"Wow, it's Moxie!" a young woman with a wide polka-dotted headband in her dyed hair said, pulling out her cell phone and frantically beginning to dial. "Hey, I just saw Moxie here. Yeah, yeah, she seemed sorta sober. Yeah, I guess. Yeah, okay, I'll try to figure out what she got and get the same thing. Let me go, I need my phone to take her picture."

As the Hummer idled outside the store, blocking traffic, June read its license plate: LOCKUP. Ten minutes later, Moxie and her entourage emerged from Sprinkles with several boxes, and the line had moved not an inch. June looked at Nora.

"I'm hotttttt, Mama. Do we have to wait much longer?"

"Well, Noony, how about a giant doughnut with pink frosting and chocolate sprinkles?"

"Do they have those here? Do we have to wait?"

"No, they are very special. Too special for Sprinkles. Let me take you to my secret place."

Delighted, Nora smacked her lips together ostentatiously, and the two left the line and walked back to their car. "I'm a little hungry, Mommy," Nora said. "Can I have some earthquake snacks?" June thought about the pile of pretzels, Goldfish, and stale cereal bars in her trunk, along with the dust-coated water bottles, all part of the car earthquake kit that was forever being picked over, eaten, and restocked. "Not now, honey, we're almost at the doughnut shop."

Twenty-five minutes later, June pulled into the tiny lot of a Winchell's and parked next to a Chrysler LeBaron missing its front bumper. Winchell's had a dirty floor, a scratched glass counter, and no line.

"What can I get you, *mamita?*" said the woman behind the counter, smiling warmly at Nora.

"I want the pink one, please!"

June paid $1.10 for the doughnut—not the $3.25 for a Sprinkles cinnamon sugar number—plunked Nora back into her car seat, and headed for a nearby playground. The two of them grabbed sand toys from the trunk, where they had been sitting under a transistor radio, another earthquake item. June wondered if the radio had any batteries, reminded herself to buy more water, and then instantly forgot. Nora went racing toward the slide as June found a bench and began to listen inattentively to a group of mothers gathered near her.

"I know. Mine never sweeps under the bed—it makes me nuts," said one in a pair of white Chanel sunglasses.

"I know. It's crazy, right? I mean, for twelve dollars an hour I expect a little housework when he's at school."

"Get a new one. I found mine on Peachhead."

Peachhead was the e-mail list for Los Angeles mothers, in which women exchanged tips on breast-feeding, child care, where to buy a diaper pail, and whether Crocs counted as open- or closed-toed shoes. June vacillated between feeling scorn for some of the mothers—"People who let their children cry themselves to sleep should be jailed"—and appreciating information about the best place to sell used child care books.

"Hey, Sarah, where did you get those cute flip-flops?"

"Can you believe, Target? I went to the one on La Cienega during a birthday party at Hey Let's Make Pottery!"

"Oh, my husband won't let me go to that Target because it's in *that* part of town. The one on Sepulveda's a little better."

"Maria took the girls there one day. I couldn't believe it."

"Is that the narcoleptic nanny?"

"No, I fired her when she fell asleep on the field trip to Santa Monica Aquarium. This is the El Salvadorian."

June glanced at her cell phone. She and Nora could stay for thirty more minutes. She looked up at Nora, fearing she would be summoned to play tag. It was too hot. Luckily, her daughter had hooked up with a small boy in an orange playsuit, and the two were digging happily away in the sandbox.

She dialed Adrian.

"Hey, sweetie! What's up? Hi, Fifty-fourth and Second Avenue please."

"Where you going to dinner?" Half of their phone conversations seemed to take place when Ardrian was in a taxi.

"A new Italian place in a weird spot, totally amazing antipasto."

"Yum, good desserts?"

"Actually, yes, original biscotti, almost as good as yours, June."

June began to whisper. "You can't believe the conversation I am overhearing in the park here."

"What? I can't hear you?"

June cupped her hand around the phone and raised her voice. "Horrible women all around me talking about how they can't go to a store where black people shop."

"Well, June, who told you to live in Echo Park? I believe that was me. M. E. Me."

"Too long a commute to UCLA. We've had this conversation a hundred times."

"Yes, I know," Adrian said. "Boring for both of us."

"Okay. Give me news."

"Welllll, I had another date with the doctor last night."

"How was that?"

"It was great when he tried to go down on me."

"In a cab??"

"June, you've been married too long. Anyway, kiss, kiss, kiss at dinner at Suba. Great wine, food so-so. Anyway. Making out at the table, him rubbing my leg. Says I'm gorgeous, blah, blah, blah. Totally great. Right? Then we get in a taxi, I mentioned what was going on there. My place, lovely, lovely—um, southwest corner please, right there, with the green awning—we had a glass of wine, talked some more, lots of kissing."

"Sounds nice."

"It takes a horrible turn."

"How?"

"Um, ten back please. Keep the rest. So anyway, we're at my place, he goes into the bathroom, comes back, sits next to me on the bed, and says, 'I like it showery.'"

"Ew."

"He said, 'You're lovely as gold. Let's get golden.'"

"You know, I've read James Joyce liked to be peed on."

"Not helpful, June. Anyway, it gets worse. But I can't tell you anything more because I'm twenty minutes late and I see Ian and Amanda waiting for me. I'll call you tomorrow . . . *loveyoumeanit.*"

Click.

June could not help but feel wistful at the vision of three of her closest friends having dinner together without her. She thought about how, back in college, Adrian had worked at Dean & DeLuca on weekends, and she would come in every Sunday and march around the store officiously, loading up on expensive cheese, gâteau nuage cheesecake, European butter, and focaccia and then stand in line at Adrian's register, where he would scan only the butter. She would then take the 2-subway journey back to 110th Street with her $250 worth of free groceries, and the four would have a dorm-room feast later in the evening.

Amanda refused to accompany June on these grocery theft outings. She said they made her too nervous. Amanda was the gentle and upright animal on their island. The only time June ever saw her lose her temper was when a professor gave her an A- on a paper on John Stuart Mill. Ian quit school a year early to cover the last year of the Croatian war. He had been a reporter ever since. Ian was rarely in the United States anymore, and June and he e-mailed and spoke on the phone only occasionally. But Adrian and Amanda remained June's New York lifelines.

June imagined Adrian closing the taxi door and walking up to Amanda, who was no doubt wearing a new outfit from Barneys, and Ian, recently back from a reporting trip to Iraq, who would provide an hour's worth of riveting tales. They would gossip about the newspaper where Ian and Adrian worked, Amanda would tell them about a new client she'd landed who had bad breath, and they would drink a little too much wine because no one had to drive. And June would sit in the arid playground listening to five women talk about a new tile store in Santa Monica.

She picked up the phone to call Mitch, then remembered he was shooting an episode of *Police Line*. It didn't matter—he wouldn't be interested in her woes anyway. She dropped her phone back in her purse.

CHAPTER 8

Mitch reached down to kiss Joy on the cheek, but she quickly held out her hand, which Mitch shook, awkwardly. She had changed. Her once-bristly hair was now pin straight, and smelled of some kind of spice—he thought June called it cardamom—and no longer of clove cigarettes. Her nose, which was once set wide across her face like a giant boulder in a river, was now thin and aquiline. The surface of her skin was almost translucent, like Nora's. Her men's Hanes T-shirt, omnipresent in New York, had been replaced by a thick black cashmere sweater; her puka shell necklace had given way to a silk scarf. He tried not to look surprised. He settled into the booth at the Roosevelt Hotel, consciously creating a foot of space between them.

"Nice to see you, Mitch. You've been doing great over all these years."

Again, the indifferent tone. Mitch began to relax. "Joy, you look terrific. It is great to see you again. You were all the buzz at Sundance this year." Joy smiled, warmly, but kind of head-of-human-resources style, as if they had never met, let alone spent years working together in the theater.

This could be a big job. Joy went on to describe his role—sarcastic Jewish mobster, slightly too loud, belligerent, annoying to those around him—things he had mastered long ago.

"Sounds like everything I can do," Mitch said, taking a sip of his coffee, now lukewarm.

"Good. I'm doing some tweaking right now, and I'll get it to your manager—whatshisname, Tad, right?—when I'm done. Then you'll read it, call me, and let me know if you wanna come in, okay?" Joy asked, looking at her watch. "By the way, David Duchovny and Fyvush Finkel are also on the short list."

"Sure thing. I really appreciate you thinking of me."

Joy smiled back at Mitch, and for a split second he thought he saw it, that glimmer of admiration, those tiny eyes covering his face with need. But it disappeared just as instantly, and Joy excused herself to make a call. This was going to work out fine.

Later that evening Mitch walked into the breezeway of the studio in Glendale where *Police Line* was shot, circumventing the "crashed" fire truck and carefully stepping over the broken "glass," pieces of the truck door, and large hoses, which were strewn about on the ground. He could still smell the sulfur from the fake fire. He glanced over his call sheet, the legal-sized paper cast members were given each day that listed the name of every person associated with the show, their call times, and every prop and vehicle needed to make the shoot happen. The cast was listed in order of their perceived rank on the show. Mitch, playing Agent Baker, the head of the local FBI force investigating a possible terrorist attack associated with the truck explosion, was number twelve, right after the regulars. Not bad.

Tracy Devern, one of the leads on *Police Line*, was suffering severe anorexia and was the talk of the tabloid magazines, whose photographers lined up outside the studio gate every day to see her car come in. Network executives had taken to supplying her with McDonald's bags to emerge from her car with, and large Jamba Juice cups and bags of Fiery Hot Cheetos to drag from the set to her trailer each day. The publicists at the network had provided a list of things that all the cast, if asked by a visiting *Los Angeles Times* reporter, should say in response to inquiries. "Tracy has a fast metabolism. Tracy loves hamburgers. Tracy is so naturally thin, and lucky! Tracy and I pigged out at Musso & Frank last night!"

But at his costume fitting a few days ago the wardrobe girl, Hannah, told Mitch that every piece of food was thrown out the back of the trailer, and that Tracy's wardrobe for her role as an undercover cop had to be modified every week, and that Hannah had finally taken to shopping in the teen department at Bloomingdale's for Tracy's pants.

Mitch could hear the scene before his being shot. He leaned quietly against a wall with a large white sign that read HOT SET, which meant that the room, which had been made to look like a coroner's office, would be used soon and should not be disturbed. A guy from the prop department walked by Mitch holding a bloody prosthetic arm for the crash scene. He was trailed by the second assistant director, who was talking into a headset. "Get hair and makeup down here. They need to gray up the dead victim, and give some cuts and scrapes to the firemen. I need shrapnel embedded in the right thigh of fireman number one. Bring the background to that little conference room near the crane so they can get their props. Remember, don't give anything out without a signature."

Mitch was careful not to make eye contact with the "background," or extras, known in the entertainment industry as the untouchables. Unlike bit players, background were not exactly actors; they would never be given a speaking part, and had little hope of upward mobility in the world of television and film. Some extras dreamed of acting, but others simply wanted to be on television, and within proximity to stars.

For forty-five dollars a day and Kentucky Fried Chicken (while the cast and crew ate steak and fresh salmon), they spent the majority of their time sitting in makeshift shantytowns, playing cards under blankets in cold outdoor spaces, waiting for their scenes, in which they would walk around in the background, their faces rarely in view.

Early in his career, Mitch had vowed to be extra nice to extras, but that only led to a number of them begging him to ask a producer to give them a line on the show so they could get into the actors' guild, nagging him to call his agent on their behalf, or trying to use the bathroom in his trailer. Hollywood was a caste system, and everybody knew his or her role. The background lined up now for their props: white lab coats, handcuffs and guns, and a few rolls of yellow tape.

"Mitch, we're ready for you."

Mitch walked past the LA Times reporter, who smiled at him—a good sign, the guy must have recognized him—and made his way onto the set. A group of writers and the director, Sadie Moss, were swarmed around video village—so named because of the group of video monitors gathered together slightly away from the set. Mitch overheard two writ-ers whispering.

"I loved that line, it was so funny, and he messed it up on purpose."

"That little shit. He always tanks a line when he doesn't like it. Thinks the network will cut it."

"Making us look bad. Asshole."

Mitch found his mark—a piece of yellow tape on the floor that in-dicated where he was supposed to stand—and smiled at Tracy Devern, playing Detective McNally, whose sunken face sent a chill up his spine.

Sadie waved to Mitch from her perch by the video monitor. "Okay, let's go." The assistant director, wearing a Mickey Mouse sweatshirt and baggy jeans, yelled, "Rolling! And background!" The extras began to move around the burned fire truck. Then Sadie called out, "Action."

"Witnesses said there was an EDP on the scene a few seconds prior to the explosion."

"That was no EDP."

"What are you getting at, Agent Baker?"

"You'll be hearing from headquarters." Tracy—Detective McNally—glared at Mitch—Agent Baker.

"Cut."

A helicopter could be heard clattering outside.

"That copter's killing me!" complained the sound guy. Everyone stood quietly waiting for it to pass.

The second AD, who had been showing her production assistant pictures of her cat on her cell phone, snapped to attention. "Copters clear. Reset. Rolling! Background!"

Tracy and Mitch shot the scene a few more times, then, after the first AD yelled "Moving in," took a break while their stand-ins were lit for the next shot. Mitch was mulling a return to his trailer, but he heard a commotion near the crash site of the fire truck.

"Don't you dare contaminate my crime scene!"

"Oh, fuck off, Marlon Brando!"

Jake Billow—Sergeant Dempsey—was an intense method actor who purchased his own home sonogram machine when he played an ob-stetrician on *Desperate Housewives*, and now wore a bulletproof vest every day of the week, even when he was not working. Another star, Felicity

Copagen, who had a love of snack food and spent half of her time on the set noshing, had placed a large platter of nachos on an evidence table at the fake crime scene, offending Jake.

"This is a sterile environment!" Jake yelled.

"Shut the fuck up. You're a nut job," said Felicity, stuffing her mouth with nachos.

One of the producers raced over. "Can you guys keep it down please? There is a reporter on the set."

Tracy, overhearing this, came rushing up. "What do you mean? I said no one can be on the set on days I shoot!"

"Well, network publicity greenlighted him!"

"Hey," Tracy insisted, "I'm number one on the call sheet. So what I say goes."

Mitch looked around for the reporter, hoping the guy had been watching his scene and would note the excellence of Mitch's performance.

CHAPTER 9

Larissa Dermot was the sort of person who frequently acted on impulse, and was then left to spend a great deal of her time correcting what resulted.

She stood in the kitchen of her Mediterranean-style Brentwood house, which when they first bought it had been big, but not big enough, in Larissa's estimation, for the Dermots, so she had spent the better part of three years increasing its size. First she went up, adding a second story, enraging the neighbors, who now looked into her guest bathroom rather than at a patch of blue sky, and whose ensuing legal action went nowhere. Then Larissa went out, adding a den to the back of the house, which contained a flat-screen television, a pool table, and an array of video games. She added an enormous playroom for Chloe and a postage-stamp-sized bedroom for her revolving supply of live-in nannies. Now she was on to her kitchen. On order: a sixty-inch six-burner Viking gas range (even though Larissa hadn't cooked in nearly five years, it would be good for caterers); a new Sub-Zero fridge, to replace the barely used old Sub-Zero fridge (but this one had deeper vegetable drawers); frosted-glass cabinets; and a stainless-steel countertop. Though she had wanted glass tile floors with LED lighting, her designer, informing her of just how over budget she was, suggested that Larissa settle for cork.

All of these changes were going quite smoothly until Larissa decided, on the spur of the moment, to host a Shaklee party for twenty women, all influential in show business, and all of whom could help her husband's career with a single phone call.

Larissa grew up in Surprise, Arizona, where she was the homecoming queen and president of the Drama Club. Her turn as Maggie in her high school production of *Cat on a Hot Tin Roof* had gotten the town talking—Larissa Bunch, with her ivory skin, thick auburn hair, and natural bow mouth, was destined for Hollywood. Infused with the notion of star potential, but mindful of her mother's lot as a housewife with no college degree who was forced to become a medical biller after her husband died, Larissa commuted forty miles every day to Arizona State University and pursued a degree in drama. In Tempe, Larissa's delicate features and creative diction ("Do unto others as you might wish they might do to you") stood out—she landed Hedda in *Hedda Gabler* and May in *Fool for Love*.

After college, Larissa packed up her Chevy Impala and drove west to Los Angeles to live with a former classmate who was waiting tables at Kate Mantilini and doing Equity Waiver theater. Larissa went on commercial auditions daily for a year, and landed a few small parts, but in the end, Hollywood offered her nothing to speak of. Except Willie Dermot.

She met Willie, ten years her senior, at the wrap party for the third season of a series they had both been on. She had one line, as Nurse Number Two; he was Dr. Louis—head of the ER. Larissa was impressed with Willie's tenacity in pursuing her—he called her every day thereafter for six weeks—and the ease with which he settled into the life of the star she knew he should be. She never felt an iota of desire for him, so when they had sex, she drew upon the image of a starting forward for the Phoenix Suns. Or a Peter Som dress. It varied.

Soon after their marriage, Larissa gave up going on casting calls and focused on helping her husband in any way he needed, whether he knew it or not. She managed every minute of his day; not a dentist appointment, haircut, or endoscopy happened without her involvement. She picked out his clothes for auditions. And she frequently badgered his agent and manager, making sure Willie was going in for all the major movies. She paid underlings at a small-time casting office to get her the breakdowns every morning, and then would spend the afternoon calling his manager, Karin, who usually didn't take the call, she noted with ire, to find out why she hadn't submitted Willie for certain parts.

After delivering Willie his first dream—a baby—Larissa worked hard to remain the girl her husband had met over his Ketel One martini.

She worked out daily; kept her face maintained with laser face resurfacing, eyelid surgery, and Juvederm injections; and never missed a season at Fred Segal. Her only indulgence, other than the occasional bite of Häagen-Dazs, was a monthly 1 a.m. run to a taco cart on Pico, after Willie had fallen asleep, which she compensated for by eating only fresh mint leaves the next day.

Larissa was never going to be a star. But she would be married to one, and she would never go back to Surprise.

Although Willie's career seemed to be exploding right now, Larissa knew that her continued maintenance of his connections could only improve his lot, and by extension, her kitchen. Besides, Larissa loved to be included in the Hollywood set. Party invitations, red-carpet premieres, wrap parties in trendy hotels, playgroups run by Romanian child care experts attended by women who had Academy Awards at home— these were the pleasures of Larissa's life. Each day she pondered how she could add more of them.

So she became an environmentalist.

Six months ago, Larissa had bought a Prius (she had gotten the dealer's son a walk-on role on *The Suite Life of Zack & Cody* in exchange for moving her up nineteen spots on the wait list) and festooned it with a bumper sticker that read: *We did not inherit the earth from our parents, we are borrowing it from our children.* She put her black Escalade into the three-car garage and parked the Prius in front of the house. Then she had her landscaper plant a desert garden in the front yard, and held an open house to show it off. She attached solar panels to her roof, and bought organic cotton shirts for Chloe and some end tables carved on a sustainable farm in Peru. She tried French hemp sheets, but quietly returned them to Jon Zabala in Hollywood after they left tiny scratch marks on the backs of her legs.

To make her commitment to a clean, sustainable, carbon-footprint-reduced life evident, she decided to host a party where people could buy organic cleaning products, like the Tupperware parties of yore. On the guest list tonight was Justine Fein, the television producer from Fein Friend Productions; Cass Martin, who had RSVP'd to come—fingers crossed!—Tina Smithers, the wife of the head of casting at ABC; Carly Zelnick, the wife of Willie's agent at CAA; Bonnie Green, creator of some new show about a school in the Bronx; casting director Donna Lawrence; Esther White, another CAA agent; and Carole King, Calista Flockhart, Daryl Hannah, Arianna Huffington, and Julia Louis-Dreyfus, with whom Willie had recently worked. Laurie David was in Nantucket and couldn't make it. Larissa had also been forced to invite June, who had overheard her talking about the party at preschool, where she had been trying to discreetly invite demi.

All around the Dermot kitchen caterers worked feverishly filling large platters with locally grown asparagus drizzled with balsamic vinegar, arranging gluten-free crackers and goat cheese on trays, and dotting tiny little plates with loads of vegan options. Looking around the half-finished kitchen Larissa started to panic. She did not want Julia Louis-Dreyfus seeing her yet-to-be-completely-installed stainless-steel kitchen counter.

"Marcus, *me encanta* what you did with those asparagus things," Larissa said. "But *mucho* people will be here soon and they can't see this horrible kitchen. It is a *mucho* mess in here. So *andale! Andale! Sí!*"

The doorbell rang. Larissa, dressed in her Pilates clothes, ran for the stairs. "Marcus, I think that is *los servers, por favor,* open *la puerta!* And remember, everyone who works in *la casa* tonight needs to remove their shoes and wear these." Larissa handed Marcus a pile of blue surgical booties, identical to the ones she had forced the caterer to wear. They had been given to her by her next-door neighbor, whose husband was a cardiologist. "I've got to get dressed!"

Larissa looked across the room and saw two boxes of Ziploc bags sitting on the counter. She didn't want Julia seeing those, either. "CONCHITA! CAN YOU DO SOMETHING WITH THESE PLASTIC ZIPLOCS? HIDE THE PLASTIC WRAP TOO, *POR FAVOR!*"

Chloe came running into the kitchen. "Mommy, can I have one of those little cakes?"

"Sweetie, you had your dessert this week."

"Mommy, please, isn't it a special 'casion?"

"It's a special occasion for grown-ups, love beans. Now run to your room and play Polly Pocket, okay? Mommy will come in soon and play a little with you. Go, run!"

* * *

Driving through Brentwood, scanning the numbers on the curbs in front of the houses, June was furious. With the second chapter of her book nowhere near finished, a page for the end-of-the-year scrapbook due at Nora's school in a few days, and a growing infestation of Argentine ants in her yard, June deeply resented fighting traffic getting to some moronic pyramid-scheme party at Larissa Dermot's.

When she heard Larissa detailing her natural-household-products party to demi at school, she had tried to slink away. But demi had un-helpfully chimed in, "June, you totally want to be part of the solution, right?" Having accepted, but planning to make up a story to get out of it, June was finally forced into going by Mitch.

"Mitch, you're joking, aren't you? I have to willingly spend a night at Larissa's house? Do you know what kind of traffic there will be around the 405 at that time?"

"Take Bundy. June, I have never asked you to go to any of these parties by yourself. *Ever*. But this is an important year for me, June-Junie. There could be people there who can hire me."

"Why is it any more important than any other pilot season, Mitch? Come on."

"I need all the help I can get, even on the margins. I need you to go. Please."

June turned her car onto La Mesa Drive. She had never been to Larissa's house but thought it was the big white one on the corner. She turned into the driveway, and then saw the house number and realized she was in the wrong place. She tried to back out but was afraid of on-coming traffic nicking her car. In the driveway were two Porsches, an SUV, and a battered gray pickup truck that clearly belonged to someone working on the property. Unwisely, June attempted a three-point turn. This attracted the attention of the pool cleaner, who came toward her, scooper net in hand. June reversed, went forward, turned her wheel, re-versed, and went forward again, praying she could clear the white stucco wall that was on either side of the driveway.

ERRRRRRCHH!

June had managed to embed her rental car in the wall like a fossil, and try as she might, she could not extract it. She got out of the car and stood face-to-face with the pool man.

"Shit," she said, looking from the wall to her rental car.

"You want me to try getting it out?" the pool man asked.

"Sure, if you don't mind. I would be really grateful."

June stepped aside as the pool man slowly detached her car from the wall and pulled it into the street. The stucco wall was unharmed, but there was a giant white scratch mark on the passenger door of the rental car, and a large dent was now punched in the side panel.

"My cousin in El Segundo can fix that for you for three hundred dollars," the pool man offered. "A lot less expensive than a body shop."

June thanked the guy, took down the cousin's number, and beat a hasty retreat.

When she arrived at Larissa's, June paused at the front door to take in the Dermot spread. The scent of lavender from the garden on the side of the house overwhelmed her, and hummingbirds pecked at the cactus in the front yard. The house was painted a tasteful putty color, and the size somewhat stunned June—how much was Willie taking in these days anyway? June was quite sure that, a million from *Super Roach* notwithstanding, it was not enough to support a two-story house on a secluded street in Brentwood. She wondered about the Dermots' Visa bills.

Larissa's live-in nanny-housekeeper answered the double doors. "Hi, Conchita." June knew her from the park.

"Hi, Miss June," Conchita said, looking toward the ground. "Come in."

June noted with confusion that Conchita seemed to be wearing the sort of blue booties worn by surgeons.

Behind June came demi, also late and talking on her cell phone. "Gotta go! Thanks for the giggles!" demi hung up, racing past June without even noticing her.

June stepped through the double doors and looked around. The entryway was enormous, with a large-scale vinyl painting covering one wall. June peered carefully—was it by Monique van Genderen? And if so, certainly it had been chosen by a decorator.

June made her way into the living room, toward a mushroom-colored sofa. She recognized Cass Martin right away sitting on a couch talking to Calista Flockhart. Justine, Rich's wife, was telling someone June did not recognize about a recent trip to New Zealand.

The room was buzzing with various other women in everything from business suits to jeans and long flowing shirts, many of them clutching ice water. June knew there were celebrities there but as usual could not remember who was who, who starred in what, who had left her husband, been in rehab, had a baby, and/or become a lesbian. She did recognize Julia Louis-Dreyfus, whose hair was in its natural curl that night. She was nodding sympathetically at a woman in white Greek sandals and giant bright orange earrings. June stood near them, enough to hear, but not to be noticed.

"They've closed the Sunday school at Our Lady of Mercy. The problem, it seems, is that lots of parents were ditching the service, skipping out on the kids at Sunday school, and then going to brunch at the Beverly Wilshire."

June would have to tell Mitch that one. Still slightly shaken from the wall incident, June picked up a glass of wine from a server's tray and began to sip it. On a large table were household cleaning products, each one sitting on a black linen napkin. On the bottles were images of small children with pinkish skin and dogs running through flower fields.

"Hi, everyone!" called Larissa, standing in the center on the room in a diaphanous rose-colored dress that fell just above her bony knees. "Everyone, hello! Welcome! *Namaste! Namaste!*" The room slowly quieted, with all eyes turned toward Larissa. "First, I want to thank you all so much for coming to our home tonight! It is so thrilling to see such a distinguishable group of women so committed to making our earth and homes cleaner places."

She folded her hands together, fingernails tastefully buffed nude to match the toes peeking out of her skinny-strapped sandals, and bowed toward the women. "Now I would love to go around the room and have everyone introduce themselves and maybe just say a few words about how you got consciousness. Even though most of you are well known to all of us, of course. Let me start. I'm Larissa"—she giggled—"and my path was first cut by my yoga teacher, who started to tell me about the asthma rates connected to the household products we use. Since then, Cass and Julia have been such an inspiration to me."

Larissa looked around. All of the women were looking back at her, except for June, who was picking at a scab on her ankle. Spider bite?

"Now I want you all to meet Conchita, who is, really is, a part of our family." Larissa pulled slightly on the gray shoulder of Conchita's uniform. "Say hello to the ladies, Conchita."

Conchita shifted a bit from foot to foot with an uncomfortable smile. "Hello."

There was an awkward silence, and Conchita looked around to see what she was meant to do next. As no one moved over to give her a seat, or indicated in any way that she should join them, Conchita, still grimacing, picked up a dirty wineglass and ran back to the kitchen. "Thank you so much, Conchita!" Larissa called after her. She looked around the room. "Okay, who'll go first? Esther? Can you share?"

"Sure. Love to. I think for me it was two years ago, when we were planning our family vacation. I really wanted an eco-friendly destination, but the hubby likes his room service and nice sheets. Then I found this amazing chain of eco-luxury hotels, and we had this awesome trip to Costa Rica, with room service, massages, but totally sustainable practices in the laundry and stuff. I realized we could really have that kind of life all the time, that we can live a high-quality life without excessive imbalance."

June prayed she would somehow be skipped over. "That is an amazing story, Esther," Larissa said. "How about you, June?"

"Um, I bought those bags at Trader Joe's that you use over and over."

"Did you make sure they were lead free? Not all of them are."

"Umm . . ."

For the next hour, June endured a room full of women providing their personal tales of eco-travel, present living, nontraditional healing, yoga at the Golden Bridge, detergent awareness, and tampon toxicity.

At one point, June noticed Arianna Huffington, who seemed to be limping—always intrigued by other people's calamities, and deeply bored with the idea of actually striking up a conversation with demi, who had managed to squeeze next to her on the couch, June leaned toward Arianna and asked: "What happened to your leg?"

"I broke my foot in New York," said Arianna, in that fun voice that always reminded June of Natasha, that old cartoon character in *The Bullwinkle Show*. "It's a funny story really. I was out to dinner and I had called for a car. I am now using a company that only provides environmentally correct vehicles. But the thing is, they didn't show up! So I had to take a taxi, and it was raining, so I ran a little toward the corner and the heel of my Jimmy Choo got clipped on a subway grate and down I went. Crack. There was my ankle."

June was fixated on a real New York City grate, as she pictured the many shoes she had lost to them, including a sandal on the way to her first job interview at Macy's, where she was trying out to be an elf. She pictured the pizza place where she ran in to use the pay phone to call Adrian to bring her a new shoe, and began to feel lonely. She smiled at Arianna.

A heated debate on vaccines started up, but Larissa artfully turned the conversation to the things she had for sale. There were organic super-cleaning wipes (fifteen wipes for fifteen dollars), soft fabric concentrate (thirty-two ounces for twenty dollars), supermicrofiber window cloths (five dollars each), and scads of laundry soap, nonchlorine cleansers, and a recycled plastic dropper for measuring it all (twelve dollars).

June dutifully bought a box of laundry soap and some wipes, and wandered over to Justine, who was wearing her little red eyeglasses and a loose Chinese jacket over a silk tank top. June studied her with fascination, unable to stop herself from picturing Justine in bed next to Rich Friend, his hands resting on Justine's breasts. She blinked and tried to erase the image, but continued to assess Justine through what she imagined were Rich's approving eyes. Thick around the waist—out of proportion with the flat chest—Justine had skin that was slightly pallid, and her small mouth always seemed to be free even of Chap Stick.

June tried to picture Rich and Justine's first meeting, wondering what he saw, what she said, what is was like for them the first time he kissed her mouth, what Justine thought about it, where they first had sex. She imagined Justine sitting in the passenger seat of Rich's car, and wondered if she threw her gum wrappers under the seat, as June did in Mitch's Saab. June remembered Mitch telling her that Justine was the brains behind Fein Friend Productions, and she tried to picture what the two of them talked about at night. Afghanistan? The state budget? Or just the fall television schedule?

Cass Martin, her long legs peering out from beneath her short skirt, was a beacon in the middle of the room, tall and effortlessly beautiful. She walked slowly, stopped to examine the laundry soap, then approached Justine and June.

Cass and Justine went back years—Justine had discovered her when she was seventeen and doing her first Equity Waiver play in Pasadena, playing Titania in A *Midsummer Night's Dream*. She had cast her in her most successful series, *Valhalla*, and from there Cass made the jump to movies, and became one of the few black women in Hollywood to have a consistently successful film career.

Though they no longer worked together, the two women had become close confidantes. Cass was one of the only people in Hollywood Justine dared to share her fears and weaknesses with, and Cass in turn went to Justine with all of her professional issues, like the perpetual problem of being offered five hundred thousand dollars less for movies than were the white actresses she competed with.

"Hey, Justine, what's going on? How's Wendy? How's Peter?" Cass asked.

"Not bad. We had a little ear mite issue but that's resolved. I was actually looking to see if they had any dog shampoo here."

"I think I saw some. So, how's the new show coming?"

"Well. Of course I wrote it with you in mind, but you're the only one of you, so I'm going to have to settle."

"Justine, if I were ever going to go back to television, you'd be the only one I'd work with. Someday we'll work together again."

"A girl can dream." Justine smiled. "Anyway, the show is good. The network loves it. But Rich and I have differences of opinion on stuff. The network wants changes and he's being a hard-ass. Sometimes I wonder if he understands that we're not making an independent film, we're doing network television."

"Huh," Cass said.

"Yeah, he just seems generally preoccupied and cranky."

"Pilot season makes everyone cranky," Cass replied. "I have to say I don't miss it for a minute. In fact, I was just talking the other day to—"

Larissa, eager to join any conversation featuring Cass and Justine, had sauntered over and tried to break in.

"Did I hear pilot season? My topic *préféré*!"

103

Justine looked at Larissa with, June was amazed to see, contempt, or at least something resembling contempt. Cass simply looked amused.

"You know, Justine, what Willie always says is, 'It is well that television is so terrible, or we should grow too fond of it.' "

"War is so terrible, Larissa," Justine said.

"That too."

"No, I mean the Robert E. Lee quote is, 'It is well that war is so terrible, or we should grow too fond of it.' "

Larissa was momentarily silenced. June looked at Justine, riveted, and Cass chimed in, "I've always wanted to make a Civil War movie."

Justine looked back at June. "Were there any significant poems written during the Civil War that are part of your curriculum?"

Larissa took one last chance. "Is that what you teach? Poems?"

Justine snorted. "She's only won the William Parker Riley prize." Her eyes narrowed. "Do you know what kind of work it takes to succeed as a woman in academia, Larissa? It's a hell of a lot harder than battling Brentwood housewives at the swag tents at the People's Choice Awards."

June's heart began to pound with exhilaration and slight fear.

Larissa stood, her smile frozen, and seemed about to reply when Willie cut his way through the living room.

"Hey, ladies, how's the cleaning stuff?"

"Hey, Willie," said Justine, amused by Willie because he always seemed in character—mildly confused but abundantly cheerful, unlikely to say something intelligent but no more so something mean.

"Hi, Justine. Great to see you."

He slapped Larissa on the ass, and she giggled. "Larissa, honey, you need to move your Escalade. It's blocking my spot!"

Larissa's smile collapsed like a fan, and her eyes darted around to see who had actually heard.

Cass looked at her. "You drive an *Escalade?*"

CHAPTER 10

"Ouch!"

It was June's own fault, really. She hadn't had a pedicure in several months, and now the middle-aged Russian woman was digging into the ingrown nail on her left big toe, killing her. Trying to distract herself from the pain, June flipped through a magazine, and stopped at the horoscope.

VIRGO: This month's cosmic energy could work for you in a big way—but it could also work against you! There's not much you can do to fight it, so do your best in every important situation and make the most of the good times.

"You don't come enough," the woman snapped. June peered down at her toes and found herself fixated by the top of the Russian woman's head, covered in hair in various shades of a banana.

"I know," June said. "I don't have time."

"You need eyebrow wax?"

June considered. "Okay."

The woman scrutinized June's face. "You need upper lip, too." June touched her skin. She felt no excess hair but became nervous. Rich Friend was coming to her office tonight: would he think she had a mustache?

"Okay. I guess I'll do the lip as well."

Almost an hour later, June emerged from Lovely Nail with deep magenta toenails, perfectly smooth hands, a strip of pink above each eye, and her lip all tingling with pain. She drove quickly to the university, where she had planned to work on her tenure package while she waited for Rich Friend to arrive that evening.

Sitting at her desk in her small office at UCLA, June stared at the piles of paper and manuscripts. Her bookshelves were tightly packed, with a few volumes protruding here and there, and she always imagined one would fall and clock her on the head. On her desk was a fading photograph of her and Mitch outside the Museum of Modern Art in New York, and two pictures of Nora, one slightly crooked in its frame, which was fashioned from macaroni, made in a toddler art class.

June looked over her tenure package. She had two academic articles from the last three years—not bad—but the progress of her book on male rage and epic poetry was what the tenure committee would be most concerned about. She flipped though her first chapter, realizing grimly how much more work it required.

She had written the narrative of her published work but had not gotten anywhere with the descriptions of the classes she taught. She had yet to write her bio for the external reviewer. As she sat debating whether or not to include her entries on a widely read poetry blog (they were not peer-reviewed, but did that matter in this day and age?), she heard a faint knock on her door. "Come in."

"Hi there." It was Gerry, from her freshman poetry class, a basketball scholarship student who failed to turn in his papers on time, and rarely made it to class. "I just wanted to come by and say, like, I just need a little more time on that *Gilgamesh* thing. March Madness killed me, and I am, like, *screwed* with the rest of my schedule."

June knew the unspoken rules about flunking a promising athlete, so she simply nodded in his general direction without even looking up from her papers. "Uh-huh. That's fine."

"Thanks, Professor Dietz. You rock."

"Uh-huh, thanks," June mumbled.

"You know what, you look hot."

June looked up, alarmed.

"Well, maybe not hot, but really nice. Your face is, like, pretty."

June felt herself blush. "Okay, Gerry. Thanks for the info." Five minutes later, she heard another knock. Irritated, she looked up to tell whoever it was that it was not office hours, but was then pleased to see Taylor at the door.

"Hi, Professor. I delved into the Mandelbaum last night. It was really illuminating, just as you suggested."

June brightened.

Taylor continued. "I know you only use graduate students to assist you. But this material is so compelling, and I feel there is so much you could teach me. Is there any way you could consider finding a role for me in your research?"

"Let me think about that, Taylor. Your enthusiasm is very much appreciated." After Taylor departed, June called Mitch, who she knew was on the golf course in Simi Valley.

"Hello," he whispered.

"Oh, hey, are you in the middle of your game?"

"Yeah. What's up?"

"I wanted to tell you that I need to work in the office tonight. I can't concentrate at home."

"That's fine," Mitch said, "but I'm going to have to call Olga to stay late. Remember, Martin and I are going to a screening of his latest after our round."

"Oh, yeah, I forgot about that."

June was unaccustomed to being out at night without Mitch. "All right, just don't forget to ask Olga to bathe her. She'll be really dirty after school—I think they did arts and crafts today."

"Okay. See you later."

June returned to her dissection of the squabble between Agamemnon and Achilles, making notes in nearly every margin. Finding it hard to focus, she began to click through her e-mail. She had gotten another chain e-mail, a recipe exchange. A sale on sheets at Bed Bath & Beyond. The Peachhead postings, which she scrolled through—one mother's posting made her pause with horror:

> My three-week-old daughter has a bit of a monobrow problem and we are having her one-month pictures taken next week. Can anyone please recommend someone to thread or wax her brow?

Or maybe I should just shave it??? Thanks in advance for your advice, as always.

June's cell phone rang again. Mitch. Had something happened to Nora? She knew she shouldn't stay late. Her panic setting in instantly, June answered: "What happened?"

"WHAT'S A NIMROD?" Mitch yelled.

"What? I don't know anyone named Nimrod."

"I need to know what it means when you call someone a nimrod. Is it racist?!"

"Whoa, calm down, Mitch. It's biblical. Nimrod was a hunter. I believe he was the grandson of Ham and the great-grandson of Noah. Oh, and he also founded Babylon. Why is there an emergency need to know of Nimrod?"

"Ah-ha!" Mitch said triumphantly. "So he came from Noah. That's a good thing, right? Not an insult!"

"Well nowadays the word denotes a klutz, which, interestingly, scholars attribute to Bugs Bunny. Now, Hebrew etymology traces Nimrod to the word 'rebel,' and vis-à-vis God's kingdom—"

"June, please, no Bible study! I'm asking if it's a pejorative, because there's this JERK standing here, pushing Martin, HARD, and accusing him of a hate crime because Martin called him a nimrod!"

"Why would Martin call someone on the golf course a nimrod?"

"Oh, he claims Martin didn't yell fore, which he *did*, and the guy got all pissed off, so Martin called him a nimrod, and he said that was a hate crime and went nuts."

Mitch was speaking quickly, almost panting into the phone. June could vaguely make out yelling in the background. "It's a crime! It's illegal! I'll get your frigging English ass arrested!" She heard Martin's voice rising above it all: "Oh, come off it, you're being daft!"

Mitch panted into the phone some more. "Hey, the marshal just walked up, I'll call you later."

June placed the phone back in its cradle. Wasn't golf supposed to be the civilized sport? It seemed like Martin and Mitch were always having some set-to on the course, whether it was facing off with a rattlesnake, getting hit in the head by a ball, or having some altercation over who was taking too long to do whatever one does at those little holes.

She went back to her e-mail as the light faded. She had lost track of the time before she heard a third rap on the door. This time she got up to open it. Rich Friend, slightly unshaven in a way June found embarrassingly alluring, was standing there, holding something wrapped in delicate pale celadon paper in one hand, a large Starbucks cup in the other. He was wearing dark blue jeans and a bright green dress shirt, untucked, with a pair of expensive running shoes.

"Hey! Nice to see you!" June pecked him slightly on the left check, and smelled that soft shaving cream scent again.

"I can't thank you enough for making the time to see me. I know how busy you must be."

"Oh sit down," June told him. "I'm not busy. Just sitting here, trying to prevent myself from being downgraded into an extension-class teacher."

June had a small toile chaise longue in front of her desk; she thought it more comfortable for students than the usual office chairs most associate professors had. She had found the chaise at the Rose Bowl swap meet, and it gave her office a charming, informal feel.

Rich sat down on her chaise, a strongly masculine presence on a decidedly feminine piece of furniture. He handed her both the paper cup and the package. "I hope you like lattes. And this is just a small thank-you in advance for your help."

June put the coffee on her desk. "I do like lattes. But there was really no need for you to get me a gift. This is beyond generous."

It glimmered across June's mind that the package might contain a collection of reggae CDs. She carefully handled the bundle, which had been beautifully wrapped in something that looked like antique paper and ethereal silver ribbons. It was almost too gorgeous to take apart, but she pulled on the ribbons slowly. She drew her breath in to discover the gift—W. H. Auden's collected works from 1945. She slowly cracked the cover to confirm what she had suspected; it was a first edition, probably worth at least six hundred dollars.

"This is too much, Rich. Honestly, I can't accept this," she said, ashamed of her instinct that he would not take it back, of course, and her knowledge that she actually did not want him to.

"June, you're the only person I know who would value a book like this. Honestly, you'd be taking my pleasure away by not accepting it."

June looked down at the book again, its cover fragile under her touch. She moved next to the chaise and began to leaf through the poems. She turned to "Lullaby," one of her all-time favorites. Rich craned his neck to see what page she had found. "Of course, you went right to my favorite, too."

June looked up at him from the book. "Is it really?" She looked at the book in her hands again. "Thank you so much. A really beautiful gift." She tried to remember the last gift Mitch had gotten her. It had been years since it was a book, although he did recently give her a muffin tin. "How did you get interested in poetry, Rich? It's an unusual interest, truth be told."

"My mother. She read poems aloud to me when I was a kid. You know how other moms read their kids *Goodnight Moon* and *The Cat in the Hat* at bedtime? My mom would recite *The Waste Land*."

"That sounds nice," said June, trying to imagine the sort of mother who pulled her child into her lap to read:

> *A rat crept softly through the vegetation*
> *Dragging its slimy belly on the bank*

She started to picture this woman, perhaps in a denim skirt, her legs needing a shave, smelling vaguely of sautéed onions. Maybe she had Rich's features, and long eyelashes.

"Actually," Rich said, "it was kind of odd. I had some freaky dreams as a kid. My mother was quite animated, really, and that wasn't the half of it."

"Really?" June had found a place on the floor, sitting Indian style next to the couch, and was looking up at Rich with a grin.

"Well, she killed every pet I ever owned."

June laughed incredulously. "Killed? Like what do you mean, murdered? She took hammers to your hamsters?"

"Well for example, we had this bunny, Rasputin," Rich said, now standing and looking around June's office.

"Rasputin?"

"I think she wanted a tough bunny," Rich answered. "Anyway, so Rasputin lived his days in a loft on the Lower East Side, and remember, this was when the Lower East Side was the Lower East Side. So he's fine and he eats well and life is good for the Manhattan bunny. But my mother couldn't stand his smell, so she insisted that he live out on the fire escape, overlooking the Hertz rental car garage where all the attendants would pass their days pissing between the cars.

"Ohhhhh, too, too sick making—" June laughed.

"Yeah, right? It passed the time when you were ten, watching them. So anyway, Mom says bunnies are outdoor creatures, apparently not understanding that when it reaches freezing, real bunnies go underground into their burrows. New York City bunnies that live on the fire escape simply freeze to death. So imagine the pathos of a ten-year-old boy discovering that his beloved pet had become a bunny-sicle on his fire escape."

"Oh, that is bad."

"So my brother and I tried to revive Rasputin by putting him on top of the radiator, sort of wedged, if you will, between the, I don't know, what would you call them, like the slats? Anyway, we figured we could defrost him. Instead he just started steaming. Soon, our entire apartment started smelling like a pot roast, with steam rising off of Rasputin's hair." Rich swept his arms up in the air, as if re-creating the steam, then rolling them down dramatically, for emphasis.

June was laughing. "That's a tragic tale."

"Yeah, it is. And then there was Fidel, the German shepherd that my mom sent off to live with my cousin on a farm in Pennsylvania. But instead of fessing up, she laid across the kitchen floor sobbing when we came home from school, pretending that the dog had been hit by a bus on Broadway."

"These are weird stories, Rich."

"Yes, they are." He was quiet for a moment. "It's funny how I haven't thought about this stuff in years. But weird childhoods are exciting really, and good material. Plus, you know what? I love *The Waste*

Land. And all the other poems I was introduced to at a young age, even when it was too young an age. Another thing I got from Mom was cooking. She taught us all how to make the perfect cassoulet. Hers is still the best I've ever had."

June could not stop smiling.

"Where did you grow up, June?" Rich said, moving to a seat beside her on the floor.

"Minneapolis."

"What was that like?"

"It was different. Not the Lower East Side, not the West Side of Los Angeles. My dad was a professor at the U, and we spent a lot of time going to documentary films about the Inuit people. My mother dedicated herself to figuring out how to appear Christian, and working for local Republican city council candidates, which enraged my father. So I would not say it was a particularly poetic environment. I discovered that whole world at Barnard. That is where I learned to bake, too. I used my waitressing money to take a class at the New School, because I got a discount."

Rich stared at her with what seemed utter fascination, and she wondered if he was imagining her small and innocent, as she was him. She wanted to run to his childhood self and comfort him in the face of the steaming rabbit Rasputin. Then she imagined what it would have been like to walk into a senior prom with a boy as gorgeous as Rich Friend must have been. But she had not gone to her prom. She had gone camping that weekend with three girlfriends, and they had gotten drunk on malt liquor and thrown up into an elderberry bush.

"Barnard, of course," Rich said with a smile.

"What does that mean? Are you pigeonholing me?"

"Never!"

Rich stood up and began moseying around June's office, fingering her books, looking out at her view of the nearly darkened campus, and the large eucalyptus, which was blocking some of the other buildings. June stared at his hands, nails unchewed, long fingers, a little calloused, which she wondered about. Raking leaves? Cycling? Maybe fixing a broken shower door, which June found exciting. A platinum ring, third finger, left hand.

"This is a nice little office, June. I could see this as a set. Is this typical for a poetry teacher?"

"More or less. All academic offices have books. Most are pretty messy, some insanely messy." June joined him at the window. "I'm lucky to have this view."

Rich looked at her, his face not more than six inches away. "I need a second lead. Who do you interact with here?"

"Well, let's see, there's the department head. That would work. If you're looking for verisimilitude points, you could have a rival poetry professor, or a slacker, who spends her entire sabbatical sailing instead of doing research on Seamus Heaney. And of course, lots of students."

"Why all these rivalries in academia?"

"Because there is so little at stake."

Rich laughed. Then he went on. "Every good show has a love interest. Who could her love interest be?"

June felt her breath get a little shorter. She inhaled through her mouth. "Oh, I don't know. Not a student. That's gross. Not a professor, that seems a cliché. Besides, academics are boring."

"You're not boring," Rich said.

"Um, I'm boring." June looked down at her sandaled feet, and was chagrined to notice that the polish on her pinky toe had already chipped. "What do you think my professor should look like?"

"Oh, I don't know," June answered. "Messy hair. No lipstick. Probably not the best shoes. You're going to have a tough time with that, because professors are not like television actresses. They're not beautiful."

Rich lifted June's chin up with his pointer finger and looked right into her eyes. "Well you're beautiful, June." He reached out and touched her hair with his other hand.

In that split second June saw before her a choice—one that she would make by either moving from the window and sipping her latte, or moving toward something that would never be easily undone or quickly finished, a choice to continue her life as is, or live in a way profoundly different from just a minute ago.

Here was Rich Friend, whose physical beauty was far beyond her husband's, himself a man she had lost long ago to auditions, trailers, bitterness, envy, and wooden swizzle sticks, and his own neurotic pursuit of security and reverence in a town short on both. He had convinced himself this pursuit was central to their marriage, when in fact it had eroded it.

She saw a man standing there now who had taken an interest in her work, who intuited that Auden was among her favorite poets, who brought her a latte without bringing one for himself, who understood the lunacy of free-range snails and excused the stupidity of giving away a car to a thief. She wanted to pretend the choice was a hard one, but in fact, she had made it days ago. She learned toward Rich and kissed him carefully on the mouth.

His cell rang. She laughed nervously. Rich pulled his phone out of his pocket and glanced at the caller ID, and June allowed herself a peek too: G. Clooney. Rich tossed it on her desk.

"Is that George Clooney on the phone?" June asked

"Yep."

June was astonished. "You're not going to take that?"

"He can wait."

June leaped onto Rich, toppling him onto her undersized chaise.

"Whoa!" He laughed, struggling to fit them both on the tiny couch.

Rich unbuttoned June's shirt quickly, and she buried her face in his neck, sighing. After nearly a dozen years of being only with Mitch, June took in the taste and smell of a new man, running her hands up his back, which was tighter than Mitch's, and smoother. Her breath became shorter as she felt him press against her and deftly reach for the zipper on her skirt. She placed her hand carefully, almost afraid, on the front of his jeans. Different that, too. Rich's kisses were at once urgent and soft, like berry cobbler in the middle of July, unexpectedly, deeply delicious. He carefully moved his weight on top of her, and she melted into the chaise beneath him.

BEEP BEEP BEEP! DEE DEE DEE DIT DEE DEE DIT!

"What the hell is that?" mumbled Rich, his face buried in June's neck.

June knew exactly what it was, and could not believe that Nora's electronic pet had woken from its electronic slumber in her purse at this particular moment, shitting electronic shit and demanding electronic food. June had confiscated the virtual pet on the way to school that morning, preventing another circle-time incident. June and Rich attempted to ignore it, but it continued bleeping as her blouse fell to the floor. Then her silk camisole, and his pants and boxer shorts, joined them. Minutes later, when they were totally naked, enveloped in each other's arms with Rich's fingers caressing June's breast, the electronic pet breathed its last with a descending final beep: BLEM BLEM BLEM-MMMMMMMM.

Rich moved to pull a pillow under June's head, kissing her and pulling gently on her earlobe with his teeth. His hand was making its way down from her breasts to her abdomen and then to the top of her thigh. Suddenly, there was a knock at her office door. June saw the handle began to turn, and realized it wasn't locked. She sat up abruptly and reached for her shirt.

"Housekeeping."

June suddenly pictured her department head's face as he learned about her being discovered by the cleaning staff having extramarital sex on her office chaise longue when she was supposedly working on her tenure package. "I'm fine! I'm busy! I am working with dangerous chemicals in here! PLEASE DON'T COME IN."

June covered Rich's mouth to stifle his laugh. They listened intently to the sound of a large garbage can being wheeled away. June looked at Rich, and they giggled together. June got up, locked the door, and dropped the shirt once again.

"You smell good, Rich. What kind of shaving cream is that?"

"Kiehl's. You smell great too, sort of like, I don't know, a sugar cookie?"

"Yeah, I must have splashed some vanilla extract on my shirt this morning." June tried to erase the image of her kitchen from her mind. As Rich began to run his fingers up the inside of her thigh, it was disturbingly easy.

Rich whispered in her ear. "Lay your sleeping head, my love, human, on my faithful arm."

June thought she heard him murmur Auden's line from "Lullaby" incorrectly, but it mattered not; he had clung to a poem that she loved.

* * *

June dialed Adrian from her car on her way home from the office. She could scarcely believe what she had just done. She was not the sort of person who cheated on her husband, and in fact, she was the sort of person who would sit next to other women over coffee listening to their tales of lusting for men other than their husbands, and find herself completely unable to identify with their longing. Her stomach twisted in a knot as she repeated in her head: *June Dietz had sex with a man who was not her husband. June Dietz is a cheater.*

She could not confide in even her best friend at that moment, but she longed to hear Adrian's voice.

"I didn't wake you, did I?" she asked him.

"Not at all. I just had a horrible meal at Casa Doña. I'm sitting here smoking my daily cigarette trying to forget about their Sysco-truck guacamole. Oh, sweetie, can you hold on just a sec, that's the buzzer."

"Are you expecting someone?"

"Just a messenger. Amanda is sending me some Ambien." June heard Adrian's muffled voice speaking into the intercom. "It's 4 D, just left of the elevator."

"A messenger at midnight?"

"It's New York, June. I can get my sleeping aids whenever I want. Too bad for you. Can you even get a taco there at this hour?"

"Yes, Adrian, I can get a taco. So, anything new?"

"Sort of. Remember the guy on eHarmony who was *supposedly* forty-one, who was *supposedly* a lawyer in private practice, who was *supposedly* living in Cobble Hill, who was *supposedly* a dead ringer for Jeff Goldblum?"

"I do."

"Okay. Try short, public defender, lives with mother in Hoboken because he lost his Cobble Hill apartment in a bad divorce, which he detailed for me ad nauseam over drinks, including the part where his ex called him from a tanning salon in Vegas to announce she was leaving him, and PS, a dead ringer for Wallace Shawn. Hey, thanks, keep the change."

"Boy, that's a fast messenger. You know, I never saw you as the Internet-dating type."

"Be glad you're married. What's with you, anyway? You sound weird."

"I'm fine. Tired."

Adrian yawned. "Me too, hon. It's late here. My Ambien has arrived, my lone cigarette of the day has been smoked, and now, so am I. So good night, friend."

"Good night Adrian. I miss you."

June pulled into the driveway, noting with relief that Mitch's car was not there. She went into the house, paid Olga, peeked in on Nora and kissed her sweaty little head. She then went into her own room and sat for a minute on the bed, taking in the memory of Rich Friend.

There was the newness of it all, the feel of a body she hadn't known, but had studied that night at Orso. She had felt desired, wildly so, and could not remember the last time Mitch expressed the same level of interest, unless she was holding a script in her hand. But, still, he was her husband, and had never had a moment of suspicion about her, because she had never given him the slightest reason. June's devotion to Mitch was sealed that night in New York after *Death of a Salesman*, and it had not occurred to her that there would ever be another.

How had Rich Friend so altered this landscape, in such a short time? There was his confidence, his utter conviction that whenever he shined his light on her, she would glow beneath it, and when he made love to her, it would be far more consuming than any sex she had had before. In both counts, as it turned out, his convictions were entirely warranted.

In a phrase, Rich Friend had lit a fire in her that she was not aware could be ignited, and was not extinguished here, three miles south of Wilshire, sitting in her bed. June peeled her clothes off slowly, burying her blouse and skirt in a pile of clothing awaiting the dry cleaner.

She rubbed her camisole against her cheek—Kiehl's. She tucked it hastily into her purse as she heard Mitch's key in the door, and ran for the bathroom.

June stepped into the shower, letting the water run down her back as she closed her eyes. She heard Mitch walk into the bedroom, and began to scrub herself vigorously with a loofah. She then washed her hair three times.

"Hey there!"

"Hi!" June called over the running water.

Mitch walked into the bathroom and began brushing his teeth. "Why are you taking a shower?" he asked.

"I felt gross after a long day. How was your screening?"

"Pissed me off, actually. I could easily have played the killer. Why doesn't Martin ever think of me for a human role? It's always monsters, zombies, or the undead. He says I'm a great actor to my face and then never hires me for a decent part."

"Uh-huh," June said. "Well, didn't he have you play a detective in that Bigfoot murder thing he did in Vancouver?"

"That was five years ago."

"Well, anyway, what happened with your nimrod?"

"Oh that." Mitch spat his toothpaste in the sink. "Yeah, Martin and I filed a police report against the guy for assault, since he pushed Martin and all. Hate crime. Give me a break. So how was your night?"

"Boring."

It was the first of what June knew would be a host of lies.

CHAPTER 11

Mitch was sitting in the Starbucks on Pico, ensconced in "his" chair, a brown fake-velvet oversized number, where he was holding court with the other morning regulars. He scratched vaguely in his ear with a coffee stirrer.

Kendall, one of the baristas whom Mitch saw most often, was arriving for her shift, tying on her apron.

"Hey, Mitch, I just got my acceptance letter from Georgetown!"

"That's great, Kendall. Someday you'll own this place."

"I'll certainly change the color." She walked behind the bar and began tidying stacks of paper cups, and picked up a DVD from behind the cash register.

"Oh, Mitch, some girl left this here for you. She says it's her reel. She wanted to make *totally* sure you got it, so I'm *totally* giving it to you."

"*Totally* fine. I'll look at it." Mitch got reels, scripts, voice-over tapes, and video shorts from young customers, baristas, and anyone else who recognized him in Starbucks, all with the misguided notion that he could help with agents or producers. Mindful of his early days, Mitch tried to be generous, but in truth, nine out of ten of the reels were met with derision—if he could even get his agents to watch them.

Mitch sat drinking his coffee, decaf this time, because today was his *My Dad Is Totally Weird* audition at the studio and he was already on edge. In an hour, he planned to take a dose of Ativan, snitched from June's supply, prescribed by her doctor for her horrible fear of flying. Mitch hoped the antianxiety drug would start kicking in as he got ready to go to the studio.

His phone rang. He didn't recognize the number.

"Hi, I have Joy Wainscott for Mitch Gold."

"Oh, sure," Mitch said, sitting up slightly.

"Hey, Mitch, Joy Wainscott." Strange that she used her full name.

"Joy, great to hear from you."

"Just wanted to let you know that I sent your manager *Dyspeptic* to pass on to you. He should have it this afternoon."

"Fantastic. I look forward to it."

"Oh, one other thing. I bought a table at a benefit honoring Dawn Greenstein in two weeks. Someone canceled and I need to fill the seat. It's next week at the Beverly Hilton. Can you make it?"

Dawn Greenstein was the head of development at HBO. There would definitely be some seriously important ass-kissing opportunities there. Done. It was mildly insulting that she had asked him only after someone canceled, but still it was good that she considered him a big-enough name to fill out the table.

"Sure, I can do that."

"Thanks. I'll have Tawny e-mail you the particulars."

She hung up. Again, without even saying good-bye.

Next, Mitch tried to flip through the *Los Angeles Times*, but soon chucked it onto the table in front of him. All he could think of were the blank faces of executives, studying him, judging him, and likely rejecting him. He tapped his fingers on the table, glanced around, took a sip of his decaf, tapped some more.

Mitch looked up as two writers from Fox who came in every morning about this time on their way to the studio ordered their coffees. One nodded at him.

"Hey, Mitch."

"Hi, Mike, how's it going?"

"Just fine. I have a part for you in the next episode of *House*. You do episodic, right?"

"If it's a good show."

"Well I do a good show."

"Oh, no question. Thanks for that," Mitch said.

Standing, pouring packet after packet of Splenda into her cup, was the woman who sold real estate and who had spent last month telling Mitch about her troubled teenager. He also saw the nurse who often came in after her shift at Century City Hospital, and a few wactors from around the way.

Mitch stared at them all impassively and made a little small talk. He picked up the *Times* again and scanned the car ads. Through the door walked a disheveled, bony man, pale of face but with arms leathery and tan. He wore a smudged white wide-brimmed hat, dirty jeans sliding half off his ass, and a white shirt spotted with grease. He carried an empty travel cup and, walking with a cane, limped toward Mitch.

"Hey, Cash, you need some coffee?" Mitch asked the man.

"Yeah, Mitch, that would great."

Mitch called out to Kendall, "Can you fill up Cash's cup? I'll pay for it."

"Will do."

Cash had been homeless for years, living on the streets of West Los Angeles, owning nothing but a pager, which was connected to a casting director who provided extras to movie and television sets. Cash was a frequent client because he needed no makeup, wardrobe, or coaching to play a street person. He just showed up, collected his forty-five dollars, and devoured what food there was available to the background.

He knew—as most extras did—to stay in his holding pen, keep away from the stars, and show up when called. Mitch had befriended Cash in the Starbucks, where they would compare notes about films they had both worked on, because they would never be near one another on the set. Mitch assumed there had been drugs or alcohol involved in Cash's downfall at some point, but he never saw any obvious signs of either.

"Mitch, thanks for the bucks. I went to Men's Wearhouse, like you said. You can't believe how far five hundred dollars went! I got three nice suits thanks to you. Now I can audition for some corporate extras."

"Good deal, Cash. Listen, I'll catch up with you tomorrow, but I need to get to an audition myself."

"Good luck, Mitch."

"Thanks, I really need it."

Mitch watched Cash, who was thirty-five but looked fifty-five, and felt a sensation he often did, that for all the ups and downs of his career, he had to admit that he had been lucky. He sometimes felt he had been two breaks away from being Cash in his early days, and it was just a matter of having been in the right place at the right time, and perhaps June, that had pushed him over.

Mitch lifted himself slowly from his chair, as if his name had just been called at the gastroenterologist, dumped his empty decaf cup into the trash. He walked home slowly, peering in the windows of Nordstrom and the Apple Pan and lamenting the fact that there were four mattress stores within two blocks. They depressed him.

He cut over to a residential street, and took in the scent of orange blossoms. He stopped to watch a hummingbird pick at its nest, gather some nectar, and pick again. He trudged on, slowly, dreading the return to his empty house, and knowing what awaited him.

Twenty minutes later, after downing an Ativan with a glass of orange juice, Mitch was standing on the lawn, swinging his club and muttering his lines. *"What is with this cell phone bill?"* He couldn't relax. He shot a few baskets in the backyard, but his mind would not stop racing. He would fail at this audition. Willie Dermot would get the job. Mitch would get dumped by CAA. This day, this moment, was all the beginning of the end. When would the freaking Ativan kick in?

He went into his office and rummaged around on his desk for the stress ball Nora had given him for Father's Day. He squeezed it several times, then noticed the stitching was unraveling. No good. Maybe toxic? He walked into the bathroom and dotted some makeup under his eyes. TV-friendly people did not have dark circles, especially in the HDTV era.

Mitch was actually feeling worse. Was this possible? Maybe one Ativan for a man his size was somehow counterproductive, teasing his system into believing it was working. Maybe what he needed was to take two more. He did so, with another large glass of orange juice.

Half an hour passed. Mitch was getting dressed and feeling no calmer. He would have to leave for Studio City soon. Traffic at this time was unpredictable, and he wanted to leave enough time.

He pulled on his friendly shirt—the one he wore to audition for roles as dads, camp counselors, and everyone's favorite teacher—a light blue short-sleeved polo.

He started to worry about sweating. Why didn't he feel better? He heard his heart pounding in his chest. His hands were shaking holding his empty glass of orange juice, and he could feel the beads of perspiration forming on his forehead. He felt angry at himself, and the world, and resisted the urge to simply start screaming. Then, he screamed a little.

If he went like this, he was going to blow it. He couldn't do it. This was the end. He was sick of this feeling, sick of this whole fucking business. He dialed Tad.

"Tad Meier's office."

"Hi, it's Mitch Gold, I really need to talk to Tad. It's an emergency!"

"Mitch who?"

"It's Mitch. Fucking. Gold. PLEASE CAN I TALK TO TAD?"

"Mitch, what seems to be the emergency?"

"Tad, I'm not going to the studio."

"What are you talking about? You have to go. This is it."

"I'm too nervous," Mitch yelled, nearly hysterical. "I'm starting to sweat! I'm gonna pass out! I'm gonna totally blow it! And then goddamn Willie fucking Dermot is going to get the job! I QUIT this business, okay, Tad? I QUIT! THAT'S IT!"

"Mitch, you say that every pilot season."

"I fucking mean it this time!"

"Mitch, calm down."

"Tad, I took three Ativans! So clearly this is as calm as I get!"

"Okay, Mitch, where are you."

"Home!"

"Do you have any alcohol in the house?"

"Yeah, I think there's some scotch somewhere here."

"Well, chug a huge shot."

"Are you serious?"

"Chug some."

"No way, Tad."

"Just do it!"

"Tad, man, that is the totally wrong thing to do!"

"You know what the wrong thing to do is, Mitch? Quit your profession at forty years old and start selling yuppies from Indiana crappy condos on Beverly Glen and stare at your hot wife who thinks you're a failure all because you got the heebie-jeebies about going to, what, your three hundred and twenty-fourth audition? So put the bottle to your lips, Mitch!"

Mitch cradled the phone on his shoulder and reached up to the cabinet above the sink to grab the bottle of Glenlivet that had been there since last pilot season. He took a deep swig right from the bottle. He stood in silence as the clock ticked, first one minute, then another. He could hear Tad clicking softly on his keyboard and a minor dogfight in the background.

"Still alive, Mitch?"

"I think so."

"How do you feel?"

Mitch assessed himself. He walked from the kitchen to the living room, and did a few head rolls. He *was* feeling a little looser. His stomach had almost instantly stopped flopping, and he no longer felt sweaty.

"You know, Tad, oddly, a little better."

"Really?"

"Really! You know, I think I can go."

"Okay. Excellent," Tad said. "But listen carefully. Do NOT tell anyone I told you to drink. I'm serious, Mitch. First, I'll deny it. Second, you'd look like shit. Third, I'll never speak to you again."

"Yeah, I hear ya. I'm good to go, Tad! I'm ready for this. Thanks, man, you're the best."

Mitch walked happily to his car, feeling normal for the first time all day. He popped a Listerine strip in his mouth and drove with confidence toward Beverly Glen, taking a left and speeding all the way up to Sunset. His arm was hanging out the window, taking in the balmy day.

Twice he was honked at for swerving into the right lane, but he scarcely noticed. Indeed, Mitch felt he had never driven better! He bopped his head and sang along to his Randy Travis CD: "*But on the other hand, there's a golden band, to remind me of someone who would not understand. . . .*"

At the end of the canyon, he took a left instead of a right, and ended up in a Ralph's parking lot and had to turn around. Heading down Ventura Boulevard, the temperature ten degrees warmer than in Rancho Park, Mitch was feeling great.

He pulled into the lot and handed the attendant his ID.

"Hey, Mitch, good to see you again."

"You are such a nice person! Wish me luck."

Mitch drove to the parking structure and turned his car all the way down, beyond the three levels of reserved spaces for studio executives and B-list series regulars who had not managed to negotiate a spot next to the sound stage. As he descended several levels belowground, the air got thicker and darker. A few fluorescent lights flicked on and off from above, humming.

Mitch pulled into a spot with a screech of his tires. He was muttering his lines, trying to connect with his character as he stepped out of the car. He noticed that his head felt strange, as if attached to the person down the street. All good!

He took one step and immediately tripped over a block of errant concrete and fell forward. The gray speckles from the concrete came toward him—or was he going toward them?—and fumes of the underground enveloped him. He braced the fall with his left arm, which instantly began to throb from his elbow to his wrist, and struggled to regain the wind that had been knocked from him. He noticed that his arm was now bleeding. Huh. That was probably not good. Well, no worries.

The lights were now flickering all around him, and the lines of parked cars appeared tilted, as if they were all parked on LEGOS. Wow. He felt something warm and weird. Was that oil? Water from a car wash? Oh yeah, there was no car wash here! Hmm. Nope, just a bit more blood. Well, he'd better get moving!

Mitch stumbled up three flights of stairs leading to the lot, and blinked in the harsh midday light. As he walked toward the building where the studio executives waited, people stared at him; sweat was now pouring off of his face, his pants had a small hole in the left knee, and he was dabbing blood off his arm with the bottom of his polo shirt.

He began to worry, just a little. But he remembered that there was a bathroom on the second floor of this building—he had used it a hundred times before. He would just go in there, wash himself, and he would be golden. He walked toward the front door to see two middle-aged casting directors in charge of My Dad Is Totally Weird. One, with shoulder-length gray curls and oval wire-framed glasses, was lighting her cigarette off that of the other casting director, who was so thin he could see her spine through her cotton cardigan.

"Mitch, what happened to you?" exclaimed Frizzy Hair, whose name Mitch could not conjure at that moment.

"Nothing. A little trip. Never better!"

Too Thin, her face twisted in horror, stared at his arm.

"That looks like more than a little trip. Yuck!"

Mitch felt his head spin, and suddenly his feet felt loose beneath him. "Actually, I think I need to lie down for a minute. That'll help."

A giant cast-iron sculpture of a lion sat right outside the building, staring menacingly at all who entered. Mitch draped himself over it, his bloody arm dragging a bit on the ground.

Frizzy Hair started tapping madly on her cell phone. "I'm calling the gate."

Mitch began to protest: "No, no stop! I'm FINE!" Sliding off the lion, then trying to steady himself, Mitch felt his head go light.

He woke up shortly after—maybe thirty seconds?—to the sound of an ambulance screaming down the lot. Three paramedics came rushing toward him, wheeling a gurney and all sorts of black medical equipment. Someone strapped an oxygen mask to his face, and the other two moved to lift him onto the gurney. Mitch looked woozily to his right, and saw seven men and one woman, all in thousand-dollar suits, walking slowly toward the building. His audition.

As the paramedics peered into his eyes and took his blood pressure, Mitch was beginning to feel slightly more stable. One paramedic, a young black guy with inhuman biceps, tapped his knee to check for reflexes.

"So, have you had any alcohol today?"

"Maybe a little."

"How much is a little?"

"A shot or two. That's all."

"Any prescription medicines?"

"No."

"No?" The paramedic flicked the light into Mitch's eyes again.

"Well, it wasn't my prescription, if that's what you mean. But I did take an Ativan. Or maybe like three Ativans."

"Well, you should not be mixing Ativan and booze, my man. Lucky for you, you're looking okay now, Mitch Gold." The paramedic began to bandage his arm. "You got any movies coming out this summer?"

"One. It's with Vince Vaughn. August release."

"That's cool, man. I'll make sure to catch that. Listen, my man, I think you need to go to the hospital. Just as a precaution."

Mitch bolted upright, as if on fire. "I WANT TO GO IN. I CAN GET THIS ROLE. I'M FINE!"

Too Thin, who had just sauntered back into earshot, protested. "It's just an audition, Mitch. Come on. You need to go to the hospital."

"No way! Absolutely not! I feel great!"

The paramedics silently continued to bandage him while Mitch looked impatiently at his watch.

"I still think this is a bad idea," said the one with the biceps. "But it's your call, man."

"I'm fine!" Mitch smiled and stood up, and tried to steady himself unnoticeably.

As the paramedics packed up the ambulance, Willie Dermot walked up.

"Hey, Mitch, what's the problem?"

"No problem. Nothing to look at here!" Mitch was wobbling a bit.

"Okay. Just checking. Did you catch the Lakers last night? Man, what a blowout." Willie was no longer even looking at Mitch, but staring toward the building, hoping to catch an executive.

Mitch walked gingerly toward the building, and then up the stairs, and tried to pretend he could not see the small drops of blood seeping through the gauze on his arm. His friendly shirt was now grimy and wrinkled. He took a deep breath, and sat down in the waiting room outside the casting session. Suddenly, daylight began to shine through the screen of Ativan. He assessed his situation: normal people do not fall down in the subbasement of parking structures, bleed, pass out, refuse medical treatment, rest in their own filth, and then go into a room and try and get a job as a television star. While he sat staring at the wall, rubbing his shoulder from time to time where it now ached, Mitch suddenly felt an illuminating sense of calm. Because, really, it could not get worse.

"Mitch!"

Mitch got up slowly, and Frizzy Hair walked over to carefully place her hand on his arm. "Will you be okay?" she whispered.

Mitch did not even answer her. He marched confidently—even though his arm and foot were throbbing, his head remained floating somewhere beyond him, and his entire being felt slightly pliable—and walked to the front of the room. He braced himself for the question, yet no one said a word about his tattered condition.

As if on cue, he decided to pretend it didn't exist.

"Whenever you're ready, Mitch," said Too Thin, now smiling brightly, as if she and Mitch had just been sharing some lemonade.

He took a breath. *"Chelsea, come down here!"*

The studio executives, the very same ones who had strolled past his ambulance only a half hour ago, laughed heartily. *"What about this cell phone bill?"*

"I told you I needed to call Kevin in Denver," Too Thin exclaimed.

"For three hundred and six minutes!?"

Mitch was oddly relaxed, and he said his lines with gusto. At the end of his audition, everyone in the room applauded.

He was elated, but as he made his way back to his car, he became aware of myriad pains, twinges, and burning sensations all over his body. His arm was nearly soaked in blood. He head was pounding, and he was inexplicably walking with a limp. It took all of his inner strength to simply push the button on his key to unlock the door.

An hour and a half later, Mitch limped in the door of his home, and found June standing at the kitchen sink, slicing garlic. She saw Mitch's reflection in the window, but did not bother to turn toward him. "Hey, how did it go."

"I would say it was an unusual day."

June turned, saw the bandage on his arm and his ruined shirt, and dropped her knife in the sink. "Good God, what happened to you? Were you in a wreck? I have told you to drive more carefully when you're stressed out!"

"No, it's not that. Let me tell you the weirdest thing you've heard today."

June raced to grab Mitch another shirt, and rebandaged his arm as he spun his tale for her from a slumped spot on the kitchen floor. Brushing the hair off of his face, she touched him slightly on the cheek. What had he done now?

He continued his story as June returned to the sink, and cutting her garlic, she listened with shock, her eyes widening at the fainting story. She did not ask how he had performed. Mitch felt some irritation about this, but said nothing.

Nora came into the kitchen and crawled into Mitch's lap.

"What's that, Daddy?"

Mitch grinned at her. "Battle wounds from Hollywood, honey."

"Neat. Can I have the Band-Aid when you're done?"

Mitch looked at June to see if she had caught this funny Noraism, but she was staring out the window at the darkness.

The phone rang, and Mitch grabbed it. Tad.

"Hey, buddy! Good news! They said it was one of the best pilot auditions they had ever seen."

"Really?"

"See, don't I know what I'm doing? You didn't mention the whole scotch thing, right?"

"Umm. . . ."

"Great. One last hurdle tomorrow, CBS."

"Les Moonves?"

"Who else, Mitch? Oh, Willie and Hasselhoff made it through too."

"Okay. So listen, did they have any notes for me for tomorrow?"

"Actually, just one. Wear a long-sleeved shirt."

CHAPTER 12

"Can you talk?"

Rich Friend's voice was in June's ear. It had been exactly one week since she had tasted him.

"Yeah, for a minute," June said into her cell phone as she raced across the expansive campus on her way to teach her afternoon Harlem Renaissance class. She dodged a group of fencers in full gear, walking en masse with iPods in their ears, who nearly clocked her with their foils.

"Did you know I have a kitchen island?" Rich asked.

"No, I don't believe you've ever shared that with me," June said, smiling slyly and guessing that her conversation with Rich Friend would not be concerned with how to properly chop tomatoes.

June sat herself into a bench next to the UCLA playing field, even though she had only four minutes to make it to class. She listened intently as Rich described the many things he had in mind for her in his kitchen, half embarrassed, half turned on.

"I am enjoying this tremendously," June said, "but I have a lecture."

"Okay. I'll let you go. But every time you say 'Langston Hughes' remember what I said about your panties."

"Like our own private drinking game?"

"Something like that."

June got up from the bench and began cantering across campus. She was laughing, and her breath was a little short.

"When can I see you again?" Rich asked.

"I don't know. I want to."

June arrived at her class several minutes late, and found a classroom of students on the brink of leaving. Somewhat disappointed, they began pulling their laptops back out of backpacks and putting their phones away. June rushed to the front of the class.

"So sorry, everyone. My computer had a virus and I needed to print some things out for you. So, who's read 'I Wonder As I Wander?'"

Larissa sat at the edge of her sparkling saline pool, in which she had not dipped so much as a toe for a year, and looked out into her yard. The gardeners had finally gotten it right. Lush green grass surrounded rows of rosebushes and cattleya orchids, which required frequent watering and fertilizing. She needed to remind her gardener to play classical music near the flowers once a week, to help them flourish. At three hundred dollars a month was this so much to ask? After all, she paid a good fifty dollars more than every one of her neighbors.

In her front lawn, her small desert garden was on full display with all of its environmentally friendly cacti. It reminded her of her mother's sad little garden, with its cactus surrounded by two ceramic Santa Claus elves—one with an ear blown off by her uncle's shotgun. Everyone in Surprise had desert gardens. Blech. She had hoped never to see another, wanted to be surrounded only by luscious flowering plants. This environmental thing was always getting in the way. And she found it exhausting to have to be thinking constantly about her car and her plastic bags. Why did Cass Martin have to humiliate her in her own house? Had she not been gracious, letting people walk around her house without taking their shoes off? Hadn't she donated Chloe's old toys and dresses to those poor people as Cass had told her to? She told people to donate presents to homeless kids instead of her child at her birthday. The last straw was when she offered to donate the dress she wore to the Emmys to Clothes Off Our Back. They told her it wasn't worth auctioning off her clothing for charity. She wasn't a star, they said.

Larissa was unnerved. She had already placed three calls this morning: one to Willie's manager, Karin Levine, and two to Willie's agent, Tim Zelnick, at CAA. The agent never returned her calls, the arrogant prick. But she usually had better luck with Karin. She dialed again.

"Hi, Larissa, what can I do for you?" Karin said, her voice a bit too starchy for Larissa's ear.

"I'll tell you what you can do for me, Karin sweetheart," Larissa oozed into her Bluetooth. "You can call me back within a reasonable time frame."

"Sorry, Larissa," Karin said evenly. "It's pilot season, it's busy. I try to be accommodating to all of my clients at this time."

"I know what season it is, Karin. That's the reason for my call, and I just need you to be receptive to my reality, to hear my message. What I need to know is, who exactly is Willie up against for *My Dad Is Totally Weird*? He claims he can't remember."

Karin put on her best nursery-school-teacher voice. "Larissa, there are three actors auditioning today for the network executives. Willie, Mitch Gold, and David Hasselhoff."

"They all made it through the studio? That's freaky, Karin. David is as fat as Jennifer Hudson. And everyone knows Mitch chokes at the studio!"

"Larissa, David has been on Trim Spa. So let's not be unkind. And Mitch Gold's a very talented actor."

"Is that what we pay you for, Karin? To tell me about the fine qualities of the two fat fuckers who are competing with my husband for a role? All I want to know is who is first choice?"

"Larissa, I don't have that information and it won't make any difference anyway. You know Les makes his own decisions. Listen, I've got another call. Take care, Larissa."

Larissa, enraged, began to pace. She kicked at the bright orange floatie sitting by the end of the pool. Who did this bitch think paid her salary anyway? Karin pocketed 10 percent of every penny of Willie's gross earnings, and couldn't even return a call. Larissa could do better herself. That much she knew, and she would start right now.

Larissa had been working hard over the last six months to befriend Ally, the ratty little gal who worked as the assistant to her husband's agent, Tim. Her efforts had recently yielded the result she had sought—an informant at CAA. Two Kate Spade bags, a reservation at Spago, and a Bliss massage had been bartered for trivia about the agency doings. After suffering through months of drivel about Ally's aborted love affair with a guy who ran the mailroom and the indignity she felt she suffered by receiving, in lieu of a Christmas bonus, a donation in her name to the Natural Resources Defense Council, Larissa finally got the big hit.

Ally revealed that Mitch Gold, if he did not get on a go series this year, would be dropped from the agency. Without CAA, Mitch was nothing but a farmers' market carrot in Larissa's new thousand-dollar InSinkErator disposal.

If she could screw Mitch, it would be a double win for Larissa. Willie would no longer have to compete with Mitch for work, and she would be rid of that blah, blah wife of his with all that hair, who was always making weird remarks about foreign countries and writers Larissa had never heard of.

Hate, hate, hate!

David Hasselhoff she wasn't worried about. He just wasn't as good as Willie, and what were his recent credits anyway—a lot of bad press and some crappy plays in Vegas. But Mitch was a threat. He had beaten Willie out for *Molar Opposites*, and even though he made far less money, critics always preferred him, morons though they were. (She once sent a large Tiffany box full of used cat litter to A. O. Scott, the *New York Times* film critic, for writing that Willie "chewed the scenery" in a movie about a single dad. The same review praised Mitch Gold as "both funny and deeply moving" as the single dad's henpecked best friend.)

She began to consider how she could orchestrate Mitch's downfall, at least for today. She could pretend to be Mitch's manager's assistant and call the casting agent to say he had to go to rehab. Problem: she heard that guy was always changing assistants. Mental note: update iPhone with all of Mitch's agent's and manager's staff numbers, and shoe sizes.

Plan A: the old nail in the tire bit. She did that at Arizona State once to a girl she was competing with for a job at Linda Lew's Dip 'N' Dunk. She had needed that job, and she had gotten it. A flat might prevent Mitch from getting to the audition at all. AAA saves no man in LA. That was the plan. From Larissa's point of view, all tactics were fair during pilot season. Deals were made behind people's backs, networks lied, friends replaced each other on shows, and in her mind, wives who were doing their part tied up the loose ends that managers and agents forgot. Willie still had to do his part—he had to be best. But she would adjust the odds a bit when possible.

It was Hollywood diplomacy, really, not so unlike what Condi Rice, one of her role models, would do. Cultivate relationships, even ones that would pay off only years later. Use a strong arm when necessary. Speak softly and carry a fat stick. Or whatever that expression was that Condi had invented.

Larissa went inside the house, flipped through the temple directory, and found Mitch and June's address. Rancho Park. Where the hell was that? She opened her laptop and launched Google maps. Oh, that place, near Fox and Century City. Spanish-style houses, small lots. Larissa marched into her house, slamming the sliding doors behind her. She pulled on a pair of bright purple mules, which showed off her tan ankles beneath her Chip and Pepper jeans, the ones with the long pockets reaching halfway down her thighs. Her emerald-colored Empire-waist shirt was pulled tightly over her breasts; her sharp clavicles glistened. She pulled on her silver bottle of Rescue Remedy, fingering the etched monogram, which she found comforting. She pulled the tiny glass stopper and dabbed four droplets on her tongue.

"Conchita, yo need usted to pick up Chloe from school," Larissa yelled up the stairs, grabbing her purse off the edge of her still-unfinished kitchen counter. "And por favor, no mas doughnuts!"

She looked in the mirror. Lipstick. She needed her La Prairie lipstick. She smeared some on. She went to the garage and rifled through her handyman's toolbox for a large nail and a hammer. Got it! She grabbed a few more, just for safety.

Peeling out of the driveway in her Escalade, Larissa was soon a few blocks from June and Mitch's house in Rancho Park. Huh. Nicer than she expected. Good yard. Tile would have looked a hell of a lot better than the concrete they had, and the backyard furniture, slightly visible from the street, looked distinctly Home Depot. Not a bad-sized house, though. Mitch was doing better than she thought. All the more reason to make sure CAA gave him the dump. Larissa turned the car into a church parking lot a block away from the house. Clutching her hammer and nails, she got out and headed down the block, only to see that Mitch was now out in front of his house swinging a golf club and talking to himself. She turned around quickly before he caught sight of her. FREAKING PLAN B!

Larissa plotted. First stop, the Pinkberry on Olympic. Larissa got almost a daily dose of plain frozen yogurt, sprinkled with cereal and bananas, usually in lieu of breakfast and lunch. Matched with her Rescue Remedy, she found it an amazing elixir, one that helped her stay thin and think clearly. Zipping down Pico, Larissa wove between cars, honking at nearly every intersection. When one car did not move quickly enough into the left turn lane, she flipped off its driver. She cranked her music—the Black Eyed Peas—and glanced in her visor mirror frequently to check between her eyebrows for wrinkles.

"Move it!" she growled to herself over her blasting music as she watched an old woman, leaning on a walker, who was trying in vain to get across Sawtelle in the nineteen seconds allotted to pedestrians.

Once at Pinkberry, Larissa parked in the fifteen-minute-only parking space. There had better not be a line, with all those idiots trying to decide between coconut toppings and raspberries. Inside the store, which looked very much like Chloe's Hello Kitty playhouse—all tiny pink plastic chairs and futuristic light fixtures—Larissa quickly edged her way to the counter, walking past a group of three Japanese girls who were mulling over their order, ignoring their muted protests.

"Nice to see you again, Miss Larissa," said the clerk in her little green apron.

What was her name again? Who remembered?

"Hi, umm. Yeah, hi. Small plain with Cap 'n Crunch and bananas, please."

A few minutes later, Larissa scraped the bottom of her cup angrily, then peeked at her watch. It was nearly 1 p.m. She hoped Willie would remember to leave enough time to get from the gym to the network audition in Burbank at three o'clock. She reached for her cell phone to call him, then suddenly stopped. Late. That was the kiss of death at a network audition. She might not be able to stop Mitch from getting there, but she could make sure he didn't get past the gate on time.

Seized with a brilliant plan, Larissa hopped up from the table, leaving her dirty cup and spoon and a few drips of yogurt behind, and raced back out to her car. She pulled out onto Olympic and drove toward the 405, stopping quickly at a cash machine for five hundred dollars.

Sitting in the traffic on the freeway, Larissa scowled. Her phone was ringing. demi. What did she want? She pressed the button on the steering wheel of her car that connected to her Bluetooth earpiece for her cell phone.

"Hi, hon!" demi said.

"Hey, what's up?"

"Listen, I heard they're starting to do classroom placements for next year at Crossroads. We've GOT to get Mrs. Branson at all cost. She is the *only* kindergarten teacher to get. It is TOTALLY important that we get our dibs in before the angry working moms. If any of them are like the preschool ones who tell me it doesn't matter what color the napkins are at the auction, I swear I'm gonna have to kick some ass."

"Can you plant the seeds and I'll help you later?"

"Okay, but don't forget. I'll see you at Krav Maga?"

"I'll be there."

"Great. Bruno is teaching tonight, and you know how I love—"

"demi, I'll let you go," Larissa said, already hanging up. She focused on the traffic with increasing rage.

A mile later, the phone rang again.

"Hi dear, it's Marvin. I've picked up some wheat linens for you to look at, and I want to get you thinking about paint for that sitting room. I think it could really be opened up with some fresh color."

"Okay, okay, Marvin, can you meet me at the house tomorrow at ten?"

"Perfecto, dear, ten it is. I'll bring that rooster I told you about from the flea market, too."

Traffic was at a standstill. Larissa stared at the clock on her dashboard. She had forty-five minutes to get to Burbank before the network audition would start. The carpool lane was zipping along. Shit. Had she driven the Prius, she would have been entitled to drive in it, even with no passenger. But she hated that damn car; it had no pickup or legroom, left her feeling low to the ground, and was so quiet it was freaky.

She glanced to her right and was momentarily startled; Chloe had left her American Girl doll on the passenger seat, and it was so lifelike it made her jump. In an instant, her next brainstorm emerged. Reaching behind her, trying not to swerve, Larissa dropped Nikki into Chloe's car seat behind her and pulled Chloe's blanket up to Nikki's realistic little nose. With that, she moved quickly into the newly constructed HOV lane and floored it. The Getty Museum flew by on her left, and next the exit for the Skirball Center. She was momentarily slowed at the 101 interchange, but she tailgated and continually weaved in and out of lanes, nearly sideswiping people three times, and was soon past that as well, and onto the 134 toward Burbank. Just two miles until the exit.

Larissa pulled her Escalade into a parking spot along a side street a few blocks from the studio and stepped out into smoggy midday air. Her skin felt dry, and she licked her lips, tugged at her thong, and then smoothed the back of her jeans. She walked with purpose toward the studio gate and reached behind her back to tighten her shirt. She approached the guard stand at the studio entrance. The guard was sitting on a stool, looking bored. Larissa came closer to make out the name on his badge: Leo.

Larissa assessed the situation quickly. Leo was maybe thirty-five, but then again he could have been one of those guys who looked a bit older than they were due to a few too many pints of Guinness. He was most likely from Riverside, or Carson, and his hair was cut slightly unevenly. He had ruddy cheeks, pale blue eyes, and prominent cheekbones. She tried to picture picking him up in a bar in Hollywood ten years ago. It *could* have happened. If it had been dark.

"Can I help you, miss?"

"Hi," Larissa said, stepping toward Leo's booth, causing him to step back an inch. She leaned toward his window, pressing her arms together to make her cleavage a bit more ample. "I need to ask you a really huge favor. It would mean a real lot."

Leo raised his left eyebrow, which startled Larissa momentarily. How did he raise just one? She pressed on.

"I think you have a Mitch Gold coming in today? He is on the list for a drive-on to audition for *My Dad Is Totally Weird?*"

"Maybe."

Larissa leaned in closer now, and Leo was able to see a wad of bills peering out from the lace of her bra. He also saw a silver vial hanging between her ample breasts, and wondered what it was. He hoped it wasn't coke. He didn't need that problem. He looked up at her again, confused. She whispered to him.

"I need you to lose his name."

"What are you talking about, lady?"

"I need Mitch Gold to *not* get his drive-on, Leo."

"I can't do that," he said, eyeing the bills again. "I'd lose my job. Whatever you got in your bra isn't gonna make up for that."

"Leo, you can blame it on the casting assistant. Casey, right? She's an idiot, everybody on this lot knows that. She forgets to give you the name, you walk away a little richer."

Larissa looked around to see if there were any other cars headed her way, knowing that people would be arriving any minute for the network audition and for other shows as well. She would have to get this done fast. "I think you know how to pass the buck, Leo. How much do they pay you here anyway?"

"I do okay."

"Not as well as you should. Here you are, watching all these assholes come in and out all day long in their fancy cars, all because they are on some crappy television show that housewives with underarm hair watch every night, folding their laundry and dreaming of California. You're better than that. And when was the last time you made five hundred dollars for doing nothing?"

Leo looked around, then back at Larissa. She was older than his girlfriend, but certainly hotter. Thin waist, lovely breasts, an actress type herself, the kind that drove through here twenty times a day, never even looking up at him from the car. And there she was, negotiating a deal with him.

"Why is this so important to you?" he asked.

"It just is."

Leo looked around to see if anyone could see him. Larissa leaned forward a bit, and he quickly snapped up the bills from her bra. Larissa stared intently at Leo's computer.

"Get rid of him."

Click. Mitch Gold's name disappeared, and the hot lady darted off before he could say another word. Maybe Leo would take his lady friend to the Indian casino near Palm Springs this weekend, or at least the Olive Garden and the dog races. He was about to play a game of cell phone blackjack, but then he glanced up and saw the hot lady staring at him intently from behind a bush. Jesus! Leo looked at her and winked. She tossed him a smile. She *did* have a nice rack.

Hiding behind a boxwood hedge, Larissa tried to ignore the twigs pricking at her ankle. She soon saw her husband pull up in his Mercedes. He was singing along to Axel Rose, very loudly, and off key—how cute! She watched his car ease past the gate. Next came David Hasselhoff in the back of a town car. Several cars she did not recognize piled in too. It was getting late. Where was Mitch?

With just ten minutes to spare before his audition, Mitch came barreling toward the gate in his Saab. Larissa peeked carefully out from behind the hedge to get a better view. It wasn't long before Mitch was screaming at the top of his lungs.

"What the hell are you talking about, Leo!? I'm going to the network, for Christ's sake! Of course I have a drive-on! What am I, an extra? Call upstairs!"

Mitch was incensed. Leo and his rules and regulations were going way too far. There had been a wreck on the 134 and he was already late, and now because of this drive-on issue, he was going to be officially late. Late for the network, lose the job. That was how it went.

Leo dialed the phone. He felt slightly guilty.

"They're in the session, Mitch. Why don't you go and street-park?"

"I don't have time to drive around looking for a parking spot, Leo. Do you realize what you are doing? You are taking food from my child's mouth with your stupid security crap and freaking incompetence!"

Leo looked at the ground.

Exasperated, Mitch threw his car into reverse and drove up and down side streets, looking a spot, any spot. Permit parking only, street-sweeping violation, failed meter, he didn't care. But there was nothing.

He dialed Tad at a speed bump. He got the office voice mail. Shit. Next he dialed Tad's cell phone. No answer. Mitch finally pulled into a spot for a car somewhat smaller than his, and slightly nicked a Honda Civic. He reached into his pocket for quarters. He had one; he needed at least three. Fuck it.

Racing back to the booth, bathed in sweat, Mitch cursed Tad, Leo, CAA, the television industry, and the person on the 134 who may have been killed, just for good measure. He approached Leo again, heaving and slightly doubled over. He was now 10 minutes late.

"Hi again, Mitch. Got ID?"

Mitch felt in his pocket. Holy shit, he had left his wallet in the car. His cell phone too. No chance to call CAA to see if someone there could resolve this nightmare.

"Leo, I am BEGGING YOU. You know who I am. You see me nearly every week. My ID is in my wallet, my wallet is in my car, my car is parked six blocks from here because for some reason some stupid jackass didn't put my name on the drive-on list, and you chose to continue with the stupidity. I am fifteen minutes late, which is nearly as good as fired from this gig. Please, would you PLEASE let me walk on this lot?"

Leo looked at his supervisor, who had come down to the booth to reprimand Leo for taking a bathroom break at a nonappointed time.

"Would it be okay, Ernie?"

"Sorry, Homeland Security."

Mitch began screaming madly, pulling, inexplicably, on his ears. Behind him, a line of cars were honking.

"Hey, asshole, maybe you could move it this week?"

Mitch approached the gray BMW and was about to lunge at its owner.

"I'm calling security!" Leo threatened loudly.

"Leo, you ARE the security!" Mitch stomped off the lot in a huff, tears in his eyes as he raced back to his car.

Mitch pulled his wallet from his Saab, and his cell phone, too, which now had five voice mail messages, no doubt the casting directors trying to find him. He didn't take the time to listen; instead he jogged back to the lot and, at long last, made it past Leo, whose firstborn children he hoped to someday have the chance to eat.

He raced across the lot, past Clara Bow, to Pickford, where the network executives had gathered to watch the final three contenders. Before he could even make it up the stairs, he saw Frizzy Hair and Too Thin smoking their cigarettes outside.

"Mitch! Jesus, where have you been?" said Too Thin.

"You're not going to believe this, but the guard wouldn't let me in. I wasn't on the list. He said it was Casey's fault."

"Casey isn't even here today. What are you talking about? You are a walking freak show, my friend. You fall down at the studio audition, practically bleed all over those executives. Now you keep Les Moonves waiting. You know what Les did, Mitch? He told a page to go and get your reel, and when he got it, he flung it out the window. Flung it, Mitch. Look over there!"

Mitch turned his head, feeling as if he were moving in slow motion, and sure enough, a DVD case with the words *Mitch Gold* sat shattered under a jacaranda tree.

"I'm telling you, this wasn't my fault."

Frizzy Hair looked sad, the deep lines near her mouth caving in slightly. "Well, it's too late, Mitch. They already picked Willie. If you want to know the truth, you were first choice, but you blew it."

Mitch reached up, rubbed his face, and tried to keep from crying. Lost job. Soon, his agency would follow. This was it. He walked slowly back to his car.

Larissa was headed south on the 405, listening to Hole at full volume. It had been a good day really, lots accomplished. Her cell phone rang.

"Hey, baby."

"Hey, Mrs. Wonderful. Guess what? Your boy is totally weird, as in dad!"

"Awesome!" Larissa cheered. "That's my man!" Her face broke into a heartfelt smile. "Who were you up against anyway?"

Back in his car, Mitch turned on the country radio station and dialed Tad.

"Mitch, what the hell is with you? I got six calls from Denise and Trish saying you never showed." Oh, Too Thin's and Frizzy Hair's real names.

"Tad, you're not going to believe this. The fucking guard wouldn't let me in. It was a total nightmare, and I tried to call you but you never picked up!"

"Yeah, well, Zeus was bit by a rattlesnake in the garden and I had to call the vet in because he passed out and I couldn't lift him into the car. We set up a triage unit in the garage, he was on an IV and the whole bit. It was panic city, Mitch!"

Mitch tried to picture Tad in his garage, standing over his unconscious rottweiler attached to a large IV. He felt the urge to laugh hysterically.

"Sorry about that, Tad."

"Yeah, well, Mitch, I have to tell you that you're dead at CBS. You don't no-show Les Moonves. And Denise and Trish? You can forget about them calling you in again. And I bet CAA won't exactly be thrilled about this either, man."

"Should I just hang it up then?" Mitch's car was getting hot, but he didn't have the energy to press the window control. He began to stink.

"Nah," Tad said.

"What? I thought I was ruined."

"Why?" Suddenly Tad was back to his normal tone, as if they had been talking about the Dodgers' record. "You got a call for Rich and Justine Fein's show. They want you to come in for the newspaper editor. Good script. Perfect for you. *My Dad Is Totally Weird* will never see the light of day. Trust me. No one makes four-camera half-hours anymore. The title alone is totally eighties. I hear the network thinks it sucks."

"Well then why are they making it, Tad?"

"I dunno. Anyway, you also have a feature audition—you'd be a guy with a really foul mouth—and I got you in for a dark wizard in the final *Harry Potter.*" Small part but with travel days and residuals probably worth doing."

"They're seeing people here?" Mitch asked. "Have they finally emptied out the Royal Shakespeare Company?"

"It had to happen sometime."

Mitch heard Tad rustling through some papers, and imagined one of his dogs trotting by, and the cockatoo flying off the pile of breakdowns, plopping white shit on them.

"Oh yeah, and there's *Too Many Cooks*. That's still not cast."

"That was the Danny DeVito thing, right?"

"Oh, he passed. He's gonna be a rabbi on an FX drama about a Hasidic community in Brooklyn."

"Huh? I'm not seeing that."

"Don't worry about him. And also I got Joy's script, which screams Mitch Gold like, seriously, I have never seen. I'll e-mail you the sides for everything tomorrow." Tad hung up.

And there it was: horrible, gut-wrenching, humiliating misery at the hands of a network gate guard for a show that was probably never going to be on the air anyway. Five minutes later, back in the game.

Mitch told June the entire tale over Mexican food that night, his stomach barely able to hold his guacamole. He never wanted her to think he hadn't tried. He wanted to please her, to let her know he was ever mindful of getting that house finished, of staying ahead of the bills, of taking care of her and Nora. And June had always been interested in his Hollywood tales; he was sure she found them fascinating. He sipped on a shot of tequila, chased by Pepto-Bismol, which he drank directly from the bottle, giving the blow by blow.

June listened intently. In truth she had lost all interest in Mitch's pilot season woes and found Hollywood stories tedious after all these years, but she had to admit, this was one for the books.

"But I do have a *Harry Potter* audition, which could be fun, and some foulmouthed thing for a film."

"That's good I guess." June's mind began to wander, and she stared off at a bullfight drawing hanging crookedly on the wall behind Mitch.

"Yup. I also have an audition for Justine's new show," Mitch said. "That'll get on the air. There is no one hotter in television right now than Justine Fein."

June snapped back to attention. "You mean Justine and Rich, don't you?"

"Well, sort of. Justine is the power in that power couple. Rich is along for the ride, in my opinion, and I'm not alone in that. But anyway, I don't know why they thought of me all of a sudden. God knows I dropped enough hints with Rich that he never seemed to hear. But whatever, that show's my best shot."

Mitch swore he saw June frown.

CHAPTER 13

Mitch stood reading the giant placard outside the International Ballroom of the Beverly Hilton Hotel: "Irritable Bowel Syndrome Benefit Gala Honoring Dawn Greenstein—Woman of the Year in IBS Research Funding." He had missed most of the cocktail hour that had preceded the dinner, which was just about to start, because he had been at a voice-over audition for the new principal on *Jimmy Neutron*, where he once again faced off with Willie Dermot.

The audition had irritated Mitch to no end. Willie was, as usual, completely placid as he sat slumped in the waiting room, flipping through *Sports Illustrated*. Willie had spent half the audition talking about the New England Patriots and taking calls from his wife, whom he referred to as "Mrs. Wonderful." Clearly it had been a long time since Willie worried about a mortgage payment. Annoying.

The guests were slowly piling into the ballroom, clutching their slightly damp napkins and nearly empty glasses of chardonnay. Mitch walked over to a small pile of place cards marked with table assignments, grabbed the one with his name on it, and headed for table two. Wow. Right in the front. He had no idea Joy had that kind of relationship with studio executives like Dawn Greenstein.

Mitch ambled over to the table, passing Kelsey Grammer and Patricia Heaton. Next to Kelsey was a woman who looked like she had been created from start to finish in an operating theater. Even by Hollywood standards, her breasts defied conventional dimensions, appearing as flesh torpedoes shooting from her low-cut snakeskin gown. Her lips reminded Mitch of two giant slabs of cow tongue—the sort June had tried once to pass off as corned beef—and her forehead was that of a seventeen-year-old girl. Mitch instantly felt guilty about his internal assessment of Woman X when she smiled at him sweetly.

"Yo, Mitch!" came a greeting from behind him. Mitch turned around and saw Kiefer Sutherland sitting at a table in the middle of the room with several cast members of 24. Kiefer was set to star in an action movie, *Pacific Daylight*, which was going to shoot in Alberta in the spring. Mitch had gone in for the role of the secretary of defense.

"Hey, man, good to see you here," Mitch said. "I don't know about you, but I've always been moved by bowels." He instantly regretted the barb. Would Kiefer tell the casting directors on *Pacific Daylight* he was foul?

Luckily, Kiefer chuckled slightly. "Well, anything for the boss lady. Where's your table?"

Mitch looked in the direction of Joy, who had her face almost pressed against Natalie Portman's cheek, and the two of them were giggling. Joy was wearing a black sequined dress, with a soft blue wrap thrown carefully over her shoulders. In all their years in New York, Mitch had never seen Joy in anything but a peasant skirt. She was something less than pretty, but certainly polished in a way that was usually reserved for wives of executives, her edges soft, her lines filled, her hair subject to significant professional attention. "I'm sitting over at two, with Joy Wainscott."

Kiefer looked impressed. "Oh right, Ridley's directing her next project. I want to get in on that."

"Yeah, I am just digging into the script," said Mitch. "Hey, I went in on *Pacific Daylight*. Secretary of defense. Great part."

"Oh yeah, I hear you've got a pin in you."

Mitch pictured his headshot affixed to the casting office bulletin board with a big red stickpin through his forehead. No doubt Willie had a pin in him, too. "Good to know, Kiefer. Enjoy your evening."

Mitch walked toward Joy and leaned down to give her a peck on her cheek but, remembering their last meeting at the Roosevelt Hotel, thought better of it and awkwardly turned his head, knocking over a wineglass onto her bread plate. He quickly grabbed it before it made more than a small puddle, felt embarrassed, and began to fumble around with a nearby dinner napkin, watching the beads of red wine stick to it rather than be absorbed. "Don't worry about it, Mitch, they have people to do that," Joy said. "Thanks a lot for coming. Have, you met Natalie?"

"No, I don't think so. Nice to meet you."

"Mitch is coming in on *Dyspeptic*," Joy said to Natalie Portman, smiling.

"That's the name of your new movie?" asked Natalie, her eyes uncommonly wide.

"Yes," said Joy. "I'm letting Ridley direct this one."

Mitch sat down at the only remaining seat at the table, sandwiched between a woman he had never seen before and the sitcom star Jenna Mills. She was immediately friendly. "Hi, I'm Jenna," she said, smiling warmly. Her streaked blond hair framed her face, which was polecatlike, and tumbled down her bare shoulders, which were a bit too bony for Mitch's taste, but he conceded that she had a good look for the camera. "You look so familiar. were you ever on my show?"

"I don't think so," Mitch said, frantically trying to remember what her show was. Oh right, that weird thing with the waitress married to the lawyer. Her show? Wasn't there a co-star named Zev?

"It's just that you're so familiar to me. But you work a lot," she said, before taking a long slug of water.

"I read in *Variety* you're doing a movie," Mitch said. "It's a romantic comedy, right?"

"I am. I'm really excited about it because I took myself out of the game there for a while."

"Huh. So are you friendly with Dawn? Or is IBS a cause you're interested in?"

"I've known Dawn a long time," said Jenna, and Mitch thought he saw tears forming in her deeply lined eyes. "I've seen her suffering, and I've tried to share with her a different way, a sort of, you know, processing that could cure her."

"Do you mean like food processing?" Mitch asked as a waiter in a black vest placed their dinner plates in front of them.

"You know, there are a lot of perceptions and beliefs about illnesses that are incorrect. It's a known fact that you can cure about seventy percent of man's illnesses through rethinking them."

Mitch had no idea where she was going with this. He tried once more. "Do you mean like mind over matter? Sort of?" Mitch stuffed a forkful of the potatoes in his mouth.

"Well, it is more about eliminating suppression from your life. Like for instance, I found that the more successful I became, the more suppression I bumped into. Especially in the entertainment industry, which really is home to rabidly suppressive people. I've achieved a whole new appreciation of the everything, you know, all of mankind, and not just animals."

Jenna reached under the table and pulled up a large book bag and rooted around in it. Mitch looked over to Joy, who gave him a look, her lips pinched together. Jenna handed him a magazine, *Source*.

"You should just check this out. I'm sure it would interest you, and maybe you'll join me and my husband, Mook, with clearing the planet."

Suddenly Mitch had a memory of Jenna giving an interview to *Entertainment Weekly* about suppressive people, something called engrams. Ugh, Scientology. Mitch played dumb, hoping she would stop soon.

"Like, with violence? The whole tree-saving thing?"

"No, just joy and clarity." Jenna answered. "Not trees, this is about your internal environment. And honestly, your career will really be enhanced once you get clear."

Mitch began to feel a deep sense of mourning that he was going to spend the next two hours eating steamed vegetables and poached pears and listening to tales of intestinal disorders and Dianetics.

When Jenna moved to put her book bag back under the table, Mitch dropped his copy of *Source* on the floor and turned to the right to start a conversation with the woman he had yet to meet but hoped would save him. But suddenly the room began to darken. The clink of glasses and forks sounded louder as the conversations hushed. Cybill Shepherd took the stage.

"Thank you all so much for being here tonight," she said. "The issue of IBS is one that has gotten far too little attention in our culture. But millions of those who suffer are silent no more, with this wonderful foundation that gives IBS sufferers a voice while working diligently on a cure. And who better to recognize in that fight than Dawn Greenstein, executive, mother, wife, sufferer, and front-runner in supporting research toward a cure for diseases of the bowel and abdomen. She is, if you will, our Katie Couric of the entire digestive system! Ladies and gentlemen, please join me in honoring—Dawn."

Dawn Greenstein walked carefully to the stage, her black velvet cape dragging slightly behind her. Tiny, with-cropped hair, she approached the podium gingerly, and Mitch tried hard to detach his image of the woman who had greenlighted over a hundred films from her advocacy of diseases of the bowel. It wasn't easy.

"Friends, for years I have been battling constipation, pain, and bloating," said Dawn, her voice so quiet Mitch could barely hear it through the microphone. "I know it is not a sexy disease, but these symptoms have gotten the better of millions of Americans, and I can only hope that by doing my little part, irritable bowel syndrome will no longer be a disease that brings shame and embarrassment. So thank you, Cybill, and thank you everyone for your generous support tonight. Before we have dessert, I just want to make you all aware of our colonics and Blahniks silent auction. You can walk right over there," Dawn said, sweeping her hand toward the right wall of the ballroom, "and find an entire selection of designer shoes and handbags worn only once, usually to an award show, generously donated by a vast array of wonderful actresses. All the proceeds will benefit digestive-diseases research. Also, as part of the auction, colonic cleanings are being offered by the Healing Nest, which has served hundreds of people in our industry. So spend like crazy, and thank you all again so much!"

The lights slowly came up, and Mitch looked around the room for an escape. A giant chandelier hung over his table, and he silently prayed it would fall onto the centerpiece of pink bud roses, thus ending the evening.

Mitch was uncharacteristically stymied. To be rude to Jenna Mills might piss off Joy, whom he increasingly, to his own amazement, longed to please. There she was, center table at a benefit for a major Hollywood executive, giggling with movie stars, a beacon that pulled others, no longer the other way around.

Mitch began to imagine what life would be like married to a woman like this. Scripts in hand nightly. Parts being written for him, no auditions necessary. No worries about being dropped by the death star. He had read in the paper that morning that Jeff Zucker at NBC was going to make a whopping nine pilots this year, most of them reality shows. Would he care with this award-winning writer and director at his side? Nope! He'd be knee deep into features. Then, another brain synapse: sex with this woman, her hair crinkling back to its natural form under his touch. Thinking about June, whose hair he suddenly missed, he cringed with shame and looked back at Jenna, who was now trying to talk to him about something called the Super Power Expansion Project.

To say something even vaguely supportive could invite more literature. He was saved, as it turned out, by the woman next to him.

"You're Mitch Gold, right?"

"I am."

"You did a pilot for us a few years ago, the one about the troubled clown. I was so sorry it didn't go. You were great. It took me months to get that scene of the twelve-year-old boy's party out of my head. I'm Elizabeth Wilcox."

Elizabeth Wilcox, head of programming at NBC. How could he have not recognized her? He could have spent the entire evening buttering her up instead of engaging a washed-up sitcom actress on her religious beliefs.

"Oh, gosh, of course, so nice to see you. You cut your hair, right?"

"No."

"Oh. You look different."

"Well I lost fifty pounds if that's what you mean."

"Um, maybe." Mitch changed the subject. "So what have you got going this season?"

"Pilots at NBC have been way down since the strike. We're more focused on reality programming now."

"Uh-huh." Mitch felt tense, as all actors did when faced with having to discuss the very sorts of shows that put them out of business. He bit into his pear. "Anything great?"

"Yes, a wonderful concept with celebrities and their mothers competing at cheerleading rounds. It's a really wholesome show."

"That sounds like perfect eight o'clock programming," Mitch said, trying to sound jovial.

"Yes, we're just reality at the family hour now. At ten we move to Leno, and that should prove to be a great lead-in to late night."

Mitch was unable to hide his frown. She went on, "Cheer up, though, we do tons of reruns after late night, which means residuals for you guys."

"Uh-huh. That is great," he said, looking back toward Joy. She now seemed to be trapped by Jenna Mills, who had cornered her at her end of the table.

"I'm just saying that IBS is a state of mind," Jenna said.

"You know, Jenna, you may be right," Joy said, glancing briefly at Mitch. Was that a wink? He swore it was. "But I learned a long time ago that religion and politics don't mix with digestive issues."

Mitch laughed, and flipped open his cell phone to see if he had missed any calls. There was never any reception in these places. Joy carefully moved the subject back to the safe world of work.

"So, Jenna, what have you been up to?"

"Well, I'm doing a romantic comedy for Fox. We start shooting in North Carolina in June."

"Nice. Good script?"

"Perfect for me. It's with Kate Hudson. We have about the same size role. She's in about ten more scenes, but still, it's more of an ensemble thing."

"Great. That's great, Jenna."

"I've turned down a few pilots. Oh, and here's something exciting! Kiefer just told me that they're going to offer me the president's secretary in the *Pacific Daylight* project."

Mitch snapped his head up. "My agent told me Anna Faris was playing that part," he said. "It's like a wacky secretary thing."

"Oh right," Jenna said. "I'm the secretary of state. No, wait a minute. Sorry sorry! Secretary of defenses. That's the part. It's a great role."

Mitch felt his face flush as rage engulfed him. Kiefer had just told him that he had a pin in him. Shit. Jenna's agent was probably negotiating her deal, and he had a pin in him in case it all fell through. And Kiefer knew it. But Jenna Mills?"

"Are you sure, Jenna?" Mitch asked. I read that script, and the secretary of defense was a man."

"Oh yeah, I think it *was* a man. But I guess they decided it would be more fun to make it a girl."

CHAPTER 14

Rich Friend. The sheer stupidity of his name was compensated for by the memory of his hot breath on June's neck. Where June once saw only browning palm trees, Piece-A-Pizza restaurants ("Had a piece lately?" inquired their signs), and red, speeding Carreras zipping down every trash-strewn street on the west side, she now heard, smelled, and tasted her lover everywhere. At every Coffee Bean & Tea Leaf, dry cleaner, and computer store, there he was. When giant, bright yellow roses began to bloom in the spot where a sewage backup had dumped human waste into the garden for a solid month last winter, June longed to call him and amuse him with the tale. When she lectured on the poem *Orlando Furioso,* she imagined Rich sitting among her students, his eyes lifted in fascination.

Even as June tiptoed down her driveway each morning in her nightgown to fetch her newspaper, dodging the stupid sprinklers that seemed only to water her car, she felt irrationally disappointed to not see Rich's silver Porsche parked out front, waiting to take her to breakfast. Since that first night at UCLA a few weeks ago, they had been together only twice, but in those two rendezvous June had lived an entire affair, so enamored was she of her new lover's funny stories, doting attention, and unwavering gaze when they were together. Rich was never in a hurry, never outwardly worried about work; he seemingly had all the time in the world just to attend to their courtship.

Their first meeting after the campus night was while Mitch was off at the network. June managed to sneak away after class and meet Rich at the Courtyard by Marriott across the street from a Ralph's supermarket, a place where no one they knew would ever spot their cars. There was no room service, of course, so Rich scooted across Olympic Boulevard, dodging six lanes of traffic, to get June a bottle of San Pelligrino, a nice touch. She felt stabbing pains of remorse when faced with her husband and child that night, especially given what happened to Mitch that day, but her elation at the memory of what she had enjoyed on those cheap sheets at the Marriott numbed her guilt.

The next time was less physical but more romantic, a three-hour lunch at La Cachette, with two glasses of red wine and a deconstruction of *The Simpsons*, in which Rich convinced her that Homer Simpson was sort of a Chauceresque antihero. She had committed parts of their conversation that day to memory, and replayed them in her head, picturing him holding her hand under the table, the first time someone had done that in nearly a decade.

Rich had gone to law school and worked briefly as an assistant district attorney in Brooklyn for two years before moving to Los Angeles to try his hand at television. His agility at leaping among evidence-based law, New York politics, ancient poetry, 1980s punk bands, hard-to-find Thai herbs, Monet versus Manet, Blizzard versus Slurpee, Frank Gehry versus Rem Koolhaas, coastal towns of Morocco, the Tour de France, and lunar positioning during a single meal both delighted and intrigued her. There were overlapping interests—food, politics, and astrology— and the things she had never thought about—Morocco, cycling, punk— that ignited both her brain and her libido.

Rich convinced her that term limits had been the downfall of the legislative and budget processes in New York City, and explained the proper way to cook skate so that it would not turn in on itself in the pan. He explained to her how the hard beats of the Stimulators originated from Nga Puhi Maori heritages. And he made the case for the dominance of the second Saturn Return—as opposed to the one people experience in their early thirties, which June felt was more transcendent.

Network television was a grace note, not the main measure; June had never met anyone so successful in Hollywood who seemed to obsess so little. And his admiration of her, she had to concede, was equally alluring. "Charming, hilarious, petite—not interested in the demo share— how could I be so lucky to have met you, June?" That day at La Cachette

154

was marred only by a scolding from the head of her department, with whom she was supposed to meet to discuss her tenure package. She had begged off at the last moment to have her lunch with Rich, rescheduling for the next week. "You're cutting it pretty close, June," said Bob. She was fine. Bob was borrowing trouble. She had missed the deadline for her grant application, but there was always next year.

But increasingly June was overtaken by an unaccustomed roller coaster of emotions that she felt unable to manage. The daily trajectory was becoming familiar, and constant: she would panic over not hearing from Rich, then dissolve into obsessive and irrational fears about the discovery of their affair (perhaps the network tapped his phone?), and arrive at the stark realization of her own recklessness, and what she imagined could only be a miserable end to this situation. And then Rich Friend would call. She would try to begin the conversation by telling him that their affair had to end and that she never wanted to hear from him again. But even as she formed the words on her lips, he would describe in some detail what he planned to do to her the next time they met, and she never spoke them. She wondered what she really wanted: for him to demand that she leave Mitch, which would force her to realize the enormity of this affair, or for him to never ask, underscoring its meaninglessness.

Her obsession with Rich followed June to the pasta aisle of Trader Joe's on Saturday afternoon, where she was weighing the relative merits of fussilli over rigatoni (perfect sauce cling versus nicer mouth feel). Rich loved rigatoni. He had eaten a particularly divine version in Tuscany during the shooting of a film he worked on seven years ago, and could still describe it in detail. Like June, Rich remembered all his favorite meals and never tired of discussing them. She reached for the box of rigatoni, but Nora, sitting in the child's seat of the shopping cart, swinging her legs back and forth to June's irritation, said indignantly, "I like the wagon wheels! Why you're buying those fat ones?" June grabbed a box of each and tossed them into the cart. She glanced at her list, scrawled across the face of Chad Wynn, one of the real estate agents who constantly left his notepads and sales reports on her lawn.

"Mommy, I'm cold! When are we going to be out of here?"

"I'm moving fast, sweetheart," June said, pushing the cart quickly.

She felt a banging on the back of her ankles, the third time. She looked back to see a woman with long black hair and an organic T-shirt dress who had run her cart into June in nearly every aisle. "Dumb twat," June mumbled, instantly amazed at her own hostility, and then something close to fearful when the woman snapped her head away from the row of fiber pills she had been examining to glare at June. It was one of her colleagues, the midcentury prose expert. Shit shit shit. What could she pretend to have been saying? Rum makes me fat? Oh *that*! Um, happy diwali?

June pushed her cart quickly down the last aisle, tossing raspberry jelly, cereal, and crunchy peanut butter into the cart. Mitch preferred the smooth version from Ralph's. She didn't give a shit. Organic and crunchy it was.

"Mommy, when are you getting me a new Tamagotchi? You keep promising after you made the old one dead."

"I'll do it, Nora. I hate electronic pets, by the way. What happened to your dolls?"

June stood at the checkout line waiting to pay, wondering what Rich was doing at that very moment. Could she call him from the car without Nora inquiring? What if Justine was around? She quickly swiped her ATM card as the bagger with white-man dreadlocks and giant, painful-looking buttons in his earlobes bagged her ice cream, milk, pasta, coffee, jams, organic peanut butter, frozen waffles, free-range chicken, butternut squash, baking soda, and raisins. What was that funny story Rich told her about his father? He wore a fur coat to his college graduation in the middle of May? Was that it? June wheeled the cart toward the parking structure, pushed it a little aside, and opened the car door. Nora resisted getting into her car seat, as usual.

"Come on, Nora, sit down."

"I want to drive!"

"You can drive later. Please, Mommy is hungry, let's go."

"Can we listen to the Dixie Chicks?"

Rich loved the Dixie Chicks too. She meant to burn him a CD later that he could download on his iPod.

Having strapped Nora into her car seat—June's car had finally been discovered by the police ditched at the Mexican border, only slightly worse for wear—June slid behind the wheel and sped home. Mitch greeted her at the door.

"What took you so long?"

"It's called traffic, Mitch. Maybe you've heard about it. It seems to be a problem in the southwestern United States."

"It's just that I'm starving. Did you get anything for lunch? Maybe some peanut butter?"

"Yeah, I got stuff."

June opened the trunk and her stomach sank. She had left her entire cache of groceries in the parking lot at Trader Joe's. Now she would have to trudge all the way back to Westwood and National to get them.

"June, what is wrong with you these days? You seem out of it," Mitch said.

June didn't answer. She placed Nora in Mitch's arms, kissed her, mumbled an apology, and got back into the car.

Having retrieved her groceries—melted ice cream, warm milk, free-range chicken that was now probably rife with salmonella—June put everything away. She wrapped one of the nine games of Twister she kept in the closet for birthday presents and forced Nora to write a card to Max G., even though Nora hated Max G. because he threw sand. She and Nora set out to My Gym on La Cienega for the fourth birthday party there in the last two months. This time June defiantly read *The New York Times* in full view of Town Crier rather than talk to the other mothers.

At the end of the day, June collapsed into a living room chair and stared at her husband. Mitch was sitting flipping channels with his teeth-whitening plates in place.

"The babysitter will be here in an hour," June said.

"Sowwy, wudyousay?"

"Mitch, can you take those absurd teeth things out while we talk? It's like living in a nursing home. I said the sitter will be here soon."

Mitch pulled the plastic molds out and carefully placed them back in the case, which June always noted resembled a diaphragm container.

"The clog dancer or the rhythmic gymnast?"

"Gymnast."

"What happened to the clog dancer?"

"She went back to Berkeley, which you would probably know if you were the one who ever arranged for babysitting. Anyway, I'm going to get dressed. What's this party for again?"

"I guess it's for Nick's wife. She published a book or something."

"A book. Isn't she a former porn star?"

"Exotic dancer. There's a difference."

"If you say so. Remind me of the dress code?"

"Casually fabulous."

"You always say that, Mitch. Is that: jeans with a silk shirt and high heels, or a cocktail dress?"

"Well, Nick Contreras is a huge director, and he's a bit on the odd side, but he isn't showy. So don't overdress. That will make us look like wannabes. I am sure his wife will be in pants. Plus she's kind of pudgy and you don't want her to hate you. What about jeans?"

"Hmm," June said, considering her wardrobe options. Rich said she should show her legs more. It was true, she had nice legs. "I think I'll wear that little black dress I bought in New York during my last trip."

"A dress? I said jeans."

"Well, I want to wear a dress. So a dress it is."

"So why did you ask me, then?" Mitch asked.

June walked through the living room, a tidy room with high arched ceilings, knotted wood floors, and shabby chic matching chairs and a formal, mint green arched couch. In the corner was a dollhouse that had been June's when she was a girl, with tiny furniture scattered around it, which she nudged out of her way with her foot. In the bedroom, she pulled her dress over her head, slipped on some Bakelite bracelets she had gotten at the flea market, and admired her look in the mirror. She was rubbing hand cream on when Mitch walked in, turned on his closet light, and rummaged for a clean shirt.

"June, is everything okay? You seem, well, really bitchy."

"I'm all right."

"Is it me? You know pilot season drives me crazy. But hang in there June-Junie. It will be over soon and our lives will go back to normal."

June looked at Mitch carefully, and wondered what her husband thought normal was. Pilot season would end, and then it would come again. And in between there would be jobs to be fired from, shows to get canceled, and Alec Baldwin stealing his movie roles at the last minute. Normal for their family was the constant ambience of moodiness, insecurity, occasional elation, and general edginess.

"I'm just worried about tenure," June said, hugging Mitch sort of sideways so that her body would not have to press against his. She patted his shoulder, as one might an elderly father-in-law who smells slightly of Winston Lights. She wanted the conversation to end.

She walked out of the room and absently picked her cell phone off the dining room table. There was a message from Adrian. "Hey, there. Adrian has been a very naughty boy. Let's see, it's the end of March, and I've slept with three different men. I think that officially makes me your slutty friend. I am very angry, however. I met some Latvian guy at a book party, and because I had heard Latvians had big ones, I took him home. Let's just say not all cultural stereotypes hold up. Oh, I have a new recipe for lemon granita. I'll e-mail it. Where the hell have you been anyway? I haven't heard from you in weeks. Okay. Loveyoumeanit."

About forty-five minutes later, June and Mitch were making their way up the hairpin turns deep in Beverly Hills, squinting into the darkness. The lack of streetlights and the tiny white street signs combined to keep out anyone who didn't own a house there, June decided, as she craned her neck in search of the name of the street they had just passed. Finally, after inching up Lloydcrest beyond squat, leafless willow trees that bent forward ominously like the mean talking apple tree in *The Wizard of Oz*, Mitch spotted the house. A valet stood outside—in Beverly Hills there were always valets at dinner parties for more than eight guests, and June always wondered where the cars were parked among those tiny winding streets—and Mitch handed her the keys. These female valets were wearing black pants and pink corsets with little name tags: Valet of the Dolls. June thought they must be cold.

They approached the giant double front door with its enormous Elizabethan gargoyle knocker, and pressed the doorbell just beneath it. Incongruously, it played "Take Me Out to the Ball Game."

They were greeted by a housekeeper, who ushered them into a large front room, where a display of the hostess's book was in full view. June blinked at the hot pink books—there must have been fifty of them—with a woman's leg on the cover, wearing a black stiletto, a white

159

feather floating down beside it. The title: *How to Get Freaky Like a Fan Dancer.*

June was intrigued—fan dancing, how positively Roaring Twenties!—but also somewhat burdened—would she actually have to pretend to have read this book to talk to people here? What if there was a dramatic reading? That could take a while. June grabbed a glass of champagne and looked around; Mitch had already made his way toward Nick, who had cast him in two of his movies and was very fond of him. Mitch was no doubt sniffing for a job in Nick's next picture—a western.

The room was the usual mix of recognizable actors—Warren Beatty was digging into a crepe—and people June never recognized, but whom she knew made all the decisions, and money, in Hollywood. She noticed a rapper whom Rich had told her about—Professor Mo Fo, whose album *Velocitized*, a treatise on freeway driving, was apparently quite seminal. Then there was the cast of hangers-on, those painfully thin women who scanned the room for other vaguely whoreish competitors, and balding men in too-casual shirts who made enough money to keep them happy. June could have sworn she saw Breasts, from the golf course, but it was hard to tell with her fully clothed.

She saw Cass Martin and felt vaguely pleased, the luscious taste of watching her become privy to Larissa's Escalade embarrassment still in her mouth. June would not have spoken to her first, but Cass approached her, with her husband, Michael Thomas O'Shea, in tow.

"Hi, it's June, right?"

"Yes, thank you for remembering. Very nice to see you again," said June, offering her hand, but Cass bent down and pecked her on the cheek, to June's surprise.

"Do you know Michael?"

"I think we may have met."

Michael turned on the face all famous actors have mastered, the one that radiated recognition and warmth toward someone he had never laid eyes on before.

"Did we meet at the Environmental Media Awards?" he asked June.

"No, I don't think so. Were you honored there?" June asked politely, not remotely interested.

"Actually, yes, it was awesome. I won Greenest Television Actor for providing carbon offsets to compensate for our travel on the show."

Michael seemed to grow a few inches taller as he leaned toward June, raising his voice like the law professor he had once played on *Boston Legal*, and began his lecture:

"It is such an honor to be involved with carbon offsets. They're a wonderful way of preserving the planet, and involve planting trees all over the world to compensate for the greenhouse-gas emissions from air travel."

"Huh. Well, what about just not traveling on private jets?" June asked.

Michael continued smiling. "That's one option. But why not make the world more breathable and more beautiful by planting trees?"

"You know," June said, "it sounds to me as if carbon offsets are a sort of modern equivalent of indulgences—the medieval practice of paying off sins with donations to the Church. Eradicating the practice of indulgences was on the list of things Martin Luther nailed to the door of Worms Cathedral."

"June, Dr. King was a great man, but I'm talking about everyone doing their part to make our earth greener."

Cass looked uncomfortable during this exchange, but said nothing.

"I understand that," June said, annoyed at Michael's tone. "I'm just suggesting that it might make more sense to fly commercial, so you don't need to offset anything."

"Wow, June. I'm experiencing you as kind of hostile. Do you hate trees? Are you a Republican?" Michael looked at Cass, inviting her to join his laughter, but Cass had stepped away with an uncomfortable look.

"Of course I don't hate trees. What a ridiculous accusation!" June answered, beyond irritated. Michael Thomas O'Shea, increasingly agitated, moved to interrupt June, but she only raised her voice. "And by the way, do you run your air conditioner in the summer? I am guessing you have, what, a ten-thousand-square-foot house?"

"What I possess is not something I discuss," said Michael, now red faced and clutching his diet Coke.

Suddenly June began to worry—was insulting Michael Thomas

O'Shea in some way going to harm Mitch? Should she begin to apologize?

Then, as if in a dream, her lover appeared next to the enraged actor. Rich was smirking under a swoop of dark hair.

"This sounds like an interesting conversation," Rich said.

"Well sort of. If you like Republicans," said Michael, looking to Rich as a possible repository for further ammunition against June.

But Rich Friend looked incredibly tickled, and turned toward June with mock shock. "June Dietz, are you a Republican?"

"I'm an Independent, actually. Thanks for asking," June replied, grinning at Rich.

Michael Thomas O'Shea had had enough. "It's nice to see you, Rich. Is Justine here?"

At the mention of Justine, June felt nervous. She looked around for her.

"Nah, she's burning the midnight oil as usual. More changes to the new show," Rich answered.

"Well I'm sure it will be a great one. I need to find Cass. Good to see you again, Rich." The actor had regained his composure, and his thousand-watt smile. "I hope you can grow on your point of view, June."

June smiled sweetly. Michael Thomas O'Shea had faded from her mind before he had even stepped away. She looked up at Rich, who whispered in her ear, "Your legs look sexy in that dress."

"What are you doing here?" she hissed back. "You never mentioned this party to me." June looked around for Mitch, trying not to look frantic. He was far across the room, talking to a group of other actors. Catching June's eye, and seeing Rich, he made his way toward them, and June's heart sank a little. Rich whispered to her quickly, "Don't worry. It's a long night." June longed to grab his hand, but Mitch was now standing between them.

"Hey, Rich, how are you, man?"

"I'm good. What's new with you?"

"Busy. Coming in for your show next week," Mitch said.

"Yep, I saw to that."

"Thanks! It's a terrific script. I have a great take on it."

June stared at Rich and was almost certain she saw derision sweep across his face. She felt protective of Mitch, yet found herself sharing a bit of what she believed was her lover's disdain for her husband and his mildly pathetic pandering. It was a confusing, deeply unpleasant feeling.

"Boys and girls!"

The three of them looked up at the winding staircase, where Nina, the hostess/author, was standing at the top. To June's amazement, she was holding two gigantic white ostrich feather fans in her hands, one in front of her body, one behind. Between the gaps in the feathers, June could see Nina was wearing only a black thong and matching pasties. "Time for fan-dancing. Girls, watch carefully—this is how you please your man!"

Mitch looked at June and made a face of horror, as if he had just taken a slug of buttermilk. She quickly glanced to her right at Rich, who winked in mock lasciviousness. She flicked her glance back to Mitch—had he seen the wink? Was he onto them? But Mitch was staring at Nina and her feathers.

Stereo speakers built into the walls above them blasted burlesque music, and Nina began to make her way down the stairs, stopping at each step to pull back one of the fans suggestively, shaking her rear end. When she got to the bottom, she began to strut from the left to the right, making little spins and continually peeking one breast from behind the feathers.

Many of the guests began to hoot and catcall, although some of the women had found refuge in the buffet table and were trying to pretend Nina did not exist. Cass Martin seemed disgusted, and looked around to see if anyone agreed.

Nina made her way toward Mitch and scooped him up in a fan while the room cheered, "Mitch! Mitch! Mitch!" Abashed, but unable to detach himself from this important director's lunatic wife, Mitch smiled gamely and tried to shake his hips. He then moved into comic mode, peeking out of the feathers and raising his eyebrows like Groucho Marx. As the Nina and Mitch show moved toward the other end of the house, June looked toward Rich, who gave her a tiny wave and mouthed, "Meet me in the master bedroom."

June glanced around nervously. No one was watching her. She nonchalantly made her way up the stairs, then rushed around from room to room trying to find the master suite. There were endless closets in this house, a small room that appeared to belong to a maid, at least three bathrooms, all of them with marble fixtures. She opened another door—pool table. This place was endless!

Once she finally found the bedroom, she huddled on a gold-tasseled daybed along the wall. Her heart was pounding again, this time with fear, but the idea of being alone with Rich for even a second thrilled her. She heard feet on the stairs. Rich. She slunk off the daybed and tiptoed to the door, the back of her high heels slapping against her feet, and stuck a pinkie out to signal him.

Rich slid inside, and they closed the door all but a crack, so as to listen for others.

"You look so beautiful. I had to feel those legs under that dress." Rich slid his hand under the black cloth and up her thigh, then into her panties.

June gasped and looked around—there were long silk robes hanging from several hooks, and heavy drapes hung on the windows. She reached up and kissed Rich's mouth. They stood there for several seconds, kissing passionately, and June began to unbutton Rich's shirt.

"No, June, we need to get back downstairs. I think your husband will be looking for you."

"Oh, he's hitting up Nick for work I'm sure. Five more minutes." There he was again. Andy Flynn. Someone concerned about getting caught at something. Someone boyish. Childish? Sexy.

Rich looked around nervously. "I wonder if there are cameras here. With a spread like this I wouldn't doubt it."

"Rich, don't be so afraid. Who would come up here?"

"No, no, we need to go. Do you want to get caught with your paramour in Nick Contreras's bedroom? I for one don't need that."

June adjusted her dress, smoothed her hair, and licked her lips. The last of Rich's vodka was on them. As she waited for him to go ahead, June had a sudden desire to return Adrian's call, and took her phone out of her purse. No bars. Too far up in the hills.

June made her way quickly down the stairs, nearly colliding with Nina, who had ended her dance and was sitting among her feathers at the bottom. As she got up and walked away June studied her form carefully, and realized that Mitch was right—rolls of flesh peeked out from behind a tuft of feathers.

June saw a line of people cued up outside a small dark room that appeared hardly larger than a closet. Curious, June peered over the crowd and saw a tough-looking woman with dyed blond hair sitting at a desk with a laptop, a pile of tarot cards, and a large martini, reading the palm of one guest, a pale, diminutive sort who appeared distressed. June watched for a few more seconds, and tried to eavesdrop. She looked at the line. A little long. She had to find Mitch. Abruptly the small woman squeezed her way out of the room, sobbing.

Seeing Mitch nowhere, June grabbed a piece of apple tart from a passing tray. She moved into the next room, where Nina and Nick's son, who looked to be about eleven, was playing a pitiful version of what June recognized as a Brahms violin concerto.

Mitch appeared at her side, and hissed in her ear: "I can't take this family inflicting their so-called talents on me for one more minute. Where have you have been, anyway? You left me stuck behind that fan."

"What was I supposed to do? You looked like you were having fun!"

"Fun? Like jock itch! Let's get out of here."

June looked to her left and saw Warren Beatty. "Are you going to eat that tart?" he asked her.

Stunned by this query, June handed the dessert to him silently. He thanked her and trotted off with it.

Then June heard Nick yelling at someone, and saw a commotion near the psychic's room. "Wait, I just need to check this out," June said, cantering toward the other end of the house, excusing herself as she made her way past the guests.

"You can't tell people at a party that their mother's gonna die!" Nick was yelling.

"I'm a psychic! I see what I see!"

"I hired you for fun, not to make people miserable."

"You should have hired a clown then! I have a gift!" the psychic countered.

After taking in this scene June returned to where she had left Mitch, and they made their way out of the house, thanking their hosts, saying their last good-byes, and making false promises to get together with the various ancillary characters of their lives. June saw Rich across the room, laughing uproariously at something Kristin Davis was telling him, her arms gesticulating wildly with her story. June felt a pang of jealousy—if they were married, would Rich flirt with actresses at parties? She wondered as she had a dozen times where they would be in six months, a year, if they would grow old together, in secret, using their AARP cards at the movies.

June and Mitch waited at the valet station, shivering, and a young girl in a maid's uniform ran out to them.

"Don't forget your gift!" She handed them each a pink bag, with Nina's book peeking out from it.

At the light at Sunset, June peered into the bag to see what else it held: a bar of Ibarra chocolate from Mexico, a small fan, and a hot pink vibrator. Overcome with the absurdity of the evening, her behavior, her life, and now, her vibrator, June began to laugh hysterically.

CHAPTER 15

Mitch had read Joy's script four times and was obsessed. It was as if she had written the role for him, just as she used to do with her plays: a mobster who was perpetually struggling with his adolescent proclivities. He wondered if the script was a bit dark for a studio feature, but it was funny. He had been longing for a part just like this one, a complicated character that would be challenging to play and would show his range.

Keeping a film profile was also essential to the arch of Mitch's career. Actors who made movies constituted the top tier of Hollywood, followed by series television regulars, episodic guest stars, voice-over actors, and then, at the bottom of the heartless heap, those who made commercials. They were just one precarious rung above wactors. Mitch moved through the top three genres seamlessly, like a helicopter diving from ten thousand feet of features back to the heliport of voice-over ads for insurance. The goal was to always be flying with a tier below to descend to.

He would never be a movie star, this much he understood. But a diet of a couple of run-of-the-picture movies a year—present on the set for the whole film, not just a few days—was a dream he felt was in reach. The role of the contemporary Dutch Schultz–like gangster, if he could get the job, could certainly propel him forward.

Mitch had had several calls with Joy since the IBS dinner, and each one was professional, if clipped. It was almost as if the perpetual-seduction Joy had unzipped her own skin, and new, blunted-affect Joy had stepped out and made her way to Hollywood. But she did agree to meet him at the Chateau Marmont for a drink to work on the audition.

She seemed to want to help him get the role, but both she and Mitch knew the decision was ultimately up to Ridley Scott.

Mitch attempted to settle comfortably into the maroon banquette in Bar Marmont, but his long legs, shoved under the table, instantly banged against its bottom. The couple next to him, with matching long black stringy hair, glared at him. He felt conspicuous, a Jolly Jewish Giant among a slew of sinewy twenty-somethings, most of them with slick heads. A waitress walked over to take his drink order.

"Amaretto and soda, please."

"You got it."

He noticed Amy Adams sitting in a booth with what he surmised was a celebrity journalist, his tiny tape recorder resting between them. To entertain himself, Mitch tried to write the reporter's story in his head. *Amy Adams is surprisingly sweet, alighting from her silver Mercedes exactly on time, dressed in an off-the-rack cotton dress. "Oh, I so hope I didn't make you wait," said the enchanting enchantress, who ate a giant hamburger (extra mustard!) while tucked into a booth at Marmont. . . .*

Mitch saw Joy before she saw him. She wore a short white dress with a strange array of buttons on the front, those skinny legs poking out. She waved at him as she made her way to the table, her phone pressed tightly against her ear.

"Well I've already given them a new third act, so I don't see why they need to wait. Okay . . . uh-huh. Well, if Keira Knightley has already committed, then why are they bothering me about this? Uh-huh. Yeah, but fuck 'em. Anyway, I've got someone waiting, Suzanne. Let me call you tomorrow. Okay. Bye."

Joy settled into the chair across from him. Mitch felt embarrassed that he had not saved her the banquette.

"Hey, Mitch. What ya drinkin'? Bourbon?"

"Actually, it's amaretto. With some soda."

"That's fun!" Joy craned her neck for the waitress, who sauntered over. "I'll have what he's having."

Mitch snorted a little. "Well that's two amarettos they've sold this month. I actually never get a chance to indulge. My wife hates when I order girly drinks."

"Really?" Joy tilted her head a little to the right, and Mitch noticed her perfectly lined eyes. When did she start wearing makeup? "Does she police all your food and beverage choices?"

"Well, sort of. I can't have girl drinks, or Fritos, or French dressing. She just hates when I order French dressing. She calls it five a.m.-strawberry-daiquiri-vomit dressing."

"Wow." Joy shrugged. "I don't get why foodies get so worked up about this stuff. They turn dining into a medical experience."

They sipped in silence for a minute.

"Listen, Joy, this script is really fantastic. It's such a compelling story and the dialogue is so real. But then you always were great with dialogue. The other thing that I really loved was Seymour's journey as a character, the way he starts out so seemingly one-dimensional and cruel, but then you realize he is so complicated and emotionally crippled. Anyway, I really want to do a good job for Ridley."

"I know. You will. Would it help for us to go over the material?"

Mitch pulled his sides from his jacket pocket. "It would help a lot, actually. And I have a question. Why is Seymour so abusive to Barry in the scene in the bar? I mean, Barry has been such a passive character up until then, and he's never really done anything directly to undermine Seymour."

"True, but Seymour's beginning to realize that his entire crew is turning on him, and Barry sort of represents that betrayal. But why don't we read it?"

Mitch felt a slight prickle of excitement to be reading with Joy again, and he recognized the familiar anticipation in her eyes as she waited for him to begin.

"*Barry, I've got a flu that no amount of fucking Airborne can cure.*" Mitch pretended to spit in Joy's face; she seemed tickled. "*Now you have my germs!*" Mitch roared, causing some of the people at the other table to stare.

"That was good, Mitch. But don't be afraid of the Brooklyn accent—it will help you get into the character. And use your body a bit: remember, Seymour is physically threatening Barry. Mitch, be creative, don't be afraid to make interesting choices."

Mitch began again, this time on his feet, scowling and throwing his body toward the table. He boomed, in an accent now thick with Brooklyn, "*Now you have my joyms!*"

Joy clapped her hands together like a child and laughed uproariously. "Perfect! You nailed it!" Mitch was thrilled. He remembered how
wonderful it had been to work with Joy.

Joy and Mitch read a few more lines together, then went back to
sipping their drinks. Joy told Mitch about her life in Los Angeles: her
house in Hancock Park, rented from Courtney Love's manager; the
German short-haired pointer she took jogging in Runyon Canyon on
the weekends; movies at the ArcLight; premieres in Westwood; rewrites
over coffee at BLD; a development deal with Fox Searchlight; being
courted for a kids movie at Disney. Work, more work.

Seth Rogen approached the table. "Hey, Joy, how's it going?"

"Great, Seth. Do you know Mitch Gold?"

"Hey, what's up?" Mitch said.

"Yo. Joy, I saw the notes on the new scene in *Bite Me, Eat Me*. Dying to talk to you."

"Sure, call me next week when you get back from New York."

Mitch felt again, as he had begun to feel at the benefit dinner, that
Joy was firmly affixed in the world he only orbited. He ruminated on the
security of Joy's position. The girl in the cloth skirts who left weird poetry on the fire escape was now the woman with the expensive haircut
that people gravitated toward at Bar Marmont. It was shamefully exciting to be there with her.

Mitch also wondered what it would be like to be able to read with
someone like Joy every night, someone who could really help him be a
better actor, instead of June, who these days listened uninterestedly
when he asked for her help. He could overlook the hair thing. And the
bony legs. Maybe. He felt guilty for the thought, yet again.

Out of the corner of his eye Mitch watched Seth Rogen sit down
at the bar next to Sacha Baron Cohen. Glancing at the clock above
their heads, Mitch realized it was 10 p.m. June would be angry—he had
promised to put Nora to bed so she could work on her book.

"Joy, I gotta run," Mitch said.

"Sure. Hey listen, an executive friend at Disney gave me a bunch
of VIP passes for a party at Disneyland Sunday." Joy reached into her
purse and handed three tickets to Mitch. "Why don't you bring your
wife and daughter?"

CHAPTER 16

During the fifty-minute car ride from Los Angeles to Anaheim, Nora had somehow rearranged the safety belt across her booster seat so that it was no longer over her shoulder, thus offering no protection whatsoever in the event of an accident. Mitch was circling the Mickey and Friends parking structure, slowly, so slowly, looking for an open spot. June, hopeful as she always was on these visits that this time Disneyland would not be packed, felt her optimism waning as they drove through the Mickey, Goofy, and Daisy levels, which were all crammed full of cars. June noticed a family climbing into a red minivan but thought better of pointing this out to Mitch. She had been with him in enough parking structures to know he was completely incapable of waiting the thirty seconds it might take for the red-minivan family to pile into their car, put on seat belts, open their respective cans of Diet Coke, and get the engine started. She didn't want to hear Mitch's mad honking.

Finally they found a space on the Donald level, and hauled a dirty umbrella stroller and a knapsack stuffed full with sunscreen, hats, extra T-shirts, a camera, and Nora's battery-operated Pluto dog, which she had gotten on their last visit, down the escalators and onto the sweltering sunbaked tram platform.

June wondered why it always seemed to be twenty-five degrees hotter in Disneyland than anywhere else in Los Angeles as she grasped Nora's hand and helped her up into the tram that would shuttle them to Downtown Disney. They sat in silence, listening to the litany of enticements and warnings over the PA: "Welcome to the happiest place on earth! Please keep all body parts in the tram, no standing, please keep all children under adult supervision at all times, no lap sitting on the tram, be sure to remember where you parked, don't miss the parade at eight o'clock down Main Street USA, please make sure all strollers and bags are safely stowed, try our Park Hopper pass, should an object fall from the tram during the journey to Downtown Disney do not attempt to jump from the tram to retrieve it, be sure to remain seated until the tram comes to a complete stop. . . ."

"Remember to wipe your ass after visiting the bathroom," Mitch said under his breath.

When they arrived a few minutes later, June was relieved that they were quickly ushered into the park courtesy of their VIP passes, because of course there was an endless throng of people waiting at the entrance to the theme park. Nora stared at all the attractions with a mixture of fear and ecstasy. "Can we go to Small World, Mommy?"

"Oh definitely," June said, trying hard to be cheerful. Disneyland had never been her favorite place, with its absurdly long lines, corn dogs, exorbitantly priced balloons, and creepily cheerful adults in polyester costumes helping thick-around-the-middle tourists sink into the cars and boats of the various rides. Having VIP passes both enhanced the experience and made it all the more distasteful. They got in for free, which was great, because Disneyland was a roughly three-hundred-dollar day. They got passes to use a separate entrance to get into the rides ahead of everyone else, which was both a lifesaver and a humiliation, as June looked back at the sweaty faces of parents in their Texas A&M T-shirts, holding their crying children, as they stared at the little sign over the Big Thunder Mountain Railroad which bore the sad news: "Wait time: 65 minutes."

June watched impassively as Nora danced around with Mickey and Minnie. She tried not to throw up on the Mad Hatter's Tea Party, holding a tissue over her mouth. She helped Nora decorate a hard cookie near the Princess Castle, munching on the Marcona almonds (smuggled past Disneyland security in a small Ziploc hidden in her bra) while Nora fumbled with the pink frosting.

Mitch had been cheerful, which was unusual these days. He took Nora on the ride where they shot at monsters, and shared a giant wand of cotton candy with her, tickling her on the nose with its sticky airspun tip. "That's my girl Nora, always up for a goodie!"

At last they were in Small World, where June opted to stand in line because it was shortish and she had had enough of cutting lines time after time.

"Hey! Look who's here!" Mitch said, looking over June's shoulder at a group—most likely Disney executives, other VIPs, and, June suspected, a movie star or two, given the largeness of the herd and the telltale muscular men in suits with earpieces. Ugh, June was not in the mood for introductions to people who expected her to already know who they were.

A spindly woman, nearly as tall as her husband, waved frantically at him. "Hey, Mitch! Quick, come here, I want you to meet Keira!"

Mitch glanced toward June. "I can't fit in that boat anyway," he said. "Why don't you ride with Nora, and I'll wait for you right here. I'm just going to talk to them for two seconds."

June agreed, and soon she and Nora were tucked into the fiberglass-bottomed boat cruising by the audio animatronics garishly dressed in native costumes of yore, gathering every ethnic stereotype known to man into a five-minute ride. Nora stared, riveted, at the hip-shaking hula girls in their grass skirts. "Mommy, do they wear those to school?"

At the end of the ride, grabbing the hands of Disney helpers dressed in Dutch costumes, the two inelegantly launched themselves out of the boats and fought the crowd toward the stroller parking area. Nora was getting tired, and June knew the internal rhythms of her child. She had about thirty minutes and one snack left in her, and then she would begin to cry. "Mommy, I want to sit down," Nora whined. "I'm so tired." June struggled to open the stroller, kicking on its umbrella center with the heel of her tennis shoes. It finally clicked into place, and she fumbled with the knapsack.

"Okay, honey, I'm trying. Where is Daddy?"

"I don't know."

June looked around with irritation. It was unlike Mitch to wander off. She felt a sunburn forming on the two inches of her forehead where she had failed to rub Coppertone. She looked behind her, then lifted her hand over her forehead to block the sun's glare. Why hadn't she remembered her phone? Where the hell was Mitch?

Nora plopped into the stroller. "I want water," she said, and June

173

fumbled around for a bottle in the knapsack. Shit, it had all poured out inside. Mitch hadn't closed it properly. Nora began to drag her feet in front of the stroller, causing it to lurch forward.

"Stop that please," June said, becoming more annoyed.

June began to walk aimlessly through Fantasyland, meandering in circles past Dumbo the Flying Elephant, beyond Pinocchio's Daring Journey (where she noticed paint peeling off in the whale's mouth), finally leaning against the railing containing the crowds at the Matterhorn Bobsleds. Nora looked up at the tiny carts of screaming strangers on the ride above them. June felt sweat trickle down her back. She was exasperated, bordering on fearful. What was she supposed to do now? She stood weighing her options: Go back to the car? She did not have the car keys; would she have to get a cab back to West LA? What would that cost, four hundred dollars? Was there anywhere around here where she could buy a bottle of water? She looked up and saw, to her astonishment, what appeared to be her husband, wedged on a brightly painted horse on the giant carousel across the park.

As she marched toward the ride, pushing Nora, who was now openly sobbing, June saw that it was indeed Mitch, surrounded by several other adults, who were laughing uproariously as they rode the horses up and down. Keira Knightley was sitting sidesaddle, an unsmiling bodyguard standing next to her, while Mitch's long legs crunched up near his chin as the horse rose. Next to him was the spindly woman—did June actually see her muss his hair?

She stood beside the ride, watching it slowly come to an end, the music clanging to its finish. "Is that Daddy?" Nora asked.

"Indeed it is," June said.

"He looks weird."

"Yep."

Mitch descended and began to follow the entourage, when June yelped out. "Hey! Mitch Gold."

Mitch walked over, still laughing. "Hi, guys! Nora, have you been crying? Did Small World scare you again?"

June began to unload. "What the hell were you thinking, Mitch, wandering off like that?"

"Sorry, honey, I lost track of time. I mean, it's a theme park, so chill out."

"Chill out? You left me with no word in the middle of this godforsaken place, and I go to find you, and the man who can't ride a Small World boat is on a carousel horse. What gives? And who is that severe-looking woman in full makeup? I mean, who wears full makeup to a theme park?"

"That's Joy Wainscott. I told you about her. June, she might actually give me a part in a movie. I am sorry, but I can't be rude to her."

"Oh, of course not, why be rude to a Hollywood writer when you have a perfectly good wife and child to be rude to?"

"June, am I detecting jealousy here?"

Nora began to cry again, and placed her hands over her ears. "Too loud! Too loud!"

"Just two minutes, honey," June said, and then looked back up at Mitch. "I'm not remotely jealous, Mitch. What I am angry about is that you are treating me like the hired help, dragging your kid around Disneyland while you hobnob with your Hollywood assholes. Do you just assume that I am going to wipe all the hands, buy all the lunches, get the stroller moving, while you do as you damn well please? And believe me, Mitch, you are the last person who would ever make me jealous."

Mitch's face fell, and June thought of those cheap umbrellas that littered the streets of Manhattan after the rain, broken and twisted. "Well, good to know," he said quietly.

Understanding she had gone too far, June tugged at the stroller, pulling it awkwardly 180 degrees and jerking Nora back into it as she pulled. She tried to make her way to the exit, and began asking anyone she could stop how to get out.

"I know where the exit is," Mitch mumbled, taking the stroller handles and pushing Nora forward. June walked five feet behind them, furious.

Back at the car, Mitch and June wordlessly tossed the stroller, backpacks, empty water bottles, and hats into the trunk. Tucking Nora into her car seat, June could see she was about to nod off. "Mommy, I never got a balloon," she said, rubbing the sides of her head with her hands.

"I know, sweetheart. The next time."

Nora tried to cry, but was too tired. "I wanted one this time. You always say next time."

"I know."

"I don't like the assholes," Nora said, then turned her head to the side, already falling asleep. June shot Mitch an angry look, which he ignored, staring straight ahead.

As June climbed into the front seat of the car, Mitch turned on WKFI, a conservative talk radio station; listening to it was an odd habit that irritated June. Through the screaming of John and Ken—"Illegal aliens are filling the emergency rooms by the thousands and this governor won't do anything about it!!!!!!!!"—June and Mitch sat silently, all the way back to Los Angeles.

CHAPTER 17

To: MitchGold@aol.com
From: Tad@Tadmeier.com
Re: Auditions

Hey—
Busy week. First, the *Harry Potter* audition at Warner Bros.
Then I will send you the sides for the dirty-mouth-dad thing.
I should have a time for you later today. Rich and Justine's
show will be at the end of the week. I think you've got a
really good shot at that. But I can't take phone calls from you
approximately every 13 seconds this week—off to Vegas with
Candy Christmas, the animal hypnotist. Does a few other
things to humans too—lol! Also, someone wants you to be
the voice of an ape for an insurance ad. Who's your voice-
over agent?

To: Tad@Tadmeier.com
From: MitchGold@aol.com
Re: Ape

Hi. Thanks for the info. Can you give the ape info to Misty Bar-
ron? She reps me for voice-overs. And, umm, Candy Christmas?
Is that her Christian name, or is it a Long Dong Silver type
thing?

Okay, I'll call Misty for you so you can be an ape. BTW, Candy Christmas is a nice girl. She could be the one!

June rolled over on the silky white sheets away from Rich Friend, who had thrown his arm over his eyes in exhaustion. Justine had gone to scout a location where they would re-create a French village for the new show, and Rich was supposed to stay behind to work on rewrites, but he had called June at the last second that morning and convinced her to meet for a tryst at the Beverly Hills Hotel. June left UCLA right after her Harlem Renaissance class and raced along Sunset toward the giant pink and white cake of a hotel perched at the entrance to the elegant hills behind it. The hotel was surrounded by palm trees, which all seemed to lean toward it, as if forming a gate. Rich and June met in the grand deluxe suite that Rich had reserved under the name e. e. cummings, which amused June.

June walked into the room, and was astounded by its largeness and the elaborate decor. "Whoa!" she said, setting down her purse on a beige wooden footstool near the bed. June had never stayed in a place like this in her life, and imagined the 1930s movie stars who once bedded down there, sipping gin and tonics in their silk pajamas. The bed—made of basket-weave gold and swathed in a white satin canopy—sat in the middle of the room; the walls around it were mauve and sage. There was a full kitchen, which of course they would not use, a spacious dining area, a gas fireplace, and, in the most dramatic twist, a grand piano sitting near the picture window.

Rich was playing something—Chopin?—heavily, hitting each note with a sort of thud that really did not resemble the raindrop notes that June remembered from her father's recordings growing up. It was hard even to make out Rich's playing as Chopin. She said in amazement, "A piano?" She walked into the enormous bathroom, its fixtures all in marble. "A bidet?" She plopped down, childlike, on top of it. "You play piano?" she called to Rich as she looked over the array of expensive shampoos and bath gels. She reflexively pocketed the shower cap.

"I've been taking lessons for a few months. My teacher wanted me to stick with 'My Favorite Things,' but I thought I was ready for the nocturnes."

Not for the first time June wondered how a television writer, in the middle of pilot season, when most of the television industry was putting in sixteen-hour days, had time to take hours of piano lessons, cook elaborate meals, shop for first-edition poetry volumes, and meet married women for bistro lunches and sexual encounters in two-thousand-dollar-a-night hotel suites (which were used for only two hours) in Beverly Hills.

Before she could ruminate further, Rich came into the bathroom, where June was still sitting on the bidet, and pulled her into the suite, then onto the bed. June found herself feeling extremely happy that she had gone to Nordstrom earlier in the week and gotten five pairs of Hanky Panky thongs (a little wider than the other brands, which she had thrown under her bed because they were so irritating) and matching camisoles in bold colors (on sale). Rich had brought his pink vibrator party favor, which they used with great amusement, and some delight. After another round of athletic and transcendent sex, June craved tuna fish. She knew there was a classic coffee shop in the hotel that was supposed to serve a mean tuna melt. She reached for her panties, which were gathered somewhere in the mass of blankets.

"What's your favorite sandwich?" she asked Rich.

"Hmm. A Reuben, maybe. I've always loved Monte Cristos, but those are hard to find in Los Angeles. I kind of hate panini, but I love the classic grilled cheese at Campanile. But not the one with tapenade. Too mushy."

"Interesting. What are three things that you believe?"

"Believe. Let's see. I believe women should dress like women and act like men. I believe that Starbucks overroasts its beans. I believe that Ally McBeal was the worst television show ever made. What about you?"

"I believe that candlelight is overrated. I believe that men over fifty should not surf. I believe that tartar is an invention of the toothpaste companies."

"I think you're wrong about that last one, and I hope to be surfing at fifty-five," Rich said, leaning on his elbow, and clearly enjoying this game. He took his own turn. "What is the worst thing you have ever done to someone else?"

Have an affair with you, June thought, but said: "I don't know. When I was in the fifth grade, I wanted another kid's bathing suit. It was a bikini, tiny and cute, with all these little alligators imprinted on it. So one day during gym, I exchanged my ratty Speedo with hers in her gym bag, and took her bikini home. Heidi, I think her name was. Anyway, of course I realized after that I could never wear it, but I relished just sort of looking at that bikini in my underwear drawer for years after. You?"

"On my first TV writing gig, I had a writing partner. We had to share our salary, and the credit, and the guy wasn't pulling his weight. So I started a rumor that my partner was having an affair with the show runner's wife. The show runner got paranoid, my partner got fired, I stayed on for another five years!"

June was appalled, and alarmed. What would it take for her lover, her kind, seductive, adoring lover, to rat her out? And who makes up a story about someone for a job? She looked at his soft face, and down at his arms, which looked oddly older than the rest of him, stained by too many years in the sun, wrinkly and veiny, like she remembered her grandmother's arms, working dough in her kitchen in Minnesota. But he was smiling sweetly at her. He kissed her nose, and went on.

"What is your idea of a perfect vacation?"

June considered the question, still disturbed by Rich's last tale. "Well, I've always wanted to go to one of those cooking schools in an old villa in Italy, where you shop for ingredients at the market, cook all day, then eat fabulous feasts at night. Or maybe a walking tour of Dublin. I don't know. How about you?"

"Morocco, for sure. I'd walk the ancient medina of Fez, dodging donkeys and hucksters, and drink mint tea. I'd go to Essaouira and walk in the wind. The women there wear these long white djellabas that are completely different from those in the rest of the country. I'd eat fish stew near the sea. I'd go to Rabat and visit the tomb of Hassan the second, and drink more tea. I'd speak French, and attempt Arabic."

June was lost in her fantasy image of Morocco, one that had been slowly shaded, like a vacation coloring book, through her conversations with Rich. She pictured sitting and drinking the tea with him, quietly, in some ancient city, but then realized that his fantasy vacation seemed to place him there alone.

June was now starving. "Let's go downstairs. I need something to eat."

Dressed and still slightly flushed, Rich Friend and June settled into the rose-colored stools that surrounded the horseshoe-shaped counter at the Fountain Coffee Room. Giggling a bit as they perused the menu, June ordered her tuna melt and looked around at the odd mix of fashion models, tourists, and older women who seemed to have been sitting at the counter since the mid-1950s, sipping ice-cream floats.

But June was still bothered by her earlier conversation with Rich. She knew Mitch was auditioning for Rich and Justine's show, but she had not wanted to mention it before.

"Rich, I need to ask you. Is this, umm, well, this thing between us going to hurt Mitch's chance to get on your show?"

Rich looked annoyed and stirred his coffee. "Casting is Justine's area. Don't worry about it. The network makes all the decisions anyway, June. I'll do my best for him, if that's what you're asking."

"No, that's not what—"

"I don't want to talk about Justine and Mitch," Rich said with his jaw set tightly. "Let's enjoy our lunch."

June suddenly realized that it was far past lunch, and that her cell phone had been off for a few hours. She flipped it on and was stunned to see five messages awaiting her. The waitress dropped her sandwich in front of her, and June took a bite as she dialed. Yum. Perfect amount of butter.

The first message, oddly, was Nora. June panicked. How did Nora get a phone? She heard an adult voice faintly in the background of the message. demi? "She's not there, sweetie. She must be working. Leave her a message." Nothing more. June quickly skipped to the next one. Nora again. "Mommy, where are you? I am waiting for you at senior spring sing. The teacher readed your name and you were not there."

Next message: "Mommy! Where are you?"

Senior spring sing. Holy shit. She was supposed to have met Nora's class at a Sephardic senior citizens home in the Beverly Hills flats five minutes ago. The children were going to sing songs and hand out oatmeal cookies. Parents were supposed to go too. She had written this down! She knew it! And then, she had forgotten it all, here at the Beverly Hills Hotel.

June pushed her sandwich away and listened to the last two messages. One was from Larissa: "Sorry, June, I know you must be at work, but Autumn wanted me to call. Nora is a little upset. I guess she was expecting you to be here."

Then one more from Nora, which June listened to as she jogged through the lobby of the hotel, waving her valet ticket frantically. She had not even said good-bye to Rich, but mouthed to him only, "I have to go. NOW."

"Do you have a validation today, miss?"

"No. Please hurry. I have an emergency."

"Certainly, miss. That will be thirty dollars."

Fuck. June reached in her purse. She had $27. "Please bring the car around, I have the rest in there." She tapped her foot anxiously. When her Honda finally pulled up—it seemed like hours—she dug around in her cup holder for parking-meter quarters. That made $29. She turned upside down to look under the seat, and realized that her skirt had gotten stuck in her thong, exposing the back of her legs and half of her bottom. Goddamn it! She found six dimes. She had $29.60.

"Sorry. This is all I have. I really have to run!" The valet slammed the door, glaring.

June pulled into the Sephardic Adult Day Care of Greater Los Angeles parking lot, and could not find a spot. She parked behind a Rolls-Royce with a license plate that read TUMYTUK, left a note on the windshield with her cell phone number, and raced inside, unable to think clearly, as sweat formed above her upper lip.

She saw only an old man in a private security company uniform slumped in a chair, reading a Farsi newspaper. The center was dark and dank, and smelled vaguely of overcooked green beans.

"Excuse me! Excuse me? Where are the children?"

The guard snorted, and barely looked up. "There's no children here. This is an adult day care."

"Yes, I know that. I mean the children who are guests!"

The man looked confused, but June heard from a distance the high-pitched wheeze of a harmonica. She ran past the guard toward the sound, and found it coming from a small meeting room crammed full of preschool parents standing over withered figures in wheelchairs. The room was hot, its walls covered with notes in Hebrew and Farsi, and a tattered Israeli flag. The other mothers—and there were only mothers—looked tan and expensive, standing next to the fading figures of people who had come from much less then they had.

Some of the residents stared vacantly at the front of the room, where two men in lederhosen were playing the harmonicas, for no apparent reason, among the tiny children, who were attempting to sing "Bingo." Where had these guys come from?

She scanned the room for her daughter. Where was she?? Her eyes finally rested on Nora, puffy eyed, with a trail of tears on her cheeks, sitting on Nancy's lap, next to Thor, who had his fingers in his ears. Oh, right, he was afraid of live music. The increasing smell of decay overwhelmed June as she tried to make her way toward her child, but she could not successfully weave past walkers, oversized wheelchairs, and the Formica-topped tables covered with Styrofoam coffee cups and plastic flowers.

"Wheeze, wheeze, wheeze wheeze OH and Bingo was his name-o!" played the harmonica guys. "Name-o!" the children said in unison, a full beat behind the horrid duo.

The concert had ended. A few of the elderly residents clapped their hands, and some continued to stare. One woman, wearing a nearly see-through mustard-colored nightgown, was slumped in her chair, and called after June. "Hi, honey! I thought you were going to bring me an egg cream. I want to drink it while I watch Cronkite!"

June finally made her way to Nora, who immediately burst into tears again.

"Where were you?"

June thought frantically. "I am so sorry, Noony. . . ."

"ALL THE OTHER MOMMIES WERE HERE AND YOU WEREN'T!"

Nancy looked at June balefully, and sort of tilted her head. June

183

felt enraged, embarrassed, sick with regret and guilt, and deeply nauseated from the smell. She pulled Nora off of Nancy's lap, and Nancy dramatically fell to the left a bit. "Careful!" she said as she tried to steady herself and Nora.

June glared in her direction and swooped up Nora, elbowing her way out of the room as the other mothers looked on. Nora continued to whimper as they made their way to the parking lot.

"You didn't hear me sing 'Little Teacup.'"

"Sing it for me now, sweetie. I want to hear it!"

"NO!"

June felt her throat tickle. Tears were coming. She knew what she had done was inexcusable, disgusting, really, and what was worse, she had no way to fix it, and no intention of swearing off its cause.

She had hurt her child, her darling, innocent, trusting child, whose sweet little face was now creased with rage and pain. She had never missed a pediatric appointment, a haircut, or a single first moment, even with her busy career. And now she could not even coax Nora to make eye contact, let alone sing her the song.

The second she stepped into the parking lot she saw it: a tow truck being hooked to her front bumper, and a long flatbed pulling up behind it.

"Jesus! I was inside for FIVE MINUTES! YOU CAN'T TOW MY GODDAMN CAR!" she screamed at the driver, who stared back silently. In her panic, she had completely forgotten she had blocked the plastic surgeon, who was sitting in his car, his face twisted in fury, waiting for her Honda to be removed so he could leave. Damn. She had left the cell in the car.

June looked around at the other mothers, now filing out of the center, either pretending not to see her as they walked with their children, or gazing on the scene with faux sympathy. Nora stared at them from June's arms, then buried her head in her mother's neck.

"Where are they taking the car, Mommy? Are they stealing it like the last guy did? Migly's in there."

June tried to keep her voice happy and light, to use the tone that had always come so naturally to her, when she thought only of Nora and her needs, and was not haunted by the distractions that now took her away from bedtime stories to look for a text message on her phone, that took her away from the dinner table to call her lover feverishly from the shower stall, that took her away from where she was supposed to have been today.

"Imaginary friends don't mind being towed. They think it is fun. Let's visit Migly at the impound, okay? We'll take the bus. How fun is that? And I'll get you a malt." June tried to keep a singsong tone to her voice as she imagined what story she would have to make up to explain this incident to Mitch.

"A malt? Yummy!" Nora flicked her tongue over her lips, like a lizard slurping up a fly.

Larissa walked over to her and clucked. "Hi, June. You didn't see that parking structure across the street? Everyone parks there."

As June watched her swaying Honda on the flatbed making its way down Olympic, she tried to think of a single thing left in her life that was under control.

CHAPTER 18

To: junejune@gmail.com
From: Amandamalone@smithbarney.com

Hey Friend. I have been wanting to call but it always seems to be 4 a.m. on your end when I have a minute. Anyway, why didn't you tell me about these horrible mothers on the UWS? Here I was quietly trying to read the paper and this one kept asking me over and over again if Rose was walking yet, if no why not, was it possible that Max is cross-eyed, had I applied for a twos program at Columbia, did I take my children for music enrichment for toddlers yet??? I wanted to take my latte and dump it over her head. And by the way, what's with these women and their Burt's Bees obsession? They are always smearing it all over their mouths. Haven't they ever heard of proper lip gloss? When Sebastian gets back from Frankfurt, I am sending him to the park for three days.

June chuckled as she read Amanda's e-mail, and hit the reply button but was interrupted by a sound at her door.

"Helllooooooooo? Is any-von home?"

June sighed with frustration. Her coffee had almost finished brewing, and she was exhausted; it had taken three hours to get her car back from the sheriff's impound, where Nora sat with her, playing on the dirty floor with a box of license plates and random abandoned car parts, listening to people scream profanities at the clerk when she informed them, one by one, that they had thousands of dollars in parking tickets that had to be paid before their car could be retrieved. June had stared at Nora, and the one section of USA Today that sat on a dirty coffee table. In it was a small article about the ten thousand carbon-offset mango tree saplings planted in India with donations made by the band Coldplay and its fans. Most had withered due to neglect.

Mitch had finally come to meet them, tired from his day of being the voice of an ape and furious with June. "Let's see, June. We've got roughly eight hundred dollars in parking tickets, I'm battling with an insurance company over the rental car, which PS you scratched in a driveway—a first in the driving world—and then took to some body shop in El Segundo who ripped us off—"

"Actually he gave us a pretty good price—" June tried to inter-ject, but Mitch cut her off.

"Yeah, right. Anyway, that was all because you gave our Honda to a car thief posing as a valet. Now, a week after getting the damn thing back, you get towed from a parking lot because you couldn't be both-ered to put your daughter's school play in your date book."

"It wasn't a school play, Mitch. It was a senior spring sing. And I didn't notice you there."

"I was at work, June!"

June was silent. She couldn't say she had been at work too. Not this time.

"Hellloooo!"

Who the hell was pounding on the door at 8 a.m.? Out the win-dow June saw a shock of white hair, perched above a giant pair of wire-rimmed glasses, attached to a matronly body swathed in an overly warm, knobby wool sweater. Ugh. Cat Empress. June walked to the door, clutching her coffee cup, and pulled her nightgown down over her knees.

"Hilda. What can I do for you?"

"Did James sleep here last night?"

"Hilda, I don't know. I had kind of a hectic day yesterday."

"Vut about a cat door, June?"

"Well, Hilda, if you'd please just stop feeding my cat, maybe he'd stay here, and I wouldn't need a cat door."

"I luff James, June, and I still vonder, does he have a happy home? Because you ahhh his mommy, June."

"Hilda, he's a cat. I did not give birth to him."

"But James has talked to me. And he tells me dat he likes Purina. Do you feed him Purina?"

Mitch walked out in his underwear, saw Hilda, scowled, and retreated to the bedroom.

"I don't know what we feed James, honestly."

"Vell, you should buy Purina. He likes ze chicken flavor. Not ze fish. I will look for him in my garten. He luffs my pansies." Cat Empress walked back across the street to her garden calling in a high-pitched voice that was almost a yodel: "James! James-y!"

June closed the door and walked back into the kitchen for more coffee. She was going to be late taking Nora to school if she didn't move it.

"Can you make Nora a waffle?" June called to Mitch as she headed for the shower. While rubbing the soap on her face, trying to rouse herself awake, she considered all she had to do, and felt daunted. Tenure package, another school event for Nora, papers to grade, two academic articles to plow through, her endless book, and she needed time for her lover.

Her thoughts remained cloudy as she went back into the kitchen to make Nora's lunch, maneuvering around a six-foot-high claw scratcher, an electric water dish with a cascading fountain, a sack of catnip, and a cat bed, purchased at a garage sale on Ilona Avenue last week in the vain hope of getting James to stick around. June heaved a heavy sigh. Where the hell was she going to put all this stuff?

As Nora and June approached the corner across from school, June saw Nancy and Thor, who was dressed in a heavy hat with long flaps along the sides, dark sunglasses, and overalls with knee patches, in spite of the seventy-degree weather. Thor was skipping slightly ahead of Nancy, who yelled after him, "Thor, you are not allowed to run outside!"

Nora looked up at June, who was feeling particularly defeated by this morning, even though it had just begun. "Mommy, why doesn't Thor's mommy let him run anywhere?"

"I don't know, sweetie. I guess she's just nervous."

They made their way into the classroom, and June rifled though Nora's cubby to make room for her lunch box, pulling out leaf prints, ironed-crayon projects, and a rotten banana, discarded from snack.

"You need to put your glasses away, Nora," June said flatly. Nora reached her face up toward June and opened her eyes widely, so their charade of putting in contact lenses could commence.

The stay-at-home exercisers chattered, and June focused on not meeting their eyes. From behind, she could hear demi walking toward her, advising another mother, who June could not identify, on the merits of waxing over threading ("Threading is great for brows, terrible for the upper lip. It so hurts!") in her flinty voice.

"Hi, June," demi said.

Don't reply, thought June. Maybe she could say later she had an ear infection that produced fluid and made her unable to hear normally.

"June!" demi tapped her on the shoulder. No escape.

"Hi."

"Is everything okay with your car?"

"It's fine. Thanks for asking."

"Yeah, we all felt so bad. Nora was so upset. Maybe it's none of my business, June. But we all can see that Nora is not getting what she needs maybe from you. Do you really need to work so much? They're little for such a short time."

June felt a tickle behind her ear, and her upper body filled with heat. The rage that such remarks inspired had always been a thing she had put in a little box, one she opened only for Amanda, to whom she complained at length about the slights that she and other working women had suffered at demi's and the other mothers' hands.

"No, demi, I can't just quit. I would lose my tenure track. And you know, your kid probably feels bad when you send the nanny to career day, but no one's perfect."

Before demi could answer, her backup had arrived. Lexi, standing in her lime green sweat suit, bent down to Nora, who had been ignoring June and demi in favor of a large toy box filled with dress-up costumes. Lexi bent down toward Nora and held her chin in her hand. "Not so sad today, Nora?"

Nora gazed at her blankly. She had completely forgotten about the concert and the ensuing hysterics, but June was further angered by this insistent reminder by the other moms. June began to juggle all of Nora's art projects, which were falling out of her arms. She needed to get out of there.

"Let me get you a bag," said Autumn quietly, who had heard the whole exchange between June and demi.

Larissa walked in with Chloe, who went racing toward Walker, Lexi's son. "I can't wait till your birthday party, Walker! My mommy says you are going to have a real tent!"

June looked up and saw Libby, who was quietly stuffing Sally Foster magazine drive leaflets into each child's cubby. Libby was flushed and her face looked pained. June realized that nearly all the moms were now standing within several feet of each other, pulling off their children's jackets, reading a last story to the more anxious of the children—who had never quite learned to separate from their mothers—or gossiping in the corner.

She saw Tasia, who was playing blocks in the corner of the room, trying not to listen. Town Crier and Charlotte were playing their daily game of See You Later Alligator, which they sang to each other near the sink. Others were straggling in—in spite of Autumn's numerous entreaties to please arrive on time, at least half came twenty minutes late each day.

June moved toward the door, then stopped and looked at Lexi, who was now laughing with Cheerleader Mom about something they had seen on *Two and a Half Men.*

"Um, Lexi, is it Walker's birthday?"

"Yeah . . ."

"Because I notice that Nora wasn't invited to his party, and it seems like some other children were."

Lexi froze. Libby piped up: "Yeah, we weren't invited either." Town Crier looked up from a stack of LEGOS and seemed a bit nervous. He stared at June, then his eyes darted toward Libby, and rested on June again.

"Hey, I can't believe Thor was left out. Walker and Thor play together three times a week," said Nancy.

"I let Walker choose," Lexi said. "It was a small party and we

190

couldn't have everyone." Lexi's eyes hardened. Several of the children stopped what they were doing and stared.

"Lexi, you invited the kids of your friends, not the ones Walker plays with." June began to raise her voice. "How do you explain leaving Tasia's kids out? Or Sophia? Or Thor?"

Lexi glared, saying nothing.

June continued: "Frankly, Lexi, I am thanking God I don't have to waste a Saturday afternoon eating stale catered food at your house. But you're the head room parent! You are the person who stood up in front of all of us this year and said that if you invite one kid in the class to a birthday party, you have to invite them all."

Autumn looked slightly afraid, but said nothing. Barbara, pulling on her beret, quickly moved the children to the Play-Doh table. All of the parents had slowly moved to the front of the room, either staring at June and Lexi or pretending to be making their way out.

June found herself floating above her own form, listening to her words spill out, as if in a movie, louder and without stopping.

"I've been told that none of you like me. Well, that's fine, because really, you are all horrible. Just totally horrible. If someone has a job, or doesn't exercise as much as you do, or her husband made money in a way that you think isn't chic enough, your answer is to . . . to . . . punish her children."

"We don't punish anyone," Lexi protested. "What are you talking about?"

June went on. "Lexi, you snub certain mothers on the playground. You leave kids out of parties. You yammer on about your so-called parenting, when half of you have nannies and housekeepers and don't do a goddamn thing all day but talk to each other about, I don't know, where you stay in Kauai and whose Mother's Day project idea you're going to vote for."

June stammered a bit. "I . . . I hope when you all get finished with your three hours of Pilates classes and deliberating over who is going to bring the fat-free crackers to your oh-so-exclusive playgroup, you stop and think about where you all are right now. This is a preschool, not your prom committee, not your locker room at Equinox. It's a school."

June stopped, having run out of thoughts for a moment. The room was silent.

"And by the way, Lexi, you look like shit in that color."

June walked to the back of the room, almost tripping over a LEGO. She pecked Nora on the head. "I love you, Noony. You're the best thing I have."

Town Crier tried to touch June's arm, but she pushed him gently away. Although she had tears forming in her eyes, she felt somewhat relieved, as if she had been waiting to sneeze and finally had. And she walked out of the class, dropping a reminder for the toddler tea hour next week. She did not bend to pick it up.

June arrived home to put her things together for the day. She had a meeting later with the head of her department, and tomorrow was the deadline for her article on homoeroticism and individualism in Byron's *Don Juan*. Standing at the kitchen counter, June read:

> *Then there were sighs, the deeper for suppression,*
> *And stolen glances, sweeter for the theft,*
> *And burning blushes, though for no transgression,*
> *Tremblings when met, and restlessness when left.*
> *All these are little preludes to possession. . . .*

She hated herself for thinking only of Rich Friend in the high-thread-count sheets of the Beverly Hills Hotel. She stared at her cell phone sitting next to her stack of papers, longing to call him—she had hastily explained her panicked departure of yesterday in a message, but wanted to hear his voice, and know that he forgave her. She had tried to never mention Nora to Rich, to keep their worlds apart. But she heard Mitch walking in from his garage office.

"*Crucio!*"

He was moving toward her, flinging his arm forward, dressed in jeans, a nicely pressed shirt, and his bathrobe. June was perplexed.

"What the hell are you wearing?"

"I was just trying to get the feel of a robe. Today is that *Harry Potter* thing."

"Oh, right." June looked back at her papers, glanced at her watch. She should get going.

"*Avada cadavra!*"

June did not look up this time; she was busily gathering her papers together.

"Wand or no wand?" Mitch asked her.

"What?"

"Should I go out in the garden and get a stick?"

"For what?" June said, not really paying attention.

"For a wand! I'm a wizard, June!"

"No. I think that's stupid. Who expects you to bring a wand? Just act."

"I guess." Mitch looked doubtful. "Hey, I also have that audition coming up for that foulmouthed-friend thing. Tad says it's straight to DVD. I don't care. I need to do a movie, even a shitty one."

"I thought you had an audition for that Joy what'shername's film?"

"I don't know if I have a chance there. I mean, a run-of-the-picture role working with Ridley Scott? I bet they'll stunt-cast that. So listen, can you run a few lines with me for another audition I have later? It's a half hour about a guy who just lost two hundred pounds."

June sighed. Not again. But Mitch had gotten almost superstitious about reading lines with her before big auditions. She understood that he needed the comfort it gave him, but she had lost all enthusiasm about reading sides and giving acting notes. "Okay, but I have to get to work soon."

Mitch tossed the sides at her, and she glanced at them, trying to summon energy.

Mitch began. "*I have another hot date tonight.*"

"*Did you meet her on the Internet?*" June read.

"*Nope, the Shell station.*"

June imagined the roar of canned laughter.

"*Well at least you don't look like you work at the Shell station anymore.*"

"*Yeah I know! I just got a facial peel!*" Mitch said, tapping furiously under his chin with the back of his hand as he spoke. The dull thud of skin on skin distorted the line.

"Uh, it's good," June said. "But that chin thing is kind of distracting. Maybe you should drop that."

Mitch heaved a huge sigh and threw his sides on the floor. "I'm trying to be creative here, make some interesting choices. I guess I'm no good."

"What are you talking about?"

"This is all I've got!" Mitch said, beating madly with the back of his hand on his chin. "The chin thing! That's what I've got! Hey, you know what? I'm done here! I'm not going in!"

"Well, one thing you could try—" June was attempting to stay calm.

"I'm not going in, June. It's not worth it. I'm a shitty actor. All I have is my instincts, and I guess you think my instincts are rotten."

"You know what, Mitch? Don't ask for my opinion if you don't want to hear it. I have my own career, Mitch, and my own problems. When was the last time you thought of me anyway? Do I ask you to read my tenure package? When have you asked me about my book? Meetings with my department head? Why is it you never even think to buy me a volume of poems?"

Mitch was startled by June's outburst. He pushed his hands into the pockets of his bathrobe and looked at the ground. June felt a dart of guilt, but not enough to apologize. And now she was late. She walked out of the house, wordlessly, and heard Mitch on the phone loudly canceling the audition with Tad.

"I'm not going in on the audition about the guy who works at the Shell station. I don't have a take on it and I won't do a good job. I'm not auditioning."

Walking toward the driveway, June saw a woman she vaguely recognized from somewhere. Where was it? School? Please no. Oh, right, the bus stop bench ad at the corner of Pico and Beverly Glen, where the housekeepers all lined up each day at 5 p.m. June almost didn't recognize her without the Magic Marker mustache. It was one of the Bizzy Blondes, from the real estate outfit.

This "blonde" was fiftyish and had a chin-length mane of thick, stiff, frosted hair, almost wiglike. She looked like a grade-school teacher, with a crinkly smile, through which sparkly overwhite teeth

194

peeked. She was wearing a dark blue suit and was carrying a giant poinsettia.

"Hi, neighbor! Do you have any special needs?"

"Not really," said June, rushing.

"It's still a great market. Are you thinking of selling?"

"I don't know, ask my husband. He's inside. I need to go. Sorry."

"Terrific! I'll ask him then!" the realtor said brightly.

June walked past the Bizzy Blonde, to her car. Parked next to it was a Lincoln Navigator. License plate: SLFSH.

Sitting in her department head's office a half hour later, June was uncomfortable. Her stomach tended to hurt when she was tense, and today she could barely stand the cramping. Ouch. She needed to go to the bathroom. The tag of her shirt was scratching the back of her neck. She wanted to leave, go home, and start the day over. She was worried about what she was going to do when she saw Lexi at school again. She didn't regret what she had said. Well, maybe the ugly-clothes remark. But on the other matters, she wished she had said more. But she didn't want to harm Nora.

"Anyway, June, the point is, while your students continue to admire you and speak well of you, and there is no denying your past success here at UCLA, we can't help but notice that you've seemed really distracted this semester," Bob said.

"Distracted?"

"Yes." Bob continued. "We understand you've been late for class a few times, you've asked for an extension on your tenure package, which is quite unprecedented here, and you have not published all that you said you would this year. And I have yet to see much progress on your book."

June's head scrambled. She could not blame family life. That would kill her. Pilot season? No chance. Certainly not the truth: *Well, I've been having a lot of sex and it has left with me less time than I might have liked to prepare my package.*

"And you postponed this meeting, which is unlike you." Bob leaned toward June carefully. She looked down at his shoes, worn Docksiders. His pants were pleated, and his shirt pulled tightly over his stomach. For some odd reason June's thoughts went to a photo she had seen

195

recently of air traffic controllers on a picket line in the 1980s. They were all so thin. When did American men all get so paunchy?

"So what I am trying to ask you, June, is this. Are you sure you want to be a tenured professor here? Are you up to it?"

June stared back, meaning to answer quickly in the affirmative. She had to get to a bathroom. "Can I get back to you? I'm really not feeling well." June bolted, assuming Bob thought she was either pregnant or menstruating. Sitting on a couch in the faculty bathroom, doubled over in pain, she listened to her voice mail. One from Rich Friend: "Don't worry, babe. We'll always have the Beverly Hills Hotel." She smiled in spite of her agony.

In class, Taylor, her favorite student, was particularly enthusiastic, which was encouraging. Taylor made a bevy of points about poetic structure, and links between Greek and Roman poetry, Romanticism, and the blues.

June listened, smiling, as Taylor said, "I know it's not fashionable at the moment, but structuralist poetics offers such fundamental insights into language and the way language creates us—if you ask me, no one ought to be able to get even an undergraduate degree in any humanistic discipline without at least passing familiarity with the Russian formalists."

It was a small moment of happiness in June's day, and she approached Taylor after class to compliment her.

"You're doing so well, Taylor, I am really considering your earlier request to be my assistant. Candidly, I could use the help right now while I work on my book."

"Terrific! Can I ask you one other thing? I know you are so busy and I hate to bother you."

"It's no bother, please."

"Well, your husband is Mitch Gold, right?"

"He is."

Taylor began to gush. "I know his work well. He is such a tender character actor. Shakespearean really. And while I love poetry, I do have other aspirations. Would you mind terribly giving him this?" Taylor handed June a manila envelope, which June opened with trepidation. She pulled out a headshot of her prize student.

It was a color glossy eight-by-ten in which Taylor was wearing a low-cut black sheath, her heavily made-up eyes staring into the camera. Taylor's usually pulled-back hair was flying all her around her face, which wore a sultry pout.

"I don't know if it might be possible for your husband to pass this on to his agent? I know it's a lot to ask, but I have done a ton of student films and even a few nonunion commercials. . . ."

June placed the photo in her briefcase, her face carefully neutral. "Thank you, Taylor. I'll try to give it to him."

June went back to her office, defeated. She reflected on Taylor's participation in class all year. How could it be possible that this brilliant girl was actually only interested in working in the entertainment world? Hadn't she been the one to give such wonderful commentary on Fagles's translation of *The Aeneid*? June went to Amazon to look up Fagles's book, now that it was on her mind. She toyed with the idea of buying a copy for Rich.

June scrolled through the book's Amazon page, absentmindedly reading the comments and reviews left by readers. She wondered if any of her colleagues had posted. One comment, from the northwestern United States, stopped her. She felt cold as she read and reread it, disbelievingly.

When he chooses to be less literal, it seems he's aiming for polish, which I don't want. No doubt he wants to avoid vulgar overliteralness—he knows that the Romans didn't feel the full specific and literal impact of every verbal stem—but instead of deepening the accuracy through attention to idiom, I feel that his choices insert just a bit too much stuffiness between me and Virgil.

Taylor had memorized every line of the review and recited it perfectly during class. June began to flip through her class list—who else was faking an interest in poetry just to get a headshot to Mitch? June felt the pangs in her stomach again. She had been cocooned in Westwood, thinking she was immune to the duplicitous, double-handed ways of Hollywood while she was safe in academia. But, she had to concede, duplicity took on many forms.

Later, as she pulled up to her house, hitting the curb as she parked, she was relieved to see that Mitch did not appear to be home.

June raced through the front door and into her bedroom. She looked frantically for two of Taylor's papers that she had not graded and returned yet, which were in a file with her other students' work. She spent the better part of the afternoon Googling sentences from Taylor's essays, occasionally finding wholly plagiarized quotes, down to the italics from online book reviews. She felt compelled to continue, Googling and Wikipedia-ing over and over in search for any other evidence against her student.

And there it was again. Taylor's commentary on the Russian formalists.

In truth, Taylor was clearly not cut out for an academic life—she had not learned anything, but rather had memorized it, like lines in a script. Her acting had been good enough to fool June, and for that, she had to give her odd credit. Yes, her methods were sleazy and lacking consideration for anyone other than herself, but on this point June knew she was no better. She would give the headshot to Mitch.

She dialed Adrian.

"Hey, sweetie, where have you been?"

"Adrian, I can't live here anymore. I hate it. HATE IT."

"What happened?"

June started to cry. "I just hate them all. They are all from the same cloth, really, people trying to stave off death with exercise, lactose intolerance, and headshots." She sobbed.

"You're not making a lot of sense, sweetie," Adrian said.

"There is nothing in this town for anyone!" June was sobbing harder now. "And . . . I have a lover."

"I knew it. I knew it. Listen to me. I am meeting someone for dinner right this very second and I can't just no-show, so I have exactly twelve minutes for you to give me the bare bones."

"It's Rich Friend."

"Yikes. That producer guy you hate?"

June had spoken disparagingly of Rich once or twice to Adrian, out of her own guilt.

"Well, I hate him sometimes." For the next eleven minutes, June told Adrian about the velvety soft blankets, the sex culled from a Japanese erotic drawing, the tuna at the Beverly Hills Hotel.

"Why are you telling me about a sandwich?" Adrian asked.

"I don't know. It was good. Anyway, it all caused me to fuck up my day with Nora. My whole life, as you can see, is a disaster."

"Listen, June honey, we need to talk more about this all later. Let me just give you three bullet points: One: I feel bad for Mitch. He's a weirdo, but he's our weirdo. Two: I still don't judge you, know that. I get it. Three: You need to end it, now, and we're going to walk through how to do that. So you call me in forty-five minutes, I'll pretend you're my stepmonster, because that hag is always calling with fake emergencies, and then I'll politely pay the check and leave and will call you back then, okay?"

June sniffed. "I'll be giving Nora a bath."

"You can talk right after. Just go sit in your car. Where you are, doesn't everybody talk on the phone in their cars? I have to go. Remember. Forty-five minutes. Loveyoumeanit." Adrian hung up.

June placed the phone on Mitch's nightstand right next to a pile of chewed-up Post-it notes.

CHAPTER 19

According to the clock on her new stove, Larissa had been on hold for nearly five minutes, waiting for Walter Vanguard to take her call. Should she just hang up? Would that be considered rude? Or was it possible that his moronic assistant had never told him she was waiting? Should she call back? She glanced at her flat-screen television, which was tuned to CNN. Huh, they caught one of those Taliban guys. He was hot. Shame those guys couldn't have come to LA to do something more productive, like male modeling.

She wished Walter would hurry. The whole environmental thing was not working out well for Larissa Dermot, she felt. Too many rules, too much inconvenience, plus she could never keep track of what lunch boxes were lead-free. Larissa had decided to move on to public education. She understood that world—after all, she had gone to a public school herself, but she had never been a melting glacier—and Walter was eager for her help.

Walter, who was head of Fast Track Productions, was developing three movies this spring, and Larissa had her eye on at least two roles for Willie. But Walter was also very interested in early education, and was putting his name behind a ballot initiative that would require mandatory public preschools with certified teachers in every class, which seemed like a good idea to Larissa. Walter and Larissa had met at the premiere of *Magical Beings*, a Fast Track blockbuster in which Willie played a priest, and Larissa had made a point of doing a deep Google search on Walter. She had eagerly agreed to make phone calls to women to help raise money to pay for signature gathering for his initiative. She had gotten several other actors' wives, a producer or two, and Helen Hunt on board.

Finally Walter picked up. "So sorry, Larissa, thanks for holding. How are you?"

"Super, Walter, thanks. I just wanted to let you know that I am about twenty thousand dollars from our goal! I should have a few more checks for you by the end of the week."

"Fantastic, Larissa," Walter said. Larissa could tell he was chewing something. "You have been a tremendous help. I can't thank you enough for this." Smack. Gulp.

Larissa heard someone yelling in the background, and squeezed her eyes together with annoyance. "Hey, who took my Quiznos? That's the third freaking time this week!"

"Larissa, let me shut my office door, hold on." Chomp.

Larissa waited. Walter finally came back. "So, great, anyway, as soon as you have those checks."

"Will do. Oh, just one quick thing. I read the *Me So Horny* script. It is hilarious! You have got to have Willie in on that. He is perfect for Marshall."

"I'll shoot an e-mail to Cathy Sandrich—she's casting it. Have Willie's agent call her." Slurp, gulp.

Larissa hung up and felt light with glee. She could get big checks from Flea of the Red Hot Chili Peppers; Jane Kaczmarek and Wendie Malick said they were good for two thousand dollars each; and Julie Kavner's and Miley Cyrus's agents said they would donate a thousand each. A few had asked if they could get a tax deduction. The lawyers said that was illegal, but she figured there must be a way around that.

Larissa had worked every possible angle she could to get to Holly-wood pockets. Jane had done a pilot with Willie, and Larissa had called her assistant relentlessly, dropping the name of the producer of that show. She had sent a giant box for Julie's toy drive, and she knew Miley's stylist, and worked her hard at a recent screening to get her publicist's phone number, with a promise that she would make a call to Anna Wintour at *Vogue* to get her name mentioned in the front of the magazine. Promises, name dropping, handbags. Those were Larissa's currency.

If she could get this thing paid for, Willie would have a major in at

Fast Track. Her plan was to move him out of television and into just doing features.

In her deepest soul, Larissa had still not let herself believe that she would never have to work again, never fold a sweater and refold it just to look busy on the sales floor of Benetton, never balance another person's checkbook, never again step foot in a Courtyard by Marriott. Maui, even at Christmas. Always at Christmas.

She needed some small donors. Who? Who? Who? She had hit up all the richest moms at school. She had gotten a check from demi. Lexi kept promising, but she was cheap. Maybe June. She was always talking up education.

"Hello."

"June, it's Larissa!"

"Hey. I responded to your e-mail, if that's why you're calling. I'm really sorry, but I can't carpool to La Brea Tar Pits again."

"I got that. I am actually calling for a different reason, June. I was wondering if you would be interested in giving money toward Prop 88, which will fund preschool for all?"

"Oh, does that thing have title and summary already?" June asked.

"Huh? I don't know." Larissa said, knocked momentarily off her game. She had heard someone use that expression, but she hadn't really been paying attention.

"I guess it must if you're raising money. I'm surprised this is your thing, Larissa. Aren't you sending Chloe to private school next year?"

"Well. Some people that we know send their kids to public school. I mean we'll look and everything." Larissa sounded uncomfortable. "Do I have to live in a housing project to care about housing? I mean you don't experiment on your kids."

"I don't know what that means. But anyway, I don't like the part in the proposition about teacher certification. It will drain all the certified teachers out of the ongoing schools," June said.

"I haven't looked into that, but I am totally sure that Walter Vanguard would never do anything to hurt any public schools. He's a huge supporter of them!"

"Yes, that's why he sent all his kids to The Willows. I've got a class to teach, Larissa. I need to run."

June hung up the phone and was vaguely haunted by the realization, which hit her from time to time, that all the people in the city of Los Angeles whom she hated probably hated her right back. This bothered her momentarily. And then she went back to her issue of *Gourmet*.

CHAPTER 20

The drive to Fox studios, where Mitch had his audition for the dirty-mouthed friend, was less than a mile long. As he made his way east on Pico, reciting his lines for the audition and not paying much attention, a gray Land Cruiser with dealer plates cut in front of him without signaling, then immediately slowed down. Mitch moved to the left lane, and looked in the open window of the Land Cruiser. The driver, who was on the phone, moved in front of him, once again without a signal. Irritated, Mitch moved back to the right lane, and found himself side by side with Mr. Annoying. Mitch leaned out his window and called to the guy, who looked to be about twenty-five, a baseball cap pulled low over his eyes and wearing a golf shirt.

"Hey, nice car," Mitch said, smiling.

"Yeah, love her," Mr. Annoying yelled over Jack-FM radio.

"All the bells and whistles, huh? Leather seats, Bose sound system, looks like some color-coordinated bumpers? Must have cost a bundle, uh?" Mitch asked.

Mr. Annoying smiled smugly. "Oh yeah."

As the light began to change Mitch called out, "Next time, why don't ya pay a little extra for a FUCKING TURN SIGNAL?"

Mitch peeled away, leaving Mr. Annoying looking confused, as if he had just driven his sixty-five-thousand-dollar car through a plate-glass window.

Mitch turned his car into the parking structure at Fox and made his way toward the studio, mumbling his lines as he walked. Another Hawaiian-shirt part. He could do this. Beep beep. A text from Joy. "At the Grill with Ridley. Talking U up and eating salad w/ French. Ready for audition?"

Mitch smiled. Joy was fun.

When his name was called, Mitch tried to sort of amble into the room, the way he pictured a middle-aged loser attempting to be hip might do. The casting team and the director, A. J. Pierce, an odd-looking string bean of a man with a head of greasy hair, who was known for a series of successful teen sex comedies, exchanged a minute of polite small talk with Mitch. They inquired about pilot season and noted his last film while the guy taping the audition set his camera up.

"Well, Mitch, so you have any questions about the part?" A.J. asked.

Mitch never knew the right answer to this question. If he had questions, would he look dumb? If he didn't have questions, would he seem incurious? He usually erred on the side of having no questions, if for no other reason than he could never think of any.

"No, no questions. I'm good to go."

In this scene, Paulie was advising his friend on how to convince his girlfriend to make a porno video with him, in order to play it for cops and distract them while he conducted a jewel heist. The scene, not to mention the entire script, actually made no sense, but Mitch was determined to give the audition his all.

"*So this is what you tell her: 'Here's the plan, babe. You get some of your friends, and we like order some Domino's Pizza and some peppermint schnapps and you pretend to be the delivery gal. So then I get the camera rolling and you start sucking me off while the other girls make a salad. Then, maybe, you grab another girl's titties, that kind of thing, and then like the other girls start like eating pepperoni off each other's titties too.' And then before she comes you tell her, 'Okay, you be my cock jockey forever and I'll get behind your whole NASCAR dream.'*"

Mitch read the lines as if they were a mere grocery list, the only way to do material this vulgar. The casting director looked at A.J.

"Would you like to see anything else?"

A.J. gazed carefully at Mitch and began his critique, his tone suggesting he was Ingmar Bergman shooting the chess-playing knight in *The Seventh Seal.*

"That was good, Mitch. But I think when you talk about the titties, you really need to connect to that more. Maybe make some hand motions, like this." The director began to grab the air as if milking a cow.

"Uh-huh," Mitch said, dutifully squeezing the air too.

"Yeah, and 'cock jockey.' Really, really sell that. Remember, it's the cock, not the jockey. You get what I mean?"

"Sure, A.J. Let me try it again with more cock, a little less jockey."

Mitch thought about Joy's movie and silently prayed he would get it.

The next stop was over at CBS Radford, where Mitch was auditioning for the part of an ex-husband on Lone Star Gals. Tad had called to tell him the part had been made a regular instead of a recurring, so he agreed to go in on the pilot. But Mitch did not feel well prepared. It was June's fault. What was wrong with her anyway? It seemed like everything had been okay until she literally woke up a new woman, one who no longer seemed invested in him. Then again, maybe he had been too hard on her. Well, whatever was going on with him and his wife, fixing the situation between them was priority number one. After pilot season.

Lone Star Gals was on the CW Network, which was jointly owned by Time Warner and CBS, but Tad assured him this would not hurt his chances. Les Moonves would never know. This seemed impossible to Mitch. Didn't Les Moonves know everything? But on he went.

CBS Radford had a no-drive-on policy. Mitch parked on the street a few blocks away, near the dried-up Los Angeles River, and meandered past the small stucco bungalows that lined the streets near the studio. He walked through the gate and checked in with security, showing them his ID and announcing his audition for Lone Star Gals.

The guard handed him a small white map and directed him to building 18.

"Come up to Gilligan's Island Road, take a left, past Mary Tyler Moore Avenue, take a right on Gunsmoke Avenue, go on past St. Elsewhere Street and My Three Sons Street, and you'll be at 18, right at Newhart Street."

As he made his way past a cluster of trailers, Mitch overheard a young production assistant in a long sweater and jeans, her hair pulled into a ponytail, talking to an even younger black guy in a Cal State

Fullerton sweatshirt, who was simultaneously chatting with someone through an earpiece.

"How far is base camp from set?" asked the girl, pulling on her hair a bit.

"About a quarter of a mile," the Cal State lover answered.

"Can I have a small holding pen for the background?" she asked, referring to the industry term for extras.

"Sure."

"Maybe some lights, too."

"What do you need, wackers?"

"Yeah, give me a bunch," the girl said.

Mitch found building 18 and went in to join a dozen other actors who were also waiting. He looked up from his sides and saw Chris Rock, with whom he had worked on a few movies. A dozen pairs of blazing eyes, attached to twelve actors seething with envy, landed on Mitch's neck as Chris greeted him.

"Hey, Mitch, wassup!"

"Hey, Chris, shooting today?"

"Yeah man. What are you here for?"

"I'm reading for *Lone Star Gals.*"

"You're reading? They've having *you* read? They're having you *read?*"

Mitch snorted at this insulting compliment. Chris seemed to expand by a foot in each direction as he threw his arms around, peering around the room in an animated way, as if he might find the director under a chair.

"Where's the casting director?"

"In the office, in session."

Chris Rock marched through the casting office, with Mitch, curious, trailing behind him. The rest of the actors quietly gathered outside the office, disbelieving. Chris banged open the inner room within the office, where Wayne Knight was in the middle of his audition. Mitch could see only the back of Chris's head and the horseshoe formation of casting people and show executives. The comedian began to yell.

"My friend Mitch Gold's out there. He's the best character actor in Hollywood. You're making him read? Why don't you just offer him the fucking part? Why is he reading?"

There was silence as the producers quickly made the calculation that, as infuriating as it was to have this unprofessional and embarrassing disruption, no one at the CW was going to stand up to one of the tiny network's biggest stars.

Wayne Knight turned his doughy, bespectacled face toward Chris Rock and began to stare impassively, wearing the Hollywood confrontation mask.

"Man, you got the mailman from *Seinfeld* in here! You're making the mailman from *Seinfeld* read? What's wrong with this fucking town?"

Chris Rock, his face contorted with rage, turned his back to the room, then began smiling. A young assistant with long braids was rushing toward him.

"Hey, baby, get me a sandwich."

He passed Mitch—"Later, man"—and breezily walked out, chatting cheerfully with his assistant about what scenes of *Everybody Hates Chris* were up after lunch.

Mitch sighed. *The best character actor in Hollywood.* So why didn't Chris put him on his show? Compliments in television could buy a Ferrari, but actual job offers kept him in an eight-year-old Saab.

Wayne Knight emerged from the casting room and glared at Mitch. "Thanks a lot, fat ass," he said, waddling away.

Mitch's name was called, and he walked into the casting room, now tarnished yet gilded, reviled but admired. No one in the room mentioned the outburst of sixty seconds ago. Mitch read his lines, using his best Texan accent.

"*Audra, if y'all expect me to me to light your barbecue, y'all need to light somethin' of mine.*"

Good, a few laughs.

June walked into Clementine feeling victorious. She had actually gotten a parking spot in the back, which was unheard of. She had been thinking about the restaurant's tomato soup, followed by a ginger snap, all day. Rich, insisting that he had already eaten the best tomato soup in Los Angeles at Doughboys on Third Street, was meeting her at the

Century City lunch haunt almost as a dare. She wondered about going to such a public place, but he assured her that no industry people ate there. In truth, she could not wait to see him.

She walked past the outdoor tables into the small restaurant and was daunted by the line that had already formed toward the door. People stood patiently, cell phones pressed to their ears, pausing from their conversations to order grilled cheese sandwiches, turkey pot pies, banana cream pie slices, and couscous salads. She walked to the right of the room and saw Rich, in yet another pair of expensive jeans and a blue dress shirt that deliciously defined his shoulders, hunched over a pile of papers, murmuring into his phone, a cup of coffee teetering close to the edge of his small rickety table. She motioned to him that she was getting in line, and he blew her a kiss. Divine.

As June moved toward the counter she felt someone staring at her. She looked closely and realized it was someone she knew.

"June, hey, what are you doing here?" said the tallish, expensively dressed man whom she recognized but for the life of her could not place. He craned his neck around the room. "Is Mitch with you?"

"No. I was, um, looking for pie. I wanted pie. I like pie."

"Yes, well they have pie here." The man laughed. Shit, shit, shit. She recognized that guttural groan instantly. Tim Zelnick, Mitch's agent at CAA. What had she been thinking? She should have known better than to meet her lover a few blocks from her husband's talent agency.

"Yep, they do have pie! I need to run, though. I need, um, some stationery."

"They have good coffee here. I always come over after lunch."

"Uh-huh," June said, wondering why he was telling her this. She wanted to leave. Tim looked around the restaurant.

"Hey, I think that's Rich Friend over there." Tim pointed in Rich's direction. "Come here, I want you to meet him—he's a cool guy. He and his wife are terrific writers. Mitch is going in on their new show. Have you ever met Rich?"

June dragged morosely behind Tim. "I think so. I mean maybe once."

Tim walked up to Rich's table, holding his coffee, and Rich seemed tickled. "Hey, Tim, how are you man?" he said.

"Terrific. Busy. You know Mitch Gold's wife, June?"

"No, I don't believe we've ever met," Rich said, shaking June's hand and smiling broadly. "What do you do?"

"I'm a professor. Of literature. Anyway, nice to meet you, Rich. I need to run, though. I am late for class."

"I thought you wanted pie," said Tim, staring at what June was convinced were her reddening cheeks.

"Um, I should make my own pies," June said, inanely, she knew. She looked toward Rich, but he was already peering out the window at his silver Porsche parked at the curb, apparently checking to make sure no one had touched it. June left without saying good-bye.

As he settled into his chair at Starbucks, Mitch could not resist calling Tad, even though he had promised to leave him be with the animal hypnotist.

"Tad, how's Vegas?"

"How's Vegas? Here's how fucking Vegas is. Candy Christmas ripped me off!"

"What?"

"The bitch stole my wallet and took off."

"What happened?"

"Well, I took her to the Italian joint at the hotel, B&G, G&G, some shit, I don't know, she sent back her pasta three times, saw some pork fleck in it or something. Then we hit the blackjack table, I had a great night, cleared five thousand bucks. Back at the room, wild time, rode me like a freakin' Appaloosa. Then, boom, I'm out!"

"Wow. You passed out?"

"No, she hypnotized me!" Tad said. "I wake up, no Candy, no five grand, and no wallet. The cunt cleaned me out and racked up four thousand bucks on my Visa at the Bellagio before I even knew what happened."

"Whoa, that's wild!"

"Anyway, listen, since you called, I can't get on a plane because I don't have my ID, and my assistant quit on Friday. Could you get me a Greyhound ticket back to LA?"

"Yeah, no problem, But while you're waiting on that, can you get feedback on my auditions today?"

"Mitch, did you listen to a word I just said? I told you I got robbed! I am about to sit for seven hours with a bunch of meth heads on a stinking Greyhound bus. So excuse me if I can't call the CW for you."

"Really? 'Cause you're kind of sitting there anyway—"

Tad had hung up.

Mitch listened to Muzak on the Greyhound switchboard from his Starbucks chair for nearly an hour to arrange for Tad's ticket for an eight-hour-and-ten-minute ride with the sort of people who, hungover and wrecked by slot machines, rode a bus between Vegas and Los Angeles.

Mitch called Tad to let him know that everything was in order.

"Thanks, man. Oh, I called the casting director on the foulmouthed thing. They said you were by far the best audition of the day, and I am quoting directly here: 'The funniest guy we've had in for the role.'"

"Great!" Mitch said, elated.

"Yeah, and I know it sucks, but they also said you're never going to get the job."

"Why?"

"Can you believe? They want a twenty-year-old,"

"They knew I was forty when I went in!"

"Yeah. Sorry. I wish I had better news about the ex-husband gig, but that one's dead too. Wayne Knight's going to the network. It's all about short, fat. You're too tall and too fit."

"Who wants a fat actor for a romantic role?"

"Fat's the new skinny for men. Listen, I need to get walking to the Greyhound station. It's almost one hundred and ten degrees here. Later, Mitch."

"Okay, see ya."

Mitch slammed his phone shut and stalked out of Starbucks and back to his car. He turned the ignition and looked in his mirror, and his mind wandered through the files of failed auditions over a fifteen-year career, landing on the ones that had nothing to do with the work itself. Too young, too old, too skinny, too Jewish, not Jewish enough. He began muttering lines from an audition a decade ago for *Suddenly Susan*. No one had laughed. Why? Why? He started saying the lines aloud trying to find the joke that had eluded him all those years ago.

As he made his way east on Pico, he was cut off again, this time by a red Jag, and had to slam on his brakes to avoid hitting it. As both cars were stopped for the light, Mitch threw his car into park and stormed toward the Jag, driven by a woman with giant round sunglasses, her hair pulled back into a curly bun. Her skin was stretched tightly, and a faint surgical line ran along her chin. A pink leather dream catcher swung from her rearview mirror.

"What the hell?" Mitch asked.

She said nothing, but flipped him off with a long, perfectly mani-cured, deep magenta nail, and zoomed away as the light changed and the cars behind Mitch began to honk furiously. Mitch, full of outrage, jumped back in his car and pressed hard on the gas to catch up to Jag Bitch, whom he in turn cut off.

At the next light she moved to cut him off again, and the two pro-ceeded to cut each other off for several lights, until Mitch, clutching his steering wheel with rage, made a right turn on Beverwil just to shake her, but to his amazement the Jag followed him, right on his bumper, the woman glaring at him, as the two cars wound their way through Beverly-wood. She was so close he could see her in his rearview mirror, her lips pursed sourly, like a small pug, her face obscured in part by the giant glasses.

Eager to escape her, but unable to turn around, Mitch pulled into a driveway on a tiny street. Before he could back out, the Jag had blocked him in, its curly-haired owner sitting glowering, unmoving. Los Ange-lenos and their cars had a relationship that was so intrinsic—as with a pet, or even a child—that zealous overreactions toward minor slights were the norm. Mitch had seen, and even participated in, much of it: road rage, drag racing among forty-year-old advertising executives on the 10 Freeway, minivan tailgating in the carpool lane at preschool.

Mitch got out of the car, popped open the trunk and grabbed his nine iron, and made his way toward the Jag, the club aloft. He tapped on the car window with his club, and called, "Are you a maniac? Can you move? I swear I will use this."

"Did you think you could outrun me in that sad little Saab? You're not going to do anything. You'll go to jail and you know it," Jag Bitch countered, sneering.

"Just get out of my fucking way, lady."

He heard Jag Bitch through her window. "Yes, operator, I do have an emergency! There's a maniac man on Sawyer Street trying to batter my car with a golf club!"

"Move the car—you're the maniac!" Mitch screamed.

Jag Bitch refused even to look through her darkened windows.

Enraged, Mitch spit at her windshield and stalked back toward his own car. He dialed June. When she picked up, he quickly yelled, "You need to get over to Sawyer and Monte Mar right fucking now. I am blocked in a driveway by a crazy lady, and the cops are on their way!"

June sounded like she was in her car, too. "What?"

"Just hurry!"

Within a few moments Mitch heard the ominous wail of a police siren. A more composed man would have tucked the nine iron back into his trunk by now. Mitch was not that man.

Instantly, it seemed, there was a Los Angeles Police Department helicopter hovering, and two cops on motorcycles soon pulled up.

"Drop the weapon!" bellowed one, his tattoo-covered arm moving toward his gun.

Mitch dropped the club, and the more burly of the cops grabbed him, frisked him, and put him in handcuffs, pulling his arms tightly behind his back.

Mitch yelled, "This is all a huge mistake! HUGE mistake. This woman was cutting me off in traffic like a crazy person!"

Jag Bitch opened her mouth, and a much higher- and sweeter-pitched voice than the one she had used to Mitch came out. "I was so scared. He damaged my car."

The cop looked closely at Mitch. "Did you damage this lady's car?"

Jag Bitch piped up. "He spat on it!"

The cop looked back at Mitch. "Hey, you were on *Alias*, right?"

"That's right."

"That was a great show. So, did you spit on her car? Or maybe did you spit *toward* her car?" The cop glanced at the Jag's windshield.

"Well, I think—" Mitch began.

"From my observation of her vehicle, you appear to have spit toward the car. Not on it." The cop stared hard at Mitch, whose wrists were chafing badly under the cuffs.

"Um yeah, toward it," Mitch said, suddenly understanding that if he had spat *on* the car, he would likely be sent to the Los Angeles County Jail.

June made her way down Pico, tapping her foot anxiously as she seemed to hit every light. The call from Mitch had been alarming. She wavered between feeling panicked and annoyed. Her near miss with Tim Zelnick earlier had already set her on edge. She knew it was just another sign that she needed to adjust her life. She had to stop seeing Rich.

June sped down Motor, toward the street that Mitch had called from.

"Where are we going, Mommy?" asked Nora from the backseat.

"To see Daddy."

"Why?"

Unsure herself, June continued to stare at the road. "Um . . . we'll be there in a sec."

June looked out the windshield to see a police chopper hovering in the sky in exactly the direction she was headed. She began to feel more alarmed as she turned the corner of Monte Mar. She saw two police motorcycles, lights strobing, pulled in around a blue Saab and a red Jaguar. In the middle of it all stood Mitch, shirt rumpled, hair disheveled, and arms twisted behind his back, wrists locked together tightly by a pair of silver handcuffs that shone in the bright LA sunshine. At his feet lay a golf club.

"OH MY GOD!" June exclaimed.

"What, Mommy, what?" Nora's face was plastered to the passenger window.

"Nothing, Noony." Longing for a distraction, June shoved *Meet the Beatles* into the CD player and cranked it up.

Nora asked in a tear-filled voice, "Are those policemen taking Daddy away?"

June turned to face her. "Um, no, honey. He's, well, he's, he's just *working*. It's a movie! Daddy's just *pretending* to be a bad guy." She smiled cheerfully. "But, you know, he seems really busy. Let's catch him at home, okay sweet one?"

June made eye contact with Mitch as she sped away.

Mitch, seeing Nora's tiny face in the backseat of June's car, felt hot with shame.

Suddenly a man, maybe seventy, wearing a one-piece, zipper-front jumpsuit, pulled up in a Bentley. "You spat on my baby?" the man snarled.

Mitch wondered if he meant his apparent girlfriend or the car.

"I'm gonna take you out!" the man said, advancing on Mitch unsteadily.

The cops moved the decrepit suitor to the side and took the cuffs off of Mitch. "This seems like a settled matter," said the officer with the tattooed arm.

Jag Bitch was furious. "What? He threatened me! And his car is a piece of shit!"

"Okay, lady, move along. Have a nice day," the officer said.

Back at home June tried to appear unruffled as she stirred a pot of vegetable soup. Nora sat at the kitchen table, feeding James a cat treat. June's cell phone rang. Adrian.

"Hi there," June said.

"Hey, I wanted to see if you're okay."

"Oh, I'm okay. I can't talk much about it right now, because I am here with Nora. You know what would actually make me feel better is if we talk about you."

"Really? Are you sure?"

"Very sure. We talked enough about me the other night. Give me your news," June said.

"Okay, hon. Well, let me run this by you. Do you think I give bad three-way?"

"Um, how would I know that?"

"I don't know, June. Intuit. Because I met this couple in a bar last night and we had this really nice time, and I have to tell you, as three-ways go, I was exemplary. I mean, I gave total attention to both parties. . . ."

"Adrian, I'm sure you give excellent three-way. You're a generous person."

"Yeah, but then today, no phone call. Nothing."

June saw Mitch's car pull into the driveway. "I'd love to continue this conversation. Believe me. But Mitch is home and he nearly clocked a lady's car today with his golf club, so I gotta go."

"Oh God, did you tell him everything? Is he wise to Rich Friend?" Adrian asked.

"No. He arrived at this point without my help."

"Wow."

"Yes, my life is a miniseries, Adrian. But yet, somehow, not nearly as interesting as yours. I'll call you later."

"Bye, hon," Adrian said.

Mitch walked into the house, kissed Nora on the head, and walked toward June sheepishly.

"Why were you playing a bad guy, Daddy?" Nora asked.

"What?" Mitch said, confused.

"We saw you being a bad guy today on your movie,"

Mitch looked at June expectantly.

"Yes, Mitch, why so bad?" June asked.

"June . . ."

"Since you seem to have averted a night in the lockup, I don't think we need to address this, would you agree?"

"I'm guessing not," Mitch answered her.

"There's soup on the stove. I need to just run to the store. We're outta milk," June said, grabbing her keys and purse off the kitchen counter.

June tucked away into her car and dialed her lover's phone. No answer.

CHAPTER 21

Mitch and Joy were supposed to meet at her office around lunchtime to work one last time for the audition, which was the next day, but her assistant had called at the last minute and said she needed to reschedule. Could Mitch come to her house in Hancock Park around six instead?

Mitch pulled into the driveway of the Spanish-style mansion, and made his way past a spread of teak patio furniture, including a tea cart and large cushion box. He had seen that in one of June's catalogs. He knew it was pricey.

People in Los Angeles always rented houses fifteen times bigger than they actually needed, and as he peeked in the window at her kitchen—which was roughly the size of his backyard—Mitch wondered if Joy ever felt lonely there. His own kitchen counter, in a house half the size, would seem empty to him without Nora's Bob the Builder lunch box on top of it. Here, on Joy's soapstone counter, there was a pile of scripts. A house full of work, some of it, no doubt, that could be his.

"Hey, thanks for coming here. Did you have any trouble finding the place?" asked Joy, giving Mitch a fast peck on the cheek. He walked into the foyer and took in the details—vintage wallpaper, heavily upholstered chairs, big shuttered windows. They walked through a formal dining room, around the corner, and to a small sitting room with what appeared to be Louis XIV furniture. Joy's dog was asleep under the table.

"Thanks again for this, Joy. I really appreciate all your help," Mitch said. The house was spotless, more like a set than a home. He didn't even see a throw anywhere. Didn't she get cold? They sat down on two matching chairs, and Joy pulled hers right next to his.

"No worries, Mitch. You know I want you to get this part." Joy was sitting about three inches too close. Was that amaretto he smelled? Joy rolled her shoulders ostentatiously and flicked her neck from side to side. "I have this terrible thing with my neck," she said, sounding in pain. "I got horribly injured throwing the racket around last week." Why was she telling him this? Shit. He hoped she wasn't going to ask him to move furniture.

"What sport do you play?"

"Badminton."

"Wow. Those shuttlecocks can be rough, huh? So do you want to start?"

"In a minute," Joy said. "You know I would love something to drink. Do you want to check out my new juicer?" Mitch, dying to get reading, obediently followed Joy into her kitchen and endured a twenty-minute demonstration of her new kitchen toy. She slammed her knife down violently through a carrot, then shoved the pieces into her new appliance. "You'll see. This juice is better than sex!"

Mitch smiled at Joy, who turned off the roaring juicer and then poured him a cup. She dipped her pinkie in the carrot foam, then massaged his upper lip with her juice-covered finger. "Wow. Hot. This reminds me of that weird guy you played on *Boston Legal*."

"You saw that? I was on only once," Mitch said, sucking the juice off his lip. He felt flattered.

"Oh, I saw it. You were great. I loved you in *Ugly Betty*, season two, but didn't agree with the shirt they put you in. *Dumb Ass* I saw three times. You were so, so funny. The whole beehive bit. You wanna know a secret? I tried to get a nomination going for you for an Oscar for best supporting for that."

"Really?" Mitch was beginning to feel more than vaguely uncomfortable.

"Oh yeah," Joy said, putting her hand on his shoulder and tilting her head a little to the left. Her eyes seemed glassy. "You had that reoccurring part on *30 Rock*. I was in London for a lot of it but I watched it on DVR. *Molar Opposites* was hard to catch, but my assistant got them for me. That was a total injustice that they didn't pick you up for the back nine. And you were wonderful as Dr. Hyatt, too. I would let you touch my nipples anytime."

Sipping on the concoction, Mitch tried to convert this conversation into banal chatter. It was hotter than usual, but then again it had been colder than usual last month. (She agreed.) Should he watch out for that one producer when he met him, because he had heard the guy didn't shake hands? (Maybe, she said.) Did Joy read about that wreck with the crane on the 405 last week that shut down southbound traffic for six hours? "Most days I could get an entire colonoscopy waiting on the 405," Mitch joked.

Joy laughed hysterically. "Mitch, you are the only one who has ever made me laugh like that. I used to think about your jokes. I still do, while I am lying in bed." She ran her hands across her breasts and leaned toward him. "I think of you a lot when I'm in bed."

Mitch began to tap his foot nervously. Was this officially a betrayal of his marriage? He thought of Nora, her Harry Potter glasses askew, a bit of brownie on her chin. His desire for Joy to be something other than unhinged had been an illusion, fueled by his dreams of moving forward and beyond where he was in this town. Now the woman was rubbing her breasts, and if he played along, she would answer those dreams definitively.

"Do you want a salad?" Joy asked. "I bought you French dressing. I want you to get what you can't at home."

His mind zipped to a random memory of June, sitting on El Matador beach in Malibu eating sandwiches slightly laced with sand. She was pregnant with Nora, and the two of them sat quietly, watching a school of dolphins breach the surface and playing "would you rather." Mitch said he would rather eat live fire ants than change the diaper of an adult; June picked the diaper. She wanted to maintain her taste buds, she reasoned, and someday, if he asked nicely, she would change his diaper, too. He remembered that her lips tasted of fresh lemonade.

"Hey, Joy, I left my cell in my car. Let me just grab it."

"Sure. I'll pour us a bourbon. You always liked bourbon, right?"

"I did."

Mitch walked out to his car and opened the door as quietly as possible and quickly started the engine, then backed his car out of her driveway, turning it toward Larchmont Boulevard. One more job lost.

CHAPTER 22

Mitch was walking along Beverly Drive talking to himself in a very loud voice, scarcely aware of it. Today was the network audition for *Sole Operator*. Justine and Rich would be there, along with the head of ABC. "Well, I'm going to the network. Again. Big whoopie. Another chance to fail, to be too fat, too skinny. WHATEVER."

It had been several days since he'd blown off his audition on Joy's film, and Tad had been none too pleased: "No one said you had to fuck her! But couldn't you just drink her stupid juice and let her touch your knee?!" It was one of the more depressing exchanges he had had with Tad in recent months, but at least his downfall had come at his own hands, and not those of a casting director or a producer or a network head or a director. That was somehow comforting.

Mitch had decided to get a haircut in Beverly Hills before he went to the network. After the barber he had time left to grab lunch and get a new cell phone battery. While walking down the street Mitch noticed a guy staring at him, and Mitch stared back indignantly, until it dawned on him that maybe he had been talking to himself loudly enough for the other people on the sidewalk to hear him.

He was dreading the network, even though he had to concede that he had killed on the initial audition for Rich and Justine. Justine could not have been more complimentary—"That was fantastic, Mitch. It was like we wrote that part for you."

Rich had been . . . what's the word? Shitty. He never laughed during the audition, not a single tee-hee. In fact, Mitch never saw the guy's lips even turn upward.

Well. That seemed potentially disastrous. On the other hand, Justine had far more power at the network. As long as Mitch was Justine's first choice, it didn't matter what Rich thought. The prick. Mitch was sure he saw him use his foot wedge in the rough at Riviera. Anybody who cheats at golf has to be an asshole.

In truth, he had all but given up hope of getting a pilot this year. He was sure he would be dropped by CAA. He pulled on the neck of his shirt. He was itchy from the barbers, even though the stray hairs had been brushed off his neck. Clonk. A young woman, the sort who insisted on wearing a belly shirt even though she actually had a belly, had bumped into him.

"Oh, sorry!"

"What the hell's the matter with you? Are you blind? Raised by moles?"

The girl stood speechless, taken aback by Mitch's tone and the fact that he was waving his elongated arms in her face. She moved away quickly, turning back once to shoot him a dirty look.

"Hey, I know you!"

A twenty-something guy in a suit stopped and pointed at Mitch. His pants were a bit short; his shoes looked cheap. Oh great, Mitch thought, an aggressive fan.

"I know you, dude. You're an actor!"

"Yeah," Mitch sighed.

"You're really losing it, man. Yelling at that woman. You're losing it!" The guy continued walking, shaking his head at Mitch.

Mitch felt his stomach drop, abashed. He did a mental calculation: he was now the sort of person who yelled at strangers, fought with old birds in Jaguars, nearly got arrested for assault, took drugs and belted scotch before auditions, made his daughter miss her school festival, and neglected his wife, who had done nothing but try to assist him and ease his burdens. Yeah, he was losing it.

He looked for the girl to apologize. She was gone. He moved more slowly down Beverly now, and found himself standing in front of Williams-Sonoma. Sitting in the window was that ten-speed mixer that June had admired so many times, the bright blue one with the dough hook. He peered in closely to see if he could the read the price tag. Had he been a four-hundred-dollar jerk this year?

After his little shopping adventure, Mitch hauled his shopping bags into the trunk of his car and made his way south on Beverly and then west on Wilshire and Santa Monica to the ABC building on Avenue of the Stars. He decided to park at the Westfield Century City Mall and walk over to the building rather than valet-park, since the executives would have all the good spots reserved.

Mitch entered the network with the familiar knot in his stomach. It was his first audition in front of the network brass this season since the fiasco at CBS had prevented him from actually getting in on *My Dad Is Totally Weird.* While auditioning in front of casting directors was unpleasant, there was still a creative tension to that process, an attempt to impress people who knew something about the craft of performing.

Of all the indignities of acting—sitting in an excruciatingly heavy nineteenth-century period costume on a set in New Orleans in August; playing the role of a patient who had his testicles nipped by a shih tzu (a role Tad insisted was fine, as long as the dog wasn't hurt in the shoot); being forced to lose twenty-five pounds in two weeks to play a POW; opening $2.45 checks—auditioning for the network was by far the worst.

As he made his way through the hallway, Mitch saw whom he was up against for the brass ring: two other character actors, Kurt Fuller and Stephen Tobolowsky. Both were tall and slightly neurotic-looking—perfect for this part. "Hey, Mitch," Kurt mumbled, barely looking up. Stephen was friendlier. "Hey, Mitch, long time no see, watcha been up to?" Mitch made small talk with Stephen until Cheryl, the casting director for *Sole Operator,* walked up.

"Hey, Mitch," said Cheryl. "I just need you to sign off on your deal."

"Sure thing."

Mitch examined the sheet of paper outlining what Tad had negotiated for him. Definitely forty-five thousand a week, an extra week's pay if the pilot got picked up. A couch of some sort in his double banger. Single card, third billing. Parking looked fine. Still no gym membership. But not bad. Not bad. He signed it and handed it back to Cheryl.

"Great, let's hit it!"

All the network executives sat scattered throughout the room in seats.

Justine smiled broadly. "Hi, Mitch, great to see you."

Rich, lounging in his seat a few chairs down from Justine, seemed to Mitch to be scowling.

"Hi, Mitch."

"Hey, Rich."

"How's June?" Rich asked.

It was an odd question, seconds before an audition.

"Good. Thanks," Mitch said.

"I bet she thinks this is a weird part for you, right? The boss? Are you the boss at home?" Rich asked in a slightly mocking tone.

Justine looked incredulously at Rich, who stared back at her.

The head of the network, looking impatient, took off his glasses and rubbed the lenses with his shirt. "Uh, can we get to the business at hand?"

Justine immediately spoke up. "Of course! Mitch, please, whenever you're ready. Cheryl will be playing the role of Sam."

What had gotten into Rich lately? Mitch had thought they were buddies. And now the head of the network looked annoyed. None of this boded well. Mitch could hear his heart in his ears.

Mitch was playing Dean Mack, a newspaper editor, and Sam was a female reporter who had recently adopted a baby from what had been Ethiopia in the original script, but was now France. In the scene Mitch's character was supposed to be getting a manicure in his office in the newsroom. Mitch sat down in the tiny chair on the stage and spread his hands in front of him as if someone were filing his nails.

Cheryl began: *"Dean, don't mean to interrupt your big story meeting. Trying to decide whether to lead with pink or red?"*

"Sam, great to have you back! Parlez-vous peekaboo?"

Laughter. Mitch drew his breath in. It might be okay. Then it was Sam's line.

"Listen, why have you pulled me out of the White House? I am as capable a reporter now as I was before the baby."

"First of all, Sam, I don't see you making wheels up at Andrews at six a.m. Second, given that you adopted a baby from France, I don't see how you

can objectively cover diplomatic stories anymore. Uh, Me-ling, please push the cuticles back, don't cut."

Mitch was thrilled to hear a giggle from the head of the network.

"That's nuts, Dean. First of all, I covered the White House, not the State Department! Second, I am quite sure what you're doing is unethical. And finally, this is a breaking story that no one can cover but me!"

"Well, someone else is, and it's Valco. But listen, Samantha, where do you think I should take the ambassador from Oman to dinner? I was thinking Café Centro, but maybe someplace more Muslim-y?"

More laughter. Mitch felt better. Rich and his odd comment faded from his mind.

June sat at the end of the bed in the tiny room at the Hotel Angeleno on the corner of the 405 and Sunset. She ran her hands up and down the bedspread, and realized that she was now a mini expert on the bedding of various hotels on the West Side of Los Angeles, a topic she knew nothing about two months ago.

Two months ago, she was the anonymous face at the bake sale, the woman in the blue suede platform shoes racing around the moms in their yoga clothes, another mom at the bank, in a hurry to deposit her check.

She was a person whom her colleagues respected, a good associate professor, someone who was never late to meetings, always prepared for her department head, the one people came to for discreet advice about their own careers. A married professional woman with a child, often spotted buying organic chicken thighs. Now she was a person who used a fake name in hotels.

June didn't particularly believe in God, and was startled to find that she was praying. There she was, in the fading light of an early spring day, sitting on a hotel bed, begging God to let this be the last time that she made love to a person who was not her husband.

She began thinking about her wedding day, how she and Mitch had laughed at the dryness of the cake, which Mitch spit out dramatically after she shoved it in his mouth. No one could have convinced her that beautiful clear fall day in New York that she would ever again be with another man.

She dug around in her purse for ChapStick. She had ripped her horoscope earlier in the day from the *New York Post*, and its edges were rough and uneven, displaying half a Macy's ad.

It could seem like a very dull and dreary day today, made worse by the fact that someone just won't be on your wavelength. Give it time, Virgo; the rest of the week shows a dramatic improvement, so for today arm yourself with a couple of calming crystals, like hematite and opal, and power through!

Her phone rang. It was Rich Friend.

"Hey," June said.

"Hey, babe. I'm so sorry, but I need to bail on you. Our director just quit for a feature and now we're in a state of crisis. I've gotta deal with it."

June felt her heart sink. She had prayed moments ago for an end, and now felt deep disappointment that she wouldn't be touching her lover's skin on that soft brown bedspread, listening to the roar of the 405 beneath them. She was hoping she and Rich would snack on anchovies and wine later, at the bar on the eighteenth floor of the cylindrical white hotel, watching the sun lower over the ocean.

"That stinks," June sighed.

"I know. I miss you so much."

"Me, too." She paused. "Tell me three things you hate."

Rich spoke quietly. "That I hate . . . Let's see. . . . I hate dessert wines. I hate the smell of furniture polish. I hate people who say, 'You go, girl!' What about you, sweetheart?"

June thought for a moment: "I hate chestnuts. I hate when I'm walking by one of those leaf blowers and the cloud of dirt and twigs blows into my face. I hate that spot on Beverly Glen Boulevard where they have Astroturf instead of real grass."

"I hate that too. I have two more minutes. Let's do love."

"I love my first cup of morning coffee," June said. "I love making Bûche de Noël. I love Wilfred Owen poems. Go."

"I love when the Reds lose. I love this ratty Baylor University sweatshirt that I've had since high school that I refuse to throw away. Let me think. . . . Love . . . Love . . ."

June held her breath. Finally Rich said, "Oh, I know! I love when a show that's up against mine tanks."

He loved something that was a show. Not even a good show. June felt something—what was it, sadness, disappointment, despondency? Fear.

"I gotta run, June. Justine's coming. Bye!"

Thinking Rich had hung up, June kept the phone pressed to her ear, unable to quite let go. She listened to the silence, and then heard something that sounded like yelling. Was Rich still there?

"Where the hell have you been? You've been out for the last two hours doing God knows what while I'm trying to replace Tommy Schlamme!"

Justine.

"I had stuff to do," Rich said grumpily.

"What stuff? Piano lessons? Tennis court time you couldn't give up? Come on, Rich! This is real life. I'm doing this entire show by myself. You haven't done shit all season."

"That is totally unfair, Justine. I have been working my ass off! Meetings, rewrites, casting sessions—"

Justine began yelling louder. "Are you having a fantasy? You were in one casting session to be exact, and that was this morning. And what was your added value there? Making distracting remarks to Mitch Gold seconds before he had to audition. I've never seen anything like that! The network is deciding right this minute who we cast, and it had better be Mitch, my first choice!"

"Oh, Justine, keep your panties on. You always get what you want."

"Don't patronize me! You're really screwing this up, Rich, and don't think everyone around you can't see it. And by the way, if you're going to fuck that bimbo, can you do it *after* pilot season?"

June hung up quickly, her heart pounding. Justine knew! She knew everything. Except the part about her being a bimbo. June wasn't a bimbo. She was more like a paramour, right? What had Rich said to Mitch?

Holy shit. Would Justine tell Mitch. No, no, no! June told herself. Her brain began to race, fueled by fear, searching for schemes. Sadly, she was schemeless. How to stop Justine? June raced out of the hotel, back to her car, and drove to the office, sobbing at each stop sign, pulling herself together through every intersection.

Back at her desk at UCLA, she stared briefly at her still-unfinished chapter, pages marked with red ink that she had barely addressed. She picked up her phone and sent a text message to Rich.

Does she know?

She waited. Beep beep.

Who she?

Justine!

Beep beep.

No. Why would she?

June was not sure how to respond to this last text message. Rich was obviously lying, thought June, but why she did not understand. Nor was there any neat way to settle the matter. Confess to listening to him on the phone, and she looked sneaky. Insisting further would make her seem neurotic. Needy, even.

For the first time since the affair began, June was forced to mull actual consequences. Would her marriage end? Or would Mitch just yell a lot? He would definitely yell. Would he forgive her? Did she want him to? And if he did leave her, would she be able to figure out where the mortgage book was? Who would turn the gas off in an earthquake? She kept promising Mitch that she would learn, but every time she went to the side of the house to find the valve—maybe it was a knob—she became preoccupied by the ant beds.

Would someone take Nora away? Who in his right mind would give Nora to Mitch? *Your Honor, he was recently detained by the LAPD for threatening a defenseless woman in a fancy car with a nine iron. Oh, and he never once wiped our daughter's behind. Not once.*

Would Rich divorce Justine? June suddenly was enveloped in the image of herself at her own wedding with Rich, and for some reason she imagined them at Carmines II on Wilshire. Would anyone come? Adrian would, for sure. He would drink a lot and maybe sleep with one of Rich's friends.

June wondered what she would wear. It was so tacky when people wore white twice, but she had never cared for second-wedding skirt suits. Would Rich dance? She didn't like grooms who couldn't dance. They gave ballroom lessons for a cut rate on Pico; she and Rich could meet there on Wednesdays, and then go to La Serenata for fish tacos.

Nora would be the sad child, at home with the elderly sitter who would cluck and pat her on the head and take her to Marty's for French fries before dinner. Nora would hate Rich; there was no room in the backseat of his Porsche, plus she would probably spill grape juice on the interior.

Of course, what if Mitch left her but Rich stayed with Justine? She'd be alone, and dating, and there was no way she had the guts to do a three-way. What if someone wanted to pee on her? She imagined herself trying to comb her hair into a chignon—that seemed to be the thing people on television did before a date. Ugh—then there would be the story. I grew up in Minnesota but I went to Barnard and I don't like chestnuts. Blah, blah, blah.

She could try the Internet thing, but that was for middle-aged women who called themselves a "Christine Lahti type." And men with hair plugs.

These thoughts were like an epic dream, one that seemed to go on for hours, but actually took place over seconds, like flashbulbs going off in her brain.

And although it was hard to imagine, June knew that the evening was about to get worse. She had agreed to meet Mitch and Nora at Aloha Burger, quite possibly the most disgusting restaurant in Los Angeles. Having blown three hours sitting in a hotel waiting for her lover who never showed up, she realized she needed to get moving. In a blur June managed to get to her car and drive south on Westwood Boulevard toward the burger joint.

"Mommy!" Nora jumped into June's arms, knocking her back a bit.

June had valet-parked, a small irritant, since the parking fee would be more than her meal, and met Nora and Mitch inside, where they had clearly been waiting for more than a few minutes. Nora had been hanging from the rail that led to the bar, and Mitch had been quietly, and ineffectively, scolding her.

"Three for dinner?" asked the hostess dressed in the Aloha Burger outfit: a pair of khaki shorts, a Hawaiian shirt, and a plastic lei. June surveyed the room. A giant surfboard hung from the ceiling, and the walls were peppered with old surfing photos. The booths, which were meant to look as though they were fashioned from bamboo, were perpetually sticky from ketchup and relish, and jam-packed with squirming children and their parents, who were nursing Coronas in various stages of defeat. June loathed Aloha Burger, but Nora, like most children in the neighborhood, adored it, and so they endured it as a family every other week.

"Yes, three please. Can we sit near the back?"

"*Mahalo!*"

June grabbed Nora's hand to keep her from darting underfoot of the khaki-shod waiters balancing trays on their shoulders. Mitch was carrying an enormous shopping bag, which repeatedly smacked June in the leg as they made their way to the back of the restaurant, irritating her.

"Mitch, what are you carrying?"

"You'll see. You look nice, sweetie. Did I buy you that shirt?" Mitch was looking at her admiringly.

June was both oddly flattered—knowing that her face had been rubbed red with Kleenex and that her eyes must look bloodshot—and annoyed. Typically Mitch had found a way to turn a compliment back onto himself. But it was the first time in months he had seemed to look right at her and study her face, as if he hadn't seen it in a while.

They had barely settled into their booth when a waiter slammed three beer mugs brimming with water in front of them, splashing a little on the table. Nora dipped her straw in one, and June reflexively grabbed it before it toppled.

"Can I have a plastic cup for her, please?"

The waiter was looking over his shoulder toward the bar. "Can I start you off with some drinks and appetizers? Maybe some Maui rings?"

"I'll have a Coke," June said, "and a plastic cup for my daughter, please."

"Let me have a piña colada," Mitch said. June grimaced but said nothing—she had grown long accustomed to Mitch's embarrassing drink orders.

"And we're ready to order. Junior Wave, no cheese for her," June said, tilting her head toward Nora. "I'll have a chicken sandwich."

"Okay," said the waiter, who looked to June to be about seventeen, scribbling on his notebook. "Sir?"

"Hmm. Let me see. Tiki salad sounds good," Mitch said.

"It's not good," June said. "There's nothing good here. Just get the burger."

The waiter ignored June's insult but looked impatient and peeked back at the bar area, where a table of seven slightly drunk UCLA students was polishing off a pitcher.

"You know what. I'll have the chicken sandwich, too. No tomato," Mitch said, handing his menu to the waiter, who went off.

June looked at Mitch. "How was your day?" She held her breath—she hoped not visibly—bracing for his answer.

"How was my day? Well, I had to go to the network, so it wasn't exactly relaxing."

The mental picture of her husband and her lover in the same room together made her feel shaky yet again, and what had she overheard Justine saying to Rich? Something about making distracting remarks to Mitch? June felt her familiar stomach cramps seizing her. She looked hard at Mitch's face to see if he knew something he wasn't telling her. Would he hold out in front of Nora, slam her later? Maybe that big bag he was carrying had all her clothing in it. But Mitch was absentmindedly chewing on a straw. Nothing.

"How about you? What did you do today?" he asked.

"Not much. The usual," June answered, trying to keep her voice steady.

Nora was standing up, dipping her head into the booth behind them. She placed a sticky finger on the back of the woman, clearly on a first date, who smiled at her.

"Sit down, Nora."

Nora returned to her seat with a bang, making both booths shake, and began to bite on the table a little.

"Sweetie, don't put your mouth on the table. It's dirty."

"If it's dirty how come we eat here?" Nora asked.

June deliberated on the question. Not a bad one, really.

The waiter returned with three red plastic baskets, each overflowing with French fries.

"Can I get you anything else?"

"Some mustard," Mitch said, already biting into his sandwich.

"Can I please, please have a plastic cup with a top?" June begged.

"Oh right! My bad, you asked me for that before."

"Don't worry about it."

June dipped her sandwich into a dab of mayonnaise she had squeezed from the little packet, trying to avoid Mitch's eyes as she asked, "So did the audition go well?"

"It was okay. I was really good. They laughed a ton. The head of the network seemed to like me. Justine was great. Rich was a jerk, which seems to be his new usual."

June felt her face get hot. She prayed Mitch wouldn't notice. Nora turned around again.

"Nora, sit down!" June snapped, more sharply than she intended. Nora began to cry.

"You hurt my feelings!"

June pulled Nora onto her lap and rummaged through her purse for the box of crayons she kept in it. "Here, honey. Draw on the paper tablecloth."

Delighted, Nora began to make large orange swirls.

"Jerk how?" June asked, looking at Nora so Mitch could not see her nervousness.

"He asked me if I was the boss at home."

"What does that mean anyway?" June said, hoping she sounded casually interested.

"I don't know. The role is a boss, so he asked about you and then said something like, 'Are you the boss of your home,' in front of all those executives. It was like he was trying to blow it for me. He doesn't want me. Justine does. I think it has something to do with their sick dynamic. Justine's the winner and Rich is, from what I can see, the loser. I mean, he cheats at golf."

Rich would never cheat, June thought. He was scrupulous about games and rules. June thought so anyway. Maybe it had been Andy Flynn who never cheated at games.

"Aren't you gonna eat, June sweetie?" Mitch asked.

June looked with disgust at her chicken sandwich. The meat was dry and tough along the edge, the bun soggy and clearly made in a factory somewhere in Ohio. Her cramps grew stronger.

"I need to go to the bathroom. Excuse me."

June walked quickly through the restaurant, past the open kitchen, where indifferent line cooks stared at overcooked burgers on a fry grill.

She stepped into the bathroom stall and locked it, sat down on the toilet lip, and called Adrian.

"Hey, I was just going to text you. Mr. and Mr. Three-Way sent me a text, so I guess I am not as bad as I feared."

"That's great, but listen, I need to tell you something. I think Justine knows. She called me a bimbo."

"She walked up to you and called you a bimbo? Where?"

"No, I overheard her talking to Rich—"

"At a party? Where?"

"No, on the phone. He forgot to hang up after we talked. Never mind about how, just listen. So she said something like, I know about your bimbo, and then I hung up because I was so scared. And Mitch auditioned for them both today and Rich made weird remarks to him in the middle of it!" June felt frantic.

"Listen. I would agree at this point you have something to legitimately fear. But if you end this thing now, you can reduce that risk a lot, June. This has gone on long enough. Think about Nora. Think about what this would do to your family, and yourself frankly. Crabs, a bladder infection, hepatitis, a stalker, loss of child custody, loss of face—this could end in any or all of those ways, or you could end it now."

"Okay. I can do that. You're right about ending it. I will. I promise. I am going to end it soon."

"Not soon, June. Consider it over yesterday. Listen, I have to get back to the table. Loveyoumeanit."

June knew Adrian was right. She needed to rethink her entire life, and she would. Soon. Really soon.

Her phone rang. It was Amanda.

"Hi, June. Listen, do you have your personal portfolio in order?" Amanda asked.

"My what? You mean do I have a 401(k) or whatever?"

"Yes. I need you to figure out your entire asset picture. And tomorrow, I want you to withdraw ten thousand dollars from your joint account with Mitch and put it in an IRA in your own name," Amanda said.

"What? What are you talking about?"

"Adrian told me what has been going on with Mitch. You need to get your financial house in order."

"Amanda, I wanted to tell you, it was just so . . ."

"*Basta.* Let's just get it dealt with."

"Amanda, I'll call you tomorrow." June hung up on Amanda and frantically dialed Adrian.

"What?" he said. June could hear the din of diners and laughter.

"Did you tell Amanda about Rich Friend?"

"Hmm. Did I?"

"Adrian! That was coned! Totally coned!"

"I know, but I didn't know it was Amanda-proof coned. She needs to know stuff like that."

"Oh, for fuck's sake," June said.

Amanda was highly discreet. June knew that. But as the circle of people who knew about her indiscretion grew, her chances of getting out of it alive shrank.

June rushed back to the table, where Nora was halfway through an ice-cream sundae, her face covered with chocolate sauce.

"Are you all right? You were in there forever!" Mitch asked.

"There was a line."

"Okay, listen—I have great news. Tad just called. I got it! I'm the boss on *Sole Operator*! I guess Rich came around!" Mitch was beaming.

June felt utterly confused. She was happy for Mitch, but absolutely devastated. Did Rich give Mitch this job so he could slowly humiliate him on the set? Did Rich give Mitch the job to get closer to her? Where was Justine in this?

"And there is something else I need to say to you," Mitch said.

June froze. It was coming. Mitch handed her the large bag he had trailed in with. She peered into it with fear. Inside the bag was a giant box. Looking closely, she saw it was the ten-speed mixer she had been eyeing for months. She looked up at Mitch, who was smiling at her.

"It's been a tough couple of months June-Junie. I know that. And I apologize. But we're really lucky people, sweetie. And everything is about to get better."

June started to cry.

CHAPTER 23

Mitch walked into his yard, which was still enveloped in darkness. The perfume from the gardenia bush was overwhelming, as if he had just stuck his nose in a honey jar. Mitch knew that he had better be working on a pilot when the white flowers began to open each spring, just as midwestern farmers know a good crop of corn must be knee high by the Fourth of July. Mitch was due on location downtown by 6:30 a.m. and he needed to move quickly if he was going to make it to Starbucks on the way.

The coffee shop was bustling, even at this early hour. There were financial types making their way to the office before the opening bell rang almost three thousand miles away on the New York Stock Exchange; random students; at least one homeless person; and a couple of kids who looked like they were on their way home from a night out at Privilege. Mitch glanced at his script while he waited for his latte—new pages had arrived in his mailbox in the middle of the night—and wondered what his day would be like. This pilot was anchored by a big television star—Jennifer English—who had worked consistently in lead roles on a variety of hit shows since the midnineties.

Her name alone would get this pilot on the air. The network had courted her for months to play the role of the political correspondent mom, Samantha. Mitch had asked around and heard only good things. "Oh, you'll love her, she's a doll." He was really excited. Good cast, good writers, a hot star. It all seemed great.

The sky was becoming illuminated by shards of early-morning light as Mitch's car made its way east toward downtown Los Angeles. The pilot was being shot in an old office building on location on Flower

Street, and as Mitch pulled up to base camp—the setup area near the location—he saw a flurry of production assistants, trucks, a craft table already covered in Lorna Doone cookies and pots of weak coffee, and row upon row of parked cars.

Mitch pulled in and was directed by a PA in a headset toward his trailer, which had his character's name on the door: DEAN MACK.

Mitch climbed the rickety steps up to his trailer and began inspection. He breathed deeply. Good, no cigarette smoke. The walls were paneled with brown vinyl, there was some industrial carpet on the floor, not badly stained, and one full-length mirror illuminated by track lighting.

There was a couch, not as long as he had wanted, but a couch nonetheless. He turned the air on and picked up the digest-sized version of that day's sides, which were sitting next to a nice Dean & DeLuca lunch box filled with chocolates, nuts, and salted crackers, and a few bottles of Fiji water. "Good Luck, Mitch!" read the note. Hmm. Fine. Network warm. He assumed Jennifer English's note was more effusive. The word "thrilled" or "honored" was probably invoked. He opened a Scharffen Berger chocolate bar, took a guilty bite, then threw the rest under the couch.

He peeked in the bathroom. Small, but it smelled like nice soap. He flopped down on the couch, and noticed it had no give. Oh well. At least he had remembered to bring a pillow from home. His trailer shook slightly with a bang-bang knock on its aluminum door. He opened it and saw a PA, his face covered in acne, standing before him.

"Hey, Mitch, welcome. Do you want some breakfast?"

"I just got here. Can't you give me a minute?"

Mitch slammed the door, but it didn't latch. He pulled it closed with a bang. It was his firm belief that it was of essential importance to be short with production assistants on the first day; otherwise he would always be the one to get the stale sandwich. Fear him first, he believed; then, as the eight-day shoot went on, he would soften.

Mitch looked at his watch. At exactly three minutes after the PA had taken his leave, Mitch opened the door and called for a breakfast burrito. The PA meandered to the craft table and returned a few minutes later, this time avoiding eye contact, and handed him a plate. Mitch examined his pile of eggs and Kraft American and pulled out a single long blond hair from the center of the breakfasty blob. Another knock.

"Wardrobe."

Mitch opened the door, and a tall woman with red hair walked in, holding a dark gray Armani suit. "Got everything you need?" she asked.

"Shoes would be nice," Mitch answered, laughing.

"Oh, right then, shoes it is." The wardrobe woman—Julia?—sort of hopped down his trailer steps. He looked again at his burrito. Ugh. A huge cheesy pile of shit-to-be. Yuk. He threw it in the garbage and walked out to the craft table in search of oatmeal. He would definitely sneak that Armani suit into his car at the end of the shoot. Nice!

When he got back to his trailer a pair of black wingtips was sitting in the middle of the floor, with gray cashmere socks folded on top. Good, wardrobe was efficient. He liked that. There was a plastic bag waiting for him to place his wedding ring and other personal items in. Sort of like jail, with pay.

Sitting in his trailer nursing his coffee, Mitch was soon interrupted again. A new PA, a woman this time, well, a girl. She looked about eighteen, her face totally nude of makeup, her smile a giant beam.

"Are you ready for a great day?"

"Sure." Mitch answered.

"Okay, I'll be back in a while," Chirpy said.

"Isn't it time to do makeup?"

"Not quite. They're running a little behind. Just relax." The PA moved to the trailer door.

Another hour passed, during which Mitch ate a few more chocolates, balled their wrappers up, watched *Market Watch* and *Good Morning America*, read *The New York Times* culture section, and became increasingly impatient to begin working. His phone rang. "Hello, is this Mr. Gold?"

"Yes, who is this?"

"This is Hector Garcia. I'm an assistant district attorney for the county of Los Angeles. I am calling to inform you that Uri Umarov, whom you engaged to remodel your home in West Los Angeles, has been charged with six counts of embezzlement, racketeering, and felony robbery. You should expect a subpoena in this matter."

"No shit. Where did you find him?" Mitch asked

"He was serving in the army in Chechnya," the DA answered.

Mitch felt momentarily sorry for the contractor who stole their life's savings. "Great," Mitch said. He knew they would never see a dime, but he did like the idea of Uri in the slammer.

Mitch was about to walk out onto the set to see what was going on, when Chirpy knocked again on the trailer. "Hi again! Let's get you to makeup!"

Chirpy led Mitch to a double-wide trailer a few hundred yards from his. At last he would get to meet Jennifer, who had been out of town during both the first read-through of the script and the cast dinner.

But now she had undoubtedly arrived two hours before him, to get the extensive hair and makeup that female leads always received and, also undoubtedly, to fight about her wardrobe. A dress would be blue when pink was promised. It would be too long, or maybe too tight. It would be too frumpy or, sometimes, too sexy. Mitch had heard all of these arguments. But Jennifer English was a veteran of these shows, known to the world as America's television sweetheart, so he was optimistic that she would be as professional as they came. He settled into the swivel chair in front of a long row of mirrors, looking for her. Hmm. Not around. Maybe she was on the set already?

"Hey, Mitch! How you been?" A short woman, her arms covered in tattoos and her left eyebrow pierced, looked up from a bag of makeup. Mitch struggled to remember her name.

"Hi—"

"Maxine. Remember? We worked together on that horror movie last year, the one about the chick who gave everyone rabies?"

Maxine smiled widely and fiddled with her iPod speakers, cranking up Green Day.

"Yeah, of course, Maxine. How've you been?"

"Cool."

Mitch looked at Maxine's workstation. Pictures of her kids playing in a sprinkler somewhere were tucked into the corner of a mirror. A large photo of a German shepherd sat in a chipped wooden frame on her table. Bags and bags of makeup, caked with hairspray, were scattered everywhere, along with a Ziploc of pretzels and a dirty coffee cup.

"Has Jennifer already been through the works?" Mitch asked Maxine.

"Oh no, she's, uh, she's running late. Production said she just called—she's not far."

"Running late" on the first day?

Luke Lemon, who was playing Mitch's nerdy underling, came wandering into the trailer, stuffing a Danish into his mouth. "Hhhhey, Mooch. Jennifer here whet?"

"Oh, she's a bit late," said Maxine, trying to hide her annoyance as she dipped her brushes into a pool of blue liquid cleaner. Staring at each other in the mirror before them, Luke and Mitch raised their eyebrows. Luke flopped into the chair where another makeup artist was waiting.

"Hey, girl," said Maxine to her co-worker. "How was your date last night?"

"Oh, it was nice," said the other makeup artist. "We went to a movie and dinner. It's all weird though, because he's an Orthodox Jew and he won't eat in regular restaurants and stuff. And his parents don't want him dating non-Jewish women, so it's just all kind of different for me."

Maxine dipped a brush in a large pot of tan base makeup and began swiping it over Mitch's face.

"Well, Trixie, have you guys slept together?"

"Oh no. He's waiting till he gets married. See what I mean? I don't know," Trixie said a little despondently.

Maxine looked back at Mitch and ran her hands through his hair. "You have soft hair. You want a little gel in the front?"

"Nah," Mitch answered.

"Are you sure? 'Cause even the baldies usually like some product."

Was Maxine suggesting he was going bald?

"I hear the network's really high on the show," Luke said, wiping some Danish crumbs from his chin. "That's what my agent said, anyway."

Mitch nodded—he'd heard that line on the first day of every show he'd ever shot, most of which never saw the light of day. Anyway, he was daydreaming, trying to picture the Orthodox guy on a date with Trixie, the punk rock hair stylist. Did they go for pasta?

The windows began to rattle, little pots of makeup jiggled, and a tinkling could be heard from the back of the trailer. Mitch felt the trailer shudder, and a tube of lipstick fell to the floor. There was a brief silence, and then Maxine leaned down to pick up the lipstick.

"Probably a 5," said Luke.

"Nah, that was more like a 4.3," Maxine said, and Mitch went back to reading his lines. "You know what, Mitch. I've got some new pancake that would be great for you. Just give me some time to find it."

Where was Jennifer? Mitch started to worry they would never get to his scene today. Another thirty-five minutes went by, and then suddenly there was a flurry of activity at the front of the trailer as Jennifer English came sweeping in, followed by her own hair stylist, an assistant, and some guy holding her Maltese.

"Oh my God, the traffic!" she said, rushing into the room as if she were ten minutes, not three hours, late. Who runs into traffic at 5:30 a.m., which is the time she would have left Malibu to make her call time, Mitch wondered. The network sent a car to pick her up, and she had clearly made it wait.

"Did you guys feel that earthquake? Hey everybody, hi, I'm so glad to be here today, whoops!" The Maltese had jumped onto her lap and was licking her nose. "Oh no, sweetie, not now! Everyone don't hate me! I am soooo sorry to be late."

"Oh that's okay, hon," said Trixie, settling Jennifer into a makeup chair.

"I'm sure we have plenty of time! They always call me here too early anyway," Jennifer said.

Mitch studied her closely. Jennifer had the classic older actress body, thin arms, a little loose near the triceps, but just barely. Her skin was smooth and mostly unlined, except near her eyes, where tiny crevasses had formed, and he could see a smattering of freckles on her nose. There was a deep valley between her breasts, a telltale sign of surgery. Her hair was whitish blond and her eyebrows seemed penciled on. She was wearing a pair of blue yoga pants, which revealed the grandma butt of the underfed, and a tight T-shirt.

"Hey, Jennifer, Mitch Gold," Mitch said, swiveling his chair toward her.

"Yeah, I remember youuuuuu. Didn't you play a shrink on *Topanga Canyon* a few years ago?" Jennifer asked.

"Yep. That was me," Mitch said. "So listen, you wanna run lines?"

Jennifer giggled. "I'd better look at them first!"

She didn't know her lines yet? Wow, Mitch thought. Was that possible? Her assistant handed her the sides, and Jennifer began to read them over, grimacing by page two. "Oh, I've got so many words. There are just too many words here!"

Luke piped up, "Yeah, I thought it was a bit overwritten."

"I've gotta talk to the writers," Jennifer said. "Okay, let's go, who's in charge of my face today?"

Trixie began to dab Jennifer's face with various emollients, powders, and glosses. As she sat, Jennifer flipped through a pile of magazines excavated from her purse—*People*, *Us*, *Hello!*, and *In Touch*.

"Ugh. My divorce has been in like total detail in *People*. I mean who wants to read crap like that?" Turning the page, she saw a picture of Moxie, the hip-hop artist. "Look at her ass! What did they feed her in the pokey? I heard she's dating Lupe Fiasco!"

She flipped some more, and landed on a photo of her soon-to-be-ex-husband, the lead guitarist for a band Mitch had never heard of, frolicking on the beach in Maui with a woman half Jennifer's age. She slammed the magazine shut. "Oh. There's Mr. One-Minute Man with Used-to-be-my-personal-assistant. Yuck. Why do people want to look at this?" She began to absently pet the dog.

Maxine found the pancake she had been looking for and began to coat it over Mitch's pores as Jennifer went on.

She continued to talk about her divorce, when the papers would be signed (a few months, apparently), where she would go on vacation to celebrate (Cabo), what juices she liked to drink (pulverized romaine lettuce with a shot of cantaloupe). Mitch noticed with increasing concern that she had not picked up her sides once.

"Well, Jennifer, I see that you're shooting first. So let me know if you wanna run lines," Mitch said, heading back to his trailer.

"I'll be fine. See you in a few," Jennifer said over her shoulder.

Mitch sat in his trailer—"forty-five minutes max," the PA insisted—

and an hour and twenty minutes later, he was flipping on the air conditioner to keep his makeup from melting. Outside, he could hear the whir of generators, and crew guys walking back and forth under the bright morning light. He heard random bits of conversation between gaffers, PAs, and others—"Hey, fuck you, man," "Copy that," "I met him in Sardinia—he was mean"—and wondered if they were ever going to get to his scene. He practiced his swing, then pulled gray hairs out in front of the mirror. Desperate, he watched the Women's Scottish Open.

A full three hours later, he finally wandered out to the set to see what the hell was taking so long.

Mitch made his way to Video Village, where executives and the director stood staring at a bunch of monitors, taking in the action slightly off the set. Mitch spied Justine, who was standing, her arms folded, her face locked in a frown, staring at a monitor with two junior writers in tight suits.

"Mitch, nice to see you," Justine said, breaking into a smile. "We're so glad to have you here. I would love to chat, but I need to talk to some of the writers."

"No worries, Justine, do your thing. Rich here?"

Justine had already begun to huddle with her staff. "Umm, not yet."

That was odd. It was the first day. Maybe Rich was doing things in the office. Mitch looked next toward the director.

"Hey, Ed, how's everything going?"

Ed appeared unnerved and ran his hand through a thick mane of brown hair. He whispered to Mitch, who had to lean toward him to hear over the din of generators and clanging sets.

"How's everything going? Well, our star doesn't know her lines. I had this beautiful long tracking shot, which is basically the shot that we rented this location for, which is costing a third of the budget, and I had to break it up into little tiny pieces because Jennifer could remember only a few words at a time. I would say it is going for shit."

A depressed-looking man with hair that had thinned prematurely looked up glumly from the corner of the room. He spoke so softly it was hard to hear him over the clatter on the set. "Hey, Ed, you got a minute?"

Jim Barry had worked as a reporter for twenty years before signing a "separation agreement" from the *Los Angeles Times*. He had recently found a moneymaking niche in consulting with film and television directors about the news business. His doctor friends, who had turned him onto the gig, did medical consulting on hospital dramas for a lot more money. But hey, it was work, and he figured he could finally make TV newsrooms and reporters authentic. But he quickly realized that his comments were seldom, if ever, absorbed.

"Sure, Jim, what's up?" Ed asked.

"Hey, um, there are a few issues with the female reporter."

"Sam? Please, tell me!"

"Well, um, her shoes are pretty high. Most female reporters wear pretty scuffed shoes actually. Kind of low-heeled. For the most part."

"Uh-huh," Ed said. "Well, the shoes were a network choice. I appreciate the insight though, Jim."

"Oh, and that whole thing about taking her off the White House. Yeah, that's illegal. I don't think that would happen in a newsroom," Jim said.

Ed tried to look concerned. "Yeah, I hear you. But that is sort of the spine of the story, you know?"

"Uh-huh. And just one more thing—I am not sure about the manicure."

"Right. Understood," Ed replied.

Jim sat down again and pulled out a ragged issue of *The New Yorker*.

The pimply-faced production assistant came toward them both. "Mitch, we're ready for you."

Mitch walked toward the set, past Jennifer, who was sitting in a low director's chair, laughing with a cameraman. Ed approached Jennifer's chair from behind, and she tilted her neck back, looked at him slightly upside down, and giggled. "God, Ed, from this position we could be doing some serious tea-bagging."

Everyone burst into laughter, including Mitch, who was secretly disgusted.

"That's our Jen, just one of the guys!" Ed smiled. "Now listen, doll, everything looks great. You're doing a fantastic job. The lines could umm, sort of, you know, come a little quicker. But it's the first day, so we can make up time later. Let's move on to the scene with Dean. Remember, you're really ticked off here."

"Okay. I got it, Ed," Jennifer said.

Mitch was incredulous. "Aren't we going to rehearse?"

Ed looked tense. "We're really crunched for time. The producers are already on my case."

Jennifer piped up cheerfully: "We can wing it!"

Mitch was a big enough name that he was offered the back entrance for rides at Disneyland, got free dry cleaning in exchange for a headshot. But in the pilot pecking order, he was by no means a big enough name to demand to rehearse a scene when the star of a show didn't want to.

Maxine and Trixie came racing toward Jennifer and began dabbing her nose and forehead with tiny sponges and fluffing and spraying her hair. Maxine called to Mitch. "Here, this is for you. A little man fan. You need it." Mitch flicked on the little yellow battery-operated fan and held it close to his neck. "Spraying!" Maxine called out. A cloud of hairspray rose around them.

The stand-ins had been blocking the scene—standing in the place of the real actors to get the scene lit and the camera angles right—and a production assistant went scurrying toward them and announced officiously, "First team has the set. Second team. Thank you!"

Mitch and Jennifer walked onto the set, under the glaringly hot lights, which caused Mitch to sweat further. "Where's my mark?" asked Jennifer, glancing around for the tiny piece of red tape that indicated where she ought to stand. A PA steered her gently into place. Mitch eased himself behind the rosewood desk at the edge of the set and waited.

The idea was for Jennifer to walk through the door, barking her lines at Mitch. A PA walked across the set, waving his hands around. "Quiet on the set!" A giant foam-covered mike began to lower slowly just above Jennifer's blond head.

"Rolling!" bellowed the first assistant director.

"Sound speed!"

"Scene five take one," said the cameraman, slapping down the clapboard. Then, Ed: "And, action."

Jennifer walked through the set door. *"Dean, don't mean to interrupt your . . . um . . . story thing . . . oh shit!"*

"CUT!"

"I'm sorry. Let's go again."

"Rolling!

"Sound speed!

"Scene five take two.

"Action!"

"Dean, don't mean to interrupt your . . . big thing . . . big story . . . big story thing! Oh for crying out loud! Why can't I say that? All I can talk about is your big thing!" Jennifer looked at Mitch and giggled.

The script supervisor, looking exhausted from her already-long morning feeding the star her lines, tried to smile. "The line is, ' *"Dean, don't mean to interrupt your big story meeting. Trying to decide whether to lead with pink or red?'* "

"Right! I know these. Okay, let's do it." Jennifer pumped her fist for emphasis.

"Rolling!

Sound speed!

"Scene five take three."

"And action!"

Jennifer began walking. *"Dean, don't mean to interrupt your big gig* OW! Story! Right! It's a newspaper! Stor-y." She tapped her hand on her leg. "Oh I am so dumb! Damn it!"

Ed walked over quickly and wrapped his arm around Jennifer. "You know, maybe it's not working for you to walk through the door and talk. How about if we do this in two shots? You walk through the door, you stop, we stop, we'll give your line, we pick it up, you say the line. Is that good?"

"Oh, great. It'll look better that way anyway."

"It will look like crap that way," muttered a cameraman, who was sitting inches from Mitch, the only one who could hear him. The camera guy raised his muttering an octave. "But that's okay with me, because I'm a blond TV star who can hold up everyone 'cause I was too busy sucking dick this morning to learn my lines."

246

Mitch looked up. "Uh-oh. Someone missed his sexual-harassment workshop."

"I don't need to go. I already know how to sexually harass. You know, we just spent three hours on a half-page scene because Meryl Streep over there didn't know her lines."

"Ready for First team," called the AD.

Jennifer scurried back to the door. She was shot, in silence, walking through it.

The script supervisor quickly fed her the line. "It's: *Dean, don't mean to interrupt your big story meeting. Trying to decide whether to lead with pink or red?* Got it?

"Rolling!

"Sound speed!

"Scene six take one."

"And action!"

"*Dean, don't mean to interrupt your big story meeting. Trying to decide whether to lead with pink or red?*"

"And cut!"

Ed walked over smiling. "That was great, Jennifer. Now let's do it again. Remember, he just pulled you off a big breaking story, and you're pissed, so let's try it a little more forceful."

"Oh no," Jennifer said. "That was good. I know when it clicks. Remember, I've done a ton of this."

"Well, how about just one more time?" Ed pleaded.

"Nope, I got it. Listen, my makeup needs a little fix. I'm going back to my trailer."

And with that, Jennifer turned on her spiked heel and marched off the set. Mitch couldn't believe it. He had been called there at six thirty, been through the works, gotten in his wardrobe, arrived at the set, and now six hours later and counting, he hadn't said a single line.

"Let's break for lunch," Ed said to Mitch. "We'll pick it up then. Things will start rocking and rolling."

"Lunch!" yelled the PA. The silence of the set was shattered as equipment began to heave, crew guys began yammering loudly, and scores of workers headed for the craft table. The five network executives began

247

murmuring nervously into their cell phones, as did the phalanx of writers. Mitch heard someone say "replace" but, for once, he was confident that this portentous word was not being applied to him.

Justine huddled with Ed, and Mitch, standing nearby, overheard their conversation.

"Steve said there is no way they're going to replace her," Justine whispered.

"Well, okay, we've gotta work with it."

"Why don't you try cue cards?" Justine asked Ed.

"Cue cards?" Ed said. "This is not the Academy Awards, Justine. I'm telling you, it will look terrible. Her eyes will be all over the place."

"At least we could get it done."

"We'll fix it in looping. Seriously, Justine. Let's move on."

Justine looked incredibly tense. This was her one shot to get this show right, and Jennifer English seemed to be bringing it all down. Unlike a movie, which could drag on for an extra month or two, a pilot had ten days, because of the network schedule and financial concerns. If it couldn't get done, the network would simply shelve it.

Mitch wandered mournfully back to his trailer and waited for the PA to bring him a turkey sandwich. It would have been faster to get it himself, if that were a thing that number 4 on the call sheet actually had to do. Instead, he watched *Playing Lessons from the Pros*.

After lunch, as second team stood in for the scene, Mitch and Jennifer sat in chairs, getting their hair combed. "Think maybe we should run a few lines now?" Mitch tried to sound casual.

"Nah, I've got it. Is your wife in the business?" Jennifer asked.

"First team!" the PA called.

Mitch wedged himself behind his desk, feeling a tad fatter since lunch, and waited for Jennifer to make her way to the door.

"We'll go from your line, Mitch," said Ed.

Mitch licked his lips a bit and twisted his neck a little, trying to embody the editor of a major newspaper. The extra assigned to polish his nails took her place at Mitch's knee and smiled brightly, trying to catch his eye. "You're doing it just great," he said to her, and she beamed.

"Hold the work. Scene seven take one. Action!"

"*Sam, great to have you back! Parlez-vous peekaboo?*"

"Listen, why have you pulled me out of the White House? I am as capable a reporter now as I was before the baby."

"First of all, Sam, I don't see you making wheels up at Andrews at six a.m. Second, given that you adopted a baby from France, I don't see how you can objectively cover diplomatic stories anymore. Uh, Me-ling, please push the cuticles back, don't cut."

"Cut! Excellent. Check the gate, and moving on!"

"Gate's clean."

Mitch looked at Ed with confusion. "Moving on? Ed, we did one take. I thought I would throw it away a little more this time. Maybe have a little glance at Me-ling."

"No, no. It was good. We have to move on," Ed insisted.

Jennifer ambled off the set to take a call, and Ed whispered to Mitch. "Sorry, man, but she got her line right. And you were great. You always are. Solid. So we gotta go. The day's burning."

"But one take?" Mitch asked.

"Sorry, man," Ed said again.

Mitch and Jennifer then did the scene three more times to get their close-up shots. But Jennifer refused to do the lines off camera with Mitch, forcing him to do it with a production assistant. It was the height of rudeness. He had done his off-camera lines for her close-up.

"Shit, hair in the gate!" a cameraman yelled. The gate on the camera had been dirty, and would have to be cleaned with an orangewood stick and an air can. "Oh, did I leave a short hair on the gate?" yelled Jennifer. Mitch seethed. Finally, it was time to move to the next scene.

"We're lighting, second team."

Mitch walked back to his trailer to get a Coke. He waited for the set to be lit, not even bothering this time to ask for a rehearsal. A half hour later, they were ready for him.

"First team on the set!"

Jennifer tucked her phone under her chin. "Just give me two shakes of a lamb's tail. I just need to finish with my lawyer."

The crew waited another ten minutes, looking around, snapping gum, fiddling with cameras, looking longingly at a soda table nearby. Finally, the star was ready.

Jennifer minced up to the set and waited for the PA to hand her a baby bottle. In this scene, Sam had brought her baby into the newsroom and was trying to keep Dean from noticing that she was taking the bottle into her office to feed the baby.

"Quiet on the set! Scene seven take one. Action!"

"Sam, what have you got there?"

"It's nothing, Dean, just my, my, my, bi bop, bop! Augh!"

The bottle of milk fell to the floor with a small thud. "Oops!" Jennifer giggled, bending to pick it up. "Look what fell out of my pussy!"

The crew, who three hours ago would have erupted in obligatory laughter, was silent. They had had enough.

Jennifer moved back into place, holding the bottle, and over the next two hours, she and Mitch managed to muddle through the scene. Exhausted, Mitch walked slowly back to his trailer to change. His day was finally over, even though the show had at least one more scene to shoot before it got dark. At the rate this day had gone, it might be another few hours. He passed by the pimple-faced PA and paused. "Hey, do you have my call time for tomorrow?" He didn't.

"It's probably gonna be a long night. We'll call you later," the PA told Mitch.

As he made his way to his trailer, Mitch saw Justine and Rich, who both looked angry. As he got closer, he could hear their sniping.

"Now you show up, Rich? With one scene left to shoot? You have no idea what kind of day this has been."

"I was back at the office, Justine, doing the rewrites you asked for. You know how that goes—I do what you say, as told."

"Oh, cut the crap, Rich. Leslie was there all day and never laid eyes on you. You know what, Mr. Friend, you're so full of shit your eyes are brown."

Mitch quietly slid by them and into his trailer, trying not to be seen. As he was washing his makeup off, there was a rap on the trailer door. "It's Luke!"

Mitch opened the door, hoping to dish about this hideous day with his beleaguered cast mate.

His mouth twisted sourly, Luke marched past Mitch to the corner of the trailer, pausing to take a sidelong look at the couch. Luke flipped out a tape measure and proceeded to measure the length and width of Mitch's trailer. Distraught by what he had found, Luke spat out, "Favored nations, my ass!" He stomped down the steps, tripping slightly on the bottom one.

CHAPTER 24

June sat in her kitchen staring at her tenure folder with her now customary unease. She had promised to publish two major articles this year. One was half written, and she could not stand to finish it. The other was done, and had been submitted to a journal that had asked her to make significant revisions and resubmit it, but she felt blocked somehow from doing it. What was more, she had been invited to write the introduction for a collection of Philip Larkin poems, and on that too she was woefully behind. But of far greater importance was her book, and she felt paralyzed by fear that it would never be completed let alone as well received as her first one. Every morning started with the best intentions: today would be the day she could polish off the second chapter, write up her recipe for the preschool cookbook, finally go to Target to buy Soft Scrub and a new electronic pet for Nora, clean out that nasty plastic bin in the bathroom that had the cough syrup coating the bottom. And every day, she would stare out the window at her gardenia bush and whisper to her lover on her cell phone.

"Quick, your three favorite movies?"

"Okay. *Blood Simple, Donnie Brasco, Casablanca.* You go."

"*Sense and Sensibility, Do the Right Thing.* And I suppose *Dead Man Walking.*"

Occasionally, their phone calls would turn steamier, and June would lie under her kitchen table, so as not to see the detritus of her domestic life.

"Tell me what you are doing to me now. . . ."

After, there was the mix of emotions that had become as familiar as a drug reaction: sexual euphoria, followed by shame and guilt, followed by obsessing over when they could talk again, followed by eating lentils with mustard and thyme with her family and wondering what kind of slimy nauseating person had phone sex under a Shaker table in West Los Angeles.

She had wanted to get together with him again, but Rich seemed fixated on it being in "exactly the right place." June fantasized about what that place would be. That great spa in Santa Barbara? A Latin bungalow at Chateau Marmont? Maybe the Ojai Valley Inn? Wherever they met next, June knew, Rich would go out of his way to make it memorable. Perhaps in time they would see all these places together.

Her home phone rang, and June recognized Rich's office exchange on the caller ID. He never called the home phone.

"Hello," she said, with some confusion.

"Hi, June. Justine here. Hope I'm not bothering you."

June could hear her heart begin to pound in her ears. This was it. This was where it would all end. A bead of sweat formed under her left arm.

"No, why would you be bothering me?" June's voice felt high, as if it belonged to someone else.

"I assume any working woman with a small child whom I call midmorning is busy. Anyway, is Mitch there?"

Oh, so the plan was to rat her out to Mitch. Why did Justine sound so friendly?

"No, he is on his way in to work I think."

"Oh yeah, right. I just wanted to touch base, tell him what a great job he did yesterday. It was a rough day, but he really pulled us through," Justine said.

"Did he?" Again, the bluebird voice.

"He seriously did. Hey, you know, it was so nice to see you a few weeks ago at that party at Larissa's. The event was so-so-ish. I hope we can have dinner again sometime, after pilot season, okay?"

"Uh-huh."

"Great. Nice talking to you, June. I'll catch Mitch on his cell."

June placed the phone down and tried to regain her breath. Okay. That was weird. What was Justine's game anyway?

An hour later, as June stared at her computer screen, her phone lit up with a text from Rich.

Home. Can u come here?
2 ur house?
Yes. It is my sanctuary. I want you there.

June had never stepped foot in Rich and Justine's home, though she had longed to see it. She had fantasized about the space many times, picturing a large Spanish estate, with those giant rounded awnings over the windows. In her imagination, there would be mantels covered with silver picture frames filled with pictures of her and Rich along the medina in Rabat.

June picked up her phone and dialed Rich's number.

"Hey, babe," he answered.

"Rich, I am *not* coming to your house. That's crazy. What if Justine finds out? What if she comes home for some weird reason?"

"Why on earth would she come home? She's on location downtown. I'm supposed to be working from here and waiting for the dog groomer. She specifically asked me to do that because she knew she wouldn't be back until ten p.m. Come on, June, I'm tired of hotels. I want you in my space. Please. I want to cook you a beautiful lunch. Let's meet at the Santa Monica farmers' market in twenty minutes, we'll get a bunch of great stuff, there are cherries already, and we'll make a lovely feast. I have an organic chicken here. Please? It might be our only shot to do this," Rich begged.

This gave June pause. Rich had never mentioned the state of their relationship—not its inception, not its present state and what it might be missing, like visits into each other's homes and lives, and certainly not its future. Was he trying to lead her down a new pathway?

June looked at the pile of papers on her desk, and the forms she needed to fill out for Nora's next doctor's appointment. She remembered her call with Justine, her prayers in the hotel toward ending this affair, the sinking feeling she had at 2 a.m., the shame and remorse and animal fear of being caught. And then, she walked out to her car, sat briefly before turning the ignition, and took Olympic toward the beach.

She saw her lone vanity plate of the week, but was too unnerved to mull its origin. MEATMEN.

June's car smelled of marjoram, its passenger seat covered in a dozen plastic bags from the farmers' market. She followed Rich Friend closely as they made their way along the Pacific Coast Highway toward the Pacific Palisades. She held on to the steering wheel tightly as Rich floored it up Chautauqua and the ocean faded behind them.

Their cars twisted and turned past the eucalyptus trees through the foothills of the Santa Monica Mountains. It was one of those neighborhoods that she somehow never managed to visit, even though she knew the surrounding areas of Malibu and Brentwood fairly well. As they climbed, June felt almost as if she were following Rich through Barcelona, making their way along tiny streets, bathed suddenly in a Mediterranean light.

They made their way up yet another hill, and Rich slowed down before what June realized was the home he shared with Justine, a dramatic structure perched over the Pacific Coast Highway below them. The house, which appeared to be built of white concrete, was shaped like a faceted diamond, jutting out from the side of the hill over Santa Monica Canyon, with long slits for windows, and a garage tucked underground.

The house seemed to have been built up, then pushed to cascade down the hill, then stopped midfall and settled into the cactus garden like a gem in its velvety case. It was a deeply modern, spare structure unique to a neighborhood filled with giant Mediterranean villas, country French homes, and bluestone marble pools.

"Would you mind finding a parking spot in the street, babe? My Corvette is in the second spot. No one's going to steal yours," Rich called to her from the Porche, apparently forgetting the fake valet at Orso. June turned her Honda back toward Chautauqua but could not find a space. Finally she managed to find a spot a few blocks from Rich's house. She parked unevenly in front of a large Tudor with a high gate, and marched back a few blocks and up the hill to Rich's birdhouse perched above the ocean.

"Wow. This is an amazing place," June said as she came through the front door that Rich had left ajar.

"Yeah, the property is actually tiny, and not zoned for much. So we had to sort of build out, if you will, rather than across. It's very private."

"Do you feel suspended?" June asked as she walked carefully into the house, and was stunned by the giant windows that met at an angle, offering a panoramic view of Santa Monica to the east and the Pacific Palisades to the west.

For a house that stuck out of a hill, this one was surprisingly spacious, filled with extremely expensive testaments to its decorator. Each room was an expanse of clean walls, recessed cabinets, and polished concrete floors interrupted only occasionally by a few perfectly arranged vintage Eames chairs, and, in one case, a handcrafted zebrawood dining table. A long wraparound window in the living room looked out over the canyon below, which June imagined must stretch out into a vast field of an illuminated Los Angeles at night. The only artwork was a wall hanging of differently colored, sized, and shaped letters arranged to look like a ransom note, which spelled out "Believe."

Each room connected to the next seamlessly, with no doors anywhere that June could see. An open, freestanding white staircase linked a large bedroom on the lowest level to the living-dining area and kitchen, which seemed to be below yet another set of rooms off a mezzanine gallery. June studied the staircase, and the polished concrete floors of this house, and imagined children falling to their deaths. This was not a home for a family. It wasn't quite a home at all; it was more a living architecture lesson.

"I like it. It feels like this entire town is looking up at me," Rich said, walking into the Italian kitchen with its knobless pantry and stainless-steel fixtures. There was his kitchen island, also stainless steel, where Rich unloaded his bags of groceries, making it look messy and almost offensive in this surgical environment. June joined him, still taking in the view, and plopped her own bags of herbs and vegetables onto the counter, vaguely ashamed of them. Rich walked across the island and held her from behind, and began kissing her ear.

"I've dreamed of having you here," he murmured. June felt cold. She turned toward him and they kissed for several minutes, and he pulled her sweater off, leaving her feeling exposed under the white light of the spare room.

"We should make lunch. I'm hungry," she said, feeling uneasy. She picked up a large knife, and instantly pictured Justine's hand. This felt wrong, uncomfortable. She saw a small tin of Darjeeling tea—Justine's?

June tried to push her discomfort out of her mind as she minced garlic for their feast of pattypan squash. It occurred to her that she was chopping in her bra, and she picked her sweater up off the floor and pulled it hastily back over her head.

"Where are the dogs?" she asked Rich.

"We actually have a scaled version of this house in the backyard, and they live there. It's heated and everything," Rich said as he rubbed olive oil over a small chicken. He reached for a jar of sea salt and began to rub the cavity of the bird with salt. June tried to make small talk as she pitted her cherries, preparing a tart for after lunch. Pretend you're the caterer, she said to herself.

"How's work?"

"Ah, I need a new way of living," Rich answered. "These stupid television shows are going to kill me. If Jennifer English is going to ruin my chance of getting on the air after all the work I have done on this, which PS she is now mutilating, I am going to freak. I planned on retiring on this show."

Rich carefully slid his finger beneath the skin of the bird, inching rosemary branches under it. June thought to herself that no matter how successful *Sole Operator* was, Mitch was the type who would keep slogging on.

June rubbed cherry juice off her hands with a white cotton towel, and was made instantly even more tense by the bright red stain it left. She thought of the faded blue tea towels that were stuffed in a drawer— one that was always coming off its runners—in her kitchen. They were stained well beyond any damage that a few cherries could inflict.

"Well, what would you do if you stopped writing?"

"I don't know," Rich said, smiling widely. That smile that June had first noticed on the All Stars night last winter, the one that greeted her every time they met, the one that shined its light onto her. She wondered if anyone she knew would see her car.

Rich tucked the chicken into the oven, and washed his hands carefully with lemon-verbena soap. Tiny bubbles puffed out of his sponge, emitting a smell that June recognized as being slightly of Justine. June wrapped her arms around him this time and squeezed tightly, closing her eyes, and tried to imagine them in the W Hotel. The steel and concrete of the house were making her crave a heavier sweater, and the presence of Justine was oppressive. Rich turned and slid his hand, warm from the hot water, under her shirt.

"If you move that bag of flour, I can do everything I've done to you on the phone on this kitchen island at last."

June was conflicted, her discomfort slowly being melted by the feel of Rich's lips hot on her neck, and his hands under her bra. She began to breathe heavier, and slid her own hand down the front of his pants. He moved her backward, and she stumbled a little as she tried to get her footing through the maze of open space of the kitchen.

Suddenly, the room filled with the booming sound of William Shatner's voice. *"Space, the final frontier."*

June jumped, and Rich laughed. "That's the doorbell. It's the only fun Justine would let me have in this gorgeous mausoleum." Rich carefully guided June toward the library, where row upon row of perfectly symmetrical books rested in the floor-to-ceiling shelves. In the room was a black Formica desk with an Aeron chair, and a small white leather love seat, the only softish object in the house.

"That's Spa Dog. It won't take long," Rich said.

"His name is Spa Dog?" June asked.

"No, his name is Dylan. His service is Spa Dog. He comes to groom Wendy and Peter every week. I just need to write him a check, and he'll deal with the kids himself. Just wait here. I'll be back in a jiffy."

"Okay," June said, mildly amused, and pulled her bra strap back onto her shoulder. She tugged on her sweater as she examined the books. There were books by journalists, arranged in alphabetical order by author's last name. There was the entire oeuvre of Nora Ephron, which made June smile. A large shelf held a gorgeous collection of coffee table books: a photo book on Moroccan henna, one of Indochina through the ages, a glorious collection of Ed Ruscha paintings.

June overheard Spa Dog at the door.

"Did you get a bird?"

"No, why do you think that?" Rich said, sounding confused.

"I thought I heard the small tinkle of a bird. I don't go in houses with birds," Spa Dog said.

June heard the tinny yap, yap, yap of a small dog. She peered around the corner carefully, hoping that Spa Dog would not see her. He was a medium-built, deeply tanned guy, about thirty she would say, with a mop of wavy red hair swept across his forehead. His aquiline nose was the centerpiece of his face, which was sculpted and handsome, with a sort of a *Dukes of Hazzard* veneer. He reached down and scooped up a Chihuahua that June noticed was wearing a strand of pink pearls.

"Golly Gee, knock it off," Spa Dog admonished his own pet. "Or no fun for you today."

"Justine said to tell you that she thinks she has the ear mites under control but wants you to take a look," Rich said.

"I'll make sure those honeypots are good as new today," said Spa Dog, rubbing Golly Gee's head.

"Okay, so let me get a check. How much do we owe you?"

Spa Dog did his calculations. "Let's see, four weeks, plus Wendy's coat treatment, that's three hundred eighty dollars."

"Okay. Does that include today?" Rich asked.

"Nope. Justine left me a message saying she wanted aromatherapy massage for both today, so that would be an extra fifty each."

"Why do they need that?" Rich asked.

"Just a little stress reduction after the whole ear mite thing," Spa Dog said.

"Well, Justine runs the dogs. I'll write you a check for everything then."

As Rich walked off to the back of the house, Spa Dog seemed to be taking a call. "Well tell her if she wants her Labradoodle to look like Jake Gyllenhaal she needs to leave me a picture of Jake, because I don't memorize these people. Uh-huh. Uh-huh. What is she talking about? We hand-blow-dry every dog! Hot dryer, spare me! I don't even know if I want her business. Uh-huh. Uh-huh. Okay, I gotta run. I'm with a client."

As Rich and Spa Dog concluded their business, June sat down on the white leather couch. As she settled into the cushions, she realized she was sitting on something hard, and reached under her thigh to pull at whatever it was. She stared down at her hand in disbelief. It was a silver vial, with the intials LD engraved on the bottom. She opened it and breathed deeply. Rescue Remedy.

Had there been a party here? No way. She would have known about that. Larissa came by to see Justine? Justine hated Larissa. June flashed to the night at Orso. It dawned on her all at once.

June was not Justine's bimbo.

Rich walked into the library and toward June, seemingly not noticing what was in her hand. He touched her hair. "Where were we?"

June opened her palm like a small child discovering that she had squished a butterfly.

"What's this?" she asked.

Rich was silent.

"It's Larissa Dermot's," June said. "What is it doing here?"

Rich's cheeks flushed, but he said nothing. He turned his face toward his desk, searchingly, as if he would find his answer there. After what was probably five seconds, but felt to June like an hour, Rich sat down on the couch and looked up at her. She looked back at his face as if seeing it for the first time. It no longer resembled Andy Flynn's; it was older, lined, and hard around the edges. His smile now seemed slick, like the grin of that guy whose name she could never remember who was running for state comptroller. She felt exposed tugging on her sweater, making sure her shoulder wasn't showing.

"This can't be happening," she said.

June heard a pinging in her ear, as though she had been hit with a large object and was just now regaining consciousness. She smelled the oily scent of cooking chicken flesh, and thought suddenly of a day at the Hell's Kitchen food festival years ago, where she had gone to eat sausages with a boy she had dated briefly her freshman year in college.

She had made a snide remark about his music, and he had slapped her, fairly hard, in the middle of the street. She had dropped her sausage and run back to her dorm, some sixty blocks or more, barely stopping. As she sat in her tiny dark room, she wondered how she had been blind to the obvious malignancy of a personality that was beguiling, in retrospect, only on its surface.

June pushed past Rich, grabbing her purse off the kitchen counter. She searched frantically for a doorknob, and found it buried in the architecture of the door. She pulled it open, and the sunlight flooded in. She looked back at her lover, who was standing in his bare feet, his jaw hardened in a way she had never seen before. "June, you're overreacting."

"Rich, I hate when people tell me I'm overreacting. It's a cliché, and I hate those, too. And since you like lists, here are some more things I hate. I hate people who butcher Chopin. I hate people who care enough about cars to ask a guest to park down the street. I hate liars. So I, I guess I hate myself."

Rich tried to interrupt, but June was already out the door.

"Oh, and by the way, Rich Friend, it's 'lay your sleeping head, my love, human on my FAITHLESS arm,' not FAITHFUL!"

June rushed out the door, past Justine and Rich's cactus garden and down the uneven polished stone steps that led down the hill. Spa Dog's polka-dotted van was parked nearby, and she heard the whir of a hair dryer. "You're my princess, Wendy, just give me that last paw. . . ."

June descended the steps of Rich's house and in a haze turned the wrong way. She found herself racing through narrow little streets of the Palisades, unable to find her car. She took a left, and then another left—was that the spot?—and suddenly found herself trampling through a large garden of azaleas. Her eyes stung with tears of frustration. Finally, after twenty-five minutes, she stumbled across her car, parked just where she left it, with a fifty-dollar ticket attached to the window, for turning her wheels the wrong way on a hill.

June collapsed into the Honda and pecked away at the radio dial, trying to find reception. The only thing that came through was Christian radio. She cranked it, and wrapped her arms around herself, trying to warm up. She felt something—it wasn't quite sadness, but what it was, she did not know.

For some reason she could not fathom, she remembered being in the third grade, and receiving the assignment of collecting signatures from all the teachers in her school for a going-away card for a departing principal. She stood outside the classroom of Miss Hathaway, feeling that it was hotter than the other rooms, and smelled of bubble gum. She had mispronounced the name of the principal, and Miss Hathaway corrected her, laughing, and the rest of her fifth-grade class laughed too.

She remembered calling Andy Flynn, and sitting quietly on the line. "I know it's you, June." She had placed the phone down in the dark.

She remembered last year when her cell went off during an important department presentation, how she had fished frantically in her bottomless purse to find it, and could see only a tiny green flashing light as it rang, incessantly and loudly, while everyone stared.

She knew the feeling: dumb.

But the worst part for June, in this moment of shameful epiphany, wasn't that she had nearly ruined her marriage, ignored her work, failed her child, broken her vows to Mitch, lied, overspent, used another woman's (slightly dull) paring knife, or compromised everything that she had ever known herself to be. The most painful, untenable thing of all was that she, June Dietz, had something in common with Larissa Dermot.

Now the memory of Rich Friend's hands on her body did nothing to excite her; it made her feel ridiculous. She tried to feel something else, anything, but only felt alone. She drove the car down the hill and toward the beach, and soon found herself parked in the Santa Monica public parking lot. There were a few surfers in the lot, and some mothers dragging tired toddlers behind them. A collection of junkies were gathered in a van, their skin weather-beaten, passing around a bottle of cheap vodka. June sat and stared for two hours, thinking about the day Nora was born—how Mitch had brought June bagels and cream cheese from Izzy's in Santa Monica and how they had eaten together on her hospital bed gazing at their tiny daughter.

June pulled up to her house, realizing that it was way past the time that Olga was supposed to go. She felt guilty for keeping Olga and also wondered if there was anything in the fridge for dinner. She walked in the house, and Nora ran toward her, bathed and smelling of Mustela baby wash. She buried her head in Nora's hair, taking in her scent.

June walked into the kitchen, holding Nora heavy in her arms, and found Mitch stirring a large pot of steamed vegetables. He asked June, "Where have you been? I was getting worried. I've been trying to reach you for an hour."

"Oh, my cell ran out of battery."

"Again? June, when are you going to buy a car charger? Jesus.

Anyway, I have some steaks on the grill. I had another WONDERFUL day at the set today. The network literally almost shut the show down."

"Where's Olga?" June asked.

"I've been here awhile. I let her go early—she had some thing at her kid's school. Anyway, are you listening to me? A crew of executives came skulking around complaining that we were behind schedule and over budget. Justine freaked on them—it was ugly. Let me tell ya. Not pretty. But I give Justine credit, she got things rolling again within two hours, and the suits disappeared. She's a pro."

Nora was now sitting at the table, playing with a Polly Pocket doll and murmuring a little ditty. "Renew! Reuse! Recycle!" Renew! Reuse! Recycle!" "Household waste! Blech. blech, blech!"

June looked at her four-year-old. "Where did you learn that?"

"School. We don't want to make landfills."

"What's a landfill, Nora?"

"Bad garbage's house," Nora answered.

Mitch's forehead was a bit sweaty, with a small patch of sauce on it. One hand was covered in a thick silver oven mitt. "Maybe they could teach them a little more lowercase letters, a little less environmentalism."

"Yeah, well . . ." June looked in the wine rack and pulled out a Barolo and poured them each a deep glass.

"Mommy, is wine a grown-up drink?"

"It is, Noony. But you can have some grape juice." June poured Nora a glass, diluting it a bit with water, and Nora grabbed it with two hands.

"What made you decide to cook?" June asked Mitch as she settled into a kitchen chair. She felt exhausted, as if she had not slept in months, and her stomach tensed with starvation.

"I wouldn't say decide. I would say forced. You weren't here. Anyway, the one blessing today was that Jennifer managed to get off one whole line on the first try."

"One line?" June asked.

"I'm kidding. Well, sort of. Anyway, we got out early because she had to present at the Environmental Media Awards."

"What are they giving an award for this time?" June asked. "Actor to use most environmentally correct tissue to wipe his ass?"

Mitch cracked up, and his laughter made June laugh too. For the next hour, Mitch and June ate their barbecued steaks, wiped down kitchen counters, read Nora three stories together, smashed some termites that were embedding in the front door, and talked about Mitch's show.

He told her how Jennifer English had taken two different band members from the Barenaked Ladies to her trailer, each time causing production to hold up for an hour. How she had to have makeup plastered over her carefully placed tattoos. How Jennifer's love interest on the show, "Jeremy," an English actor named Hugh Oliver, would chain-smoke unfiltered cigarettes between takes and mutter, "That fucking slag! That fucking slag! What is she playing at, not knowing one bloody word. Fucking cow."

June finished the last bit of inky wine and sediment in her glass, laughing at Mitch's rendition of Hugh Oliver, of the cameraman, of desperate Ed slugging Red Bulls at Video Village, of America's foul-mouthed sweetheart. June wiped up the last bit of crumbs from the table and turned off the kitchen light.

"Oh," Mitch said, "I forgot to tell you something. I could swear that Tad is having an affair with Kathy Griffin."

"Who?" June asked.

"That D-list star. Do you know her? Apparently they met at the Bow Wow Wein. You know that party where you dress your dogs up. I guess Kathy has one of those runty dogs, and apparently she dressed one up as Juliet for this party, and it just so happened that Tad had dressed up Zeus as Romeo. Isn't that weird?"

"Well, Tad's weird," June said.

"That's true. Anyway, after that thing with Candy Christmas he started talking about Kathy Griffin this, Kathy Griffin that. Love is odd, don't you think? I mean, what do you make of it?" Mitch asked.

June stared out the window into her dark yard. She wondered if it would be cold in the morning. "I haven't the foggiest idea."

She picked up her overflowing milk carton of compost and headed into the yard. She pushed away a large palm from her now-blooming bird-of-paradise plant and walked to the compost bin. As June pulled the top off, she heard a rustling in the container, and peered down to examine the source of the sound. Suddenly she heard the wild screech of a small animal leaping up at her—a medium-sized brown squirrel with a scruffy tail—and she could see from the garden light its dirty mangled claws poised to defend its trash. June yelped in fear and skidded back as the squirrel's nails swiped at her sweater, ripping a large hole where Rich Friend's hand had been hours before.

Shaken, she brushed madly at her front as she made her way back into the house, watching the irate scatter-hoarder scurry off into the bushes. June had bought the sweater one day last year on her lunch hour when she was cold. She pulled it over her head, and stuffed the sweater in the kitchen trash.

CHAPTER 25

"So, what have you heard?" Mitch had been trying to reach Tad all day, and he had finally unearthed his manager, who had been having lunch at Craft with his top client, Jessica, visiting another client on the set of *Big Love*, and doing a home visit for the dog adoption agency he volunteered for.

"I've heard what you've been hearing—a lot of crap from people who don't know anything,"

In the three weeks since *Sole Operator* wrapped, Mitch had been obsessively checking online for gossip, signals, predictions, and hints about the fate of the pilot. People who had been in the focus group blogged about their experiences, and their reactions were all over the map. Jennifer English seemed to sell well to younger guys, but women were less than charitable.

The Futon Critic, a television blogger, claimed to hear that ABC loved the show, but Nikki Finke, another Hollywood blogger, said it was toast. Both of them were wrong as often as they were right, but no matter. Luke Lemon had called Mitch daily, trying to deconstruct every bit of information he had heard, most of which was totally inconclusive, like the men had tested well, but the show had tested poorly, and vice versa. All of this Mitch repeated frantically to Tad.

"Mitch, chill," Tad told him. "Nobody knows anything until the networks announce later today what they're picking up. You know the game: network suits leak fake stories to bloggers to trick the other networks about what their fall lineup will be. Sometimes the show that is

266

the least talked about is their ace in the hole. You've been going through this for years. Stop."

"I can't stop! This is my life."

"Okay, well, stop calling me, then."

Tad hung up, and Mitch, frustrated, went back to Googling *Sole Operator.* He soon got an e-mail from Tad: the ABC travel department had called to confirm Mitch's availability to travel to New York for the upfronts, which was a good sign. But then again Mitch had heard through the grapevine that CBS had called the entire cast of *My Dad Is Totally Weird,* and everyone knew that it was not getting picked up.

The doorbell rang. Mitch peered out the door and saw a young guy standing on his step, holding the telltale clipboard of a magazine salesman, so ubiquitous in Los Angeles. Mitch opened the door carefully, and with dread, too guilty to simply ignore the knock.

"Hello sir, you might note from my dress that I am a young man on my way upwardly mobile through the system of selling a product for points," the kid said, staring at the doorbell. He looked up at Mitch to continue his pitch, but instantly recognized him.

"I know you! You're in the movies, man!"

"Yeah, I am."

"You live here?" The kid craned his neck around to see behind the house. "Where's your good car, man? I know that Saab ain't yours. Where you hiding your Mercedes?"

"I don't have a Mercedes," Mitch answered.

"Oh come on, man. Why you living here with the regular people? You're in the movies."

"Because I am a regular person," Mitch said. "Listen, I don't need any magazines."

"Oh man, you can buy ten subscriptions for the Boys Club of America. People always need magazines, and then I get one hundred points toward my mobility."

"You know what, I'm kind of busy here. So how 'bout I give you a hundred dollars and we call it a day, okay?" Mitch offered.

"Man, you're in the movies. How about a grand?"

"A thousand dollars! Are you nuts?"

"Oh, did I scare you? I didn't mean to scare you," the kid said.

"You didn't scare me, you repulsed me."

"All right, all right, with one hundred dollars you can get ten magazines—"

"Just take the hundred. I don't care what you do with it." Mitch took out his wallet.

The kid pocketed the five crisp twenty-dollar bills and was on his way.

Mitch went back to his office, and saw he had two voice mail messages. Before he could listen to them, the doorbell rang again. Furious, he marched back to the front door, ready to let the magazine kid have it. Instead, he found a messenger standing on the stoop, his face obscured by a humongous gift basket covered in red cellophane, its enormous handle sticking out from the top. Mitch tipped the delivery guy and carried the basket back to his office. Excited, he tore open the card. *"Mitch, welcome to the ABC family."* Ecstatic, he picked up his phone and hit Tad on the speed dial.

"I got a gift basket! It's HUGE! The show got picked up!" Mitch yelled into the phone exuberantly.

"I know. ABC just announced a few minutes ago. Didn't you get my message?"

"What, no!"

"Yes! This is exciting—just the break you were waiting for this season. Justine and Rich, well Justine anyway, hot, hot, hot! Congratulations, man!"

"Does Tim know?"

"Yes, he's thrilled for you. He says he'll call you later."

"Yeah, I bet he's got other clients to congratulate. And some to drop."

"I didn't say it. You did. Oh and I just got an offer for you—*Viva Elko*. Starts tomorrow. It's a pretty good part, town sheriff."

"Tomorrow? Wow, this is my day! Did the guy they cast for it tank at the table reading?" Mitch asked.

"Something like that. You wanna do it? It's a few day's work for top of the show, sixty-seven hundred and change."

"I'm in. Thanks, Tad." Mitch hung up and dialed his voice mail.

"Hey, it's Tad. ABC announced—you got picked up. Congratulations!"

Next message, Angie at CAA. "Hey, Mitch, great job. Congratulations. We knew you would do it."

Mitch collapsed with glee on his couch and called June, who was happy, but frazzled, because she was on her way to meet with her department head. Next Mitch called Luke Lemon, who had also gotten his gift basket.

"Yeah man! Woo-hoo! See you in New York, man!" Luke said.

"See you in New York! Ritz Carlton! Thank you, ABC! First-class all the way! Here comes the swag!"

Mitch carried the fruit basket to the kitchen, tilting a little as he walked, the thing was so damn heavy. He carefully placed the basket in the middle of the kitchen table and pulled at the cellophane. In the center was a giant snow globe, its glycerin-coated snow dribbling along a night scene of the Empire State Building. Mitch smiled—Nora would love it. He wound it up and set it on the table, listening to a soft, tinny rendition of "New York, New York" as he dug around a little bit in the basket for a snack, pawing over organic pears, oranges, grapes, Medjool dates, Godiva chocolates, kiwis, and two passion fruits.

He grabbed an apple and bit hard into its underripe surface. An episodic job without an audition, a go series, a trip to New York this weekend to present the new show to advertisers, and a snow globe. Excellent life, his. He made a mental note to run up to 107th Street when he was in New York to pick up Absolute Bagels. June liked the pumpernickel ones.

June pulled her car into the UCLA faculty parking lot, under a jacaranda tree in full purple bloom. They were by far her favorite trees in Los Angeles. She hopped out of her car, slammed her skirt in the door, then fumbled for her keys, reopened the door, pulled her skirt out, and slapped at the black line of dirt left by the door. She heard a text message bleeping on her phone, and looked at it as she made her way toward the department head's office.

Pls call. Pls.

It was perhaps the tenth text message from Rich Friend since that afternoon at his house on the hill, on top of several phone message, e-mails, and a bunch of anonymous flowers sent to her office, which she dropped at the reception desk at the UCLA hospital on the way home, asking the receptionist to give it to someone without flowers in her room. It wasn't that she didn't still crave to hear Rich's voice, or wonder what he was doing, or deconstruct what had happened. But every day at school, as she watched Larissa standing by the children's cubbies in her skintight yoga pants, June reflected on a deeper desire, which was to fail with pride at fitting in.

Of course, no one at school spoke to her anymore. They dipped their heads at the stoplight on Pico so as not to have to make eye contact. Once or twice she heard a few moms whispering about her as she walked down the hall. "She didn't even bother to bake a cake this year for the shelter fund raiser." Or, "She had better not try and take credit for that after-school project. I don't care that it was her idea." Town Crier tried to intervene—he scheduled a class barbecue (boneless breasts, no sauce) at his house, but June declined the invitation. At this point, to make amends would be to become *them*. And all of Rich Friend's entreaties went unanswered.

June sat in the large black chair of her department head's office, watching him flip through a pile of papers. Was it possible he had gained even more weight since the last time she was in here? She looked at the frosted glass Mikasa frame surrounding the photo of his wife and children, all of them overweight.

She tried to picture dinner at their house. What went on there? Did his wife serve those canned pears in syrupy juice? She imagined a slightly soiled tablecloth, and lots of challah, maybe a large bowl of ice cream after, drizzled with Hershey's chocolate sauce. She was so lost in her fantasy, she failed to notice that Bob was looking at her with concern.

"June, this is going to be a hard conversation. There are few people in this department whose company I enjoy more, or whose intellect I respect as much."

"Bob, let me just say that I know I have been slow to publish over the last year. I had a few things that were blocking me, which I can't really explain to you. I do see things picking up soon."

"June, you're stellar in the classroom. Your students constantly give great feedback in your evals, and I know you are always prepared. Your curriculum ideas are inventive, and your administrative service is exemplary. And honestly, the work you have published is penetrating and masterful."

June knew there was a "but" coming.

"But the truth is, we have found you increasingly, and adamantly, inner-directed. It seems while everyone is confident in the brilliance of your work, you have almost pathologically ignored my constant reminders that brilliant research alone is inutile if one doesn't put it before an audience."

June felt tears forming, to her anger, and she stared at Bob. He continued speaking.

"Everyone here loved your first book, and they find the concept of your second book compelling, but we've seen only a single chapter of it, and you haven't submitted anything for a journal." Bob paused, waiting for June to respond, but she felt paralyzed and said nothing, so he went on.

"I feel certain that if you were able to get your book moving, the department would rally behind you in a tenure vote. Your brainpower alone is probably an insurance policy toward future productivity. But I feel equally certain that given your poor publication rate with this book, the academic personnel committee would give you a no."

June continued her stare, saying nothing. Her first instinct was to be furious—how many lesser academics had she watched founder, writing nary a sentence fragment once granted tenure—and to protest in the strongest terms what Bob was laying before her. But her mind went to an image of herself, splayed under her kitchen table, her ear to her cell phone. She thought of the velvety soft bedspread at the Hotel Angeleno and the smell of inky red wine and fresh cherries. If June had wanted to be a tenured professor of English at the University of California, Los Angeles, her choices would have been different. And now it was too late.

"I can't tell you not to complete your package, June. I can only discourage you from what I think would be an unpleasant outcome for you and your family." Bob looked saddened. June thought of Nora: *My mommy is a failed tenure-track instructor of ancient poetry.* June thanked her department head, and quietly slipped out.

June walked back to her car slowly, as if there were mud pulling at her shoes. Sticky pollen had covered her car, and tiny purple petals were stuck in the windshield wipers. June brushed futilely at them, then opened the door, sat down, and, without bothering to close the door, dialed Adrian.

"I'm not getting tenure."

"What? Honey, what happened?"

"It's the damn book. I had an affair and the man I was having an affair with had an affair and I failed to write about poetry and male rage and lost my job. More or less," June said.

"Oh, honey, I'm so sorry. Do you want me to come there?"

"No, it's okay. Of course I would love to see you." June sniffed and wiped at her eyes.

"You know, June, I seriously think you need to blow La La Land and come back to New York."

June sniffed again, drawing in a shudder. She imagined herself walking across her old stomping grounds at Columbia, with red leaves falling around her. Well, she got tanked for tenure at UCLA, so maybe she would have to imagine herself walking around the Sixty-eighth Street subway stop near Hunter College instead. That would be okay. There was a good soup place near there. New York. She could leave LA—where everyone was trying to Botox, exercise, and juice-fast his way toward immortality—and go back to the world of the living, where people ate and drank and stayed out late, accepting the joyous toll of life.

June sniffed, "I don't even own a winter coat anymore."

"That's insane. I'll take you to Searle and you'll get a huge bubble coat on sale this summer."

"I don't know. Mitch just got a series."

"Oh. Well," Adrian said, "I didn't necessarily think you'd be bringing Mitch, not after everything that's been going on."

June felt a little punch in her stomach. She imagined herself at Café La Fortuna—was it even still there?—drinking espresso by herself and staring at the photos of John Lennon. She imagined walking with

Nora on the cobblestones near the entrance to the Museum of Natural History, without Mitch. She thought about getting on the subway, with no one on the opposite side of the track, going the other way, waving. Their town, without Mitch. She realized she missed him deeply, and she hadn't even left.

June pulled her car into a parking space a few blocks from school and walked slowly toward the car pool lane. Libby was talking to demi, and moved to smile at June, who waved. But when demi looked up, Libby pretended to be waving at someone behind June. June saw the one other working mother from her class and tried to catch up with her, but that mom was walking stridently, clearly with no time for chitchat.

June found Larissa in her Escalade, hunched down and yelling at Autumn, who was assigned to deposit kids into their cars that day.

"Sorry, Larissa, it's the temple rule. If you're talking on your cell phone in the car pool lane, you have to circle the block again. Sorry."

"Oh, for crying out loud! I'm holding for my husband's manager. Am I supposed to say, 'Oh, they've got a rule at the Jewish preschool. No phone calls!'"

"Sorry, Larissa. I'll get in trouble. Chloe will be waiting right here."

June sidled up to Larissa's car and dropped the Rescue Remedy vial in the driver's-side window. Larissa looked down at her lap as the vial fell onto her crotch, and then up at June with astonishment.

"You heard her, Larissa, move your eighteen-wheeler."

June walked away, her hand feeling oddly empty without the vial that she had stared at at every traffic light for the last few weeks. She had considered sending it Federal Express, without a note, but realized that people were no longer allowed to send anonymous FedEx packages. She considered both keeping it and throwing it away, but somehow both options spelled a missed opportunity. It belonged to Larissa; let her brood over how June got it.

June walked into Nora's classroom, dodging the scramble of two dozen four-year-olds moving like little calves toward their mothers and nannies, and greeting them with the litany of preschooler complaints that befell them each day: *Why did you pack me that yucky sandwich? I don't wanna go to the dentist! My banana got mushy.*

June made her way toward an ebullient Nora, who was putting on her shoes as she walked up. "Mommy, I was bathroom monitor today!" June smiled and kissed her head as she gathered Nora's artwork and watched Nora put her Harry Potter glasses on.

"Do you want to go to the market with me, Noony?"

"No, I want to have a playdate with Charlotte."

"Okay, I'll drop you there, and pick you up after I go to Whole Foods."

After a brief exchange with Town Crier—"How are you?" "Couldn't be better. I'll see you in an hour." "Would you mind bringing me a quart of soy milk?" "Sure." "Make sure it's Silk, though. I don't like the other brands." "Yeah, okay, Brant."—June made her way to the store. A new mom, Carol, glared at her. Had she ever even spoken to her?

June wandered the aisles aimlessly, trying to think about what she might make for dinner this week. Maybe just lasagna. She couldn't imagine much more. A cake would make her feel better, and she picked up a bag of sugar and a vanilla bean. Her mind kept returning to Bob's ruddy, chubby face. "Adamantly inner-directed." That was a good characteristic for baking, anyway.

June stopped in front of a display of watermelons. They looked so luscious, and she imagined Nora with sweet red juice running down her chin, and spitting the seeds into her tiny hand. June grabbed the biggest one she could find and made her way to the line. As she filled her car with groceries, she realized she had forgotten to take her beach chairs out of the trunk, and would not be able to wedge all her bags back there. She tossed one bag in Nora's car seat, and the watermelon on the passenger seat, and turned her car toward home.

June made her way through the late-afternoon traffic, annoyed with the thickness coming from the 405, and decided to get off of Wilshire. She took a right on Selby and took her foot off the accelerator as the car slid down a large hill. Suddenly, her watermelon rolled off the seat, past the empty space between the two seats, and landed on the accelerator, causing her Honda to lunge forward at fifty-five miles an hour.

Panicked, June kicked furiously at the giant melon, to no avail. Then, manically beeping, she pressed hard on the brake as her car sped toward a blue BMW. June instantly thought of Town Crier telling Nora that her mommy had been killed on Selby, murdered by a fruit.

SCREECH! POW!

June plowed into the back of the BMW, and her head snapped forward. Instantly, a young guy with a thin gold chain came racing toward her. June's leg shook with terror, but she was paralyzed by her billowing air bags.

"What the fuck?" he asked.

"Sorry, my watermelon fell!" June stammered.

"Your water fucking what?"

"I had this fruit in the passenger seat! Oh God I am so, so sorry."

The BMW guy manically dialed his cell phone as the traffic behind them began to honk and swerve. He made another call, and she heard him yelling into the phone in Russian. Within minutes, two police officers on motorcycles arrived and put up some flares around the mangled cars, while indignant drivers slowly maneuvered around them.

"You okay, miss?"

"I think so," June said, rubbing the back of her neck. The watermelon, peeking out from under the air bag, was largely intact though its red fleshy interior was emerging somewhat and leaking sticky juice.

"Have you had any alcohol, miss?" the officer asked.

"No. I had a fruit problem. I can explain. See, my gearshift is up by the steering wheel, so there's this big space between my two seats, and stuff is, stuff is always rolling around down there. My daughter's doll shoes and stuff."

"Yeah," the officer said. "So let me get this straight. You were approaching Selby from the north when the fruit item on your front seat began to roll forward with some amount of speed. Could you estimate perhaps how fast you were going?"

Over the next thirty minutes, June soon learned all about her victim, Bogdan Egorov, who had calmed down only slightly as the police made an accident report: he was twenty-five, lived in West Hollywood, really liked his car, did not know how to change a tire, was a former world champion vaulter and now worked as a gymnastics coach in Mar Vista, was allergic to almonds, and had a girlfriend named Zoya, who soon raced up to the accident scene and tumbled out of her car in a panic.

Zoya was tall and slim, with dark hair and thin eyebrows, which were met by wings of sparking blue eye shadow. Her shapely legs, covered partially with knee-high leather boots, tumbled from a metallic minidress. Seeing Bogdan unscathed, she tottered toward him, wrapped her arms dramatically around him, and covered his face in kisses. June, who had been finishing up her Breathalyzer test with the police officer, approached them both sheepishly.

"I'm really sorry," June said. "It was a terrible accident."

Zoya slightly turned her face from her almond-averse, BMW-driving lover, holding on to his championship triceps, and kept her cheek pressed to his as she gazed at June. "Don worry, darling. These are only material tings. Life is much more than all of this."

CHAPTER 26

"With just one call I can shut this whole operation down."

"Sheriff, you don't own this town. I do."

"And cut! Everyone in the bar area for rehearsal," the AD called.

Mitch meandered off the set, grabbing a granola bar off the craft table as he made his way through the Morongo casino, where he was on location for *Viva Elko*. It was near the end of his day in the desert town of Cabazon, and he was hoping to hit the freeway before rush hour. His head was already in New York, and he had been mentally running through a hypothetical question-and-answer session with the entertainment reporters.

> Q: What was it like to work with Jennifer English?
> A: It was a dream. She's an actor's actor, the most professional person I've ever worked with. And she's so funny, I mean we blew so many takes just laughing.
> Q: Have you ever gotten a manicure in real life?

Mitch walked toward a blackjack table, adjusting his oversized brown sheriff's hat. His gun holster hung uncomfortably, rubbing against his leg, and his gold badge was slightly open under his shirt, poking him in the chest. It was a hot costume, and Mitch was looking forward to getting back into his jeans.

"Hey, Mitch, I can't thank you enough for helping me get this gig."

"No problem, Taylor," Mitch said, waving in her direction. The original roulette girl had looked too much like the star, so they'd fired her the day before. Mitch, at June's urging, had recommended June's student for the one-line part. He kept walking, so as not to have to talk to her further.

Mitch slid down into one of the oversized tan chairs near the bar and waited for his next and last scene to be up. He turned on his phone, and saw that he had a message from Rich Friend. "Hey, Mitch, can you give me a call?" Mitch quickly dialed Rich off his caller ID, wondering if they were planning a cast dinner in New York already.

"Hey, Mitch, thanks for calling back," said Rich, sounding formal.

"No problem. What's happening?"

"Well, I have some good news, and I have some bad news," Rich said.

"Okay, good news first."

"The good news is *Sole Operator* is going to be the lead-in for *Ugly Betty*."

"Great! They must love us!" Mitch said.

"They do. But the bad news is it doesn't look like you'll be with the show."

"What?!" Mitch could hardly breathe.

"Yeah, sorry, man. The network wants to go another way."

"Rich, are you telling me I'm fired?"

"That's a strong word," Rich answered. "More like replaced."

Mitch sank to the floor of the casino, the heat from the blue overhead neon lights burning into his neck. He felt absurd, sitting there in a brown sheriff uniform, with a cell phone pressed to his ear, his throat tightening with rage.

"So where exactly is the good news in this for me?" he asked Rich.

"Yeah, huh, well, you got me there. Sorry about this, Mitch. Ya know, I'll let you go." Rich hung up. Probably off to a casting session for Mitch's part.

Mitch dialed Tad, his hands shaking.

"Tad, I got fired! The fuckers fired me!"

"Yeah, I am sorry, man. I heard this morning."

"So why didn't you tell me?" Mitch asked desperately.

"I wanted to wait to call you at home tonight, not ruin your day on the set."

"What happened? Did I test badly?"

"No, not at all. My friend Mike in programming at ABC said your numbers were really high."

"Did the network hate me?" Mitch asked. "Was it Jennifer? Did she get rid of me? And by the way, where was Justine in all of this? I thought she was in my corner."

Tad sighed. "No, the network was fine. Jennifer English had some medical thing, so she hasn't even been around. And yes, Justine fought for you. Really hard. The issue was Rich. He just had something about you. He said basically it was you or him. To be honest, I think Justine would have picked you, but the network would never go for it. Did you and Rich have one of your things?"

Mitch did a frantic mental inventory of how and when he might have angered Rich Friend. He did always beat him at golf, but they hadn't played lately. Did he laugh enough at his stupid jokes? Was he too nice to Justine, and maybe Rich thought he had been flirting?

"I can't think of anything offhand. My affronts are usually pretty out in the open."

"Yeah, that's true," Tad agreed. "The whole thing sucks, but honestly, Mitch, these guys are idiots to fire you. I saw the pilot—you were great, and you absolutely should not have been replaced. You wanna know what I think? I think Rich Friend has been rendered ball-less by his absolute inferiority to his wife on this show, and was trying to pull a power play. That's what I think."

Mitch was devastated by Rich's enmity. But it didn't matter. All he knew was that he had just lost a huge job, maybe the only one like it he'd ever get, and now he had to go home to tell June, who had been crushed by her own professional setbacks.

"Tad, listen, do you know who's replacing me?"

"Yeah, I know."

"Who?" Mitch demanded.

"Ugh, Mitch, I don't wanna be the one to tell you."

"Come on, it can't get worse."

"Well," Tad said, "it's Willie Dermot."

Mitch threw the phone across the bar, and it separated as it hit the wall, the battery landing in a highball.

For the next two hours, Mitch muddled his way through his final scene in *Viva Elko*, a man split in half. When it came time to shoot, he said his lines expertly. When the director yelled cut, he immediately began to crumble in front of the other cast members.

"I'm so sorry," said Kelly Connell, who was playing the role of the blackjack dealer. "I was fired from *Picket Fences* in 1996 and I won an Emmy later that year. So keep your chin up." Mitch took a bit of balm from his co-workers' sympathetic remarks, but at each cut, he still fell into a daze. Fired. Shit! And Willie Fucking Dermot. That was "another way"?

A twenty-four-year-old Thai woman. That would have been another way. Isaiah Washington, that would have been another way. A hugely fat bald guy thirty years his senior, that would have been another way, too. But another forty-year-old white character actor with whom he had been competing for roles for over a decade? That was not "another way." That was the same way, minus fifty IQ points.

During the two-hour drive on the 60, which Mitch had hopped on in a futile attempt to beat the rush-hour traffic on the 10, his thoughts turned in an endless loop to the set of *Sole Operator*. What had he done? Why had this happened? Was that PA with the breakfast burrito Rich's cousin? And Mitch felt with distinct certainty that this failure would only presage a dozen more.

Mitch made his way past Riverside, and breathed in the smell of cow dung and burning chemicals. His car inched through Pomona in heavy traffic, behind three tractor trailers, and he watched the spewing diesel smoke pour toward him, the world an ugly place.

Tomorrow, anyone who read *Variety* would know what had happened, and he would be tainted. And he was as good as dead at CAA.

Mitch walked through the door and saw June combing Nora's hair, still wet from her bath, as Nora quietly sang yet another environmental ditty from preschool. "What is the solution to storm water pollution?" The ABC fruit basket sat on the kitchen table, its red cellophane still covering one corner.

"Hey, are you okay?" June asked him.

"Well, I was fired from *Sole Operator*, and replaced by Willie, and all I have to show for pilot season is this fruit basket."

"Oh my God, Mitch, what happened?"

"I wanted to call you from the road but I broke my phone. Rich called and fired me. He hated me, apparently. I don't know. I just know I'm off the show."

June's face hardened, but she said nothing. Nora looked at Mitch. "What's fired?" June's mind raced. Did Rich fire Mitch to get back at her? Or was this his plan all along? Was the hiring of Willie a treat for Larissa, and was that her motivation for being with him, as well? Was it possible that Rich had thought all the time that they were together that he had a tacit agreement with June, too? She was entirely culpable for Mitch's loss. The completely obvious reality of her affair—one she thought she had indulged in as a balm against pilot season—was that she had damaged her marriage in the one way she had never considered, by striking at the one thing that most threatened Mitch's security and sense of self, his career. For the first time since she pressed her lips against Rich Friend's, she felt the full gravity of what she had done.

June picked up an overripe pear from the basket and rubbed it carefully with her hand. "This is what I would like to do to Rich Friend," she said, and, to Mitch's amazement, June lobbed the pear against the back wall of their kitchen. The pear exploded with a thud, smashing against the wall, and slid down slowly, landing in several pieces.

Nora looked afraid, but June handed her a handful of strawberries and smiled brightly. "Nora, people in the television industry are very bad and naughty, so we're going to pretend that they are fruit, and that will make us happy. Here, you throw one."

Nora looked shy, and tossed the strawberries lightly on the floor. She looked back at June for approval. "More like this, sweetie," June said, grabbing an orange, which she lobbed at the pear stain on the wall. Mitch grabbed a handful of kiwis, and smashed them against the side door that led to the garden.

For the next ten blissful minutes, they all created an angry fruit salad against two walls and a door of their kitchen, mushing a few dates and Godiva chocolates on the floor under their shoe heels for good measure.

"This is for Les Moonves!" Mitch yelled, hurling an orange, which ricocheted off the door, "and for every drive-on I was never given!" He picked up a passion fruit. "This is for Bonnie Green, and her stupid lattes. This one is for the acting teacher in college who told me I'd never even make a commercial!"

June threw a few more strawberries, thinking of Bob, and of Lexi. Poor James took a kiwi between the eyes and a date on the back, which he then licked off his fur slowly, with some pleasure.

"I love the fruit game!" said Nora. June soon wiped the juices off of Nora's hands, changed her nightgown, and settled her into bed. The fruit basket had been decimated, save a single passion fruit, which June had reserved for a smoothie. The paper "grass" that had lined the basket had fallen into a little mound on the floor.

After Nora was asleep and the last bit of orange juice had been wiped from the kitchen door, June fell into Mitch's arms, and they made love for the first time in months, with a desperate passion that reminded June of the beginning of their relationship. She had forgotten the smell of her own husband's skin, and she felt comforted by its familiar—if slightly citrus—taste. He was thicker around the middle than Rich, but somehow that charmed her. All that time, she thought, Rich must have been comparing her legs, the curve of her waist, and her hair to Larissa's, and somehow she could now see him thinking of her as she quickly recalled their steamy afternoons in hotels. They were never quite alone. Mitch stared at her, with something—was it gratitude?— and she could feel he was only with her. God, her husband was tall!

Lying breathless next to him, June thought back to the other day when she came home and told him she wasn't getting tenure. Mitch had said nothing, just held her as she sobbed. He had softly told June that he would do anything to help her, that he felt to blame for not having supported her as she tried to write her book. He had made thoughtful suggestions about what she might do next, and reproachful remarks about her colleagues at UCLA. June had felt a deep sense of loss and shame. She had forgotten over the last six months to actually look at Mitch.

"You know, maybe you'll be able to get on a better show now. I thought *Sole Operator* was pretty insipid anyway," June said.

"Like that stopped a hit show before. Anyway, I'm done with this," Mitch said. "I'm not going to go on any more auditions. I can't deal with being fired for no reason again."

"Mitch, I understand what you're saying. But I confess I've heard it all before. You don't have to quit. You'll get another gig. There has never been a year without work for you since we got here."

"But this is the first year since we got here that I don't feel the hunger anymore. There's a lot more to me than a thirty-second audition."

"Well, one could argue that this is a time for clean slates all around."

"Yes. New ways of living. Hey, on the topic of new beginnings, your car will be ready next week," Mitch said.

"Oh great."

"I hope you can sort of, you know, avoid incidents for a few months?"

June smiled, feeling genuinely warm. "If you don't make me Google 'nimrod,' don't call me from the scene of road rage incidents, and try not to freak when I tell you not to tap your chin during an audition, I think so."

"You know what? I told Greg about the chin thing, and he asked me if he could use it because I wasn't going in. So I said yeah, and when he went on the audition the director told him it was distracting."

"Well, what can I say. I'm a regular Martin Scorsese. Anyway, yes, I'll try to keep up my end with the driving issues."

"Speaking of which, June, did you get a parking ticket in the Palisades?"

June saw her opportunity in that moment: to tell Mitch why he had been fired, to confess another man's hands had taken off her panties in the dark of her office, to apologize for her enormous transgressions, and to explain them, too.

"Palisades? Who knows. I'll take care of it myself this time, Mitch."

CHAPTER 27

"This is a beautiful book." June stared at the hands of the buyer at Book Alley in Pasadena, struck by how they seemed to belong to a much older man. While his hair was not yet gray and his face was only just beginning to wrinkle, his hands were covered in age spots and looked fragile as they carefully thumbed through *The Collected Poetry of W. H. Auden 1945*.

"It's in great condition. I can give you four hundred dollars," the buyer said.

June suspected that he anticipated she would bargain, but her mouth turned up with the sort of smile that suggests something other than happiness, and she nodded. "Fair enough."

As the elderly hands fumbled with the large checkbook ledger, the sort June hadn't seen since her high school job at the shoe store, she glanced at the *Los Angeles Times* resting on the counter. She swore she saw Larissa's photo on the front of the California section, and turned the paper slightly so she could read the accompanying article.

> The wife of a popular television actor who gave the voice to a Super Roach character was arrested Monday and charged with three misdemeanor counts, including leaving the scene of an accident after hitting the car belonging to Laurie David, the environmentalist and former wife of Larry David. According to the police, Larissa Dermot, who is married to Willie Dermot, a well-known character actor, rammed her Cadillac Escalade into Ms. David's Prius in the parking lot of Yoga Works in Santa Monica and raced

*off before Ms. David, who suffered minor injuries, had time to
exit her car. Security cameras in the lot identified Ms. Dermot's
vehicle, and police arrested her at her Brentwood home Monday.
Calls to Mr. Dermot's agent were not returned.*

June read the article three times and stared at the photo of Larissa,
taken on the red carpet at the ABC All Stars night last winter. She then
took her check and left, driving slowly up to the 210 Freeway so she
could glance at the *Thomas Guide* on the passenger seat. There were so
many freeways in Los Angeles County that she had rarely been on—the
51, the 27, the 14—that she often wondered where they actually went,
and what kind of people lived off the exits they traversed. What in God's
name really happened every day in the Newhall Pass anyway?

The rain that had pelted the freeway all morning was suddenly
cleared by a giant sunburst, and instantly, an immense rainbow stretched
above her, an endless pastel ribbon headed toward the undulating hills
and downtown. She took a picture with her cell phone and sent it to
Amanda. A text reply came right away: *Wow. You live in a Dr. Seuss
book.*

June parked at the Brookside Golf Course and walked carefully
into the pro shop, fearing that she would be discovered as a person who
should not be there. June pulled slightly on her skirt, hoping she didn't
look naked.

"Umm hi . . ."

"What can I do you for?" asked the formerly muscular pro shop
manager.

"Umm, yes," June said, glancing at a Post-it note where she had jot-
ted down her golfing information culled from the Web. "I guess I need
something called a burner?"

"You mean a TaylorMade Burner?"

"Yes, that's it," June answered.

"Is this for you?"

"Oh God, no! I hate golf. I mean it's great and all, but not for me.
Anyway, this is for my husband, who I guess is good at golf. Anyway, he
seems to think often about burners, so do you have one?"

"Yeah, the Burner's good," the pro shop manager said, "but you might want to check out the Cleveland Launcher because it has the lowest and deepest center of gravity of that kind of driver. What's his handicap?"

"I actually don't understand a single word you just said. But if you sell that burner thing, I'll take it, as well as"—June glanced back at her Post-it—"a box of Titleist Pro V1 golf balls."

"Sleeve or box?"

June was dismayed by all these choices. "Uh, box?"

After her purchase at the golf course, June had a few dollars left from her sale of Rich Friend's book, and felt a deep urge for a slice of banana cream pie at the Pie 'n Burger, since she was so rarely in Pasadena.

Sitting at the counter, licking the meringue off the back of her fork, June suddenly felt a numbing sensation fill her legs and a deep hot flush move from her waist to the tip of her head. She had nearly ended her marriage, destroyed her family, and made a colossal fool of herself, all for absolutely nothing. Sheer terror, the sort she imagined plane crash survivors must feel after the fact, enveloped her for many minutes as she sat, staring at the young mother trying to manage her newborn and her toddler as she ate a hamburger at a nearby table.

The sensation passed after many minutes, and June began to reflect on where they were now. Already job offers from Claremont McKenna and USC, neither of which really interested her, but still they existed; a new Burner thing; a husband who was back to telling knock-knock jokes, drying the dishes, and taking Nora to school in the morning, returning to tell June what horrible thing Lexi was wearing or how harassed he felt by the school director, who was always trying to con him into doing dramatic readings of *Weiner Dog* for the children. He had removed Nikki Finke from his bookmarks and had yet to replace his cell phone. Nora had learned almost all her lowercase letters. June had mastered the perfect Gruyère soufflé.

Was this what they dreamed of ten years ago when they boarded that American Airlines flight for LAX? Was it where they pictured themselves, in a place and situation where small pleasures and getting through the day were often the best they could hope for? It wasn't. But it was enough.

CHAPTER 28

"You'll never believe what I saw today walking around the golf course."

Mitch was looking out his driver's-side window at the two blondes in a Mini Cooper, its top down, music blaring from its speakers. "You walked around the golf course?"

"No, Mitch," June said. "Did I have a personality transplant?"

"So what did you see? Breasts in her summer outfit?"

"She is decked out in the white spandex now. But anyway, that's not what I saw. I saw a mother, about my age I guess, speed-walking next to her nanny, who was pushing her toddler in a stroller next to her."

"Yeah, well, that happens."

"No," June said. "It gets better. On the other side of her was a young black guy, I don't know, maybe twenty, in a track suit, pushing her Pomeranian in a doggie stroller."

Mitch cackled. "Get out of here!"

"I'm serious, it was a stroller. For a dog."

Mitch shook his head and laughed a little more. They were heading north on La Brea toward the Hollywood Hills, where they had been invited to the wrap party for the movie *Welcome to Pussytown*.

Mitch had originally lost the part of the foulmouthed friend to Leif Saxton, a troubled actor almost half Mitch's age, who had made a name for himself in sex comedies. However, a week into the shoot, Leif was found by his on-set acting coach unresponsive in his trailer. He was soon pronounced dead, an unfortunate result of mixing OxyContin, Restoril, Vicodin, Xanax, and Allegra.

Mitch was called in as an emergency replacement. The money

had been good enough to overlook that fact that he was forced to use the double banger in which Leif had croaked, because there wasn't another trailer available.

When the invitation to the party arrived, Mitch moved to toss it, but June stunned him by saying she wanted to go. He was so surprised by her concession that he easily agreed, and so it was that they were climbing into the hills toward the house of A.J., the *Welcome to Pussytown* director.

June was reading from a slightly ripped printout from MapQuest. "Um, let's see. Turn right at Hillside. Then right at El Cerrito, this street here."

"What do you mean, right on El Cerrito? That takes me into a ficus tree!"

"Oh, sorry, I mean take a left. Okay, now another slight left on Outpost Drive. Do you see Outpost Drive?"

"Yeah, I think that is the street we just passed, June. Listen, honey, you need to tell me what street to turn on before we actually pass it, okay?"

Mitch stopped the car, but with the road as narrow and twisting as it was, there was no place to turn around. He began to back tentatively down the hill, and a black Mercedes that was making its way in the opposite direction honked madly.

"Oh shove it!" Mitch said, to no one in particular, then finally found Outpost Drive.

"Okay," June said, staring at her directions again. "Then take a slight left at Mulholland, and then another one at Baseline Trail."

The car wheezed up the hairpin turns and stopped at the street. They saw the telltale valet in a black vest standing expectantly, as if he had been waiting for them alone all along. "Welcome to Pussytown, lady and gentleman," he said as he took their keys. June stared at him, and realized that she was glaring.

June and Mitch walked into a giant great room, every wall a window, which seemed to make up the lion's share of the house. A sound system blared music that June didn't recognize, as she surveyed the room. Vintage pinball machines lined one wall, and an enormous flat-screen television illuminated another one. Several people were gathered around it, playing Guitar Hero. June had to smirk. She had friends with teenagers who spent their entire Saturday afternoons in front of Wii. Who knew they had so much in common with forty-year-old movie producers?

A woman in a tight cocktail uniform meant to look like a NASCAR jumpsuit, unzipped down to the center of her chest, approached June with a smile. "Would you like a pussypower?"

"What would that be?"

"It's our specialty cocktail. Vodka and Red Bull."

"Sounds, um, uplifting. Do you have any red wine?"

"You got it!" the waitress said, and looked at Mitch.

"Pussypower?"

Mitch smiled. "Well, since you put it that way, sure."

The two stood side by side, taking in the crowd and making notes together, as they used to do, years ago, before Mitch used parties as job interviews.

"Blond at four o'clock," Mitch said. "Quick! Escort or wife?"

"Hm. Wife. But second one. No kids," June countered. "Check out the superhigh-waist-jeans dude. I haven't seen jeans like that since freshman year in college. Is that an intentional look?"

"I don't know, it might be. He looks like he's wearing a hot-water bottle."

June laughed. Mitch rubbed her head and kissed her just above her right eyebrow. "As usual, the prettiest girl in the room is my wife."

Farther back in the room was a craps table, where several men, most of them in jeans and striped shirts, and a few women in tank tops, were hooting. Across from that was an oval racetrack, one June recognized from a child's birthday party, on which kids race remote-controlled cars. Another dozen men were gathered around it, their faces contorted in concentration as they worked the cars.

June sipped her wine and tried to imagine actual children in this glass house. She suddenly had a small fantasy of throwing rocks from her cactus garden at each wall, just to see how hard she would have to toss them to chip the windows.

She was about to ask Mitch to weigh in on this daydream when a fleshy-faced man with long stringy hair made his way toward them. It was less a man, actually, than a very large head attached to rail-thin legs and arms, the latter flailing as he walked and spoke, quite loudly, as it turned out.

"Mitch, my man, you fucking saved our asses!" said the head, his stringy hair flipping slightly to the left. June noticed he was balding, and that his hair had at one point been artfully combed over the spot, something that the act of walking quickly undermined. "Who expects your third lead to ice himself in the middle of a shoot? Or have an accident or whatever that shit was. Man, the industry is still mourning. Or whatever."

"Hey, A.J., meet my wife," Mitch said, wrapping his arm loosely over June's shoulders. "June, A.J. He was the director, I told you about him."

"Nice to meet you," June said, cringing slightly at having to touch his hand. It was only then June realized that some of the waitstaff were topless. She wondered if she had a baby wipe in her purse, because she craved to wipe her hands.

"Mitch, there's someone here I think your bro Tad would really like. You wanna come meet her?"

"You know, A.J., I think Tad is pretty deft at getting his own ladies these days," Mitch said, and June was struck. A mildly insulting turn toward a successful director. She tried to think if she had ever seen it before.

As A.J. ambled away, June considered whether it would be okay to ask to leave soon. But Mitch was yet again embroiled in a conversation with someone June was certain she knew, but had no idea from where. Short, dark curly hair, black-framed glasses, tiny mouth, rosebuddy, small in proportion to his nose. Who was it?

Mitch looked toward her. "You remember Jacob, honey. Our playwright in residence back on Thirteenth Street?"

"Oh God, yes of course, Jacob. Oh God, it's been years!" June was suddenly flooded with warm memories of Jacob Mnookin, who had indeed written several plays that Mitch's theater company produced in New York all those years ago. There was one about the Black Panthers, and another concerning the Triangle Shirtwaist factory fire, which had to be shut down early because the set had caught on fire.

"Jacob, it is great to see you," June said warmly. "What on earth are you doing here?"

Jacob smiled back. "June, I'm jazzed to see you! You look amazing. Um, I actually wrote *Welcome to Pussytown*. And in fact, I produced it, too."

"Oh, okay," June said. "I can't believe Mitch never mentioned that." June instantly regretted the remark. Mitch probably had told her, during that period when she had only pretended to listen to half of what her husband said. "Well, this material seems a long way from the fires on the Lower East Side."

"Yeah, can't quite get that stuff made in this town. But this shoot was fun. We had a ton of laughs."

A woman from across the room, who June believed officially had even larger breasts than Breasts, called toward them. "Jacob cutie! Hey there!"

June looked at Jacob with amusement. "Someone your mother set you up with?"

"No, actually that is one of my actors. She plays a girl who eats Cheerios off the breasts of other girls on the racetrack to distract her boyfriend's opponent. Actually I have to tell you, I felt so uncomfortable, you know, as a man who's always considered himself a feminist, asking her to strip during the audition."

"Why did you?"

"Well, to make sure, you know, to see what we were going to shoot."

"Didn't you write the scene?" June asked, somewhat dumbfounded.

"Yeah I wrote it."

Mitch began to wince a little, as if he had just taken a bite of a raw lemon. But June went on.

"So if it made you uncomfortable, why did you write a scene that's topless?"

"Um, June, that's the story."

"Right, so why be uncomfortable?"

"Well," Jacob said, laughing a little, "I'm not in the habit of telling girls to strip on demand."

"Well you wrote it that way, Jacob. I guess I don't get where you're going with this, I don't know, sort of manufactured discomfort. You write a scene with two girls eating breakfast off one another's breasts, but then you feel sad actually watching it."

291

June waited for the anger she had long grown accustomed to in these conversations to darken Jacob's face, but was surprised to see sadness instead. She looked at Mitch, who, to her amazement, piped up.

"Hey, everyone needs to make a living in this town," Mitch said. "You don't need to act like you wrote and produced this under duress. You've got five scripts. Four of them are worthy. This is the one you could get made. But be for real."

Jacob nodded. "Yeah, it's true. But I still felt uncomfortable. I'm telling you that."

"Yeah," Mitch said. "Discomfort is a permanent state in this town. Was for me, too."

There was really nothing left to say. June was staring at Mitch with admiration in her face. "You know, sweetie, I promised the babysitter we would not be out too late. Do you mind if we hit the road?"

"Not at all," Mitch said, and they exchanged a stilted good-bye with Jacob, who smiled wanly at them both. June tried to feel bad, she knew she should, but she couldn't locate the feeling.

Back at home, June kissed a sleeping Nora on the head while Mitch paid the babysitter.

"June come to bed," he said as the door shut behind the rhythmic-gymnast sitter, who was still in her leotard. "I need your company."

"One second, sweetie, I just want to check my e-mail."

In the dark of her home office, June's computer screen illuminated her face. Four e-mails: One was from a cooking magazine. There was a Peachhead posting ("Hi Everyone—I've completely forgotten the lyrics to a couple old-time songs that my daughter's Fisher-Price toys are churning out. Listening to them is part of our crucial interactions. Does anyone know the names in the following songs? I know they are both 2 syllables: 'someone's in the kitchen with——blank. Someone's in the kitchen I know oh oh oh.'—and—'——blank won't you blow,—— blank won't you blow,——blank won't you blow your horn.' CAN ANYONE HELP ME WITH THIS MYSTERY?") One was from an account that she knew to be Rich Friend's, under the screen name Gilley. She sent it directly to the trash before having to even contemplate her own curiosity. And, to her shame, mild desire. Still.

The last one was from Amanda.

To: junejune@gmail.com
From: amandamalone@smithbarney.com

Hey friend. Saw some curtains online that you would love.
Should I send you the link? How's life west of America?

To: amandamalone@smithbarney.com
From: junejune@gmail.com

Well, I went to a party tonight for a movie Mitch is in called
Welcome to Pussytown. They served a drink made with Red Bull
called pussypower. Half the waitstaff were topless, either by de-
sign or inadvertently, because their tits could not fit in their
NASCAR uniforms. Saw an old playwright friend who wrote
this incredibly cerebral film—which apparently centers around
naked girls eating meals off each other's private parts—and he
told me he felt really sad to ask women to audition for it, as if
he had nothing to do with the material. So, um, I think you get
the idea.

The reply was immediate. June was surprised; Amanda must have been
pulling an all-night deal for a client.

To: junejune@gmail.com
From: amandamalone@smithbarney.com

Admit it, if you ever left LA you'd miss parties celebrating, um,
pussies. Here we only have *Lingua Franca* alumni gatherings.

To: amandamalone@smithbarney.com
From: junejune@gmail.com

In fact, I would not. There are of course things I would miss
about Los Angeles. I would miss my butcher. I would miss the
months when the whole town smells like jasmine, signaling
the beginning of spring. I would miss clear days, when I can see

the mountains from Olympic, the guy who has framed all Nora's artwork, the rocks at El Matador beach, the brown bread ice cream at Scoops, and, weirdly, the clatter of LAPD helicopters at night. I would miss *The Sound of Music* sing-along at the Hollywood Bowl every summer. And I would miss e-mailing you, across the Continental Divide, wondering who you are making millions for in the middle of the night.

June closed her e-mail, and went to join Mitch in bed.

CHAPTER 29

June and Mitch were perched on slabs of travertine on the edge of the giant fountain outside the West Pavilion of the Getty Museum. They had just walked through the Dutch painting collection, where the two had sparred genially the way they used to over whether or not Rembrandt's paintings were too dark (June's view) or perfectly lit, like a theater stage (Mitch's take), and whether or not looking at the illuminated manuscripts was a fascinating (June) or hideously boring (Mitch) way to end their tour. June won, but agreed to sit at the fountain, even though it gave her a chill, because it was Mitch's favorite thing to do. The sun was beginning to lower over the Santa Monica Mountains, and June pulled her sweater tighter.

They were taking advantage of a rare Saturday afternoon alone. Town Crier had agreed to take Nora with Charlotte to a birthday party in Santa Monica at Magicopolis, which gave June great relief, since she hated both magic and children's parties. Town Crier, who took his wife to the Magic Castle for Valentine's Day, loved nothing more than a great card trick, and cheerfully carted the children off in his minivan for the afternoon.

"So how are you feeling about everything?" June asked Mitch, who was staring out at the purple light to the west.

"Well, let's review. This year, I had one show cancelled, got fired from another, and lost more than a handful of movie and television deals to other actors. I am barely hanging on at CAA. I think it is fair to say that it this year has been, shall we say, suboptimal."

"Well," June said, contemplating her own failures, "I really do believe that next year things are going to look up. I have two job offers already from USC and Claremont McKenna, and you have a few new auditions pending. I seriously feel like what we just went through was one shitty, rotten, but ultimately anomalous year, Mitch."

Mitch shook his head. "I don't want my whole life to revolve around whether I get a job or don't get a job. I don't want to feel that my marriage can be happy only if I am assured that I will be dressed in a suit from wardrobe playing a district attorney three times a week. I want to eat a taco in the middle of the winter and not worry that it will make me too fat to play the father of someone five years younger than me. I don't want to talk about trailers and deals and residuals. I don't want to make a movie I would never want my child to see. I want to rejoin the world of the living, and not remain moored here among people who can only talk about the demo share."

She grabbed his hand and held it tightly. "I know that. But I feel like you are on the precipice of something huge. I also feel like if we turned a little more focus on us, on what we need in our marriage, in our home, in our lives outside of Hollywood, we have room to come together again."

Mitch looked at her with some confusion. "Had we grown apart?"

June felt that wave of guilt sweep over her. "Not apart in any permanent sense. But we were both just visiting other places, I think. We need to come together more."

"Well, one thing that I think is obvious is that we need to leave LA. I am still thinking seriously about Oregon. Do you remember Jean Intrick, who ran that theater company on Thirteenth Street with me? He's now on the board of the Oregon Shakespeare Festival, and he's called me three times this year about a job there. The artistic director is leaving. I think I could get that job, and that would allow me to be in a few plays a year too. This year they're doing *Macbeth, Henry V, The Norman Conquests, Our Town. . . .*"

June stared ahead. Leaving Los Angeles had been a fantasy for so long that the idea of it actually happening filled her with an odd fear, as if she had willed it to happen through her own series of mistakes and misjudgments.

She had realized something of late, as the days without running lines with Mitch had turned to weeks, and she was no longer forced to watch his face on the phone, looking for telltale disappointed frowns, or ebullient smiles, to discern what was happening on the other end. Staring out at the clear skies from her perch at the Getty, she could see Brentwood. At that moment, nothing sounded more horrible to her than living in Ashland, Oregon.

Fog. Bed-and-breakfasts. River rafting.

"What about going back to New York? Did you ever consider that?" June asked hopefully, picturing herself with Adrian at the Spotted Pig, teaching Nora to eat offal.

"I've considered it. And what I concluded was that a one-bedroom apartment on 106th Street for nine hundred thousand and no good public school nearby and being unable to make my SAG insurance minimum because I'm only doing commercials and indie films is not for me. It's not for us, because I'd be back here every two months, trying to get the same pilots once again to pay the mortgage. I want less stress, not more. I want more of you and Nora, not less. New York is for the young and the rich, June. We aren't either."

June considered this, and realized she had no counterargument. But, Ashland? Oregon? She became momentarily fixated on paprika. Would she find the good Hungarian kind there? As she started to form her laundry list of why-nots, she began to see clearly the only why that mattered: she had cost Mitch his job, and betrayed his trust. It came to this: she owed him Ashland, Oregon, even if he would never know it.

June snuggled Mitch on the Getty tram as it made its careful slide down the mountain back to the parking structure. He kissed the top of her head.

"I'm a shitty wife," she mumbled.

"You're the only wife for me." Mitch flashed to a vision of Joy in her kitchen, with carrot juice on her finger. He had never told June why he lost that job, and felt grateful that she had never asked.

Back at the car, June opened the trunk and smiled devilishly. "Close your eyes."

Mitch squeezed his eyes shut. "Are you going to pick me off here on P3 Orange level at the Getty Museum, June?"

He opened his eyes and saw June holding a golf club wrapped

clumsily in tin foil, with a giant Hanukkah bow left over from last December tacked to the head of the club. "Oh man, that's a beauty!" Mitch said, caressing the club. "Wow, June-Junie, why the club?"

"Just a reminder that you're more than your job."

Mitch swung at an imaginary ball. "Thanks so much! A burner! You remembered! How did you even know where to get this?"

June just grinned. It felt nice to make Mitch happy.

In the car on the way home, June held Mitch's hand, and they laughed about the guy they had seen with the giant black glasses and Andy Warhol hair at the museum and noodled about where they would take Nora for dinner. Not Aloha Burger. Louise's?

Pulling up to the house, June squinted out of the car. "What the hell is wrong with our windows?" As they slowly inched up the driveway, June made out a thick layer of pink frost that seemed to have settled on every window of their house, thin toward the center, thick and muddy toward the panes. There were giant handprints in the center of some. "Jesus, what the fuck?" Mitch asked, and they ran in opposite directions around the back of the house, to confirm with disbelief that each window was the color of old salmon.

"God, what is that smell?" June asked, wrinkling her nose. Mitch knew immediately. French dressing. June quickly unlocked the doors of the house, but Mitch stopped her. "Let me just make sure no one is in there," he said, making his way gingerly through the door. June looked genuinely frightened as she stood shivering on the porch while Mitch checked the closets, looked behind opened doors, and flicked the lights off and on for good measure.

"All clear," Mitch said as June made her way in and began to dig around under the sink. She pulled out a large bottle of Shaklee window cleaner, then grabbed a handful of paper towels and newspapers and walked outside. She pulled on the garden hose, tangled under a group of fallen palm fronds, and turned it on full blast toward a side window. The force of the water splashed pinkish water into June's hair. "Goddamn it!" she said, rushing to turn down the hose, turning it up instead. "Never in a million years would I think that some asshole kid would put salad dressing on my windows. What a stupid, disgusting prank." She rubbed angrily at the window while Mitch walked down the street to the corner, looking from one side of the street to the other, in hope of finding the window assailant.

As it turned out, it didn't take him long. Sitting in a gray Lexus on the corner of Beverly Glen was a woman in a giant red wig and big tortoiseshell glasses, staring straight ahead, her hands gripping the wheel. She might not have been recognized by her colleagues at Sony, but Mitch knew Joy Wainscott in every disguise she had.

CHAPTER 30

"This part is perfect for you, Mitch. It's a straight offer! You don't even have to go to the network."

"I thought Wayne Knight got that. Remember? Fat was the new skinny."

"First of all, they've done a total rewrite. They are still lone star gals, they still live in Texas, but now they're witches casting spells on their exes, who are warlocks."

"Okay. So why I am more warlock than Wayne Knight?"

"It's a visual thing. When they got Wayne Knight in wardrobe and set him off to fly, he looked like the Goodyear blimp. So they need more athletic, someone who can sell levitation. And I haven't even told you the best part yet! I got them up to fifty-one thousand five hundred a week! That is every week, and its pay or play, thirteen episodes guaranteed. You have never had an offer like this in your entire career. And let me just tell you one more thing. Jay and Erin are doing a feature for Paramount this summer too, and they have something in mind for you for that. They love you. Please. This is your year."

Mitch began the calculations. With thirteen episodes pay or play, a few film roles, and a voice-over or two, he could easily clear over a million dollars next year. He thought about how he would be listening this time next year to his agents on a conference call about ratings. About fighting over a trailer. Another year of fifteen-hour days just as Nora headed for kindergarten, and fearing visits to the set from network executives who might decide to fire him. Listening to his next-door neighbor tell him how stupid witches in Texas were: "*Bewitched*! Now that was a show!"

It was never what it seemed, and whatever success he was having, it already felt to Mitch firmly affixed to his rearview mirror.

"You know what? It sounds great. Probably the greatest show that will never see a second season. But I came here to say good-bye, Tad, and to sell your assistant—what's her name again?—my car. We're closing on our house this week, and we're out of here. I got a theater gig in Ashland, Oregon—"

"Theater? What century are you in? This is major money. MAJOR, Mitch. You're out of your mind!"

"Squawk! Squawk! No talent! No talent!"

"God, Tad, does that bird have anything nice to say?"

"He just picks stuff up," Tad said as his latest rescue dog, a rather smelly Jack Russell with a cast on its left foot, jumped into his lap. "Anyway, Mitch, I can hold them off at casting for a couple of days. But then you gotta take this."

"I'm going to do theater because that's what makes me happy. You haven't been listening to me for the last month. I'm done with this crappy business. June got a gig as a pastry chef apprentice at Chateaulin and a part-time teaching gig at Southern Oregon University."

"But this moves you from B- to A-list, Mitch. No one will remember *Sole Operator*. All they'll say is Mitch Gold was in thirteen episodes of *Lone Star Gals*. It changes the whole equation for you."

"You're not listening to me. I want to live somewhere where my whole worth to the world is not measured in whether or not I tested well in a focus group. I want to live somewhere where how deeply you live in a canyon, how expensive your car, how good your table, how high-powered your agent, who will probably be fired next year anyway, is not the marker of whether or not you deserve to breathe air each day. I want to be in a place where acting is another job, like painting houses or managing someone's taxes, not a status symbol, where people aren't constantly whispering that you're a person who never quite had it. Saying no to this town is what makes someone a winner, Tad. This place is the big nothing."

"I can't believe it. I can't. Ugh." Tad stared, still disbelieving. "What about the weather? You'll miss the weather, man."

"I actually like the rain, Tad."

"You get a chance like this only once a career, Mitch. You'll regret it."

Mitch was already down the hall.

June looked out at the window. Trash Lady was having a field day with the Gold family's garbage—discarded Barbie dolls, broken chairs, old dish towels, dented cans of baked beans that June could not remember buying, a quarter container of ginger, and a ratty Ace bandage. June ran her hand along the front-door frame, now exposed as badly in need of a paint job, and felt a tinge of sentimentality. This was the door she and Mitch had walked through when they brought Nora home from the hospital. How many dinners had she cooked in this inadequate kitchen with its heat-surging stove she had never managed to regulate? She would never know when it was six o'clock without St. Timothy's bells ringing hymns each night. "You can have ice cream after the bells, Nora."

But then she thought about how she would never again have to look at Lexi's ass in her yoga pants, never receive a birthday party invitation addressed to "Princess Nora" from "Queen Chloe" with the return address written as "Larissa, the Royal Mother." No more staring at the sheet of plywood covering the skylight that Uri had never finished. No more tank tops on Thanksgiving. Never again hearing the phrase "I'm going to the network." Nora would start kindergarten in a nice neighborhood public school, where parents rotated the job of room representative and the mothers wore high-waisted jeans and fleece jackets. June could not stop staring at Trash Lady as she methodically examined each piece of garbage, dropping some back in the trash can, and less than half into her shopping cart. What was her method? What was she looking for? June felt compelled to understand her, though of course it was impossible. The doorbell rang. Maybe it was the movers again. She opened the door, and the bright July sun filled her dark house, which thanks to the Spanish roof tiles was far cooler than outdoors. For a moment June was slightly blinded, and flush from the blast of heat.

"Hi, June, so sorry to bother!" It was one of the Bizzy Blondes, who had sold the house to the Everetts, an English couple, both actors, who were moving from London to try their luck in television. They had played husband and wife in *Blithe Spirit* on the West End, and were hoping that smash success was going to translate into American living rooms.

"No bother, umm . . ." Sally? Jessie? Carrie?" June said. "No bother at all, umm, you busy lady you!"

"Well I know it is very unusual for the buyer to do a walk-through with the seller still in the house, but Pauline and Derek are here for only two days before they need to go back to London to close on their flat, so they were wondering if you'd be terribly upset if they did it now?"

June peered out over the Bizzy Blonde's head and saw a young couple sitting in the back of her car, smoking out the passenger window. June could see that Pauline was a tad plump by Hollywood standards, and Derek had one of those English haircuts. Curious about who would be using her washer and dryer next week, bathing in her bathtub, maybe carrying their own newborn through the front door one day, June welcomed the blonde and her two clients inside. Pauline had creamy skin, with rosy cheeks, and wide blue eyes that seemed to actually expand when she spoke.

"Hello there! Lovely to meet you. Very kind of you to let us take a look on such short notice."

Derek, who was very thin, his pants nearly hanging off his bottom, smelled of cigarettes and, oddly, tomato juice. June inhaled, wanting to remember the scent of the new owners. "Oh yeah, June is it?"

"Yes, it's June. Nice to meet you both. Come on in." She noticed that the bottom row of Derek's teeth were somewhat brown.

The two craned their necks toward the ceiling, no doubt taking in the chipped paint. June remembered how much smaller the house had looked when she first saw it empty, and wondered if they felt disappointed. Would they smoke inside? June felt sad to think of that. Pauline tried to measure the windows, but could not quite get the tape across. "Could you give us some help, Derek?" Her husband stalked across the room and grabbed the end of the tape measure, holding it awkwardly, as if he'd never seen a tape measure before. "It looks like one hundred and twenty centimeters."

Pauline looked at June. "Your husband's an actor, yes?"

June considereded the question. "He was. Well he is, but we're leaving. He's going to do theater in Oregon."

"Is that another state?" Pauline asked.

"Yes, it's in the Northwest," June said. "It's nice there."

"Funny that, being an actor and leaving Hollywood. Most people who want to act live here, no? That's why we came. Bloody sick of the theater actually. If I had to do one more matinee in my life I'd go mental!"

June was charmed by Pauline's odd expressions and her rather plain yet somehow gorgeous face and the tiny lines between her eyebrows. June wondered if a year from now, the lines would still be there, if Pauline would still be a size 8, and use phrases like "mental."

Mitch walked through the door, holding Nora, whom he had just picked up from her last playdate with Charlotte. Town Crier had been busy plotting his next export franchise—rice cakes for the gluten averse. He looked startled by the English couple who were just wrapping up their measuring, reimagining, and stock taking of his home.

"Hello! Mitch Gold, right? Love your work!" Derek said.

"Hi. Thank you. And you are . . . ?"

"Oh sorry, Derek and Pauline Everett. Adore the house. I know we'll be really happy here," Pauline said, and then asked, "So, Mitch, who is your representation?"

"We're both going with Endeavor," Derek chimed in.

Mitch stared at the two of them, and June could feel his impatience. "I used to be CAA. I quit the business, though."

An awkward silence ensued, and Pauline inched toward the door. "Well carry on then. Thanks again so much for letting us in!"

The Everetts made their way out, and Nora sat on the bare floor of their bare living room, pushing an empty cereal box that had somehow gotten left behind along the floor, pretending it was a car. "Beep! Beep! Move it! Only selfish people have minivans." Mitch laughed. The doorbell rang again, and June's stomach tightened. She remembered Cat Empress was coming by to say good-bye to James, who had been locked in the house the last few weeks to avoid an abduction. Hilda walked right past June, Mitch, and Nora to the cat, who was curled up in a slice of sunlight by the window.

"James darling. I vill miss you." James looked up at a Cat Empress, then began to chew on the inside of his leg. "Good-bye, James." She looked tearfully up at June. "Promise me that you will feed him Purina. Don't let him get vet. I understand Oregon is very vet."

"Hilda, James will be fine. I'll send a picture," June said.

June had not been to LAX in almost two years, and the mere smell of engine fuel, overpowering even at the Randy's Donuts a mile from the airport, caused her to start panicking. Flying terrified her, and she discreetly tucked an Ativan under her tongue before sipping her coffee. Nora licked the sprinkles off her pink frosted doughnut, and Mitch, after saying three times he didn't want one, chewed on a plain one, dipping it into his milk carton, creating a flurry of crumbs as he shoved it into the undersized container. Randy's Donuts was a famous Los Angeles landmark, a giant doughnut-shaped stand on a busy intersection, where honking was overwhelmed by the roar of Southwest Airlines jets landing on final approach.

"We need to go," Mitch said. "We're going to be late otherwise."

June, Mitch, and Nora, who insisted on lugging James's cat carrier even though it was too heavy for her, piled into the polka-dotted Parking Spot van and made their way to the terminal, staring out the window in silence. Mitch dialed Tad, as June had watched him do, she thought cloudily, her Ativan haze taking over, perhaps a million times.

"Hey, Tad. I left the car on the roof level. Tell, umm, what's the new assistant's name again? Oh yeah, tell Bethany the registration papers are in the glove compartment and I'll send her the keys once her check clears. Yes, we are really going, Tad. Uh-huh. Right. What? Wow. Jesus. No kidding. Really? You're shitting me. Well, you always knew my opinion of Rich Friend. Okay. Thanks, man."

June looked at Mitch expectantly.

"Get this. The network shut *Sole Operator* down. Apparently that medical leave that Jennifer English was on was for a face-lift. Now there's an issue of something called facial immobility."

"What is that?" June asked.

"It's when an actress has so much Botox and stuff that her face won't move anymore. It makes her expressionless. It just doesn't work on camera."

June started laughing, becoming more and more giddy as they neared the airport. "Did you hear that, Nora? Facial immobility!"

"And guess what else?"

"Else? Hee, hee, hee!"

"Yeah, June, hold it together. So listen to this; Justine and Rich are getting divorced. Sounds really nasty. I guess he is suing for custody of her damn dogs, and for alimony. He wants like three million a year. So then she is suing him over her collection of rare books, which apparently he had been pilfering and selling on eBay."

June felt a little cold, and pulled her sweater around her. "Well, that's a story. Want an Ativan?"

"Yeah, let's both take Ativan and drool on Nora in coach," Mitch said. "Come on, we're at the terminal."

On board the plane June was having a hard time convincing Nora to wear her seat belt. "I don't like it, Mommy!"

"Just wear it, sweetie. Then we'll look out the window and count the clouds together!"

June no longer felt afraid. She knew that was illogical—the important thing was to realize how fundamentally unsafe this experience would be—but she could not locate her fear center. The captain came on the intercom—their flying time would be about two hours and twenty minutes, at an altitude of thirty-three thousand feet. Wow. That was high. June grabbed Mitch's hand as the plane began to speed down the runway, and the thumping of the rear of the aircraft as they became aloft startled her. The plane headed out over the Pacific Ocean, and Nora looked out, amazed. "Is that where we swim, Mommy?"

June didn't answer. The plane banked slightly east as June saw the Los Angeles skyline fading under them, and the outline of the Santa Monica Mountains. The shoreline seemed edged with silver, and she could still spot sailboats making their way toward Catalina Island. She felt amazed by the beauty of Los Angeles, just as it faded away.

ACKNOWLEDGMENTS

Every book has many authors, and this one would simply not exist without the careful, honest, and profoundly diligent work of Tad Friend and Amanda Hesser, for whom no amount of thanks will ever be enough. For believing in the book, we are indebted to Suzanne Gluck and Erin Malone at the William Morris Agency, and Deb Kogan for introducing us to them. We are deeply grateful also to Elizabeth Beier at St. Martin's Press, for her amazing ear, humor, and support, and the fabulous copyediting team who backstopped her. A huge shout-out is due to Judith Hendra, who pointed out more than once that we had misspelled YouTube, and Bill Pierce, for the photos. We also want to thank Susan Brenna, Frank Bruni, Clifford Levy, Jennifer Farrington, Esther Fein, David Firestone, Ian Fisher, Alexandra Foote, David Kim, Jamie Lynton, Jennifer Mnookin, Elisabeth Schmitz, Todd and Tali Slavkin, Lynn Steinhauer, and Mark Wilding, for taking the time to read and give thoughtful suggestions. We thank our children, Julia, Hannah, Charlotte, and Sadie, who agreed to watch hundreds of Looney Tunes while the mommies wrote their chapters. And to our husbands, Kurt Fuller and Edward Wyatt, who make all things possible.